DAY AFTER DAY

BY

JENNIFER TAYLOR WOJCIK

ISBN: 0615756417
ISBN 13: 9780615756417
Library of Congress Control Number: 2013901862
Jennifer Taylor Wojcik, LLC
St. Petersburg, Florida

FOREWORD

NOVEMBER 3, 2012

The culmination of one's dreams doesn't always happen until we are at the end of life; sometimes even then it might go unrecognized. But my dream to write a book and be able to call myself a published author happened with *From Day One*, the first of the Day Trilogy.

My most recent dream culminated today with the completion of the second book of three: *Day After Day.*

The book you are holding in your hands or reading on your e-reader is actually the second version of Book Two. Allow me to explain. When *From Day One* was published in October 2010, I immediately began writing the second in the *Day* series. Some 45,000 words into it—*half finished*—I suffered a computer hard drive failure. No—it wasn't backed up. I know, I know. *Now I know.*

After exhausting all of my geek contacts, as well as a forensic geek group who have the ability to take a dead hard drive and retrieve data from it, I was faced with starting over. On June 3, 2011, *Day After Day* began for the second time.

Having long realized that "bad things do happen to good people" and even that "everything happens for a reason," I swallowed hard and immersed myself in more research. The result is here. I think I produced a better book through this effort. Perhaps *that* was the reason, or perhaps it was a valuable lesson learned the hard way. I'll quickly add that I back up off-site and on-site—backing up my backups to my backup. I even resorted to printing a hard copy.

If you read *From Day One*, you will be happy to be reunited with the same characters; their lives continue here. This story begins where the first one left off, and it is with all humility that I say this one is even better than the first.

If you haven't read *From Day One*, well, you're not alone. It's still in print by the way; feel free to order a copy. *Day After Day can* stand alone on its own merit, and I believe you will find it a good read as well.

Enjoy *Day After Day* and stay tuned—*The Final Day: All Clear* is in the works (and backed up!).

Blessings,
Jennifer Taylor Wojcik

DEDICATION

For Larry A. Trimmer: for *everything*.

SPECIAL THANKS

To the Sassy Seniors of the First Baptist Church of St. Petersburg who welcomed me as a "Junior Senior"—pushed me (constantly yet gently) to finish this book and doted over me for writing *From Day One.* Photography credits are gratefully given to "Phil DeMille" for my *close up.* And to my close-knit gal pals who keep me centered and empowered, I could not do what I do without you in my life: Carol, Mary, Joanie, Kathleen, Maggie, Jean, and Shona; thank you from the bottom of my heart.

Finally, thank you, Carbonite. I am now your customer for life.

CHAPTER ONE

TALLAHASSEE, FLORIDA

SEPTEMBER 1960

It was a Saturday in September that no one would forget. Joanie and Matthew were now man and wife, and after a pristine ceremony at the Serenity Chapel, the bridal party and family arrived at The Tea Room for the wedding reception. Everyone arrived, save the bride's father, Detective Bovier, who had stayed behind to contact the police department in New Orleans. He had promised his wife he'd be along as soon as he checked in with the station.

Mrs. Bovier was not surprised that he would lag behind his only daughter's wedding reception. This was standard operating procedure for him, and she had long ago stopped nagging or asking anything more of him. Mrs. Bovier busied herself by helping get Marc and Lucy's twin daughters, Sandra and Amanda Winters, nestled into a table at The Tea Room. Lucy appreciated the help since Marc was preparing his "toast" to his twin brother, Matthew.

The Tea Room had never looked more beautiful. Billowing white gauze was draped from the ceiling's simple but elegant chandelier down to the head table. The wedding cake stood on a crystal stand and had been adorned with fresh flowers and chocolate candy pieces.

As soft music played in the background, the new Mr. and Mrs. Winters stood at the head table with glasses raised to their family and guests. Marc proposed his well-planned toast to his brother and Joanie.

As glasses were clinking, a lone shot rang out near Serenity Chapel. Detective Bovier had been shot once in the back of the head.

His body was discovered shortly thereafter by a passerby who later swore he had seen nothing except a man in a tuxedo lying on the steps of the garden by the church. In his front tuxedo pocket, there was a note with only one word on it—*omerta:* the Mafia code of silence.

Joanie had just leaned over to whisper something to her new husband when the ear-piercing sounds of sirens filed the air.

"Wow, that sounds serious," said Joanie.

"And close," Matthew added. Quickly looking around the room, it was obvious to him that everyone from the wedding was here, except Detective Bovier. Catching the eye of his twin brother, Matt motioned for him.

When Marc approached his brother, Matt leaned over and asked him to take a quick walk back to Serenity Chapel and check on Bovier. Without saying a word to anyone, Marc quietly left The Tea Room.

What he discovered would change the course of everyone's lives.

CHAPTER TWO

SERENITY GARDEN

TALLAHASSEE, FLORIDA

By the time Marc arrived, the Tallahassee police were stringing crime scene tape around the perimeter of the incident. Stopped several yards away, Marc was asked a series of questions: his identity, why he was there, and what, if any, knowledge he had about what had happened. Marc caught only a glimpse of Detective Bovier's lifeless body as the questioning continued. After explaining his twin brother's wedding and the fact that it appeared to be Detective Bovier who was lying prostrate on the ground, Marc was asked about the next of kin. Marc agreed to take them to The Tea Room so they could inform Mrs. Bovier. He carefully explained that the detective was the father of the bride, hoping that their announcement would be handled with the utmost care.

Marc and two TPD lieutenants made their way to The Tea Room. The first person they encountered was Matthew. Joining them outside the restaurant, Matt was informed about what had transpired. After quietly reentering the restaurant, Matt sequestered Mrs. Bovier and his new wife into a private room. Marc and the police lieutenants followed, where they reluctantly reported Detective Bovier's death.

"Dead?" Joanie shrieked. "You're saying he was murdered—at my wedding no less?"

Mrs. Bovier stood stoically next to her daughter, one arm around her waist. "Darling, I'm so sorry," she whispered. "Oh my God Joanie, this is horrible! We knew it could happen at any time, but today? It's a bad, bad thing that has happened. We just have to get through this and find out who did this to your father," Mrs. Bovier said.

Matthew had a thousand questions, but knew this was neither the time nor place to begin asking them. He consoled his bride as well as his mother-in-law, after which he asked Marc to make the other guests aware of the situation.

The Tea Room accommodated the couple and their guests by packaging up the food, drinks, and desserts and transporting them back to Haven, where the wedding party was staying. Ron, who had officiated at the wedding, and his wife, Cynthia, were owners of Haven and assisted The Tea Room personnel in getting everything successfully transferred to the Bed and Breakfast.

Marc called cabs for the wedding party and made sure that the chosen route to Haven be conspicuously out of the way of Serenity Chapel.

Taking a moment to console his own wife, Lucy, he suggested that she and the twins ride with his sister, Vera, her husband, David, and their infant son, Daniel.

"What about you, Marc?" Lucy asked.

"I need to stay and help Matt in any way I can. Get the girls settled and get them something to eat. I'll join you as soon as I can," Marc said, giving her a kiss on the cheek.

"Be careful, Marc. I couldn't take it if—"

"Shhh," said Marc with a finger to his lips. "I'll be fine."

Vera quickly made her way to Joanie and Matthew. "What can I do?" she asked.

Matthew pointed out that she needed to do what she did best—take care of everyone headed back to Haven.

Joanie and her mother had been seated near a window at The Tea Room, each staring off into nowhere, neither of them uttering a word.

Vera approached the two bereaved women and, bending down on one knee, put a hand out to each of them. She prayed an audible prayer and asked for guidance, comfort, and peace. She then quietly got up and left them.

The Boviers were scheduled to spend the night at Haven. Matt realized this was not the best place for his mother-in-law to be and called the hotel where he and Joanie were spending the night. Given the circumstances, the hotel accommodated him with an adjoining room for Mrs. Bovier. He then called Haven and asked Cynthia to transport Mrs. Bovier's belongings to the hotel. He asked that the detective's personal effects be kept at Haven so that he could personally deal with them.

Matthew shared the change in plans with Marc and asked if he would accompany both Joanie and her mother to the hotel. Marc agreed and ushered them to a waiting taxi.

Being the last to leave The Tea Room, Matthew walked to Haven, weary and saddened that something so hideous could happen on this, his wedding day. His beautiful bride would never escape this tragic memory.

Purposely walking by Serenity Chapel, Matthew silently watched the police personnel scurrying around the site where Detective Bovier had been murdered. The crime scene was, of course, off-limits, but Matt took a few moments to make mental notes.

He watched as items were bagged and labeled, with investigators surveying the entire area. He noticed a policeman on the roof of the garden shed. He too was surveying distances and directions.

Matthew was not surprised when a policeman approached him.

"Afternoon, officer," said Matt.

"Yes, sir, can I help you?" the policeman asked.

"I am Matthew Winters, albeit briefly, I am the deceased's son-in-law," answered Matt.

"While I am sorry for your loss, this is an active crime scene investigation, and you should not be here, sir."

"I understand, officer; I don't intend nor want to hinder your investigation. I just have a lot of questions that I'm grappling with and have no means at this point of getting any answers. Is there anyone on the police force who could speak with me?"

"Just a moment, sir," the officer said as he walked over to a nonuniformed policeman.

"This is Detective Sutherland. Detective, this is Matthew Winters—son-in-law of the deceased." As soon as the officer had made the introduction, he left the two alone.

"Detective Sutherland, could you at least tell me how my father-in-law was killed?"

"It appears as though he received a single shot to the back of the head," said Sutherland.

"I see. You know, sir, that my father-in-law was a detective for the New Orleans Police Department?"

"Yes. His badge and paperwork were on his person."

"And if I may ask, was there anything out of the ordinary about his murder?" Matt was attempting to tread lightly.

"Mr. Winters, I don't find any murder to be ordinary. This case will be investigated thoroughly, and we will report our findings to the next of kin as soon as our investigation is complete. Until then I really cannot comment further. I am sorry for your loss. Now if you will excuse me please, I have work to do." With that comment, Sutherland walked away.

As Matthew turned to make his way to Haven, he noticed one item in particular that was being tagged and bagged. It had been removed from the detective's tuxedo prior to them putting his body into a body bag, and it appeared to be a note of some kind. From this distance he couldn't make it out.

Arriving soon at Haven, Matthew checked on his family members and then made his way to the Boviers' room. Cynthia had packed everything that belonged to the detective and had it waiting for him. As he left Haven, he thanked her and asked that she look after his family. He promised to come by the following day.

The cab ride to the hotel gave Matthew just enough time to sort through the detective's personal effects from Haven. The only thing that he reserved for further review was the flip-top notebook that every detective carried to keep notes in. Perhaps something in there would answer a few of his fast-growing list of questions.

Before taking the elevator to his room, Matt thoughtfully placed the detective's belongings in the hotel safe. There was no need for his new wife to endure any more agony today.

CHAPTER THREE

NEW YORK CITY

"So, is it handled?" asked Alex Mineo.

"It is, sir."

"Then let's take care of the enforcer next," Alex responded.

"Sir?"

"Get him out of the police department in New Orleans. His work there is done. And I don't care how you get him out—just make it happen, and let me know as soon as it happens. Got it?" Alex was not mincing words.

"Alex, if I could just speak to you for a second before the soldier leaves?" Benjamin Moriani tentatively asked.

"Ben, what?" asked an already agitated Alex.

Pulling Alex to the side and away from the ears of the soldier, Ben said, "Look, with all due respect, we may be drawing unwanted suspicion by pulling our enforcer out right now. Why not just let the dust settle a bit and then remove him? What can it hurt?"

"So have you decided you should be running things instead of me?"

"Come on, Alex, we've been friends for a lifetime, and you know I would never challenge your authority. John put you in charge, and you're in charge. I just have a bad feeling about making a move on this guy right now. It's your call." Ben walked away, leaving the uncomfortable situation for Alex to resolve.

Alex walked around the hotel suite rubbing his chin. "We're leaving things as they are in the NOPD for now. You are dismissed."

The soldier left immediately.

Alex then turned to his longtime friend and accomplice and said, "If you ever question me again in front of a soldier, it will be the last time. Do we understand one another?"

"Understood," said Ben.

Alex was a driven man. He'd been left in charge of John Ward's underworld empire when John had disappeared. While he had years of tutelage under the Mafia kingpin, he was understandably naïve about many of the intricacies of running an organization.

Rumors still flew about John's sudden disappearance, and while both Alex and Ben had tried to garner information about his whereabouts, they had been unsuccessful. It was as though John and his wife, Ruth Winters Ward, had simply dropped off the face of the earth. And because of how cleanly it had happened, Alex was convinced that one of the rival families had a hand in it.

Trying to appear in control, Alex was forfeiting time with his own wife and kids. He was drinking more and enjoying it less. He ate infrequently and poorly, and his health was being affected by both.

Things were changing in the mob world. The labor unions were becoming an issue among rival families as each vied for control. Alex had spent hours plotting control of the New York locals, and with Ben's sleuthing and connections, they were poised to take control of the waterfront.

Alex's mantra had become "show no weakness," yet what had he done today?

GAINESVILLE, FLORIDA

The telephone call from Matthew came as a complete shock to everyone at the law firm. Matt had recently been made partner, and his mentor, William Brown, was the first person he had called. As Matt explained the few available details of Detective Bovier's death to Brown, Brown instinctively started taking notes.

Committing to do whatever he could do in the way of support, Brown assured Matt that his safety and welfare were the top priority of the firm. Matt shared what he knew and what he had observed at the crime scene. He then asked his partner and mentor for only one thing—that Brown dig around and garner what, if anything, he could about his father-in-law's demise. Just prior to hanging up Matt mentioned the mysterious note that was found in Detective Bovier's pocket.

"It appeared to be only one word," Matt said. "And while I could not decipher it from that great a distance, I think it's substantive to his murder."

William Brown reassured Matthew and urged him to look after his bride as well as his grieving mother-in-law.

Promising to do so and to inform the law firm about funeral arrangements, Matthew ended his telephone call to his office.

CHAPTER FOUR

NEW ORLEANS, LOUISIANA

Moving a murdered corpse from Florida to Louisiana proved to be difficult. Autopsies were required by both states, and the respective medical examiners each had to adhere to his or her own laws and/or rules when it came to homicide.

When the detective's body was released to the funeral home, Mrs. Bovier took his dress uniform to the morticians. She was of course accompanied by Joanie and Matt, who had infrequently left her side, and arrangements were made to transport the body to the Bovier home.

The Boviers were well-known in their community, having lived in the Ninth Ward for some thirty years. Friends and neighbors had willingly stepped in and prepared meals, washed and dried the laundry, and prepared the Bovier home for the detective's final return.

The undertakers would open and close the casket for specified hours of "visitation," and the detective's remains would lie in state in his casket at the foot of what had been his bed. After two days of viewing, the service would be held at the home, and the body would be transported to the cemetery for burial. A brief graveside ceremony would be held at which time all nonessential members of the NOPD would be present and given an opportunity to salute their fallen comrade.

Joanie felt this custom was both morbid and unsettling, but there had been no point bringing that up to her bereaved mother. This was the way death was handled in New Orleans, and that was that.

Detective Bovier would be laid to his final rest in what was known as a "Society Tomb." These above ground monuments served as common burial housing to administer to the burial needs of members of a recognized group such as physicians, fire department staff, policemen, and even societal groups or societal members having some function or work in common.

St. Roch's (pronounced "rocks") cemetery, one of many so-called *Cities of the Dead,* was selected by Mrs. Bovier because of her Catholic upbringing. St. Roch lived during the Middle Ages and was well known for his work with individuals who suffered from the plague. The cemetery was named for him after a priest prayed to him during the yellow-fever epidemic in 1868. That priest pledged to name the cemetery after the priest if his prayers were answered. The cemetery became a shrine and Catholics began holding Sunday morning mass there as a result. Mrs. Bovier had attended that mass on a regular basis, and several of the detective's fellow officers and friends were interred there.

The next few days were excruciating for the family. Flowers and food arrived, while people meandered in and out of the Bovier home, settling in the living areas to chat with one another. There were tears and laughter, stories and reminiscing, but at the end of each day there was silent mourning. When the processional made its way through the Ninth Ward to St. Roch's cemetery, closure had begun.

The interment ceremony was reverent and brief. Members of the New Orleans Police Department honored Detective Bovier with the traditional twenty-one gun salute, a lone trumpeter played "Taps," and the service concluded with a prayer from the priest.

Mrs. Bovier, Joanie, and Matthew made their way to the waiting car and traveled home in virtual silence. The three were emotionally spent, and all needed their own kind of solitude. Mrs. Bovier thanked the ladies who were preparing food and setting the table for the three of them and urged them to return to their own homes and families.

When Joanie and Matt appeared, Mrs. Bovier asked them to sit and said, "I cannot thank you enough for all you've done, but it is time now for you to relax a bit, have some food, and plan your trip home." "But, Mom," Joanie said, "I could stay with you for a bit longer, and Matthew could go back..."

"No," said Mrs. Bovier, "it is time now for you to get on with your life—your lives together. You haven't even had a proper honeymoon."

"We have a lifetime to take a honeymoon, Mom," said Joanie with a catch in her throat at using the word *lifetime*.

"That's right, Mrs. Bovier. We wouldn't feel right leaving you alone," Matt said.

"But I *am* alone now son. I have friends who will help me as I need help. But it's time for me to learn to adjust to my new surroundings, just as the two of you need to adjust to yours. So please, don't argue with me about this. This is what I want." Mrs. Bovier seated herself behind a plate and prayed a silent prayer.

Joanie and Matt joined her, saying nothing more.

When the telephone rang, it startled everyone. Matthew took the liberty of answering the phone. It was a policeman named Jack Palace asking to speak to Mrs. Bovier.

"So was that a friend of Dad's?" Joanie asked.

"Yes—our very dear friend and your father's partner," Mrs. Bovier responded. "Matthew, I believe you met him at the house the first day, well the first day of the viewing."

"Yes, I believe I did. Seemed like a nice guy."

"He was offering any support that I might need going forward," said Mrs. Bovier. "I wouldn't hesitate to ask Jack for anything."

"Good," said Joanie. "It never hurts to have friends at a time like this."

"Jack also made a promise to me at the cemetery today," said Mrs. Bovier, staring at her still-filled plate. "He vowed to find out who did this, and bring them to justice."

Matt's ears perked up at that news. "Would he be willing to talk with me?" he asked.

"Well, I'm sure he would dear, but why?"

"I have a lot of unanswered questions, and this might be a good start in getting some of those questions answered," Matt stated.

"Mom, let me draw you a warm bath. You look totally exhausted," Joanie said sweetly.

"I am tired, and a good soak sounds good to me. Thanks, Joanie, you're a good daughter."

While Mrs. Bovier made her way up the steps, Joanie poured three glasses of wine. Carrying one to her new husband and putting the second glass next to his, Joanie simply said, "I'll be right back" and carried the third glass up the stairway to her mother.

Joanie returned to find her husband talking on the telephone to William Brown. All she heard was that they would be returning to Gainesville within a couple of days, and he'd like to discuss things further with Brown.

"Already back to work, Counselor?" Joanie asked.

"You know me too well. Where's that wine?"

The two settled in together on the couch in the home where Joanie had grown up. Her mind was racing in several directions, and she felt the urge to drink until she could no longer recognize a thought.

"A penny for your thoughts, my love," said Matt.

"They're not worth a penny, Counselor. I was contemplating getting drunk so that my mind would be quiet for a while."

"Tempting, yes, but you'd pay for it tomorrow."

"That I would, and speaking of tomorrow, are we going home?"

"Let's see how your mother is doing in the morning, and we'll make our travel plans accordingly," said Matthew, wrapping his arm around her shoulder. "For now, let's just try to regroup."

"Are you going to call Detective Palace?"

"As I said earlier, you know me too well. Yes, I'm going to try to call him tomorrow morning. I'd like to meet with him before we leave. He's not the only one who wants to know who did this, and if I can assist in any way, I want to do just that."

With a sigh, Joanie settled into Matthew's arms. Blowing him a silent kiss, she mouthed *I love you.*

Morning brought new perspective. New Orleans was sunny and humid. Mrs. Bovier had convinced her daughter to make travel plans to return to Gainesville and resume her life with Matthew.

Matthew obliged by making the airline reservations for the following day, which gave him sufficient time to make a few telephone calls to his office and to try to connect with Jack Palace. He arranged a luncheon meeting at one of the Brennan Family Restaurants that he loved so much. They agreed to meet at 12:30 p.m.

Arriving first as he had planned, Matthew arranged for a relatively secluded table toward the rear of the restaurant. Palace was at the host stand promptly at twelve thirty.

"Detective Palace, it was so kind of you to meet me on such short notice," said Matt.

"No problem, Matthew, even flat-foot cops don't turn down a free meal at a Brennan Family Restaurant!" Palace chuckled.

"I have some questions," started Matt.

"I have more questions than you I'd bet," said Palace.

"Perhaps some of our questions are the same. I'd like for you to tell me what you will about Detective Bovier. You've been his partner for a long time, I understand."

"Oh, just about twenty-five years, and Bovier was the partner everyone wished they had," said Palace.

"And why is that?" Matt queried.

"He's, excuse me, he *was* old school, just like me. We believed in the same things, followed the letter of the law, and didn't allow for any shenanigans."

"That's an interesting word to use," Matt said.

"It's about the only one you can say and not get sued for these days. I guess we could use the term *lagniappe*—a bonus or a little something extra. To me, *shenanigans* describes it best, and Bovier agreed. Some of the newbies on the force seem to feel they're entitled to a little something extra because they wear the badge." Jack Palace's voice was firm and his tone sounded bitter. "Yeah, some of our brothers needed to grow up. Some will, some won't, and I could name you names of those who won't."

"May I call you Jack?"

"Sure, if I can call you Matt."

"Deal. Jack, I have to know about my father-in-law, and it's just not appropriate for me to ask these questions of Joanie or her mother. They're dealing with more than their share right now. I was hoping you could describe Detective Bovier to me. Tell me what kinds of cases he enjoyed working on, what if anything he was involved in that might have gotten him killed?" Matt was nothing if not direct.

"Well, Matt, you sure don't beat around the shrubbery now do you?" asked Jack.

"Look, Jack, my father-in-law was murdered, and from what I can tell, it was a well-planned and equally well-executed murder." Matt moved in closer to Jack and said, "And he was shot in the back of the head and killed with a single bullet."

"Experienced marksman, no doubt," said Jack.

"And from what I witnessed at the crime scene, a lot of people were looking for something they did not find."

"Like a bullet casing?"

"I'm unsure, but the entire Tallahassee Police Force Crime Scene Unit was on hand and combed through every blade of grass, the sidewalks, the street, the building next door—including the rooftop, and they seemed dissatisfied." Matt sipped his sweet tea.

"Well, Matt, I've investigated a lot of these homicides myself, and our crime scene guys are told to cover every inch of everything within the defined radius. Now, if they were poking around on a rooftop, that would indicate to me that they thought the shooter may have taken the shot from there. But without any information, it's just hard to say." Jack went silent admiring the soft-shell crab sandwich that was just placed in front of him.

"Everything we say is speculative, Jack; neither of us has concrete information to draw on."

"Right, at least for the moment we don't," said Jack.

"Right," said Matt. "Back to Bovier—would you call him an honest cop?"

Jack Palace nearly choked on his sandwich. After wiping his mouth, he leaned over to Matthew and said pointedly, "He was old school—honest. In all the years we worked together, I never saw the man so much as jaywalk."

"I hope you understand, Jack, I had to ask. I barely knew the man, and he and Joanie were somewhat at odds, and I'm not sure why."

"I can tell you why. Joanie has grown up to be a fine woman—a lot like her mother actually, but she's always had this streak in her that made her seem impenetrable. That's why Bovier changed her name to Booth, although I told him at the time that he may as well pin a target on her by naming her Booth. Anyway, Bovier didn't want his daughter caught up in his work. He was just trying to protect her, but she made it mean that he was embarrassed by her or didn't want people to know about her. Foolishness, I say, but he never sat her down and talked to her about it like he should have. He had his own stubborn streak too."

"And Mrs. Bovier—what was his relationship with her?" Matt asked.

"They made a great team. When he joined the force, he warned her that a lot of nights and weekends would be required of him. She didn't like it, but she understood it—or so he said. She stayed with him. I'll give him that. My wife left me after twenty years—couldn't deal with it anymore, and I can't say that I blame her. If the shoe was on the other foot, I'd have bolted too. But Mrs. Bovier kept to herself and wrote her stuff. She went to church, kept up appearances in the community, and raised Joanie as best she could. I admire and respect that woman a great deal."

"It sounds as though you do. By the way, I appreciate your offer to help her if she needs something. She and Joanie think they can handle things on their own when sometimes they just need a little helping hand, you know?" Matt was smiling.

Nodding in agreement, Jack said simply, "I guess you know Joanie and her mother better than you realized. So what now, Matt—you going back to Florida soon?"

"Yes. Joanie and I will be flying out tomorrow. I need to touch base with the law firm, and then I think I'll be planning a trip back to Tallahassee."

"Funny—I was thinking a change of scenery might be good for me too. Who knows—I might just end up in Tallahassee too," said Jack with a wink.

"I'd welcome your company, Jack, and you have police connections that I simply don't have. I did meet the lead detective investigating the murder. His name is Peter Sutherland. Know him?"

"No—can't say that I do, but by the time I cross the Florida line I'll know a lot more about him than I do now," Jack chuckled softly.

Matt simply smiled and nodded his head.

"Thanks for lunch, Matt. Here's my card and my telephone number. Call me anytime." Palace stood, shook Matt's hand, and quietly left the restaurant.

CHAPTER FIVE

GAINESVILLE, FLORIDA

Matt was eager to get to the firm and talk with his partner and mentor William Brown. Taking the necessary time to thank everyone for their well-wishes on his marriage and their sympathy at the tragedy that had occurred immediately after, Matt finally made his way to Mr. Brown's office.

"Come in, son," said Brown. "Sorry not to have your new office ready, but there just hasn't been time. We'll see to it right away. So, how are you and Joanie coping with all this?"

"It's difficult, to say the least. Joanie is a strong woman, but this has really been a terrible shock. Her attitude is like mine; we both want to find out what happened and who is responsible for the murder of her father."

"After speaking with you on the phone, I put some feelers out just to see what I could find out that might be of help. While I don't have a lot of information yet, I have been in touch with some confidants in Tallahassee who should have some news soon."

"Thank you, sir," said Matt. "Any Tallahassee information is more than I have right now. Other than the detective I spoke with at the crime scene, I have nothing to go on. His name is Peter Sutherland, and from our brief encounter, he seemed like a decent sort. He appeared to be conducting a thorough investigation." Matt stood up, wandering around the room as he continued to relay what he had witnessed at the crime scene. He mentioned the investigator on the roof of a nearby building, the investigators who were shoulder to shoulder covering every inch of the cordoned off area, and the comment made by Detective Sutherland.

"It sounds as though you were pretty thorough yourself, Matt. At the very least you have something to go on. You know as well as I do that an investigator wouldn't climb up onto a roof unless he expected to find something relevant."

"I need to just run something by you too, sir," said Matt.

"Sure—whatever," said Brown.

"I suspect Bovier's death was an ordered assassination—a *hit* perhaps," Matt said

"First thought that came to my mind as well," said Brown. "Planned, orchestrated, and carried out without witness? Sounds like a hit to me."

"So having had that thought, I met with Bovier's longtime partner—Jack Palace. He swears that Bovier was legit and an honest cop. He even made the statement that he'd never seen the guy so much as jaywalk in twenty-five years."

Brown interjected, "And you doubt that's true?"

"I wouldn't say 'doubt it' but I am more than mildly curious how an undercover detective could amass a small fortune and hand it over to his daughter as a wedding present." Matt stopped his pacing and faced Brown. "He gave Joanie a cashier's check for thirty thousand dollars. Now tell me how could that be possible unless he was playing both sides of the law?"

"Good investments, perhaps," said Brown facetiously. "It's not unheard of. Perhaps he had some old family money lying around earning interest?"

"Well, I'm sure that Joanie is wondering about it as well. I think if there had been some 'old family money' lying around her parents would have helped pay for her law school tuition. Joanie borrowed every cent of that. And she's never mentioned anyone in her family having any sort of valuable anything."

"Piques your interest, doesn't it?" asked Brown.

"It piqued my interest to the point that I blatantly asked Palace if Bovier was a crooked cop," Matt said. "He kept telling me they were both 'old school cops' and that they despised the 'newbies' ho took advantage of the system. I don't know. I don't like thinking Bovier was on the take, but the pieces I have don't fit together. I need more info and more time to figure it out."

"You know that you have the resources of the firm to investigate this, Matthew. You're a partner now, and you have earned the right to follow any course of action you deem necessary, particularly since your own family has been hurt by this heinous action."

"Thank you, sir, I appreciate your support. I would like a bit of time to go to Tallahassee, have a look around, and question a few people. Obviously, we'll be suspending our honeymoon plans indefinitely."

"What can I do to help you, Matthew?" asked the fatherly Brown.

"Any information you can get about the shooting or the police investigation would be most helpful and appreciated. Jack Palace has offered to meet me in Tallahassee. He wants to look at the crime scene firsthand and talk cop-to-cop with Sutherland."

"That's a good idea and a good resource. While I have connections with several law firms and a couple of private detectives, one cop talking to another cop will garner information more quickly and perhaps more accurately than any other source."

"Then we can compare notes?" asked Matthew

"Of course we can. How soon do you plan to head over to the capital?"

"I'd go tonight, but I have to make sure that Joanie is OK and settled as much as she can be before I take off. I'm going to urge her to take at least a week off from the State Attorney's office just to get her bearings. If all goes well, I could leave in a couple of days," Matt said. "In the meantime, I'd like to get some information on Jack Palace from the NOPD. Do you have any connections there?"

"Let me see," said Brown, flipping through a Rolodex card holder on his desk. "Ah—here's an old law school buddy who lives near New Orleans in a town called Metairie. I'll give him a call and see what he knows about Bovier as well as Palace." Brown was picking up the telephone before Matthew left the room. There was an eerie silence in the apartment that Matt and Joanie would now share as man and wife. The living area was littered with wedding gifts from friends and coworkers. Joanie opted to clear the room by moving everything to what would ultimately be a guest bedroom. Just the mere act of clearing out the space seemed to lift her mood and make her feel more peaceful. There would be plenty of time for her and Matt to open the gifts.

Having that done, Joanie went out for a walk. She wandered down the street to a nearby new and used bookstore simply and aptly named *Volumes.* The bookstore was run by a sweet, middle-aged woman named Bella. Joanie had frequented the store since moving to Gainesville and had gotten to know Bella pretty well.

Joanie and Bella shared two great loves—good books and hot tea. Bella almost always had a pot of tea brewing and shared it with her favorite customers.

As predicted, the tea was brewing when Joanie entered the store. As the bell rang, signaling a customer had entered, Bella looked up with a start to see her customer and friend Joanie.

"What? Cherie?" said Bella. She called all her favorite women friends *Cherie.*

"Why are you here, my Cherie? You should be on your honeymoon now."

"Hi, Bella—you're right. I should be on my honeymoon. How about tea, and I'll tell you all about it?"

"I have your favorite Earl Grey on hand. Sit and I'll bring the tea," Bella said as she turned toward the back of the store. "You sit at my desk."

Joanie sat on the customer's side of the big wooden desk. Its familiarity comforted her. There on the side was the large silver tray with two petite and mismatched china teacups, two silk napkins trimmed in embroidery, spoons, sugar cubes, and cream. All that was missing was the teapot itself.

In the middle of the desk, Joanie spotted a very old book of poetry. It was turned upside down no doubt to mark the page where Bella had left off her reading. Curiosity got the better of her, and she picked up the volume to look more closely. It was called *Best Loved Poems of the American People; circa 1936.* No sooner had Joanie started to read a passage when Bella appeared with the Earl Grey.

"You like poetry, Cherie?"

"I'm so sorry, Bella—I didn't mean to pry," Joanie quickly replied.

"What? I didn't think you were prying—it's a book, not a ledger sheet. Please, relax. Have tea and talk to Bella."

Bella gingerly poured the tea into the two china cups and placed one, along with a napkin and spoon, in front of Joanie. She then poured her own cup and sat down on the other side of the desk.

"I don't know where to begin this story, Bella. It's so unbelievable."

"Start where you start. Bella will catch up or ask questions. Please."

Bella was talking about herself in third person again. She did that sometimes when she was a bit flustered or when her French country accent appeared.

Joanie took a long sip of tea as Bella watched her intently.

"The wedding was beautiful, Bella. I could not have asked for anything better. Matthew's original vows were sweet and perfect. He was so incredibly handsome, and he had the biggest smile on his face. After the ceremony, we went to The Tea Room for the reception. Everything there was just as we had requested. The place was stunning, and the cake was exactly what we had wanted. The world was mine at that moment, Bella. I had never been so happy in all of my life." Joanie hesitated for a moment before she continued. Bella sat silently.

"Then we heard sirens—loud, screeching tires, and I saw Matthew's face go pale. I saw him look around the room, and I guess he noticed that my father wasn't there. I had noticed that too, but I've told you what a driven man my father was—a man who put his work above his family no matter what. I just assumed he was off somewhere making a telephone call or whatever. But Matt must have feared the worst. He sent his twin brother to the Serenity Garden Chapel where our wedding was held, and the next thing I knew, Matt was pulled out of The Tea Room by his brother and two men I'd never seen before. They were policemen, Bella, coming with Marc to tell my mother that her husband had been murdered." Joanie sat quietly sipping her tea.

"Your father was murdered?" Bella could not believe what she had just heard.

"Yes, just outside the wedding chapel where Matthew and I said our vows. He was shot once in the head and died instantly."

Bella made her way around the desk and wrapped her arms around her friend Joanie. She didn't utter a word.

Joanie was the first to break the silence.

"It's a bad thing, Bella. I knew that one day this would happen to him. I just didn't know it would be the day that I married the love of my life."

CHAPTER SIX

NEW YORK CITY

It had been a mere two months since John disappeared, but to Alex it felt like an eternity. Everything in his life had changed, and it wasn't all for the better.

Alex was spending less and less time with his wife and family. He was working around the clock at times, and at other times he was researching new ways to keep the organization profitable.

Putting out fires was a big part of what he had Ben working on. That appeared to be a full-time job. Ben was loyal to a fault, but he openly disagreed with Alex on some things, as evidenced by his reaction in the meeting with the soldier.

He would have to deal with this. He could not allow anyone to openly show disrespect. He didn't have time for it, nor did he want to try to replace Ben as his second. John would never have wanted that to happen.

And then there was the situation with John. Pouring himself a drink, he paced the floor of the penthouse suite the organization had rented and reconsidered all that he knew.

He recalled the day that John had made him first in line to be in charge should anything ever happen to him. He distinctly remembered the conversation that John had with both Ben and him. Thinking back to the days leading up to that particular conversation, Alex recalled being in on a meeting between John and his attorney, Samuel Jackson Graves. John did not like that man, nor did he trust him after he had advised John to divorce his wife, Ruth.

Alex opted to call Graves and get his take on John's disappearance.

CHAPTER SEVEN

NEW ORLEANS, LOUISIANA

Ignacio Graceffo was spending much of his time in the NOPD station house. He was pushing papers across his desk when he was approached by Jack Palace.

"Didn't see you at the funeral," said Jack.

"Nope, being the low man on the totem pole, I had to pull a shift on the desk here," Graceffo replied. "Sad about the old guy, though."

"Yeah, sad," said Jack. "It's a shame you didn't know him better."

"Yeah, why?"

"You could have learned a lot from Bovier. He was a good cop and a good person, but he was also like me—a pit bull when he was cornered."

Graceffo simply smiled and nodded his head as Palace walked away.

Palace walked straight to the chief's office. The chief was out, but his assistant and deputy asked Jack if he could help.

"I just wanted to come by and thank the chief for the show of support at Bovier's funeral," said Jack in a solemn tone. "It was amazing that he had so many of the brothers on hand."

The assistant said, "It was a mandatory appearance—and that's standard operating procedure when one of our own is killed. You've been around long enough to know the only exception to that is a seasoned officer has to be on desk duty and in direct radio contact with key personnel in the event of a robbery, shooting, or disturbance."

"A seasoned officer—yeah, I did know that."

"Yes, sir—someone who knows who's who and how to handle anything that might occur during that period of time," replied the assistant.

"Excellent plan—sounds like he has things well in hand. Well, give my best to the chief when you see him. Just wanted to stop by and say thanks," Jack said as he turned to leave.

CHAPTER EIGHT

TAMPA, FLORIDA

Carmine Lorenzo was pleased that things had gone according to plan. With Bovier out of the way, he could proceed without fear of interference. He was confident that no one even suspected a connection between the good detective and his organization, and that was just the way he wanted to keep it.

Bovier had done Lorenzo a favor by leading him to Giuseppe D'Agastino. And while he hadn't realized it, Bovier had given Lorenzo just the ammunition he needed to infiltrate John Ward's empire.

"Who is it?" asked Lorenzo when the knock came to the door.

"It's the attorney from New Orleans, sir; says he has something important for you," said the voice from the other side of the door.

"OK, let him in."

A man dressed in a three-piece suit entered Lorenzo's office, closely followed by two of Lorenzo's bodyguards. As soon as he entered the room, Lorenzo dismissed the bodyguards.

"So, you've done well, I hear," said Lorenzo.

"I have, sir, and everything has been carried out according to your wishes."

"Then I'd say you've earned not only a bonus, but also my respect, Mr. Graves."

"Thank you, sir, but I'm just doing my job," Graves answered.

"And Graceffo?" asked Lorenzo.

"He's still with the NOPD for the time being, sir. He's still under the impression that the order for the hit came from Alexander Mineo."

Carmine Lorenzo slapped both hands together at this news and said, "Good work, Mr. Graves. Let's keep that ruse going for now."

"Graceffo knows to call me with any changes or questions. He's really not the sharpest pencil in the box, but he's an excellent marksman."

"We didn't hire him for his brains. I just need to know he's smart enough to keep his mouth shut," Lorenzo said.

"Well, sir, I'm convinced that if Graceffo opted to shoot off his mouth, he'd be fingering Mineo, not us," Graves said with a laugh.

"Even better," said Lorenzo, "but let's keep an eye on him just in case things get iffy."

"I'll see to it personally," said Graves. "The report I've prepared for you gives you full details of the plan and the execution of the plan. It was well done, if I say so myself."

"Great," said Lorenzo. "Now get back to New York and see what's happening there. I'll expect a report within forty-eight hours."

"Good day, sir," Graves said and headed for the door.

CHAPTER NINE

TALLAHASSEE, FLORIDA

Detective Peter Sutherland was a tall, handsome man with a slender build and piercing blue eyes. His dark, thick hair added to his good looks, and he was the consummate gentleman, adding even more charm to his persona.

Pete was a hardworking detective, an honest man with a beautiful wife and family, and his reputation was stellar. He had graduated with honors from the police academy and had worked his way up the ranks from a beat cop to detective in only five years. While he preferred working alone, he had been required to mentor a younger, less experienced detective. His assignment was a nice, young man named Scott Wood.

Scott Wood was honest and bright—a straight-up kind of guy; he just lacked experience. Sutherland knew that with experience comes patience, the ability to be a big-picture kind of guy, and

that experience was the ultimate teacher when it came to reacting to a knee-jerk situation.

Scott was learning and seemed eager to do his best, but at times it was frustrating to have to rein him in.

This was the situation Pete faced in working on the Bovier homicide. Scott Wood had shared his thoughts on the murder confidentially with Pete, and Pete, in as gentle a manner as possible, poked holes in his assumptions. That's the way you learned to be a good detective. It was also better than Scott going to the precinct and spreading his not-so-well-thought-out scenario to the chief.

Pete and Scott sat in their unmarked patrol car on the street in front of Serenity Chapel. They recounted to one another what they knew and how they knew it. They evaluated the facts and reviewed the ballistics report that had just come in.

The ballistics report contained the following information:

Detective Bovier was shot with an M1 Caliber .30 Carbine semiautomatic rifle. This semiautomatic rifle fires a single bullet each time the trigger is pulled, automatically ejects the spent cartridge, chambers a fresh cartridge from its magazine, and is immediately ready to fire another shot. The evidence at the scene indicated that a lone shot was fired. No casings were found or recovered on the garden lawn or in adjacent areas. No casings were found on the rooftop of the adjacent building where it is believed the shooter was positioned. This will be confirmed or denied based on the autopsy report and a closer examination of the bullet's trajectory.

"So what do we know about the weapon?" Scott asked. "Is this a military firearm, and if so, is it used in the US military?"

"Good thinking, Scott. The M1 Carbine has been used as a standard firearm for the US military as far back as World War II and the Korean War. It wouldn't be hard to get your hands on one of those if that's what you're thinking," Sutherland replied. "They're lightweight—easy to maneuver, even up to a rooftop, and because the magazine feeds from underneath the rifle, you have an accurate count of how many shots you've fired. It looks as though our rifleman was a sharpshooter and only needed one bullet. With that casing ejected where he was positioned, he could easily pick it up and walk away with it."

"And how does a guy with a semiautomatic rifle walk around a public park, climb up an equally public building, and position himself on the roof without being noticed?" Scott asked.

"Perhaps he gained access to the roof from inside the building," Sutherland posed.

"Perhaps we should check to see if there is access," Scott said proudly.

The two detectives bounded out of the car and walked the perimeter of the building. Their crime scene investigators had examined the roof by way of a ladder. They were looking for another access point.

Coming to a door disguised by some overgrown bougainvillea, Scott tried the door and found it locked. "It's search warrant time," Scott said.

"Excellent," replied Sutherland. "I didn't want to see you try to break down that door."

"And get cut to shreds by that bougainvillea?" Scott replied.

"Right but we follow protocol even if there's another good excuse," Sutherland retorted. "We'll get the search warrant and come back."

CHAPTER TEN

GAINESVILLE, FLORIDA

Bella and Joanie were well into their pot of tea, and Joanie had related all the details she knew about her father's murder. Bella, being a kind and caring friend, listened intently without offering any opinions or asking questions. There would be time enough for that, but she recognized that now what Joanie needed most was to expel everything in her mind that was haunting her.

When Joanie reached for her teacup, Bella laid one hand on hers and said simply, "I am always here for you, Cherie; whatever I can do for you, I am happy to do."

"At this moment, you've given me just what I was in need of most—someone to confide in; someone I can trust," Joanie replied. "I probably should look around for a book to read—maybe short stories that I don't have to read over long periods of time. My concentration isn't the best right now, but I could use a literary escape."

Bella reached across the desk to the old leather-bound poetry book and handed it to Joanie. "This will be the perfect thing," she said with a smile. "You read a little, you ponder a little. It will bring you laughter and tears, but it will also bring you to a new place of understanding."

"But you were reading this—I saw it here when I came in," Joanie protested.

"Ah, but it was on my desk for a reason, and I believe you are that reason. Take it. Keep it as long as you need to. I know it's in good hands." Bella again offered the poetry book to Joanie.

"I've never read poetry before. Well, except 'The Wreck of the Hesperus' when I had to read it for a class," Joanie said.

"That's in here too. Read it again with your newly formed thoughts and feelings. You might find that you take something from it that you did not recognize before. But more than a poem that tells a story, this book is filled with many sections that deal with everyday issues," Bella said to her friend.

"I'll take it because you recommended it, Bella. Thanks."

Joanie stood up from Bella's desk and kissed her friend on both cheeks before leaving the store with the leather-bound book of poetry.

Propping herself up on the couch, Joanie opened the book and began to read. Bella had been correct in that the book had several sections including *Love and Friendship, Inspiration, Poems that Tell a Story, Faith and Reverence, Home and Mother, Childhood and Youth, Patriotism and War, Humor and Whimsy, Memory and Grief, Nature, Animals,* and a catchall called *Various Themes.*

Joanie found that she preferred the nonrhyming pieces best. After some time she came upon a poem that she immediately copied onto a piece of paper. It was entitled *Along the Road* and was written by Robert Browning Hamilton.

I walked a mile with Pleasure;
She chatted all the way,
But left me none the wiser
For all she had to say.

I walked a mile with Sorrow
And ne'er a word said she;
But oh, the things I learned from her
When Sorrow walked with me!

Something tugged at her heart when she read the words. For once in her life she was reading something that was not necessarily literal, but it was imaginative, haunting. Perhaps Bella had known she would find such a poem that would move her and make her think. She *was* walking with sorrow, and perhaps she too would learn a great deal from the experience.

CHAPTER ELEVEN

NEW ORLEANS, LOUISIANA

Jack Palace was no fool. He suspected Graceffo was lying, and now he knew it. So the question that puzzled him now was where was he? If he wasn't at the station, and wasn't at the funeral, wonder where he was and why would he lie about it?

Jack knew there was no love lost between Graceffo and Bovier. More than once since Graceffo joined the police force, Bovier had expressed his on-sight dislike for the guy; he had even called him a thug with a badge. Jack wondered now if there had been something specific that caused the mutual dislike or whether Bovier just had a gut feeling about the guy.

Jack knew everyone who was anyone and decided to ask around. Amazingly no one seemed to know very much about Ignacio Graceffo, and more than one cop told Jack they wanted to keep it that way.

"So the guy doesn't have any close friends on the force?" Jack asked a lieutenant.

"Nah, pretty much a loner," replied the lieutenant.

"Does he have family here?"

"I don't think so. I think he's from New York."

"A New Yorker?"

"Yeah, and obviously Italian with a name like Graceffo." The lieutenant continued, "He's real touchy about his name too."

"How so?"

"Oh, Jack, you know how the guys in the squad room like to tease. They started calling him "Iggie," and he got all bent out of joint. It was just boys being boys, you know, but he threw a couple of punches before the sergeant broke it up."

"Well, well," said Jack. "That's interesting."

"You know, Jack, I don't know much about the guy, other than he likes to hang around Foxy's in his spare time."

"Foxy's bar in the Quarter?"

Bovier used to like Foxy's, and used to frequent it. Jack himself had been there a couple of times with Bovier, but he didn't remember ever seeing Graceffo. Maybe he'd make a trip to the Quarter to see what he could find out.

CHAPTER TWELVE

GAINESVILLE, FLORIDA

Matthew was preparing for his trip to Tallahassee and had gotten some information from Mr. Brown about the police department there. All reports were positive about Peter Sutherland and his capabilities as a police detective. Matt was glad to know that the lead investigator on Bovier's case was described as one of the best of the best.

A sense of anxiety encompassed Matt as he packed his briefcase for the trip. He dreaded leaving Joanie at this time and probably dreaded telling her more than anything. She had endured so much in such a short amount of time.

Matt knew that Joanie would understand and that she was as eager as anyone to get to the heart of what had happened to her father. Still he hated leaving her alone.

Just before heading home, Matthew made a telephone call to Jack Palace.

"I'm heading to Tallahassee tomorrow," said Matthew when he made contact with Jack.

"OK," said Jack. "I have a couple of things to look into here, so I'll plan to meet you in Tallahassee day after tomorrow. Hopefully I'll have information that's worth sharing."

"Great," said Matt. "I'm staying at Haven—it's a Bed and Breakfast near the chapel."

"You attorneys get the preferential treatment don't you?" laughed Jack. "I'll be at the hotel in the economy suite. I'll phone you when I get in."

"See you in a couple of days."

Joanie was sound asleep on the couch with the thick leather-bound book draped across her lap when Matthew entered the apartment. She looked so peaceful he hated to awaken her. He tried to put his briefcase quietly on the hall table.

"Is that you, Counselor?" Joanie yawned and stretched.

"Guilty. Sorry I woke you."

"No, don't be. I was reading and just fell asleep, I guess. What's up?"

"I think dinner will be 'out' tonight, my love," Matthew said.

"OK, but what are you buttering me up for?"

"I'm going to Tallahassee tomorrow for a few days."

"I see. Well, you'd better take me someplace really special then."

"Your choice, my love."

"OK, then I must change clothes," said Joanie. "And so must you, Counselor. You look like an attorney in that outfit. I'm donning jeans and boots. I want ribs. Big, juicy, fattening ribs from Porker's."

"Porker's?" exclaimed Matthew. "I love that place."

"I knew that—now let's change and go." Joanie was up and bounding down the hallway to their master bedroom before Matt could blink an eye.

Matt poured himself a beer, took one to Joanie, and sat down on the couch. He picked up the leather-bound book and saw that it was poetry. He'd never known Joanie to read poetry before. They usually shared books since their preference was political fiction, suspense, or intrigue.

"Yes, I'm reading poetry," Joanie said. "Of course, it did put me to sleep." She laughed as she said it.

CHAPTER THIRTEEN

NEW YORK CITY

Alex called a meeting with Ben and spoke candidly about his blatant disregard for appearances. Ben assured him he meant no disrespect. The subject then changed to John and Graves.

"I think we should meet with Graves and get his take on John's sudden disappearance," said Alex. "He may have information we aren't aware of."

"With all due respect," said Ben, "what kind of information?"

"A threat—perceived or otherwise—a deal John hadn't shared with us. There could be a number of things."

"But, Alex, wouldn't Graves have come forward with that information? He knows we're in charge of the organization in John's absence, and to my knowledge he's still the organization's attorney, so wouldn't he have a vested interest in keeping us apprised?"

"One would think," said Alex, "but I've called him twice today and gotten no call back. Maybe he's too busy to work for us anymore."

"Maybe so. I'd suggest giving him twenty-four hours to call back or else," Ben said.

"In the meantime, Ben, what exactly do you remember about that last meeting John had with Graves?"

"I remember John being angry enough to kill Graves on the spot when he recommended John divorce his wife."

"Yeah, and then he dismissed Graves," said Alex. "That's when he went to South Carolina to see his wife, right?"

"Right. "

"And on the second trip to see her, he and she both vanished into thin air."

"Right again, Alex, what's your point? We've been over this a thousand times," said Ben.

"My point is, we need to review everything that happened between those two trips. We need to look at what John did and with whom, what he said to you, what he said to me, and we need to corner Graves and see what, if anything, John had *him* do." Alex was into a fast pace around the suite.

"I'll do my best to reconstruct those days if you think it might give us answers," Ben said.

"And I'll look back at every appointment we had together as well as what the subject matter was," Alex said.

"We'll give Graves twenty-four hours. If we haven't heard from him by then, we're going to find him and bring him here, agreed?"

"Agreed."

CHAPTER FOURTEEN

TALLAHASSEE, FLORIDA

Cynthia and Ron welcomed Matthew back to Haven, asking about how things were going and what, if anything, they could do to assist him. As predicted, Matt had no special requests other than "if you hear anything that you think might be important for me to know, tell me." Matt recognized that someone living here full time might be privy to word on the street about Bovier's murder.

After settling in, Matthew took the short walk to the Serenity Chapel. Everything looked the same as it had before the shooting death of his new father-in-law. As Matt strolled around the grounds, a familiar voice came up from behind.

"Taking an afternoon stroll?" Peter Sutherland asked.

"Why, yes, detective, I was doing just that," replied Matthew. "And you?"

"Actually, I've been here several times since we last met. And by the way, this is my partner, Detective Scott Wood. Scott, this is Matthew Winters, son-in-law of the late Detective Bovier."

The two shook hands as Detective Scott Wood expressed his condolences.

"At the risk of prying, do you have any additional information or new leads on my father-in-law's killer?" Matthew asked.

"Actually, Mr. Winters—"

"Matthew, please."

"Actually, Matthew, we are looking into several details regarding the exact positioning of the shooter. We've just retrieved a search warrant for this building," Sutherland said pointing to the single-story structure adjacent to the gardens.

"So do you have the ballistics report?" Matt asked.

"We do, and we also believe the shooter was positioned on the top of this building," Sutherland replied. "There's no easy access from the outside, but we have found a point of entry on the other side of the building."

"Could you show me where that is?" Matt queried.

"Certainly, Matthew, but I cannot allow you to interfere with our investigation," said Sutherland.

"I wouldn't dream of it, sir. I am a partner in the law firm of Baxter, Brown, Newman, and Winters, and am more than mildly interested in assisting you in your investigation—not botching it for you," Matthew said. "Please, lead the way."

The three men circled the small building, coming to the side where the bougainvillea grew abundantly and wild. Detective Wood reached into the plant to show Matthew where the door was.

"We believe the shooter gained access to the rooftop through the interior of the building," Wood said confidently.

"Ah, that would certainly conceal their ingress and give them plenty of time to set up their shot without being noticed," said Matthew.

Sutherland looked a bit stunned by Matt's spot-on observation. "Guess you've been involved in situations like this before, Matthew. "

"I can't say that I have. Let's just say that I've dealt with enough criminals—white collar and otherwise—to look for reasons behind the clues." Matt smiled, knowing that he had just scored some points with Sutherland.

"If you'll step back, Matthew, Scott and I are going inside. I'd invite you in, but that wouldn't be appropriate, now would it?"

"Please—don't let me detain you." Matt smiled as he said it.

Before the two detectives entered through the doorway, they fully inspected the door jam and the surrounding casings and observed a recent abrasion on the lower edge of the door. It was obvious that it had been pried or jimmied open at some point. The foliage adjacent to that spot had been pushed aside and obviously put back in place. Bougainvillea was hearty enough to survive much worse. It basically grew wherever you put it and could be trained to cover a structure or grow vertically on a trellis.

After gaining entry, Sutherland and Wood closed the door behind them. Within a matter of a couple of minutes, the two appeared on the rooftop.

"Very quick and easy access," said Sutherland nodding down at Matthew.

"Anything up there worth looking at?" asked Matthew.

"We're going to take a look around up here and then make another sweep of the inside of the building. If you want to stick around, you're welcome to do so," Sutherland said.

"You can bet on it," said Matt.

Matthew went back to the garden, unable to push the memories of his wedding day aside. He and Joanie had been so blissfully happy for those few moments before Bovier was gunned down. He strolled through the garden, edging his way toward the door where the chapel spilled out into the garden. Looking up toward the adjacent building's rooftop, Matthew realized how vulnerable he, Joanie, and his family had been on that day. The gunman could have fired into the crowd, killing anyone and everyone at the wedding. He had a clear shot. Yet he waited until everyone left, except Bovier.

While Matthew had never entertained the notion of the killing being a random act of violence, he shuddered to think what *could* have happened. There was clearly no doubt—the lone gunman came there to kill Bovier and had accomplished his task in one fatal shot. Still lost in his thoughts, Matthew was startled by Sutherland's voice.

"A penny for your thoughts," Sutherland said.

"Lone gunman, single shot, waited until Bovier was alone and then did what he was hired to do," said Matthew in an eerily calm voice. "Anything you can share with me from inside or on top?"

"It's obvious the gunman had ample opportunity to hide inside the building, probably after he set up the shot on the roof. There's no way he would have been noticed unless he stood up. It's an easy crawl from the attic onto the rooftop," Sutherland said. "We've had CSIs cover the roof more than once. I'm going to request that they also come back and do a sweep of the interior of the building just in case Scott and I missed something. Once I have their report I'll know more."

"Thank you, Detectives," Matt said. "I'll be in town for a few days and would appreciate hearing from you. I'm staying at Haven. Here's my business card. I put Haven's number on the back."

"Have a good day," said Sutherland as he turned and walked toward his car.

Realizing his hunger, Matthew made his way to The Tea Room for lunch. He wanted to be sure to express his appreciation for the way they had handled the interrupted reception after the shooting. He also wanted a quiet place to reflect on what he knew and, more importantly, what he hoped to learn from this trip.

CHAPTER FIFTEEN

NEW YORK CITY

Alex finally received the return telephone call from Graves and made it painfully clear that he was more than mildly upset by being ignored. Graves made his apologies, and the two agreed on a meeting time later that day.

After informing Ben about the time of the meeting, Alex reviewed his calendar, reconstructing the time line leading up to John's disappearance. Sure enough there was more than one meeting with Graves, and Alex could not recall any meeting between John and Graves as cordial. He could not help but wonder why John hadn't simply gotten rid of Graves and put a new attorney in charge of the organization. He made a mental note to talk with Ben before their mutual meeting with Graves.

Without being summoned, Ben arrived early for the meeting and shared his thoughts about Graves with Alex. Ben had taken an immediate dislike to Graves and described him to Alex as a "troublemaker." In the course of their conversation, Ben reminded Alex that during the planned and rehearsed turnover from John to Alex, Ignacio Graceffo had been named his enforcer, yet neither he nor Alex knew much about Graceffo. Dominic Raia had long been a good soldier and would have been the logical choice.

Alex flipped through his calendar and realized that, coinciding with a meeting between Graves, John, and himself, Dominic Raia had been dismissed by Graves as an untrustworthy marksman. It was at that meeting that Graceffo's name came up. Alex was almost sure he had been recommended by Graves to fill that particular position.

"Ben, we need to find out if there is a connection between Graves about Graceffo. I don't want either of them to suspect that we're looking into it," Alex said.

"I agree, Alex. I don't have a good feeling about this guy—never did," Ben added.

"Which one, Graves or Graceffo?"

"Both."

The knock on the door came at the precise time the meeting was to take place. Alex had the soldier open the door to a smiling Samuel Jackson Graves.

Making his apologies once again for the delay in responding to Alex's call, Graves calmly took a seat facing Alex and Ben.

"So, Graves, what's your take on John's disappearance?" Alex blatantly asked.

"My goodness, sir, I, I, uh…well I really couldn't say, just like that," Graves stammered.

Alex was thrilled to have startled the guy as well as rattled his smooth demeanor. "Come now, you must have a theory that you'd be willing to share."

"If I had to guess, I'd say that his wife talked him into bailing out on the organization," Graves said. "I advised him to divorce her, but he wouldn't hear of it."

"So, Ben, did you hear that? Graves thinks it's John's wife's fault." Alex walked around behind Graves's chair.

"That's about the dumbest thing I've ever heard," said Ben. "Like John would abandon everything he'd worked his entire life for because a woman asked him to? That's not the John who taught me about the business."

"So, Graves, want to venture another theory?" Alex asked.

"With all due respect, sir, I don't believe my theories matter much in the grand scheme of things. I'm here to advise you on legal matters. Beyond that, everything is just conjecture," Graves retorted as a thin bead of sweat gathered on his upper lip.

"OK," said Alex. "Let's assume you are correct in your original *conjecture.* How would John's wife pull that off exactly?"

"I would not have an opinion on that, sir," said Graves.

"Really?" asked Alex.

"With all due respect to both of you, I don't understand the purpose of this meeting. If you have some legal situation that needs to be addressed, I'm more than happy to assist you. As far as the logistics of your business, I find myself at a loss." Graves stood up.

"Did I say we were finished here?" asked Alex.

"Not that I heard. I thought we were just getting started," said Ben.

"Sit," said Alex, and Graves again took his seat.

"Do you keep a written calendar, Mr. Graves?" asked Alex

Graves nodded affirmative.

"Now, here's what I want you to do, Mr. Graves. I want you to reconstruct your calendar from the time you advised John to divorce his wife, to the time he actually vanished. I want you to write down everything you talked to John about—what he said and what advice he took from you. I want dates, names, and descriptions—all the details. Understood?" Alex was pacing.

"Yes, sir, but—" Graves stammered.

"There is no *but*, Mr. Graves. I'll expect your written response in forty-eight hours. You may leave now," Alex said.

"Graves, we'll see you in forty-eight," said Ben.

It was obvious the two had gotten to the slick attorney. He'd been summoned and now was given a relatively simple task for a competent man with nothing to hide, but the turnaround time was tight.

"He was nervous, Alex," said Ben.

"Yeah, a little more rattled than I've ever seen him," Alex replied. "Wonder where John found Graves to begin with?"

"I was wondering the same thing. I'll sniff around and see what I can find out about the barrister," Ben said as he stood to leave.

Samuel Jackson Graves was not a stupid man. He knew that Alex and Ben were up to something, and he was at the crux of the matter. Heading downtown to his hotel, he asked the cabbie to step on it. He had a very important telephone call to make.

CHAPTER SIXTEEN

NEW ORLEANS FRENCH QUARTER
FOXY'S BAR

The minute Jack walked into Foxy's all heads turned to the open doorway. The daylight streamed in, as did the humidity, and everyone went back to what they were doing as soon as the door closed and darkness enveloped them again.

Taking a seat midway along the bar, Jack Palace ordered a tonic rocks with a lime. The bartender looked at him a little longer than Jack thought necessary but said nothing and poured the tonic. When he delivered it, Jack said, "You probably don't get too many folks in here asking for a nonalcoholic drink, do you?"

"I get all kinds in here," said the gruff bartender. "If it's your pleasure, I'm making it for you. I don't get paid for asking questions."

"Wow, sorry, man. I didn't mean to ruffle your feathers," Jack replied as he sipped his tonic.

"But do you ever get paid to answer questions?" Jack said in a whisper.

"Depends on who's asking and what the pay is," said the bartender.

"I'm looking for some info on a cop named Graceffo. He and I drink the same drink. I just thought you might remember him," Jack took another sip.

"Don't know the guy really," said the bartender. "He comes in once in a while. All I know about him besides what he drinks is that he's not from around here with that name and that accent. He's not a big tipper either."

Jack laughed and said, "Yeah, that's him all right. He's Italian or whatever. I heard he's from New York."

"Could be," said the bartender.

Jack put a twenty dollar bill on the bar and pushed it toward the barkeep.

"I think I heard him tell someone he was Sicilian. Got sort of ticked when someone said Italian and Sicilian was the same thing," said the bartender as he pocketed the twenty.

"Interesting," said Jack. "He used to come in here with a friend of mine named Bovier. You know Bovier too?"

"I know of him. He's a detective with the NOPD. Guess maybe the two of them worked together."

"Ever hear anything they talked about?" asked Palace.

The bartender looked up and down the bar, leaned in toward Jack and said, "I can tell you they didn't talk cop talk." He quickly walked toward the end of the bar as Jack sat wondering what that meant.

Jack was done here, and he knew it. He would not garner any additional information from this bartender. Finishing his tonic he nodded to the bartender and left.

CHAPTER SEVENTEEN

TAMPA, FLORIDA

Carmine Lorenzo was lighting a Cuban cigar when his private line rang.

"Why, Mr. Graves, you sound nervous," said Carmine. "This had better be important since you're calling my private line."

"I know these two jokers well enough to know that they're up to something. They've asked me for specific details about my meetings with John and my recommendations from the time I recommended a divorce until John's disappearance."

"So? Give them all the nitty-gritty details you can conjure up. Why are you bothering me with this?"

"They seem to be on a fishing expedition, and I wanted you to be aware of it. I also wanted to give you the heads up in case there was something you wanted me to share with them," Graves said.

"Tell them whatever you want, Graves. But you'd better be convincing, if you know what I mean," Lorenzo replied.

"Convincing, sir?"

"Sounds as though they think you might have had something to do with John's disappearance. Did you, Graves?"

"Why no, of course not. I thought—"

"I don't care what you thought, Mr. Graves, nor do I care what you think. Just defuse the situation and report back to me on Graceffo as instructed." Lorenzo was obviously annoyed.

Graves sat in silence after the telephone call, wondering how he should handle Alex and Ben, and wondering if Lorenzo had anything to do with John's disappearance. Graves had convinced himself that Lorenzo was the mastermind behind the whole disappearance. Had Alex and Ben arranged the getaway? They certainly had a lot to gain, but so did every crime boss on the Eastern seaboard.

Thumbing through his calendar, Graves made notes of meetings and topics of discussion between John and him. On a separate sheet, he made the same type of notes about meetings and telephone calls with Carmine Lorenzo. Nothing jibed for him, save his recommendation to John to employ Graceffo as a bodyguard and shooter. That he had done at the direction of Lorenzo. Lorenzo had assured Graves that his recommendation would take him far in the eyes of the organization, but now that he recalled the entire conversation, Lorenzo did not mention *whose* organization would benefit.

Playing both sides was becoming tedious. He was openly employed by Alex Mineo's organization and silently working for Carmine Lorenzo's group. With heat rising on both fronts, he needed to come up with a way to protect himself from both. The biggest disadvantage was that Lorenzo held all the cards and controlled his actions. Lorenzo was responsible for the double cross, and until today Graves had believed Lorenzo had removed John. Now he wasn't so sure. The only thing he could be sure of is that bargaining with either group was not an option.

Sleep came only as desperation set in. Samuel Jackson Graves spent a fitful night filled with nightmares and scenes of destruction.

CHAPTER EIGHTEEN

NEW YORK CITY

Alex and Ben met to discuss every aspect of their business between John's first visit to his new home near Charleston, South Carolina, and his disappearance. The only common denominator was Graves, his recommended divorce, and his recommendation that Ignacio Graceffo be hired as an enforcer and bodyguard. And although Dominic Raia had been a long-standing soldier who had earned his stripes, John had not opposed giving the job to Graceffo.

"I think John had other things on his mind," said Ben.

"But John's first and last thoughts were about the good of the organization," said Alex, "and admitting a virtual stranger into that position was at best *odd*."

"Agreed," said Ben, "but what if there was an ulterior motive behind that move?"

"Such as?" Alex asked.

"Such as, what if John suspected something foul about Samuel Jackson Graves? Graves was adamant about hiring Graceffo. Perhaps John wanted to give the man enough rope to hang himself?" posed Ben.

"OK, but why was John suspicious of Graves? Did he have something on him that we don't know about?"

"Just a guess on my part, but perhaps he had *Graceffo* on Graves? Perhaps John knew there was a connection, and he wanted to see who was at the root of it," Ben said calmly. "Remember, Alex, this was all happening during the shooting and attempted murder of John, and ultimately the meeting of the five families here in the city—make that five families plus Carmine Lorenzo's sudden appearance."

"I remember that vividly, Ben. John was inconspicuously appalled at Lorenzo's inclusion in that meeting. He told me that once upon a time Lorenzo intimated that he, John, join forces with his group in Tampa and cover the state of Florida in one fell swoop. John graciously declined that offer."

"Yes, and shortly after that his house in Miami burned to the ground," said Ben, "and his wife built a new home in South Carolina."

"Enter Samuel Jackson Graves," said Alex, "and right out of the box he recommended divorce. His next recommendation was Graceffo."

CHAPTER NINETEEN

TALLAHASSEE, FLORIDA

Detective Sutherland had filed his report with the department outlining what he and Scott had discovered as a result of their investigation. After meeting with the chief, he requested that a reward be offered for any information leading to the arrest and conviction of the perpetrator. The chief agreed that offering a reward was a valid option since Serenity Chapel and its garden were in open public view. The amount of the reward was set at $1000, and posters would be placed in public places including the library, post office, police station, fire stations, and on light poles throughout the city.

As a courtesy, Peter Sutherland informed Matthew Winters of the precinct's decision.

Jack Palace had arrived in Tallahassee and immediately contacted Matthew. They arranged to meet at the Serenity Garden later that day.

"Well, I see there's no grass growing under your feet," said Matt as he approached Detective Palace.

"Just looking around; that's what I do, you know," said Palace as he stretched out his hand to greet Matthew.

"I have some information for you as a result of Detective Sutherland's investigation. He obtained a search warrant and went inside that building," Matt said, pointing toward the one-story structure on the edge of the garden. "There were obvious signs of forced entry, easy access to the roof from inside, and a clear vantage point from the roof."

"They let you go up there?" questioned Palace.

"No, not yet, but I have a good ear," Matt jokingly said. "I just heard from Sutherland. The police are offering a thousand dollar reward for information from the public. Maybe we'll get lucky, and someone will come forward who either saw something or knows something."

"Either that or every Joe Blow will say he saw something to try to get at the cash. That's a fourth of what the average bloke makes in a year!" Palace commented. "But I think it's a good idea. You never know what it may turn up, and even a less-than-great lead is better than no lead. What it says to me is that the police are really trying to get information quickly."

"That suits us just fine. The sooner this is resolved, the better for all concerned," said Matt.

"This is a fairly labor-intensive process for the police department. They have to put enough manpower together to respond and follow up on every single lead that comes in. It could be time-consuming and costly to them in man hours," Palace interjected. "But all it takes is one solid lead to blow the case wide open. We'll hope for that."

Palace walked up to the chapel steps and surveyed the distance between the steps and the shooter's presumed position. Holding up a thumb and finger as an imaginary gun he simply shook his head.

"What?" Matt asked.

"I was reversing the situation in my mind," said Jack Palace. "It's a technique that I learned from Bovier. I thought he was nuts the first time I saw him do it, but it's panned out as helpful more than once. It gives you a different perspective on the crime."

"But Bovier wasn't shot on the steps. The body was found in the garden near the sidewalk," said Matt as he pointed toward the street.

"Yep, and the shooter watched him from here to there. That means he had to move his rifle as Bovier moved, all the while keeping his finger on the trigger. He had to time everything to the split second and not give his position away too early. Had the shooter stood up two seconds before he pulled the trigger, Bovier could have seen or heard him. Obviously that didn't happen," Jack Palace appeared pleased with his summation of what occurred.

"So you believe the shooter stood up and shot Bovier?" Matthew asked.

"I do, my friend. And I think the trajectory of the bullet will prove that. Does anyone have the autopsy?"

"The police were expecting it, but I haven't been made aware of its results. I think we should follow up with Sutherland. Come on, I'll drive."

On the short drive to the TPD, Matthew asked what, if any, information Jack had gleaned from New Orleans.

"I'm looking into a cop on the force. He's relatively new and appeared to go to some lengths to become chummy with Bovier."

"And?"

"And don't you think that a buddy of Bovier would be at the funeral? He wasn't—even though the commander ordered every nonessential person to be there. And on top of that, he *lied* to me about it," Jack said flatly. "Every time someone lies, there's more to the story, and usually it's because they have something to hide."

"So what do you think this guy is hiding?" asked Matt.

"Not sure yet, Matthew, but I'm still digging. Seems that this particular policeman was 'off duty' the day Bovier was killed. Makes me wonder where he was on both occasions."

"Hmmm," said Matt. "It sounds suspicious to me. What do you know about this guy?"

"Not much—just that he's Italian and sensitive about it—and that he's from New York. I know he was hired on a recommendation from some bigwig the chief knows and probably owed a favor to. Other than the fact that the guy is a liar, a jerk, and a hothead, I don't know much at all, but I will." Not only did Palace sound unwavering, he had a very determined look on his face.

What Palace did not see was the recognition on Matthew's face when he heard that this cop was Italian and from New York. Matthew was immediately putting two and two together based on his working knowledge of the Mafia and how it operated. *Put someone in a position to get to know the target, have day-to-day knowledge of the target, and strike when the target least suspects it.*

With a glance over at Matthew, Palace said, "Did I say something that struck home with you?"

"Just thinking it all through right now; no conclusions yet," Matt replied. "Here we are. Let's see if Sutherland can give us some new information." Matt bounded out of the car, avoiding any further comment on his thoughts.

The TPD squad room was abuzz, and the desk sergeant greeted the two men. "Can we help you with something?" he asked.

"Yes, I am Matthew Winters and this is New Orleans Detective Jack Palace. We'd like to speak with Detective Sutherland."

"Have a seat, and I'll see if the detective is available," said the sergeant. "In the meantime, please put these on," he said as he handed them each a "visitor" badge. "You'll return them when you leave the station."

Within minutes, Palace and Winters were across the desk from Peter Sutherland.

"Thank you for seeing us," said Matthew. "This is New Orleans Detective Jack Palace. He was Bovier's partner and friend, and he has been a great help to Mrs. Bovier and to my wife and me. I hope you don't mind sharing information with him as well."

"It's a pleasure, Detective. I am seeing you gentlemen as a professional courtesy, but until my investigation is complete, there is little I can share with you." Sutherland was kind but firm.

"I completely understand, sir," said Palace, "and we in no way want to hinder your investigation. I have a very personal reason for my involvement with Matthew. Detective Bovier and I go back several decades. He was not only my partner, but my friend. I'm sure you understand."

"I appreciate your loyalty to your partner, but I assure you we at the TPD are doing everything in our power to find the perpetrator and bring him to justice," Sutherland said.

"We're confident you are, Detective," said Matthew, sensing animosity lurking just below the surface. "We were wondering if the autopsy report was in and what, if anything, it exposed."

"Yes, I received a copy of the report today. I should really share the details with the next of kin before I can release anything to you," Sutherland said.

"I completely understand, sir," said Matthew, "but we're in a tenable situation here. My mother-in-law is in New Orleans, my wife in Gainesville, and those women are the next of kin. They've both sponsored my trip here to hopefully discover leads to the murder of my father-in-law. While I appreciate your rules of order, I don't believe that the autopsy results should be communicated via telephone, and that leaves you with me."

"You make a good argument, Matthew. You're probably a first-rate attorney," Sutherland said. "But I would have to speak to my police chief to get clearance to relay the report to you."

"Would you please ask?" Matt queried. "It's not as if we don't all know that my father-in-law died of a bullet wound to the head. The detective and I want to know if there are any anomalies or specific bullet patterns that will assist in the investigation."

"I'll be right back," said Sutherland as he headed away from his desk and across the squad room to an office.

After just a few moments Peter Sutherland returned to his desk. "I'm afraid my chief won't release the information in the report to you. I'm sorry," Sutherland said. Looking over his shoulder toward the chief's office, he turned back to the curious duo and said, "I'm going to the hallway to get some coffee. Would either of you two like a cup?" He winked as he laid the report *open* on his desktop.

"Black for me," said Matt, "but only if it's fresh."

"I'll just walk along with you if you don't mind," said Palace. "It's not often I get to see a real squad room in another berg."

Matthew stood as if to stretch and peered at the report on the desk. Sutherland had left it open to the exact page that described the trajectory of the bullet, the caliber, and an X-ray of the wound. While Matt did not understand all that he read, he was able to get enough information to be knowledgeable about how the bullet entered the head of Detective Bovier, where it exited, and noted that the report said that the bullet shot would have caused "sudden, unexpected death." Seated again across the desk, Matthew noted that the bullet's trajectory began near the top and back of the right side of the head, and exiting through the carotid artery on the left side. While not his area of expertise, he knew that with a carotid artery severed, the victim would bleed out quickly.

As predicted, the victim had died as a result of a single gunshot wound, and more importantly, the single shot entered and exited the victim's body. Not only did that tell Matthew this was indeed the work of a trained assassin, it also told him either the shooter or an accomplice removed the bullet and its casing after it exited Bovier's head.

An accomplice? Matthew had not predicted that nor was he sure of it. What he did know is that the shooter would have had to leave his perch on top of the building, stow his rifle, approach the body, locate the bullet, remove it, and then make his way back into the building, all the while going unnoticed. Matt thought that unlikely but reserved the information for further consideration.

Sutherland and Palace were back with coffee.

"Here you are Mr. Winters, fresh, hot coffee—black as you requested," Sutherland said. "I trust it will be to your liking."

"Thanks—thank you, Detective. You've been most kind," Matthew said.

As Sutherland sat down at his desk, he flipped the file closed with one hand and moved it to another area of his desk with the other. "Is there anything else I can do for you gentlemen?" he asked.

"At this moment I don't know what it would be," said Matt.

"We'll be in touch with you, Detective. Thanks for the coffee and your time," Palace said. "I'd be proud to have a partner such as you. I did once—Bovier—a stand-up guy. "

"Call me if you need anything or discover anything that might help in our case. The reward posters will be up tomorrow, and the paper is picking it up as well. We hope to have some leads as a result of it." Sutherland stood and extended his hand. "Good day, gentlemen."

The ride back to the hotel was spent filling Jack Palace in on what Matt had seen in the report. The first words out of Palace's mouth were, "Then he must have had an accomplice."

"That was my thought at first. I think it would have been risky to leave the roof and approach the body. That would take some amount of time, and I'm not sure the killer felt it important enough to get the bullet. Besides that, why would he care if the bullet was found?"

"You're right, unless it had some significance that we aren't aware of," Palace said.

"Or perhaps there was another reason to approach the body?" Matt asked.

"I don't follow," said Palace.

"I just remember the police surrounding Bovier and removing something from his jacket before they put him on the gurney. I couldn't see what it was, but I know they bagged it as evidence," Matthew said.

"Well that would be a great question for our new friend Detective Sutherland, wouldn't it my boy?"

"I agree, but I think we've pressed our luck as far as we can for today," said Matt.

"Probably so," said Jack Palace, "and besides that, I'm starving. Want to catch some dinner together?"

"Sure. I'd love the company."

"Great—your treat," laughed Palace.

CHAPTER TWENTY

ATLANTA, GEORGIA

Getting life back to any sense of normalcy was difficult for all of the Winters siblings after the murder of Detective Bovier. While Vera and David had been helpful during the initial moments after the shooting, Vera did not feel she had done anything lately to support her brother and his beautiful new wife.

Vera was in touch with Matthew and was fairly current on what was happening with the investigation, but just talking to him didn't seem enough.

"David, we're so fortunate, and we have so much," said Vera, "and while I feel blessed and am thankful, I wish we could do something for Matt and Joanie."

"I feel a little survivor's guilt myself," said David as he bounced baby Daniel on his knee. "If you know of some manner of help we could be, just tell me."

"That's just it, I don't. Well, other than keeping them in our prayers. Matthew is resourceful, and I know if there is a way he can help solve this mystery, he will. I just hope it doesn't tear him and Joanie apart. They got off to a very rocky start." Vera was obviously worried.

"Perhaps we should invite them to come here and spend some time with us," David said. "We have lots of room, and with the holidays just around the corner, it would be a nice gesture."

"Perhaps we should invite the whole family, including Mrs. Bovier. She will inevitably have a lonely, sad holiday season. And besides, if we could get everyone together, we could share the holiday as a family. That would be best for everyone concerned." Vera looked for David's approval of her idea, and naturally she got it.

"Having everyone from the Winters family here for the holidays would be great!" David said. "I'll leave the inviting to you, and I'll help with whatever you need me to do."

"Great. I'm going to review the calendar and see what dates will work for everyone. Thank you, David," Vera said with a wink. "I think I'll call Lucy and make sure that they haven't made other plans. Marc's schedule is hectic this time of year, but I'll get some probable dates when they could travel here."

CHAPTER TWENTY-ONE

BIRMINGHAM, ALABAMA

Lucy was thrilled to get the call from her sister-in-law. "I think that's a great idea Vera," said Lucy, "and I think Marc will agree. I'll talk with him as soon as he comes in."

"Have you talked to Matt or Joanie lately?" asked Vera.

"I haven't. I know that Marc and Matt have spoken a couple of times, but I haven't had the nerve to call Joanie. I just feel so bad for her, but I really don't know her well enough to know if I should reach out of not," Lucy replied.

Vera said, "I think she would be very happy and very touched to hear from you, Lucy. You and she are not that different, you know, and you're married to twins."

"I promise I will call her this week," Lucy replied.

"Just don't mention the holidays yet," said Vera. "I'd like to speak with her personally about that. I want to include her mother."

"What a great idea, Vera!" replied Lucy. "You always know just the right way to handle things. I could take a lesson or two from you."

"And I could take a lesson or two from you about raising children. Daniel is getting so active. He's growing so quickly; I feel like I don't have a little baby anymore."

“I know,” replied Lucy, “the girls are as impulsive as can be. It takes all of my energy to keep up with them.”

“Guess I should hang up now. Please give my love to Marc and to the twins. Let me know if you can make the trip and dates that work well for you,” Vera said.

“I’ll call you, Vera, as soon as I have an answer from Marc. Take care and give our love to David and Daniel. Thanks for calling.”

CHAPTER TWENTY-TWO

NEW ORLEANS, LOUISIANA

Ignacio Graceffo was not the sharpest pencil in the box, but he was good at what he did, and he did what he was told. He had long followed orders to the letter and, because of his lack of interpretation, he was known to do things "literally."

Obviously not well-liked by his fellow police officers, he was a loner unless and except when he was required to work with someone else. He begrudgingly did that only when ordered to and truthfully was tired of this entire New Orleans scene.

Hating not only this job, he hated the stale swampy air that seemed ever present, even in the fall and winter months. He preferred the snow, the cold, and the food that the northeast offered. But for now he presumed he was stuck here.

Graceffo was neither creative nor personable. His family life had been disrupted abruptly when his parents were killed in a drive-by shooting in New York. As a young man he was forced to make ends meet and find work where he could. That led him to a life of criminal activity, which had, up until now, provided him with enough money and satisfaction to live his solitary life.

He had always hated the name Ignacio, but it was the last remaining vestige of a connection to his mother whom he dearly loved. Her grandfather had the name, as had her father, and changing it wasn't an option in Graceffo's mind.

The name Graceffo was made up. He dreamed it one night and liked the sound of it, so he kept it. He didn't have a driver's license until he came to New Orleans, and even though he was forced to have a fake ID made, he still did not drive a car. In New York that was useless and an expense he didn't need.

The fake ID and driver's license had been given to him by his boss, Samuel Jackson Graves. He had been told where to go, how to act, and what to do by this man, and he'd been paid handsomely—in cash of course. He sent Graves his paychecks from the NOPD and never gave another thought to that. As long as he was taken care of, he didn't worry about anything else.

It had been Graves who ordered the hit on the flatfoot detective named Bovier. Graceffo had gotten to know Bovier just well enough to know the guy who was on his hit list and knew little if anything else about him. Graceffo had learned as a kid not to ask questions—just to do as he was told.

He never wondered why he was told to do these things; he really didn't care why. Actually Ignacio Graceffo didn't care about anyone or anything. A loner by choice, an outcast by personality, and a foreigner in this part of the world, the only thing he was ready for was a change—a new job. And even in his limited thinking and planning for the future, Ignacio knew his job was nearly concluded, and he was ready to move on.

The only thing left to do for Graceffo was to eliminate his accomplice. He had never liked depending on someone else when a job was imminent, but in this case, he couldn't be in two places at once, and the hit required some tricky timing that Graves had laid out in great detail. Graceffo had no choice but to work with another soldier. Graceffo would be "the" hit man, and his partner would pose as a bystander who just happened upon the crime scene. All the partner had to do was plant some stupid piece of paper on Bovier and then act shocked and dismayed that someone had been killed. Now Graceffo had to find him and get rid of him permanently.

The call from Graves came saying that Schnauzer could be found at a motel on the outskirts of Tallahassee called "The Fountains" and provided Schnauzer's room number to Ignacio. He would leave tonight for Tallahassee to eliminate Leonard "Lefty" Schnauzer from the earth.

CHAPTER TWENTY-THREE

TALLAHASSEE, FLORIDA

"Hello, this is Detective Sutherland," answered Pete.

"Matt Winters here, Detective—do you have a minute?"

"Sure, Matt, what can I do for you?"

"Just wondering if you had considered the possibility that the shooter had an accomplice?"

"Wow, that came out of the blue," said Sutherland. "But, yes, I am considering that as a possibility. But tell me, why would you consider that a possibility?"

"OK detective—I'll let you in on something that I noticed the day my father-in-law was killed. I saw a CSI remove some sort of note or communiqué from his lapel or his pocket and bag it as evidence or at least *potential* evidence. I have restrained myself from asking you about it, but I am thinking now that if someone planted a note on Bovier, it most likely would *not* been the shooter. That totals *accomplice* in my mathematical column."

"I see," said Sutherland. A lengthy silence followed.

"Detective Sutherland, are you still on the line?" asked Matt.

"Yes, I am, but I am at a loss as to exactly what I can or should share with you at this point." Sutherland was the consummate professional, and he had already taken a risk by allowing Matt a sneak peek at the autopsy report.

"I understand," said Matthew, "but can you just confirm that there was indeed a note of some kind placed on my father-in-law's body?"

"That's affirmative," replied Sutherland.

"Thank you, Pete. Just one more question if I may?" asked Matt.

"OK."

"I understand that there was a person who called in the shooting to the police. I'm wondering if that person has been questioned about what he or she saw?" posed Matt.

"Affirmative as well," said Sutherland. "He gave us a statement at the scene, and we are actually planning to question him further in the next couple of days. And in order to answer your *next* question, yes, I plan to do the questioning myself."

"Great. I'd love to be a fly on that wall," Matt said. "So I guess it's safe to assume he lives in or around Tallahassee?"

"He's a developer out of Tampa who is looking at some land here," said Sutherland. "His statement was fairly concise and didn't send up any red flags to my people, but I'd like to chat with him anyway while he's still in town."

"Good. I'd feel better knowing you had talked with him."

"If there's anything I can share, I will," said Sutherland.

"Thanks, Pete. Have a great day."

Matthew's mind was whirling. He opted to call his partner and mentor at the law firm to share this information. When he had reported it all to Brown, he invariably told him he felt he was at a dead end and perhaps he should just come back to Gainesville.

Brown urged him to follow through with Sutherland and reminded his junior partner that he had already established a rapport with him and that he would most likely share any pertinent information he found or didn't find as a result of questioning this witness.

Matt agreed and told Brown he would stay a couple of more days to follow this through.

Matthew called Joanie that evening with the news that he would stay in Tallahassee a bit longer.

CHAPTER TWENTY-FOUR

HAWAII – THE BIG ISLAND

SEPTEMBER 1960

Riana Tavares had settled into the new house in record time. Her husband Jarrod was desperately trying to settle in as well, which was easy enough, but settling into his new life had proven complicated.

The past few months had been difficult to say the least.

Everything was foreign to them. Riana and Jarrod were in new surroundings, sharing a new life with totally new identities. They were required to learn every day. Memorizing the data that told the story of their lives was complicated simply because someone had made the details up for them. But their choice was a simple one: stay, learn, forget, and live or suffer permanent incarceration and/or death.

Their choice was not made lightly. They knew they had to give up everything and everyone in their lives. There would be no contact whatsoever with anyone they had known before, save the FBI suits with whom they were in scheduled and carefully executed communication. Jarrod met with one or more of them weekly, giving them details and information they asked for and often feeling gut-wrenched afterward.

Sadly, this was the deal. At least he was with his wife of many years, living in a tropical paradise and had at long last felt safe enough to venture out a bit.

Riana and Jarrod strolled along the coarse brown shores of the Pacific Ocean and marveled at its clarity and purity. There were points in the mountains where they could drive and look down into the sapphire blue water, still able to view sea life in its natural habitat.

Surrounded by beauty and calm was yet another new part of their lives. Never had either of them been able to share a meal, a drive, or even a walk without fear, without being on constant alert. It wasn't easy to get used to it. Jarrod was still hesitant and looked over his shoulder often. Riana would remind him they were safe—not with words, but with the loving look she had had on her face from day one.

As they began their new and relatively safe life, they were unaware of the turmoil that was brewing on the other side of the United States.

For the time being, Riana and Jarrod practiced their memorization of their separate and collective past. Nothing was the same—not even their anniversary date. Everything had changed except their devotion to one another.

Riana couldn't help but wonder about her "old" family. At times she would even dream of Vera and her brothers. She knew better than to ask about Matthew, even though he had brokered their deal to go to Hawaii, to change their identities and begin a new life. Asking the FBI could indicate that she was unwilling to live up to the terms they had been given.

Similarly, Jarrod Tavares never asked about the organization. While ever cautious about directly implicating Alexander or Benjamin, Jarrod gave the FBI all the information they could want on Carmine Lorenzo, Senior and Junior, Francesco Patron, and last but not least, Samuel Jackson Graves.

Providing the FBI with as much information as he was comfortable giving meant telling the FBI about the Mafia's influence in the unions; specifically the mention of a name that would go down in history, one James Riddle Hoffa. What Jarrod was unaware of was that Hoffa had been reelected as president of the Teamsters Union earlier that year.

Jarrod knew all about the McClellan Committee, which had been set up to investigate the influence of organized crime in labor unions. He was aware that Robert F. Kennedy, Esquire was the chief counsel of the Senate Labor Rackets Committee (aka the McClellan Committee). He also knew that John Fitzgerald Kennedy, an up-and-coming Democratic senator from Massachusetts and brother to Robert, was running for president of the United States. Many discussions ensued about the Kennedys and their anything but discreet stance on organized crime.

Having surmised that Carmine Lorenzo had a hand in undercutting his organization and outing him to the federal authorities, Jarrod eagerly shared everything he knew about the tensions between the Lorenzo family in Tampa and the admitted communist, Fidel Castro of Cuba. While the FBI had long been aware of Castro, this inside information was most valuable.

Fidel Castro had come into power in 1959, and when he did he closed down the Mafia-owned casinos in Havana. At that time he jailed Tampa mob boss Lorenzo Carmine, Jr. Jarrod had provided the feds with another name, one Sam Giardeli of Chicago, who he believed to be recently aligned with Lorenzo, in an effort to get back at Castro.

CHAPTER TWENTY-FIVE

TALLAHASSEE, FLORIDA

Just before sunset, Detective Sutherland and his partner Detective Wood arrived at "The Fountains" to question the lone witness who reported the murder of Bovier. "Leonard Smith" answered the door to his motel room, dressed casually, and invited the two men in.

Detective Wood started the conversation by saying how much he appreciated Mr. Smith taking the time to speak with them, while Detective Sutherland remained quiet.

"We'd like to review your statement, Mr. Smith," stated Wood. "Could you tell us exactly what you saw or heard, or have any firsthand knowledge of?"

Smith sat down on the end of the bed, offering the policemen seats in the two side chairs.

"As I told the other officers, I had been looking at some property near the chapel. I was across the street on the sidewalk when I noticed a person lying near the gate to the garden. I walked over and found this guy who had been shot. I looked around for a pay phone and called the police. That's it."

"Thank you, Mr. Smith," said Wood. "Did you see or hear anything else that might be helpful?"

"Nope, just what I told you," said Smith.

As Sutherland stood up, he walked closer to Smith and said, "Come on. Give us the real story. We're not leaving here until you do."

"I don't know what you want from me," said Smith. "I've told you everything already."

Sutherland sensed a tension and noticed a slight twitch in Smith's left hand. "Really?" said Sutherland. "Then why are you so nervous, Mr. Smith? We're just trying to get at the truth here, and you don't seem to want to help us. Is that my imagination?"

"No," said Smith. "I mean, I'm telling you all that I know."

"Well let me ask you this," said Sutherland. "Who are you protecting? I promise you we will get to the bottom of this homicide, and you will be in serious trouble when we find out who you are working for."

"Look," said Smith nervously. "I'm just a guy from Tampa who is researching property, and I just happened to be walking by there when I found the dude."

"Dude?" said Sutherland. "Do you have any idea who that 'dude' was? He was an undercover cop there to celebrate his only daughter's wedding. He wasn't a 'dude.' Now how about we get serious?"

"Listen, Detective whoever you are, I don't have to answer any more questions. I've given you my statement, and if you two would excuse me, I have to pack," Smith said.

Detective Wood said, "Packing, sir?"

"Yes," said Smith. "I've been given another assignment, and I have to leave in the morning."

"And this new assignment," said Sutherland. "Is someone going to die there as well?"

"Look, I get the good cop/bad cop routine. Now you need to leave," Smith stated and walked toward the door.

"OK," said Sutherland. "We can leave with you or without you, but you need to tell us who you work for and what happened in that garden."

"What does 'with me or without me' mean?"

"Let me be clear, 'dude,' so you can get it. You either tell us who you were working with or for, or we'll arrest you as an accomplice to murder." Sutherland didn't mince any words.

"You've got nothing on me," said Smith as he opened the door to his motel room. "Now leave, or I'll report you for police harassment."

As Wood and Sutherland started toward the door they heard gunfire. Diving for cover and simultaneously drawing their weapons, they saw Smith lying on the floor in a pool of blood. Sutherland darted for the doorway, pistol drawn, and Wood quickly checked Smith for a pulse. There was none. Smith was dead.

All Sutherland heard was a screeching of tires coming from a pickup truck leaving the parking lot. It was too far away to warrant a shot. The shooter had escaped after killing Smith.

"Clean shot to the head, Detectives," said the crime scene investigator.

"All we heard was a single shot," said Wood.

"And now we have a second murder by a sharpshooter, and a reluctant piece to a larger puzzle," said Sutherland. "We'll need ballistics ASAP to see if the same weapon or a similar one was used."

"Right away, sir," said the CSI. "We'll be bagging everything here as well."

Sutherland walked around the room, careful to not disturb anything. He noticed Smith's wallet on the dresser. Picking it up with a pen, he noted the driver's license said Leonard L. Schnauzer from New York. The photo matched the dead man lying in the room.

"What is it?" asked Wood.

"Just another piece to that puzzle," said Sutherland. "Let's go."

Television news reports broke into regular programming to report that a second homicide had occurred in Tallahassee. Matthew Winters happened to be in his room at Haven but was not watching television. Cynthia knocked on his door to tell him what she had heard on the news.

"Matthew, what on earth is going on around here?" asked a somewhat terrified Cynthia. "That's two murders here, and this one was at a motel. "

"I don't know, Cynthia. Maybe it's not even related, but thank you for letting me know. Don't worry, OK? I'm sure the police have things well in hand," Matt said, hoping he was right.

"Cynthia, what do you know about this motel?"

"It's a seedy little place on the outskirts of town—you know cheap room rates. Let's just say you get what you pay for with that place."

"I see. Again, thank you. I'll let you know if I find out anything, OK?"

"Thank you Matthew. If you go out, be sure to take your key to the front door. I'll be locking it promptly at six from now on."

Matthew knew he should wait before calling Peter Sutherland. He also knew that even though night had fallen on the city of Tallahassee, the good detective and his partner were in the squad room filing their report.

Pacing about, Matt opted to place the call. When he did, the detective answered simply "Sutherland."

"Pete, it's Matthew."

"I knew it would be you. Did you hear about it on the news?"

"Sort of, but tell me, was this the suspected accomplice?"

"Affirmative; can we talk tomorrow?" asked Sutherland.

"Of course," Matt said. "Thank you."

The click on the other end of the phone let Matt know it was not the time to question the detective. Tomorrow would be soon enough, and having the confirmation that this was the suspected accomplice to his father-in-law's murder solidified a lot in Matthew's mind.

Sitting at his desk, safe in his room at Haven, Matthew made a diagram of what he now knew. It was becoming more and more obvious that these murders were related, planned, executed, and orchestrated by one or more persons. Jotting furious notes, Matt penned the words—"planned hit"—then simply "hit." Then came the dreaded but expected thought—"Mafia hit."

Everything Matt knew about the Mafia had cost him dearly. It had taken away a beloved sister and forced him into lie after lie to protect that sister. Now they were striking at his new family—the Boviers. Was there a connection?

Trying to stop his mind from racing, Matthew phoned Joanie. A sleepy wife answered the phone.

"I'm sorry if I woke you up," said Matt.

"Why, Counselor—you want to talk to me, don't you?"

"I do, and I miss you. I wish I were calling to tell you when I'll be home, but—"

"But you're *not* coming home yet, are you?"

"Not tomorrow, but soon, I hope. There's been some activity on your father's case, and I need to see it through. I hope you understand."

"Of course I do, Matt, but what kind of activity?"

"The person who allegedly discovered your father in the garden was shot tonight and killed," Matt said.

"Wow, that sounds like a conspiracy to me," said Joanie.

"You're right. I think you're absolutely right, and I intend to find out all that I can about it."

"OK, just promise you will be very careful. I don't need any more bad news right now or maybe ever," Joanie said, trying to lighten the moment.

"I promise, and I love you. I will keep you posted on everything. Goodnight, my love."

Matt knew that his sleep as well as his wife's would be fraught with questions that as yet had no answers. He prayed that God would lighten his wife's load and that He would protect them and give them courage and wisdom to find the truth.

Ignacio knew something had gone wrong back there. He had no idea that Lefty had company. His mind raced as he and his driver sped down the back roads of Tallahassee. The one thing he was sure of is that he had to get out of town quickly. If anyone at the motel had seen them, they might remember the pickup truck.

Without giving it another thought, Ignacio told the driver to take him to the bus station. Once there, Ignacio made the driver go inside and purchase a one-way ticket to New Orleans. While the driver was inside the bus terminal, Ignacio rigged a rustic but effective bomb and set it to explode inside the truck. It would detonate in about fifteen minutes.

When the flustered driver returned, he was shaking with fright. Ignacio took the ticket, gave the driver fifty dollars, and told him to drive to the nearest train station. He patted him on the back, thanked him for his work, and said simply, "Not to worry, old boy, you will never see me again." With that, he lunged out of the truck and headed inside the terminal.

Feeling relieved, the driver headed out to the main highway. About twelve minutes later an explosion ripped through the cab of his truck, sending the fiery auto over an embankment.

The bus to New Orleans left on time but was delayed for a time due to a fiery crash on Route 41. Ignacio peered out the window of the bus admiring his handiwork, then sat back in his seat, and slept.

CHAPTER TWENTY-SIX

ATLANTA, GEORGIA
NOVEMBER 1960

With the holidays quickly approaching, Vera decided it was time to plan a family gathering, making certain that this one would not be fraught with angst or fear. It would soon be Thanksgiving, and while Vera would have been happy to have the whole family stay from Thanksgiving to New Year's, she knew full well that everyone would probably want to be in their own homes for Christmas.

After discussing her thoughts and plans with David, Vera set about making her telephone calls. She called Lucy and Marc first since she had already mentioned a get-together to Lucy.

As promised, Lucy had gotten Marc's schedule and told Vera they would drive over to Atlanta and could be there on the Wednesday evening before Thanksgiving. They would return to Alabama on Sunday afternoon so that Marc could work on Monday.

Next, Vera called Joanie. She said a prayer before she rang her number. Vera had not spoken with Joanie since she and Matt had returned to Gainesville, although she had spoken a couple of times with Matthew.

Joanie was quick to answer the phone and was happy to hear from her new sister-in-law. After the two exchanged pleasantries, Vera asked how Matthew was doing. Joanie related that Matt was in Tallahassee tracking down clues about her father's murder.

"I'm sorry to hear that you're all alone," said Vera.

"It's really OK. Matt is doing exactly what he needs to be doing, and he'll be home soon," Joanie said.

"And how is your mother doing?" Vera gently asked.

"I speak with her 'most every day, and she appears to be doing as well as she could be," Joanie said. "She's a trooper, you know."

"I keep her in my prayers—as I keep you and Matthew in my prayers," said Vera. "And David and I were so hoping that you, your mother, and Matthew could all plan to come to Atlanta for Thanksgiving."

"Wow, Vera, I don't know…," said Joanie.

"It's a time when family should be together," Vera said before Joanie could finish her thought, "and we have plenty of room for everyone. Please, Joanie, think about it. Talk to Matt about it—and your mother of course, but please give this some serious thought. We want to do this for all of our sakes."

"I will, I promise," said Joanie. "It's just very hard to think about a family celebration right now."

"I understand, dear. We just would like to have the whole family together to give thanks for all the good things in our lives, and for having one another to lean on," Vera said.

"You aren't going to take no for an answer, are you, Vera?"

"Not unless I am absolutely forced to," answered Vera. "Besides, Marc, Lucy, and the girls will be here, and having you, your mother, and Matthew join us would be so very special."

"I promise that I will talk with my mother, and of course Matthew, and I will call you in a couple of days."

"Excellent. I look forward to your phone call. Give my love to my brother when you talk with him," Vera said.

"I will," answered Joanie. "Give our best to David and Daniel. Thank you for your call and for the invitation."

CHAPTER TWENTY-SEVEN

NEW YORK CITY

Alex and Ben reviewed every entry on their calendars, as well as the one John had left behind to highlight every meeting any of them had had with Samuel Jackson Graves. After comparing notes, the two shared their thoughts about the barrister and came to the same conclusion—*he was trouble.*

Ben pointed out that it had been Graves who brought Graceffo on board and that it was he who strongly recommended that Dominic Raia be skipped over as the enforcer to give Graceffo the job.

"But where did Graceffo come from?" asked Alex.

"Good question. John knew, but didn't say anything to me. Did he mention the guy to you?" Ben asked.

"Just that Raia would have his opportunity soon enough. That's all I remember," Alex responded.

"So where's the connection?" asked Ben. "We have to be missing something."

"Wait a minute," said Alex as he pointed to the calendar. "Here's where John went to Tampa to see Carmine Lorenzo and that Patrone fellow. Remember when John came back, he said that Patrone had off-handedly offered him a position in their organization if he'd leave New York and come back to Florida?"

"Yeah, so?" posed Ben.

"So when John comes back to New York, he tells us he's decided to move his wife to South Carolina," said Alex. "Shortly after that, their house *in Florida* burned to the ground."

"Patrone is obviously the mouthpiece for Lorenzo. Shortly after John's trip to Florida, and his meeting, Lorenzo and Patrone show up at a meeting of the five families, although he is technically an outsider," Alex related. "Then Lorenzo wants to meet John privately to make sure John knew he meant no disrespect, and look here—John met with Graves that same day."

"And Graves attended that meeting with Lorenzo as well," added Ben. "I drove them to the pier myself."

"And the tenor of the meeting was what?" Alex asked.

"Let's see," as Ben tried to recall all the details. "We met on the docks. It was John, Graves, and me. The whole purpose of the meeting was said to be that of showing no disrespect to John. I thought that was a bit of overkill, but then John said he was pretty sure the Lorenzos from Tampa were trying to align themselves to one of the five families."

"So obviously Lorenzo had planted the seed with John when he was in Tampa, perhaps trying to align with John or vice versa," said Ben. Alex simply nodded. "So then," continues Ben, "Lorenzo shows up at a meeting as the guest of *someone,* and fears he has tipped his hand to John. Wonder who invited him?"

"I think we need to take a hard look at the other families and see who may have a connection to Tampa," Alex stated.

"There's only one that I know of, but that's a Chicago family with no jurisdiction here in the City; that's one Sam Giardeli," Ben said. "I researched him for John."

"So maybe John was onto Lorenzo and taking a look at known associates," Alex commented.

"Always," replied Ben, "and I'll bet you dollars to doughnuts that Samuel Jackson Graves relates directly back to Chicago."

"Why don't we find out?" Alex asked. "In the meantime, see what else you have on this Giardeli character. Maybe there's something there that will help put the pieces together."

"I'll pull the file. Be back soon," Ben said as he hurried off.

Alex picked up the phone and called Graves.

CHAPTER TWENTY-EIGHT

NEW ORLEANS, LOUISIANA

Jack Palace was trying to find Ignacio Graceffo in the squad room. He was nowhere to be found, and no one seemed to know where he was.

Within the hour, Graceffo darted in, looking as though he hadn't slept in a week, or bothered to shower and shave.

When Jack caught up to him, he said, "It looks like it was a rough night."

Graceffo looked up disgustedly and said, "You could say that."

"I thought it was odd that no one knew where you were. Do you squad room guys get special treatment or what?" asked Jack.

"Yeah, we get special treatment all right. What were you asking about me for?"

"Just trying to keep up with you—you know—to see how the other half lives," an agitated Jack said.

"Well, you see me now, don't you? This is how I live. Now, I have work to do, so you'll excuse me. Or are you looking for something to do yourself?" snipped Graceffo.

"You might want to check that attitude at the squad room door, you being a rookie and all," said Palace. "You just might give me the wrong impression about you." With a half salute, Palace turned and walked away.

Graceffo made an obscene gesture at the detective and then took his seat at his desk. He needed to get the hell out of New Orleans and this joke of a job. He decided then and there to call his friend Graves. He dared not use the telephone there—someone might overhear. He would bide his time until he could leave the station and find a pay telephone.

CHAPTER TWENTY-NINE

TALLAHASSEE, FLORIDA

Matthew awakened early and called the police station to make an appointment with Pete Sutherland. After he had done that he phoned his office in Gainesville and shared this additional information with William Brown.

"It certainly sounds mob related to me," said Brown. "I may be jumping the gun here, but it seems that the information and moves keep circling back to the same conclusion."

"I reluctantly agree, sir," said Matthew. "I hope to know more after I meet with the detective. He's been a great contact, and he's a bright guy. I suspect he knows more than he is able to tell me."

"I am confident that he does, and you may not be able to garner too much information from him without divulging your—shall we say 'firsthand knowledge' about the mob. It is my opinion, Matt, that it's a little premature to do that just now." Brown was both methodical and wise.

"I agree, sir," said Matthew. "I'll call you once I have additional information. I also want to call Jack Palace and let him in on the latest information from here. I think he may find it interesting as well."

"Good. Just keep your head down and stay in touch. I will be eager to hear from you," said Brown.

Matt opted to head to his meeting with Sutherland before calling Jack Palace.

Sutherland ushered Matthew, along with his partner, Scott Wood, into a private office where the three of them could talk openly. After hearing the events of the past evening, Matthew sat shaking his head in amazement at what had occurred.

"You're both lucky to be alive," said Matt.

Nodding in agreement, Sutherland simply said, "Timing is everything. We almost had the guy to the breaking point. He was agitated, nervous, jumpy, and eager to get us out of his room."

"Yeah, and he didn't act like any developer to me," said Scott. "The guy was shabbily dressed, staying in a dump, and didn't appear to have taken notes on anything."

"He was obviously the accomplice, but that really doesn't give us a lot to go on unless we can surmise who he was actually working for," Sutherland commented. "His driver's license was issued in New York, yet he said he was from Tampa, and we're expecting a complete report from the Tampa police within the hour. We're not sure if he has a record there or not. The Tampa folks are trying to locate a next of kin to claim the remains, such as they are."

"I'm guessing here, but he was obviously registered at the motel using an alias, right?" asked Matt.

"Yes. The name on his driver's license was Leonard L. Schnauzer with a street address in New York City that doesn't exist," Scott Wood commented.

"Anything else we know about Mr. Schnauzer?" asked Matt.

"Just that he was left-handed," said Scott.

The meeting was interrupted with a policeman bringing a report into Sutherland. After looking over it, Pete said, "Well, he has a record about a mile long, but most of it is for petty stuff. He's known as 'Lefty' and used to hang out in Ybor City with known felons, but there isn't much on him specifically. No known next of kin and no real address. It's like the guy just drifts around."

"Isn't Ybor City the cigar manufacturing area?" asked Matthew.

"Yes, and it is well known for illegal activity and corruption," Pete commented.

Matthew was staring down at his shoes. Pete Sutherland picked up on the fact that Matthew was being particularly quiet and said, "Are those heavy thoughts?"

"Just mulling it all over at the moment," said Matthew, reluctant to share too much at the moment. "Thank you for the information and your time. I'm glad neither of you was injured. If you hear of anything else, will you let me know?"

"If it seems pertinent, we will," replied Sutherland.

"Any lead on the shooter?" asked Matthew.

"Just that he got away in a pickup truck," said Scott.

"And we think that's the pickup truck that wrecked on US forty-one last night," added Sutherland.

"Cause of the wreck?" asked Matt

"Explosion with no survivor. Looks like the truck may have had an incendiary device on board," Sutherland said. "How long are you here for, Matt?"

"I'm probably here for only a couple of more days. I need to get back to my wife and my job," said Matt. Shaking hands with both men, Matt left.

Matt thought about the course of events on his ride back to Haven. As soon as he could he called his office, spoke with Brown again, and then opted to call Jack Palace and fill him in on what he had learned.

Palace intently listened to Matthew as he related what had transpired in the past thirty-six hours. Even though the wheels were turning in Palace's mind, he said nothing to Matthew.

"I need to check something out here, Matthew, and when I do I'll call you back," Jack said hurriedly. "Where can I reach you?"

"Call me at Haven. I'm in for the rest of the day," Matthew replied.

Jack Palace hung up the phone and made an immediate but discreet inquiry into transportation to and from Tallahassee, Florida, to New Orleans, Louisiana. What he discovered was that a Greyhound Bus route was an overnight ride stopping once in Pensacola and again in Baton Rouge en route to New Orleans. He learned that a commuter leaving Tallahassee at seven o'clock at night could be in New Orleans by ten in the morning the following day.

Arriving at the Greyhound Bus terminal in New Orleans, Jack made his way to the ticket agent. Showing his police identification, he asked if he could see the manifest from last night's Tallahassee to New Orleans run. While the agent referred him to a supervisor, Jack ultimately looked over the list. He did not see the name he was looking for. He quickly made note of all the male passengers' names and returned the manifest to the supervisor.

There were only three male passengers who had embarked from Tallahassee and ended their ride in New Orleans: *Donald Adair, Mike Bowers, and Carl Smith.*

Feeling a bit defeated, Jack headed back to the station, where he proceeded to call Matt.

"Did you happen to get the make on the gun that was used in the shooting at the motel?" asked Palace.

"I did," replied Matt. "It appears to be the same make and model Bovier's shooter used. Why do you ask?"

"Matt, you're going to think that I've lost my mind, but I need to see you and run a scenario by you. This thing is making me a little nutty, and it's just this kind of thing that I used to use Bovier for; running the whole thing by him, you know?" Jack Palace had urgency in his voice that Matt quickly picked up on.

"Sure," said Matt. "It's probably easier for me to come to New Orleans than for you to travel back to Tallahassee. I'll see what arrangements I can make and call you."

"Make it soon, my new friend," said Jack.

Without knowing any more details, Matthew picked up the phone and called his office. Having spent very little time there of late he hated to impose on his assistant, but he asked her to get him a ticket to New Orleans as soon as possible. She then transferred him to Brown and Matt shared what he had been told with Brown.

"If you trust this guy, then by all means follow through. It sounds to me as though the detective has a lead that he doesn't want to share by telephone," said Brown. "Be safe—go—and let me know what happens as soon as you can."

Matthew hung up from his office and proceeded to call Joanie to tell her he was headed for New Orleans to meet with her father's ex-partner.

"I hope this isn't a waste of your time, Matt," said Joanie. "But Jack is a good man, and I've known him all my life. I don't think he would lead you on a wild goose chase."

"I'm banking on that, Baby," said a weary sounding Matt. "I promise I will come home as soon as I possibly can. I love you, Joanie."

"And I love you," she replied. "Be safe, my love."

Within the hour Matthew Winters was booked on a flight from Tallahassee to New Orleans leaving the following morning. His return was open ended as he had requested.

CHAPTER THIRTY

NEW YORK CITY

Alex reached Samuel Jackson Graves and requested a meeting the next day.

"Any particular agenda I should prepare for?" asked Graves.

"Well, you might bring any notes you have from your last meeting with John," said Alex, "particularly all the information you have on Carmine Lorenzo."

"Lorenzo?" asked Graves. "Is that the guy from Tampa?"

"Yes," said Alex.

"Why, I'll have to look back at my calendar, but I really don't remember any dealings that I had with Mr. Lorenzo," Graves responded cautiously.

"Well, if you don't have anything, then there won't be anything to bring to the meeting, right?" Alex queried.

"Right, sir. I'll see you first thing tomorrow," Graves responded.

Before he had a moment to process that telephone call, the phone rang again. This time it was Graceffo calling from New Orleans.

"Listen, Graves, I've taken care of the other situation, and I need to get out of town—yesterday," said Graceffo.

"Bide your time, Ignacio. While I know you have remedied our other problem, I need you to stay in the NOPD until further notice. I'll be in touch soon. Just do what you have to do to look like a good cop, and we will get you out of there shortly, I promise," Graves told him.

"I want out of here, and you can make it happen, so make it happen sooner rather than later. You get it?" said an angry and agitated Graceffo.

"I hear you. Now calm yourself and keep a low profile until I can make arrangements to move you, got it?" replied an angry and nervous Graves.

Mentally reviewing his plate, Samuel Jackson Graves realized it was quite full. While he knew he needed to work out a plan for Graceffo, he correctly surmised that his first order of business was shutting down Alex's curiosity about Lorenzo. He had no idea how that had come about. He toyed with the notion of calling Lorenzo, but there was nothing substantial to report about the inquiry. Graves assumed he could hold his own in a conversation with Alex and knew it was more important to say nothing rather than *something*. He also decided he would need Lorenzo to bless his actions with Graceffo and that he had some time on his side with that one.

CHAPTER THIRTY-ONE

NEW ORLEANS, LOUISIANA

Landing on time, Matt left the plane and headed for the luggage station. There, as promised, was Jack Palace. After shaking hands and retrieving Matthew's bag, the two headed out to the gray sedan that the city provided their ace detectives.

"Thanks for coming so quickly," said Palace. "I have a great deal of conjecture to share with you."

"Conjecture?" asked Matt.

"That's what I'll call it for now. When I tell you what I'm thinking, you may think I'm absolutely nutty," Palace said.

Arriving at the hotel in downtown New Orleans, Matt rented a room and dropped off his luggage. Turning to Palace, Matt said, "What now?"

"We're going to my place where I know we can be assured of no interruptions," said Jack. "I think we need to be sure that no one overhears our conversation."

"OK, let's go," said a curious Matthew.

Jack Palace's home was located in the Ninth Ward, old but quaint, and very simply appointed. There were only two bedrooms, one bath, and a kitchen that had seen happier times. Jack walked to the stove, put on the tea kettle, and asked Matthew if he liked hot tea.

"Hot tea would be great," replied Matt.

Pulling two teacups out of the cabinet, Jack set them on the old, wooden table that served as his dining spot. While the water came to a boil, Jack began. He told Matthew he had a suspicion about this character at the precinct who had been "dropped" into the squad room without anyone being aware of an opening. He then shared the fact that he was from New York, had a short fuse, and was, in his words, "shady." That, he told Matt, coupled with the fact that he had maneuvered his way into Bovier's life, made him a bit more suspicious.

"So you were *jealous* of the cop?" Matt joked.

"Yeah, enough that I kind of tailed him," said Palace.

Pouring the tea, Jack related more of his uncertainties about the cop. He highlighted things like the frequent meetings with Bovier at Foxy's Bar in the Quarter, the guy never drinking when he was there, and then the fact that he blatantly lied about why he did not attend Bovier's funeral.

"You'd think that a guy, who got that tight with a fellow officer would want to pay his respects, wouldn't you?" Palace rhetorically asked.

"One would assume he would," replied Matthew. "And does this guy have a name?"

"Ignacio Graceffo," replied Palace, "from New York City, no less."

"Was he a NYC cop?" asked Matt.

"Nope—at least not under that name," replied Jack. "And, when I asked Bovier about it, he told me not to meddle in it, that it wasn't a big deal. That the guy knew the chief, and the chief was trying to give him a start in law enforcement."

"So even Bovier was suspicious enough of the guy to ask the chief about him," said Matt.

"Yep, and him telling me to stay out of it made *me* more curious than ever," said Jack.

"And?" asked Matthew.

"I had him tailed—unofficially of course," said Jack. "And even though he'd only been on the job for a short amount of time, he got a weekend off near the end of September."

"Now you have my attention," said Matt. "Would that have been the weekend of my wedding?"

"Bingo," said Jack. "I began putting the pieces together after what happened this week, but I'm getting ahead of myself here."

"What I hear you saying without saying it, is that you think this guy was involved in my father-in-law's murder," said Matt.

"You are a quick study, and that's not all; I think he was hired by someone to kill Bovier," Jack said finally sipping his tea.

"A hired assassin?" Matt posed.

"A hired assassin, indeed. The only thing the guy can do as far as police work is fire a gun. He goes to the shooting range four or five times a week and is an excellent marksman. Some of the guys in the squad room said he's the best shot they've ever seen." Jack studied Matthew's face for a reaction.

"Interesting," said Matt.

"And, Graceffo was late for his shift last week. Came into the squad room about 10:30 in the morning looking like he hadn't slept in a week. I think it's because he may have slept on a bus coming to New Orleans from Tallahassee."

"Wouldn't be too much of a stretch to believe he might have been in Tallahassee to eliminate his accomplice would it?" asked Matt.

"Not too much of a stretch, but if he did it, he used an alias for the bus ticket. I got my hands on the manifest, and the only three names that popped up were a Donald Adair, a Mike Bowers, and a Carl Smith," Jack said.

"So here's some information for you." Matt then related everything he had heard from Peter Sutherland and filled Jack in on the fact that the detectives were suspicious of the lone witness in the Bovier case and had gone to his motel to question him. "That's when he was murdered," said Matt. "With both detectives in the room. All they saw were two men in a truck—the same truck that was blown up that night with only one person on board—the driver. The driver was a local and had no powder residue on his hands."

"So the shooter rigged a bomb inside the truck to rid himself of yet another accomplice," said Jack. "Yeah, and the shooter made sure the bomb went off *after* he was dropped off at the bus terminal.

"As a matter of fact, the truck was headed down forty-one toward the *train station*!" Matt exclaimed.

Matthew was now pacing the floor of Jack's small kitchen. When he finally stopped pacing, he sat down and asked Jack, "Who would have hired this guy to kill Bovier?"

"I hate to say this, but I swear it has all the markings of a mob hit," Palace said and went silent.

"I've thought that all along," said Matthew. "I didn't want that to be true anymore than you do, but it fits too neatly to be anything but."

"And what on earth would a young attorney know about mob hits?" Palace asked.

"More than I ever wanted to know. But if we're going to talk about that, we'll need something stronger than hot tea," said Matthew.

"What's your pleasure?" asked Jack Palace. "I've got all night."

Well into the night the two chatted. Matthew related *most* of the story about the FBI sting that he and his law partner had been intricately involved in. Leaving out specific details about his personal relationship with the Mafia kingpin was of course a priority for Matthew, and he saw no reason to divulge any information related to that.

"So is there a connection there to *this* situation?" asked Jack.

Somewhat taken aback by the question, Matt simply said, "None that I currently know of, but we should find out." That answer would have to suffice for now. Matt had maintained his integrity and had given the most truthful answer he could provide.

"Is that why you asked me originally about Bovier being 'on the take'?" asked Jack.

"Honestly, Jack, I asked that because of the gift Bovier gave Joanie and me on our wedding day. It was a certified check for thirty thousand dollars, and I can't figure how a cop—no matter how good he is—could amass that amount of money." Matthew studied Palace's face as the information sank in.

"Oh my God," said Jack. "I find this very disturbing, indeed. I had no idea the guy had that kind of cash." Shaking his head and pacing the floor now himself, Jack said, "No, I still don't believe he was crooked, money or no money. He just wasn't that kind of guy."

"I hear you, my friend, and Joanie doesn't believe it either, but none of us can explain how Bovier came up with that money. It just looks bad," Matthew said.

"Well I for one want to look at this more closely after some rest. It's late, and we've both had long days. Why don't you just bunk out here, and I'll take you to your hotel in the morning?"

"Sounds good to me, but just one more thing," Matt said.

"Sure—name it," answered Jack.

"I'll take a shot of bourbon if you have it."

"Well I can do you one better—we'll share a shot or two and talk about everything else tomorrow."

Jack poured two shots of Kentucky bourbon and, raising his shot glass to Matt, said, "To you, Bovier, you old so-and-so."

"To Bovier," said Matt.

Two shots later both men retired for the night.

CHAPTER THIRTY-TWO

NEW YORK CITY

Ben arrived promptly at 8:30 a.m. for the meeting with Alex and Graves. Alex briefed him about his conversation with Graves the evening before.

"So you sort of warned him?" asked Ben.

"Not really, but I did want to hear his reaction to the name *Lorenzo*," said Alex, "and it was too smooth. We'll see if he comes with any notes or information."

"If it's all the same to you, I'd like to ask him directly about Lorenzo and his mouthpiece Patrone. I want to see his expressions," Ben said. "I'd also like to ask him where Ignacio Graceffo came from and how he knew so much about him."

"Be cautious, Ben," warned Alex. "I have a feeling that Graceffo is trouble with a capital T, and I don't want Graves warning him about anything."

"I'm with you," said Ben. "We haven't had a report from Graceffo for a while, so asking about him would be natural."

"I think we should start with what's happening in New Orleans—we could even ask that Graceffo be returned to the fold—and put off our conversation about Lorenzo to the end of the meeting." Alex was clever and shrewd, and he wanted to watch the barrister sweat.

"Excellent thinking," replied Ben.

"Before he gets here, did your notes reveal anything?" asked Alex.

"Yeah, just as I thought I remembered: John suspected that the Chicago boys had a relationship with Graves at one time. He was watching Graves for any sign of disloyalty, and while I can't prove it, I think the boss thought Graves was disloyal by insisting that he and the missus split up."

"Maybe we should ask Graves how he got hooked up with John to begin with," said Alex.

"Maybe we want him to think we already *know* and that we're interviewing new candidates for his job," replied Ben.

"That could only be implied," said Alex. "I don't care for the man, but I don't want to tip our hand. I think implying that his position might be in jeopardy would be to our mutual benefit. He might roll over on someone we need to know about."

"So is it Good Gangster–Bad Gangster that we're playing?" scoffed Ben.

"Actually, that's a brilliant idea, Ben. He might just think that the two of us are at odds. His reaction to *that* would be interesting."

"Well since you're the boss, I guess I'll have to be Good Gangster," chuckled Ben. "Besides, you've already put the fear of God in him with that phone call."

"Let's do it," said Alex.

Shortly afterward, Graves arrived replete with a briefcase, folders, and files.

"Thanks for meeting us on such short notice," said Ben. "Won't you have a seat?"

"Thanks," replied Graves as he took a seat on the couch. Looking around the suite, Graves saw that he and Ben were alone. "Where's the boss man?" asked Graves.

"Oh, sorry—he's just finishing up an interview in the next room. He should be in any time now. Want some coffee?"

"Sure, I'd love some. Just black, please," said Graves.

As Ben poured the coffee, the salon door opened and out came Alex and a tall middle-aged man wearing a three-piece suit.

"Thank you for your time, Mr. Mineo," said the man. "I look forward to hearing from you with your decision."

Alex nodded and walked him to the door. He patted him on the back and said, "We will be in touch soon."

Turning back into the suite, Alex blew past Ben, offhandedly asking for coffee, and sat down at his desk across the room.

"So, Graves, did you bring us a report on New Orleans?" asked Alex.

"Sorry, sir, I was under the impression that you wanted to discuss a meeting between John and Carmine Lorenzo. I can give you a verbal report on the situation as it stands in New Orleans." Graves was stumbling over his words and rustling paper.

"If a verbal report is all you have, then let's get on with it," muttered an obviously disgusted Alex.

"Well, sir, I spoke with Graceffo just yesterday, and he said the entire situation had been handled."

"Handled, Graves? What does *handled* mean?" pushed Alex.

"The accomplice in Tallahassee isn't breathing anymore," Graves retorted, "and Ignacio is eager to get back to the city. I told him to sit tight, play the dutiful cop, and we would get him back here as soon as possible."

"That's good news, Graves," said Ben. "I for one am happy to have that loose end tied up."

"What's not good news is you making promises to Graceffo that you have no authority to make," snapped Alex. "He stays in New Orleans until I say where he goes. Is that understood?"

"Yes, sir, I meant no disrespect by telling him that, and I certainly didn't promise him anything," said Graves. "He's your employee, not mine."

"Look, Alex, we really don't want to leave him there much longer do we? I mean what if someone gets suspicious," Ben asked.

"I can't believe I have to repeat myself, Ben. When I want him out of New Orleans is when he will leave there. Sometimes I wonder about both of you," Alex retorted.

"Do you think someone in New Orleans is suspicious of Graceffo?" Ben asked Graves.

"I have no reason at all to believe anyone has even looked at him twice," said Graves. "He keeps his head down and does what he's told like a good soldier. My only concern is his fervent desire to get out of that town. I fear that if we don't move him, he might get antsy and slip up somehow."

"Slipping up somehow gets one removed all right," said Alex. "Is that your suggestion, Graves, that we eliminate Graceffo?"

"No," Graves quickly replied. "I just mean that he's probably more valuable to you up here than down there."

"He might have a point there, Alex," said Ben. "Graves, how well do you know Ignacio?"

"Not well at all. I know him from my association with this organization—nothing more."

"Funny—I could swear that John said you recommended him over Raia because you knew of his excellent record and experience," said Alex.

"No, that can't be," said Graves. "Graceffo was John's idea all along."

"Wow—you have a great memory, Graves," said Ben. "And so how did you get hooked up with Sam Giardeli in Chicago?"

"Mr. Giardeli and I are only acquaintances, and he had a great deal of respect for your employer. I did some work for a friend of his at one time, and he liked my style. Mr. Giardeli knew that John was looking for an attorney, and he urged me to apply for the position. The rest is history. But may I inquire why you are asking me that now?" Graves was focused on Alex.

Alex spoke clearly and plainly without taking his eyes off Graves. "Because I am the boss now—that's why, and furthermore John isn't around to give orders *or* hire and fire, is he, Mr. Graves?"

"Again, I mean no disrespect—"

"Yeah, you keep saying that," Alex interrupted, "yet you keep disrespecting me at every turn. I am not happy with this situation."

"My apologies, sir," said Graves. "I did not mean to anger you."

"I'm not sure that Alex is angry, Graves. I just think he has a lot to deal with and needs our help and cooperation," said Ben.

"Thank you, *Gentle* Ben," retorted Alex. "Now can we continue with business and leave the hand-holding and coddling to someone else? What can you tell me about Carmine Lorenzo?"

Ben watched the face of Samuel Jackson Graves as he pulled out some paperwork and relayed some already known information to both Alex and him about Carmine Lorenzo.

"Fine, and what about Patrone; is he just a mouthpiece or what?" asked Alex.

"I really don't have much information on Patrone, sir," said Graves, "other than that he has been with Mr. Lorenzo for a long time, actually since Lorenzo, Senior passed the reins to Lorenzo, Junior."

"And the meeting that you, John and Ben, attended on the docks—what was that about?" Alex was prompting Graves to answer quickly.

"Well, Alex, I was there too," began Ben.

"And I've heard from you, Ben. I'm asking Mr. Graves for his take on that meeting if you don't mind," Alex stated.

"As I recall, and in reviewing what few notes I have on that particular meeting, it came as a result of the Lorenzo family's interference in a five family meeting here in New York. Mr. Lorenzo wanted to assure Mr. Marconi that he meant no disrespect and was not trying to horn in on the Marconi territory."

Graves became silent and continued flipping through his notes.

"And isn't it true, Mr. Graves, that Lorenzo and Giardeli are more than acquaintances?" Alex glared at Graves.

"I would not know about that, sir," said Graves.

"And you wouldn't know that Lorenzo offered Marconi a job in Florida, would you?" Alex was pushing the envelope here.

"No, sir," said Graves.

"OK, Graves. Do you have anything else to share with us about that meeting?" Ben asked.

"Nothing comes to mind," he answered. "Would you excuse me for just a moment to go to the bathroom?"

"Great, now we need a recess. You two are making me nuts," a disgruntled Alex stated. "Hurry up—we don't have all day."

While Graves excused himself, Ben simply nodded to Alex and, without uttering a word, the two decided they had gotten all the information they were going to get from Graves.

"I've decided to let you earn your paycheck this month, Graves. I want all the information you can obtain on Carmine Lorenzo, his connections to Sam Giardeli, and I want it in writing, understood?" Alex said.

"Yes, sir, and when do you need this information?"

"Yesterday, but day after tomorrow will be generous of me, don't you think?"

"Day after tomorrow you will have it. Now if there's nothing else, I will leave to begin my research. Good day, gentlemen."

"Graves was as nervous as a cat on a hot tin roof when you asked about Giardeli and a connection to Lorenzo," said Ben. "I think we can write that one down in the 'connected' column."

"Yeah, and he knows a great deal more about one Carmine Lorenzo, Junior than he's telling. He also lied about John selecting Graceffo. It was all I could do not to dismiss him on the spot. But now I'm thinking there just may be a connection with the lot of them."

"You mean a triangular relationship between Giardeli, Lorenzo, and Graceffo?" Ben asked

"Exactly," said Alex. "Graves alluded to it when he was skating around the issue of Graceffo and again when he said a 'friend' of Giardeli—I'm thinking Lorenzo—recommended that he talk to John about a position."

"That would put a hit man and two kingpins in the mix for John's territory," said Ben.

"And it would explain why Lorenzo tried first to get John to come on board with his operation," said Alex.

"And the icing on the cake would be the retaliation on John's house in Florida when he flatly refused him," Ben added.

"Ben, I want you to call Graceffo in New Orleans and tell him we need him back in New York in one month, that he just needs to stick it out thirty more days," Alex directed.

"OK, but can I ask why?"

"So we can see how quickly he contacts Graves, if at all. If he lets Graves know we've contacted him then you can bet that he's looking to Graves as his boss, not me. If he doesn't, then we'll bring him back and keep close tabs on him from here. "

"My money is on you, Alex," said Ben.

"And my money says that Graves and Graceffo are in cahoots," said Alex. "That's not a good situation for us, my friend. After all, if John figured it out or was on the verge of figuring it out…"

"Right, look what happened to him," Ben said.

CHAPTER THIRTY-THREE

NEW ORLEANS, LOUISIANA

It was a steamy fall day in The Big Easy. Matthew awakened first, started the tea kettle, and made his slightly disrupted bed. He hadn't slept soundly, but rather dozed on and off, thinking of everything he had heard the night before from Jack Palace.

"Morning," said Jack. "I see you've assumed the duties of a good host by putting on the pot for tea."

"Yeah, but I think I could use some of that strong, dark swill you guys call coffee; I didn't sleep much last night and I could use a jolt this morning," Matt commented.

"We'll go by Café Du Monde and have beignets. Maybe you should have the café au lait. It's cut with a bit of milk and probably more to your liking."

"I want to go to the station, Jack, and I'd like to talk to the chief of police," Matt said firmly.

"What on earth for?"

"I'll meet with him on the premise of setting up a benevolent fund in Bovier's name. That way I can get a handle on him, and if I'm lucky I'll get to meet Graceffo while I'm there. Could you arrange that?"

"I can try, but I have to say that I don't really know you well enough to anticipate how you might handle a face-to-face with the guy we believe may have killed your father-in-law."

"Let's just say that I have had to deal with more delicate situations than this one, and I don't flinch. I can assure you that the guy will never know I suspect him of a thing."

"And the chief of police?"

"My suspicion is that someone manipulated your chief to hire Graceffo, and I want to know who and why," said Matthew.

"But I may have a better way to get that information," Jack said. "You meet with the chief and do your benevolent duties and let me do some snooping around about the chief's *connections*."

"Agreed. I have to go to the hotel, make a few telephone calls, and get presentable. Hopefully that will give you time to set up a meeting with the chief. Oh—and let's grab that thick coffee on the way to the hotel."

The first telephone call Matt made was to William Brown. He shared all the new information with him and told him what his plan was. He then called Joanie and told her he would be home tomorrow if all went well.

CHAPTER THIRTY-FOUR

POLICE HEADQUARTERS
NEW ORLEANS, LOUISIANA

Jack had done as Matthew asked and arranged for his COP (Chief of Police) to meet with him. As expected, Matt was greeted warmly.

"Mr. Winters, I am happy to meet you albeit under these sad circumstances," said the COP.

"Thank you, sir. I appreciate your taking this time on such short notice. I had to be in New Orleans on a separate family matter and took the liberty of asking Detective Palace to set up a meeting with you."

"I'm happy to meet with you—and Jack tells me you want to set up a benevolent fund for police officers?"

"My wife, Joanie, and I have decided that the best way we can pay tribute to her father is by starting a fund for families of fallen officers. We would like to see it mature over time and be a fund-raising effort on the part of all your officers who knew and respected Detective Bovier."

"I don't know what to say, Mr. Winters. It's such a nice thing you are offering to do here."

"We'd like to set up the funds in a local trust account and designate its use on an as-needed basis. We would also like to include you as well as Jack

Palace as trustees for the account, given your history with Detective Bovier. Naturally, my wife and I will serve as guardians on the account as well." Matt paused to open his briefcase and extract a cashier's check. "We're initiating the account with a donation of thirty thousand dollars."

Matthew watched the face of the chief as he eyed the check. He didn't imagine the grimace he saw: it was obvious and real.

"Is there a problem, Chief?"

"No, it's just an overwhelming donation. Thank you so much, Mr. Winters. I will make sure that the department is made aware of your generosity. Thank you."

"I'll leave it up to you and Detective Palace to work out the details for a fund-raiser, but my suggestion would be an annual event of some sort," said Matthew. "I'm headed to First National to set up the account now and will, of course, send you a copy of the paperwork for the trust."

"What? Oh, of course," said the COP. "We can get our public relations people involved in the event planning, of course."

"Thank you, Chief, for your time this morning. Joanie will be pleased to know that you were receptive to our offer." Matthew stood, shook the chief's hand, and made a motion for the door. "Before I leave, would you mind if I just chatted with Jack Palace? I'd like to tell him personally about our donation in the memory of his partner."

"Of course, let me get him for you."

"Well?" Jack asked when he and Matthew were alone.

"Please check those connections you talked about. There's something to discover for sure," said Matt.

"That's Graceffo," said Jack, nodding his head a bit backward and to the right.

"I see. Just as I pictured," said Matt.

"Could I have a tour around the squad room?" Matthew asked in a louder, more audible tone.

"Sure, not much to see but a bunch of cops, but that's what we have to offer here," replied Palace.

After a brief walk-through, Matthew shook Jack's hand and headed outside to hail a cab. They arranged to meet in the Garden District for a late lunch.

CHAPTER THIRTY-FIVE

MOM'S PLACE
GARDEN DISTRICT

"You beat me here?" asked Matthew.

"Didn't want you to have to wait. Plus I want to know what you know."

"As I said, I suspect your chief of police has a connection with the money that Bovier gave to Joanie and me. When I showed him the cashier's check for thirty thousand he nearly choked."

"I have to hand it to you, Matt—you were pretty darn clever using that exact amount to start the benevolence fund."

"Let's just say I got what I paid for, and now it's up to us to figure out where that money came from and what your COP's connections are to it. I know what I saw, Jack, and I know that money was given to Bovier by him or *through* him."

"Plot gets thicker by the minute doesn't it? That's what keeps me hanging around this cockeyed business. Like the weather in New Orleans—if you don't like it, stick around a day or two, and it'll change on you. Same is true with the NOPD. But what about all that money? That's a chunk of change to just hand over."

"It's obviously tainted, and neither Joanie nor I want any part of it. Besides, if it can be used for a charitable purpose, why not?" Matthew knew he was taking the high road, and now Jack knew it as well. "My guess is that Bovier knew it was from a questionable source, and giving it to his daughter was most likely the best use of the windfall from his perspective."

"That would be the Bovier that I knew," said Jack.

Once the two had ordered, Matthew told Jack that his next steps were to return to Gainesville and do some digging from a distance; Jack committed to discreetly dig from New Orleans. The two agreed to share their suspicions about Graceffo with Detective Sutherland in Tallahassee. Matthew felt the safest way to do that was by a conference call set up by his firm. The lines would be secured, and the three could openly converse.

CHAPTER THIRTY-SIX

NEW YORK CITY

Ben had done as Alex asked and contacted Ignacio Graceffo in New Orleans. Reporting the results to Alex, Ben said that Graceffo was pleased to hear that his stint in The Big Easy was coming to an end. Now they waited—but not for long.

"Hello," said Ben, answering Alex's phone.

"Hi, Ben, this is Graves. Could I speak with Alex, please?"

"Sure, hold on."

"Yes?"

"Alex, I just wanted to give you a heads up. I just had a call from Ignacio in New Orleans, and he says that he's been cleared to leave there and come back to New York *per Benjamin*. Is that correct?"

"I see, well that's something I need to look into. Thanks for the call. And I'll be meeting with you tomorrow, correct?"

"Indeed, sir. Thank you."

Alex hung up the phone and looked at Ben. "Well, well—Counselor Graves just threw you under the bus! Our good gangster/bad gangster routine worked like a charm. And, I was right. Graceffo is taking orders from Graves, not me," he said pounding his fist on the table.

"So who else is involved—Lorenzo?"

"I'd bet my life on it; maybe I already have."

"So Graves will be here tomorrow reporting on Lorenzo?" asked Ben.

"Yes, and I can hardly wait."

"As I recall, John thought Lorenzo was trying to become a major player in New York but didn't have the right connections," Ben said.

"He may well be trying to work his way into New York via Chicago connections. And how better to maneuver your way into New York other than to get rid of John?" Alex posed.

"The only other information I've been able to find out about Lorenzo is that he got himself into trouble with a numbers racket in Florida last year and ran some casinos in Havana. About the same time, Cuba came under Castro's leadership. Castro didn't like the money that Lorenzo was taking out of his country, and he closed all of the casinos. When Lorenzo went into retaliation mode, he got himself planted in a Cuban prison. Heaven only knows what he's up to now, least of all who he may have sidled up with." Ben was good with details and took his research seriously.

"There's a lot we don't know, Ben," said Alex, "but we're onto something here. I just feel it."

CHAPTER THIRTY-SEVEN

THE BIG ISLAND, HAWAII, HAWAII

It was that time again and Jarrod was preparing for his next meeting with the FBI. He was somewhat surprised that they had come this time with one lone name on their agenda: one Carmine Lorenzo, Jr. of Tampa.

Jarrod saw this as an excellent opportunity to *crucify the guilty.* He had never cared for Lorenzo nor did he trust him as far as he could expel spit. When he was *John* he knew him as an adversary rather than a comrade, and while he couldn't prove it, was sure his organization and his own home had been compromised by this man.

"I can tell you that Carmine Lorenzo, Junior is not half the man his father was. Of his two sons, he should have selected Harrison over Carmine." Jarrod continued relating story after story to the agents about Lorenzo, including his offer of an affiliation in Tampa. Later in the conversation, Jarrod shared what he knew about Lorenzo's connection to the Chicago crime families and his ties to New Orleans.

"Jarrod," one agent asked, "do you have any idea why Lorenzo would partner with Chicago and New Orleans?"

"I can't prove it—it's just what I have surmised, but I believe it's in an attempt to do a couple of things. One—to take over someone's territory in New York City; the other is to retaliate against Fidel Castro for his not-so-nice vacation in that Cuban jail." Jarrod stared directly at the agent, who did not seem surprised at all at this news.

Riana Tavares never knew what she was expected to do during these sessions with the FBI. As she had done most of her life, she opted for a long walk.

Unfortunately, Riana was aware that she had her mind set on things she had agreed not to even think about. She was thinking of the brothers and sister she had left behind nearly five months ago.

Riana walked the dark brown beach deliberately. She knew it was almost Thanksgiving and that meant that someone in the family—most likely Vera—would try to get everyone together. She was such a sweet, caring person, always doing the right thing, no matter what. *Ah Vera, if you only knew how often I think of you.*

Deciding it was time to get her mind off what she had forsaken, Riana changed her direction on the beach and headed back to her modest but comfortable home. She would plan a Thanksgiving feast for her and Jarrod and, if he would agree, she would invite friends over to celebrate as well.

Upon her return, the agents were gone. She found Jarrod standing in the kitchen looking out over the green, lush landscape. Walking up behind him, she simply wrapped her arms around his waist without uttering a word.

In response Jarrod turned to her and returned her embrace. "I love you, Riana," he said. "I will prove it to you and to myself every single day, and I want you to know, I have no regrets."

"No regrets," said Riana.

CHAPTER THIRTY-EIGHT

GAINESVILLE, FLORIDA

Joanie took extra care in prepping herself for today. Matthew would be home, and she wanted to look and feel her best. He told her he had news, and while she was eager to hear what he had to say, she dreaded it as well. The news had to be in reference to her late father. While two months had gone by since his murder—to Joanie it felt as though it happened yesterday.

She had gladly agreed to use the money her father had handed her the day of her wedding for a benevolent fund for families of fallen officers. Without knowing exactly why that had to be done so quickly, she knew that Matthew had a reason, and it had to be hard for him to even broach the subject with her.

Happy that she had talked with her mother so often, Matthew had asked that she not tell Mrs. Bovier that he made the trip to New Orleans. With her husband's promise to explain it all in person, Joanie again exercised her faith in Matt's judgment.

She had done as Vera had asked and invited her mother to come to Atlanta with Matt and her for Thanksgiving. While Mrs. Bovier was reluctant to accept, Joanie had pulled out all the stops and convinced her mother that this was the best thing for everyone. Joanie was eager to tell Matthew she had pulled that off. The two of them would work out the logistics of getting everyone to Atlanta, and she would tell her mother when she would be taken to the airport.

Matthew landed safely at the airport and headed straight to see Joanie. Several hugs and kisses later, they sat down together to discuss what had transpired.

Matt was happy that Joanie had gotten her mother to agree to the trip to Atlanta and promised to look into flight schedules immediately.

"OK, Counselor, you're bursting at the seams to tell me what happened in New Orleans, so let's have it," said Joanie, curling her legs up under herself on the couch.

Matt related the story in its entirety. While he felt uncomfortable with some of the information, and purposely left out some gruesome details, he shared his conclusions and the conclusions of Jack Palace.

"So what are the next steps?"

"Jack and I are planning to have a three-way telephone conference with the detective heading up the case in Tallahassee," said Matt. "The steps beyond that are still unclear. We have to find a way to prove our allegations, and that could take some time."

"This won't interfere with our Atlanta trip, will it, Matthew?" asked Joanie.

"I really hope not, and I don't imagine it will. But I can't promise anything until we talk with Peter Sutherland. I also need to share all of this with Mr. Brown and get his perspective on it. But I can promise that I will make every attempt to be with you and your mother in Atlanta."

"I need to call Vera and let her know something. What should I say?"

"Just call her, tell her we accept her kind invitation, and that your mother is coming as well. No need to alarm Vera if my part of this can be worked out in the next couple of weeks," Matt said.

"Good thinking. And, from your lips to God's ears, Matthew Winters."

"I know you're not going to be happy about this, but I need to go to the office and set up a meeting with Brown. How about we have a nice quiet dinner for two tonight—you pick the place, and I'll pick up the tab."

Joanie stuck out her bottom lip and said, "All right, Counselor, you win as usual."

Scheduling a meeting with William Brown wasn't a challenge. Brown was eager to get a report from Matthew in the privacy of his mahogany office, and before Matthew could do more than unpack his briefcase, Brown appeared at the doorway.

"Glad you're back, son," said Brown. "Hope you like your new office. I had your assistant supervise the move so that she could put everything in the same order as you had left it. She's a bright lady, that one. But then bright ladies seem to flock to you, Winters."

Matthew simply chuckled, telling Brown that the office was great.

"So I see that we have an appointment tomorrow morning."

"Yes, sir. I will have everything summarized for you so that I don't skip any details. There's a lot of information that has come to light, and I'm eager to share it with you as well as get your take on what the appropriate next steps should be."

"Great, son, I'll leave you to get settled in and see you in the morning. Don't hang out here too late; you have some make up time with your bride." Brown winked at Matthew, tapped the doorframe, and walked next door to his office.

Matthew made a summary of everything he knew, everything he suspected and why, and what his tentative plan of action was to be. He included every detail that was at his disposal, and when he finished, he pushed back his chair and stared at the huge wooden desk in front of him. Mahogany Row; that's what all the interns and first year associates called it. Here he was a part of Mahogany Row in two short years. He was a blessed man.

Thanking his assistant for her help in what appeared to be a seamless move, Matthew headed for home. He made one stop—at the florist, purchasing his wife a beautiful bouquet of fresh flowers. Tomorrow would be here all too soon.

Day after day they all dealt with their individual and collective reality. Bovier: murdered at his daughter's wedding and suspected to be a crooked cop. John and Ruth: vanished from the face of the earth. Some believed them dead; some believed them to be in hiding; some just tried to forget all they knew. Vera: stripped of her sister, who had truly just become a friend; her new sister-in-law, who had been robbed of her father; and Vera's brother, who was caught in the middle and no doubt traumatized by all of it. Marc and Lucy: trying to keep their children out of harm's way without knowing why these tragic things were happening in the Winters family. And Mrs. Bovier: unaware of anything other than her agonizing loss and the sadness she saw in her daughter's eyes. And it was almost Thanksgiving.

As the sun came up in Gainesville this late fall morning, Matthew made his way to the law firm. Meeting with William Brown and sharing all of the information he had gathered along with his suppositions, he found Brown predictably agreed with the scenario that Matt and Jack had put together. His only recommendation was that the three-way conference call between Matthew Winters, Jack Palace, and Peter Sutherland be made sooner rather than later.

CHAPTER THIRTY-NINE

NEW YORK CITY

After Graves arrived, Alex and Ben suggested the three of them "talk" as they drove to collect the daily deliveries.

Graves sported a briefcase with a dossier on Carmine Lorenzo, Jr., another on Carmine Lorenzo, Sr., and some information on Harrison Lorenzo as well.

Seated opposite Alex and adjacent to Ben in the backseat of the limousine, Graves could not see the route nor the direction they were taking.

Listening attentively to Graves's ramblings about the Lorenzo clan, Ben was the first to interrupt.

"So refresh my memory here, Sammie. You said you really didn't know Lorenzo?"

"That's correct. He was a friend of a friend," said Graves.

"You remember now, Ben—Graves was buddies with Giardeli from the Windy City. That's how he knew of Lorenzo, right Graves?" a probing Alex asked.

"I knew of Mr. Giardeli—knew of him enough to be recommended by him—"

"We think you knew him well enough to work a deal with him *and* Lorenzo. Isn't that right, Ben?" asked Alex.

"Yeah, I guess Sammie here left out a few details. He left them out with John, and he left them out with us. Bad to be so forgetful when you're an attorney, don't you think, Alex?"

"Wait a minute, you two. I didn't leave out anything that was pertinent to our business relationship," stammered Graves, now recognizing he was in trouble.

"OK, Graves. You meant no disrespect, right?" Alex asked.

"And how long did you think it would take us to figure out that you are working for Lorenzo and so is Ignacio Graceffo?" said Ben.

"Why I've never heard of anything so preposterous. I don't know where you are getting your information but…," a nervous, stammering Graves said.

"But nothing," said Ben. "We have you, Sammie. The only thing that hasn't been decided just yet is what's best to do with you." Silence filled the limo as it sped over the bridge toward the waterfront.

"Wow, Graves—nothing to say now?" queried Alex. "No snappy come-back? You may as well have your say, and now would be the time to do it."

"Look, here's all I know," the suddenly meek and frightened barrister continued. "John wouldn't work for Lorenzo and Lorenzo wanted in. So Giardeli suggested an infiltration of the organization and that put me in the midst of all this. I never wanted to be part of any of it. And Ignacio is just a soldier, nothing more. He doesn't even know who he works for. He depends on me to get information to him about where to be and what to do—"

"And you had him kill Bovier?" Alex asked.

"I was ordered to tell him to make that hit," said Graves.

Ben asked, "Who ordered it?"

"Lorenzo," said Graves.

"Why? What did Bovier have to do with anything?" asked Alex.

"He knew Lorenzo was after John's old man down in New Orleans. He's a cop, for God's sake, why would you care about him?"

"I think we'll ask the questions—you just answer them," said Ben.

"Look, Lorenzo knew that Bovier was a straight cop. But when Bovier made the connection between John and his old man, Giuseppe, he went to his police chief. The police chief owed Lorenzo a favor, so Lorenzo asked that the COP ignore that info and hire Graceffo. See, he planned to have Graceffo become close friends to Bovier and then kill him when he knew he could get away with it." Beads of sweat were dripping off the barrister as he spoke. "And he did that at Bovier's daughter's wedding."

"Nice way to end a wedding, huh?" scoffed Alex.

The limousine came to a stop near the docks.

"But let's go back. What about John?" Ben asked.

"I don't know anything about what happened with John. I've heard nothing, and I swear to you if I knew I would tell you."

"Right now you're betting your life that we believe that crap, Graves," said Alex.

"I swear on my life," said Graves, "that I have no firsthand knowledge of anything that may have happened to John. I was as shocked as you two were."

"Right," said Ben, "shocked."

"Look—I can try to find out what Lorenzo knows about it. He trusts me, and he would most likely tell me if I asked," Graves said pleadingly.

"Why did you tell John to divorce his wife? Was that Lorenzo's idea too?" asked Ben.

"Yes. He thought if he came between the two of them, he could force John to turn over his business dealings to him. He didn't care about the wife—he just knew that she was John's Achilles heel, and obviously he was right."

"A little late to think about what's right and what's not, isn't it?"

"Alex, I swear if you will just—"

"Maybe I should have Graceffo take you out as his first official duty upon his return to New York," said Alex as he nodded to Ben.

"No. I think I'd rather not wait," said Ben as he put a .45 to Graves's ribcage and pulled the trigger.

A second limo appeared. Benjamin Moriani and Alexander Mineo exited the limo they had arrived in, taking with them Graves's briefcase and tossing their shirts and blood stained jackets atop the body of Samuel Jackson Graves. Two soldiers immediately doused the limo with gasoline and ignited it.

CHAPTER FORTY

GAINESVILLE, FLORIDA

The conference call between Matthew Winters, Jack Palace, and Peter Sutherland took place with Matt initiating contact with the others. Detail by detail was related to Detective Sutherland, who immediately said he would issue an arrest warrant for Ignacio Graceffo of the New Orleans Police Department. Since it was outside his jurisdiction, Jack Palace offered the NOPD's assistance in serving that warrant and securing the prisoner until he could be extradited.

Urging Palace to take great care in sharing this information with his chief of police, Jack assured the two men that it would not be problematic. He asked Sutherland to wire over the warrant, and he would take care of the rest.

Within an hour of Jack's receiving the warrant, Ignacio Graceffo was placed under arrest for the suspicion of the murder of Detective Bovier and a secondary charge of suspicion of murder in the death of one Leonard "Lefty" Schnauzer, both killed in Tallahassee, Florida. A third arrest warrant was issued naming Graceffo as the suspected bomber and murderer of an as yet unidentified civilian presently referred to as *John Doe* pending dental records which would produce an exact identification.

MEANWHILE IN TAMPA, FLORIDA

Carmine Lorenzo, Jr. had not heard from Graves and had placed more than one call to him without a response. Additionally, he was quite obviously being followed by a black sedan. Calling the New Orleans police department, one of Lorenzo's soldiers was told that Officer Graceffo was out of the station. When asked if a message could be left for him, the answer was *no*.

Placing a call to the New Orleans chief of police, Lorenzo spoke to a guilt-ridden police chief who was reluctant to take his call. The content of that call would never be shared. Three hours later, the New Orleans COP died by his own hand. He left a note addressed to Detective Jack Palace that said simply, "Bovier was clean. I gave him the $30 grand to try and *feel* clean, but Omerta is real."

CHAPTER FORTY-ONE

NEW ORLEANS, LOUISIANA

Jack Palace placed a telephone call to Matthew Winters, sharing the news of his COP's actions as well as the contents of the note.

While the note was confiscated as evidence, the entire police department was aware of its contents within minutes of the chief's demise. Without exception, there was surprise and angst over what the officers had just learned. Their very own chief had betrayed not one, but all, of them.

It was a sad day indeed for the New Orleans Police Department.

After notification of the chief's next of kin, the mayor of New Orleans issued a brief statement to the press announcing the sudden death of the police chief and naming Jack Palace as interim COP.

Under the circumstances Jack had no choice but to accept. He was the only person on the force who knew the far-reaching tentacles of this suicide as well as the reason behind it. He was also the one who would have to initiate further actions against Graceffo and make sure that he did not escape or take his own life.

As his first act, Chief Palace ordered a 24/7 suicide watch for prisoner Ignacio Graceffo. He would be allowed no visitors other than his attorney, who would be allowed to talk with him only from an adjacent cell and only with an armed guard present.

Palace was determined to see Ignacio Graceffo brought to justice.

At his arraignment, Graceffo stood alone, shackled at the wrists and ankles. When asked if he had an attorney, he requested to speak to Samuel Jackson Graves of New York City. When he was told that Mr. Graves was deceased, Graceffo opted for a court-appointed attorney.

Jack Palace telephoned Mrs. Bovier and asked if he could stop in to see her. When he did, he shared a good bit of the story with her, opting not to get into details that would compromise the prosecution of Graceffo, but letting her know that her late husband was a clean cop who was caught up in an untenable situation.

Jack took the time to answer Mrs. Bovier's questions about how her husband's case was solved. She was pleased to know that her son-in-law was such a bright and talented individual, and she repeatedly told Jack Palace how indebted she was to him for seeing this through.

Jack very simply said, "You're welcome," hugged his late partner's widow and left to return to the station.

CHAPTER FORTY-TWO

GAINESVILLE, FLORIDA

Joanie was ecstatic to know that her father's murderer was behind bars. Matthew had come home early to share the news with her and was there to chat with Mrs. Bovier when she called from New Orleans.

"It's cause for celebration," Mrs. Bovier told her daughter. "Your husband and my great friend Jack solved the mystery, and I will forever be in their debt."

"I am relieved as well and happy to know that I'll have my husband back," said Joanie. "It will be a great Thanksgiving after all."

"We have much to be thankful for," said her mother, "not the least of which is your new marriage. Maybe you two can schedule that long-awaited honeymoon?"

"Maybe so, Mom; first things first," replied Joanie while mulling over the thought of a getaway with her new husband. "We will talk again soon. I promise!"

Looking over at her husband, Joanie could see both relief and exhaustion on his face. He had truly borne the brunt of this murder investigation, and it was nearing its rightful conclusion. Putting her arms around his neck, Joanie lightly kissed him on the cheek. Reaching up to clasp her hands, he simply said, "Thank you, my love."

Matthew knew there was much to do to make sure that Graceffo was convicted. And while he had been made aware of a connection between Carmine Lorenzo and the COP in New Orleans, he had mentally made the leap to further ties.

Going to the law firm the next morning added some normalcy to Matthew's life. It had been a long time coming. No sooner had he arrived than William Brown appeared at his office. Brown had news from their clients at the FBI that couldn't wait.

"First of all, welcome back—job well done."

"Thank you, sir, and your assistance and support were so valuable," Matthew said.

A smiling Brown turned serious as he said, "Matthew, it appears that Carmine Lorenzo of Tampa has been named in a plot to assassinate Fidel Castro of Cuba. Furthermore, this Lorenzo character is suspected of trying to infiltrate the five families of New York—*within the last few months*—and is working on taking over the territory of a rather large player to this day." Brown winked as he clearly made the statement.

"I see," said Matt. "So the plot thickens."

"Our clients from the FBI are interested in learning more about Mr. Lorenzo and want to know if you're interested in helping them out?" Brown looked inquisitively for Matt's reaction.

"With all due respect, William, I am beginning to wonder who I really work for."

"That's easy—you work for us. Your name is on the marquis along with mine and the other partners. If you aren't inclined to take this on, we can assign it to someone else or pass on the opportunity altogether."

"There's no one else in the firm with this kind of experience," said Matthew, "and I know the FBI has been a strong client for us. They pay their bills on time, and that's no small chunk of change. May I think about it?"

"Of course you may, and I want you to feel free to say no. Forget about the billing and think about your own career. This firm is solid, our reserves are strong, and our annual billings will grow as we grow. We've proven that over and over again. Take your time—within reason of course—I'll call the client after you've given it some thought."

"Thank you, sir; I could use a bit of time to think this through. My involvements with this client have been gut-wrenching to say the least, but I don't want to make a snap decision. I commit to you that I will let you know as soon as I possibly can."

Matthew couldn't help but think about the Thanksgiving plans, his new bride who deserved a proper honeymoon, and the unspoken fact that the FBI didn't observe holidays. By the same token, he was honored that he was highly regarded by the investigators and, because of *Ruth*, he felt a tug of obligation. No doubt his mentor and partner had been passing along information that the Bureau had gotten from *John*. At least that was happening as planned, and it eased his concern for his sister a bit.

He would rest overnight and then give the offer the attention it deserved. As always he would weigh the pros and cons and come up with an answer that best suited the situation.

Joanie immediately went to see Bella to tell her the news and finally to return the book of poetry she had borrowed. Bella knew immediately that she was about to hear good news.

"Ah, Cherie, you look so radiant and beautiful today," said Bella.

Joanie blushed from the toes up and handed Bella the book of poetry, a small but lovely bouquet of flowers and two sterling silver spoons for tea. "I had to rush over to tell you that Matthew and my father's old partner solved the case. I can't really go into details, but the murderer is behind bars where he belongs!"

"Bella doesn't need details, just good news! That news shows on your face, Cherie. I am so happy for you, but why the gifts for me?"

"The sterling silver spoons were going to be my gift for you for Christmas, but I couldn't wait. The flowers are just to brighten up your desk. The poetry book brightened up my life when I needed it most. It helped me see things from another perspective, and that's always a good thing."

Joanie hugged Bella, whispering thank you.

"Now then," said Bella, wiping her eyes. "We must have tea and try out these new spoons. Sit while I heat the water."

The two friends shared their tea and chatted about the upcoming holidays.

"I am always busy during this time," said Bella, "and it is the time of year when people are most friendly and happy. But what are your plans?"

"We're planning a trip to Atlanta for Thanksgiving. Matt's Sister Vera invited the whole family to stay at her home and share Thanksgiving. She even invited my mother and said she was now a part of our family. It is truly good to have so many things to be thankful for."

"We should always be thankful, Cherie, in good times and in bad. The bad makes us stronger, and the good feels even better when you've experienced the bad. See? Bella's a smart old lady!"

"Indeed, Bella, indeed."

CHAPTER FORTY-THREE

NEW YORK CITY

It didn't take long for the news of Graceffo's arrest to reach Alex and Ben. Though they had only a skeleton-sized staff in the Big Easy, their ears were fine-tuned to the scandal. Their sources also reported the chief of police's suicide.

Alex was made aware that Graceffo was in jail without bond and had a court-appointed attorney to represent him. The report included the fact that Graceffo was on a 24/7 suicide watch.

Alex and Ben were pleased with their actions. They had been right about Graves and Graceffo, and they were right about Lorenzo. Now they knew that retaliation would be in order.

"We have to be vigilant, Ben," said Alex. "Lorenzo will most likely be out for our blood."

"No doubt about it, and that means that he could come at us from Florida or Chicago," said Ben.

"It's my gut feeling that Lorenzo has more of a hold in New Orleans than we originally thought. He may have moved some of his operation there after John's ties were severed."

"May have been recruiting soldiers all along, for all we know," said Ben. "I remember John showing me a newspaper ad that was recruiting foot soldiers."

"We need to rethink our business, get our priorities in order, and move forward. All that's happened says to me that John isn't coming back."

"Reluctantly, I agree, Alex. John is gone for good."

"First thing is to review our ties to the unions. I'm going to put you in charge of that entire operation, Ben. You're a tough negotiator, and you can talk the talk. We need to strengthen our relationship with the unions and avoid running over Lorenzo and Giardeli in the process. In the meantime we need to find a new attorney. Who knows what Graceffo might say?"

"Good point, Alex. I'll get on both things right away."

CHAPTER FORTY-FOUR

ONE WEEK LATER
GAINESVILLE, FLORIDA

"Mr. Brown, when you have a minute, we should talk," said Matthew.

"Now is good; come on in and close the door," said Brown.

"It's about the Bureau asking for my involvement in researching Carmine Lorenzo," Matt paused. "In all good conscience I cannot say no, but having said that, I cannot say yes without a caveat. That would be that I not start working on this until after the holidays."

"I understand your conundrum, son," said Brown. "I would have the same concerns if I were in your shoes."

"I appreciate your understanding, and I know it's putting the client off for a few weeks, but I would assume they would want a refreshed, renewed Matthew Winters rather than the one standing here today."

"Let me talk with them. Even though they're eaten up with deadlines and deals, they're people with families too. I'll remind them that it is my esteemed opinion that the Bureau deserves the firm's best when he's at his best. I'll let you know what they decide. In the meantime, take some time off. I don't want to see your face around here until at least December tenth—even though I don't know what day that is—it's a good long time from today. Now pack up and go with my blessings. I am still your boss, you know!"

"God bless you, sir."

Matt called Joanie before he left the office to let her know he was on his way home. She was thrilled that he'd be home early. She had no idea he would be home for so long.

CHAPTER FORTY-FIVE

ATLANTA, GEORGIA
THANKSGIVING, 1960

Vera, David, and Daniel welcomed everyone to their beautiful home in Buckhead. The weather was picture perfect, and the leaves along Peachtree Road were adorned in their best colors for fall.

As the Winters family gathered together for the first time since Joanie and Matthew's wedding, there was a momentary but noticeable silence as they looked around the room at one another. Vera, being the consummate hostess, broke the silence by saying that their home had never been filled with so much love.

Daniel, now six months old, was crawling all around the marble and wood floors, inspecting everything and everyone as he encountered them. He would make little squeaking noises as though he was greeting everyone, and without exception, he garnered all the attention.

The twins, Sandra and Amanda were quite the little ladies and dressed alike. They were now nearing five years of age and enjoyed playing with Daniel. Unlike the baby they met at the wedding, this was now a moving target, and they took to him immediately.

Marc and Lucy were obviously proud of their girls, enjoying parenting as much as any two people possibly could.

Matthew, Joanie, and Mrs. Bovier rounded out the group, and the love between the three of them was palpable. They had experienced a great deal in a short amount of time and knew their resiliencies had been tested.

Moving to the screened-in porch that swept the back of the house, the adults gathered for wine and snacks. Mrs. Bovier stood and made a toast to Vera and David for inviting her into their home. Marc responded with a "here, here" and told Mrs. Bovier that she was now a full part of the Winters Clan and with that accolade came a great responsibility—to make sure everyone's glass was never empty!

Mrs. Bovier committed to do her duty and announced that she would prefer to be called by her given name now that she was "family." As people stared one to the other, they suddenly realized that no one except Joanie knew her name. When all eyes turned to Joanie, she softly said, "Beatrice."

"To Beatrice Bovier!" said David.

"To Beatrice!" said the group.

After quietly sipping her glass of wine, Vera stood a minute later and said, "And to our sister Ruth, wherever she may be..."

"To Ruth," they all said.

Matthew sat with his arm around Joanie. Marc had his hand on Lucy's knee, and David smiled adoringly at his wife, Vera.

CHAPTER FORTY-SIX

WASHINGTON, DC/NEW YORK CITY

As 1960 came to an end, political struggles arose on many fronts. Newly elected President John Fitzgerald Kennedy had appointed his brother, Robert Kennedy, chief counsel of the Senate Labor Rackets Committee, better known as the McClellan Committee. The committee's task was to investigate the influence of organized crime in labor unions. Beginning with the Teamsters Union, Kennedy and the committee unearthed a plethora of information about one James Riddle Hoffa, head of the Teamsters Union.

Robert Kennedy, speaking to a national television audience had plenty to say about Jimmy Hoffa and the Teamsters Union. Host Jack Paar sat quietly across the desk from Kennedy, who openly named names and accused Hoffa and others of attempting to create a superpower stronger than the government.

Robert Kennedy had openly pointed the finger at gangsters and used their real names. Subsequently, he made no bones about his desire to "get Hoffa," saying he would not abide corruption on any level and asserting that the Teamsters Union was rotten to the core.

Hoffa had been elected as president of the Teamsters Union, replacing Dave Beck who had been imprisoned for using Teamsters money for personal financial gain. In 1960 Hoffa was reelected.

Hoffa was a well-known supporter of the Republican Party and was known to be a generous supplier of funds to Richard Nixon in his presidential struggle with Robert's brother, John F. Kennedy. And as Kennedy's election victory took place, he appointed his brother Robert as his attorney general.

Once in office, Kennedy resumed his investigations into Hoffa's activities, eventually charging him with taking money from the union's pension fund.

Hoffa believed in *any means to an end*. According to him, the only thing that mattered in life was success, no matter how one achieved it. To Hoffa's way of thinking, dealing with gangsters was necessary for the success of the Teamsters. In fact, dealing with Hoffa was more necessary for the success of the mob.

While the mob provided Hoffa with the kind of muscle he valued, Hoffa provided the mob with money—and lots of it. That jackpot was none other than the Central States Pension Fund.

The hardworking rank and file of the Teamsters trusted the union with their retirement savings with the promise that it would be soundly invested and yield high dividends. Unfortunately, Hoffa made loans to gangsters, including one of the underworld's architects in Las Vegas. The infamous and grand Desert Inn as well as the Stardust Hotel in Las Vegas were built with the teamsters' hard-earned investments.

Jimmy Hoffa reportedly did not take "orders" from gangsters; he rather took "cues." That may well be when and where his troubles began.

CHAPTER FORTY-SEVEN

1961–1966

It was a time of social change, when moral ethics were challenged, violence was erupting through the country, and vigilante justice was becoming more common in the South. The sixties were the age of youth, as seventy million children from the post-war baby boom became teenagers and young adults. The movement away from the very conservative fifties continued through the decade and eventually resulted in revolutionary ways of thinking. Young people wanted change. Those changes affected education, values, lifestyles, laws, and entertainment. College campuses became centers of debate and, ultimately, scenes of protest. The "Generation Gap" as it was later to be coined, started in earnest.

Matthew Winters found himself ensconced with matters relating to the Federal Bureau of Investigation. Little did he know how involved he would ultimately become in the changes that were taking place stateside and beyond.

Matt and Joanie had finally settled into marriage and were casually chatting about where the future would take them. They discussed children, careers and opportunities. And unfortunately, they were forced to discuss their safety as it related to Matthew's position in representing the FBI for his law firm.

Both shared the painful memory of Detective Bovier's murder at the hands of the mob, which in retrospect may well have been a warning sign.

Neither Joanie nor Matt had been accustomed to fear, and while the risks were mounting with each assignment from the FBI, both agreed that Matthew should pursue the path he had begun.

Many evenings were spent in conversation about their personal safety and what to do if something or someone appeared to be "out of place". If it appeared odd, the agreed upon action was to call the police immediately.

Joanie had recently completed a course in self-defense and had enrolled in a martial arts class for further training. Matthew had achieved his black belt in karate, and had joined a firearms training session at the local shooting range.

They felt they were as prepared as they could be, when or if trouble were to come knocking on their door.

CHAPTER FORTY-EIGHT

CUBA

Since the Cuban Revolution of 1959, Fidel Castro had grown increasingly antagonistic toward the United States. The Eisenhower and Kennedy administrations authorized the CIA to find ways to remove him. As a result attempts were made to poison him, anticommunist groups inside Cuba's borders were actively supported, and a radio station beamed slanted news at the island of Cuba from the Florida coast.

Meanwhile, thousands of upper- and middle-class Cubans were fleeing the island, legally at first, clandestinely later. These Cubans had lost rights to their properties and investments when the communist government took over. Most of them settled in Miami, seething with hatred for Castro and his regime. Enter the CIA, who upon government orders made use of the disgruntled Cubans, offering them a chance to overthrow Castro. All this was on the heels of Carmine Lorenzo having his lucrative casinos confiscated and spending time in a less-than-posh Cuban jail. While in Tampa, Lorenzo kept tabs on what the CIA's intentions were. He, along with many others who had been scavenged by Castro, wanted him ousted.

While the CIA had many volunteers, many of whom were professional soldiers during the reign of Batista, they took great care to keep Batista's cronies out of the top ranks. Groups of exiles formed their own coalitions and often argued among themselves. The CIA sent its recruits to Guatemala, where they were trained and received weapons. The force was named the Brigade 2506 in honor of a soldier who had been killed in training. (His enlistment number was 2506.)

In April of 1961, the 2506 Brigade was moved to the Caribbean coast of Nicaragua, where it made its final preparations.

In April of 1961, President John F. Kennedy ordered the Bay of Pigs Invasion. US Air Force bombers were to bombard Cuba's defenses and take out the small Cuban Air Force. However, the bombing raids did not destroy all of Cuba's airplanes, as some had been hidden. Believing their mission completed, the bombers then landed in Florida. Two days later, the 2506 Brigade, consisting of over 1400 well-organized and armed soldiers, landed on Cuban soil. They were joined by rebel groups within Cuba.

The attack failed largely because of the selection of a poor landing site—the southern coast of Cuba, called the Bay of Pigs—the failure to disable the Cuban Air Force, and the overestimation of the Cuban people's willingness to support a strike against Castro.

Hearing of the attack on the Bay of Pigs, Castro ordered his military units to respond. The small fleet of aircraft that were available responded, attacking the invaders, sinking one ship that carried food and supplies for the rebel troops, and driving off the rest of the fleet. The invasion was thwarted.

The diplomatic fallout from the failed Bay of Pigs invasion was considerable and escalated the already-heightened Cold War tensions.

CHAPTER FORTY-NINE

USA AND BEYOND

In 1962 the Cold War continued to worsen when the Russians placed Ballistic Missiles on Cuban land, a mere ninety miles off the coast of Florida. President Kennedy threatened war unless those missiles were removed. While the Russians removed them for a short time, the world was on the brink of nuclear war and ultimately self-destruction. The Soviets ultimately agreed to dismantle Soviet silos in Cuba and did so between October fifteenth and November twentieth, 1962.

President Kennedy ordered a United States embargo on all imports from Cuba, including tobacco, seafood, fruits, and vegetables.

In 1963, President John F. Kennedy was assassinated in Dallas, Texas. Lyndon B. Johnson was thrust into the role of president.

While most of the nation wept and grieved, those whose lives were not so patriotic ran rampant. Rumors flew regarding who was responsible for the assassination, and those rumors would perpetuate for years to follow. The believed assassin was Lee Harvey Oswald, who never lived to see trial but was gunned down in the Dallas Police Department basement by Jack Ruby, a well-known Texan nightclub owner with ties to organized crime.

Mr. Ruby had worked for the mob in his teens when he worked as a runner for a leading mob boss.

CHAPTER FIFTY

GAINESVILLE, FLORIDA

Matthew Winters had been working exclusively with the FBI on special projects. His skills as an investigator were widely recognized and respected by the Bureau as well as his growing law firm.

There was little surprise when Matthew was asked to discreetly investigate any mob connection to the assassination of the president and, in particular, one Jack Ruby.

The FBI analysis on Jacob Rubenstein, aka Jack Ruby, provided a great deal of information about his background. As Matthew pored over the reports, he noted that Ruby grew up in Chicago and was the son of poor Polish immigrants.

His first "job" was running errands for Al Soldierne, aka Al Capone, and he ultimately became a "union organizer" and "secretary" for a local branch of the Scrap Iron and Junk Handlers Union in Chicago.

He had served in the US Air Force during World War II and entered into business with his brothers. After that business venture fell through, he left Chicago and moved to Dallas, where he opened his first nightclub that he named the "Silver Spur."

In 1957–1958 he had been running guns to the followers of Fidel Castro, who at that time were fighting to overthrow Batista.

The next phase of the report knocked Matthew for a loop. There in black and white was deposition testimony that said in 1959 Jack Ruby went to Havana to try to gain the release of one Carmine Lorenzo, who had been jailed for his role in Mafia gambling and narcotics activities. Further, that Jack Ruby helped supply arms to the anti-Castro Cubans.

Matthew sat speechless as he worked to put the pieces of the puzzle together. The connection was obvious, the motive unclear yet compelling. Confirmation of Ruby's connections to the mob was within the FBI document, and Matthew wondered why they asked him to investigate it. He shared the information with his partner William Brown, who suggested they meet with their FBI contact to substantiate the testimony made by their CI (Confidential Informant).

CHAPTER FIFTY-ONE

WASHINGTON, DC

 newly appointed Lyndon B. Johnson found this a difficult time to become president.

With mounting trouble in Vietnam where Viet Cong guerillas had killed more than eighty American Advisers, the continuing campaign for civil rights by the black community caused violent reactions from whites. Black civil rights leader Martin Luther King, Jr. had recently been arrested in Alabama, and much protest ensued.

The Warren Commission, formally known as the President's Commission on the Assassination of John F. Kennedy, was established in 1963, merely seven days after the president's assassination. The Commission's summation and conclusions presented a year later concluded that Lee Harvey Oswald had acted alone.

President Johnson was briefed on La Cosa Nostra (now known as the American Mafia), the foremost organized criminal threat to American society. Literally translated into English, the name means "this thing of ours," but the organization became more commonly known as the Mafia—a nationwide organization of criminals. Most active during the time in the New York City metro areas, additionally parts of New Jersey, Philadelphia, Chicago, Detroit, and New England were becoming prominent members of the Mafia society as well.

The *Mob*, as it became known, was in full-blown action with families vying for other families' fortunes and with omerta (or the code of silence) becoming more or less a *requirement* of *past* regimes. The old rules were now being broken; the factions had divided from all-Italian to a mixed heritage entity. It was painfully clear that the Mafia's point was to make money, and one of the simplest—*extortion*—or forcing people to give up their money by threatening them in some way, was becoming a prevalent technique.

President Johnson recognized that the Mob had far-reaching, international connections.

During 1962 and 1963, the Mafia had left many dead in Italy. The Italian government fought back, but the Mafia reorganized itself thwarting the government's best efforts. Thanks to cigarette smuggling and drug trafficking, its reorganization resulted in an expansion into Northeastern Italy, Canada, South America, Australia, and Western Europe.

In 1963, Joseph Valachi became one of the first La Cosa Nostra members to *openly* provide the FBI with a detailed look inside the organization. Having been recruited by FBI agents, he revealed to a United States Senate committee numerous secrets of the organization, including its name, structure, power bases, codes, and swearing-in ceremonies, and he divulged members' names within the organization.

THE KENNEDY RUMORS

Joseph Kennedy, patriarch of the Kennedy clan was suspected of having had ties to some well-known Mafia kingpins. Joe Kennedy, who reportedly earned much of the family's fortune as a bootlegger, was believed to have had connections to mobsters during that venture.

During the Democratic primary in 1960, John F. Kennedy faced Hubert Humphrey in seeking the nomination. Many claimed that the Kennedy clan called on their mob connections to ensure a favorable vote, and similar accusations were made during the presidential election against Richard Nixon, which Kennedy won by *only* a slim margin.

Several theories tie JFK's assassination to the Mafia, including the mob ties that existed with Jack Ruby, who openly murdered Lee Harvey Oswald, on camera, as the people of The United States watched their television sets.

One theory attributes motive to the Mafia through the Bay of Pigs invasion of Cuba because of the Mafia's hatred of having its lucrative Cuban casinos closed when Castro came into power.

Another theory points to JFK's brother, Robert, who, once appointed, immediately began an open and well-publicized Mafia crackdown.

Numerous connections appeared that were either compromised or had an inherent threat of becoming public knowledge. Regardless of the reason(s), the Kennedy family appeared to be "cursed" in their political careers.

The lone brother who served as a congressman without being assassinated was Senator Edward (Ted) Kennedy. He later had his reputation tarnished when he left the scene of a fatal accident that took the life of a young woman under his tutelage. Her death at the crash site was considered more than suspect.

CHAPTER FIFTY-TWO

GAINESVILLE, FLORIDA

Having made the connection between Jack Ruby, Castro of Cuba, and Lorenzo of Tampa, Brown and Winters scheduled a meeting with their FBI contacts.

Because Matthew was aware that the FBI was running a full-scale investigation of their own, he couldn't help but wonder why they were involving him in these most-recent situations.

The firm's FBI contact made it clear; they were utilizing every resource on as wide a scale as possible, to find any confirmation that there was a conspiracy to commit murder relating to the assassination of the President. That included the inner workings of the Mafia, any attempts by any group or individual to cover up an assassination plot, and/or an order to remove any eye-witness or informant of the underworld.

Brown questioned the safety of Matthew's continued involvement in the Mafia investigations as well as the firm's continuing role.

The FBI agent told Brown and Winters that there was an inherent risk in everything they were doing, but that the bureau was doing, and would do, everything within their power to protect the firm and its employees.

Citing all information transmitted as "confidential" the agent offered them as much anonynimity as was possible in these situations.

The meeting ended with Brown's suggestion that he and Matthew talk with the Board of Directors concerning their ongoing involvement, and committing to give the bureau a swift response.

CHAPTER FIFTY-THREE

NEW YORK CITY, NEW YORK

While the FBI looked for answers to the assassination of President John F. Kennedy, Carmine Lorenzo Jr. was flexing his muscle in the Big Apple.

Having now moved most of his operation from Tampa to New York, Lorenzo maintained many of his Florida connections.

Graceffo had been incarcerated and "handled" by some prison insiders and of course Samuel Jackson Graves had mysteriously *disappeared.* When those things occurred, Lorenzo reorganized and made substantive changes within his organization. That necessitated a new attorney for his growing New Orleans business interests, and he opted to hire Frank Ragano, a brilliant attorney who had a direct relationship to James Hoffa. Lorenzo felt that Ragano's connection to the unions would be beneficial.

Without having had the pleasure of personally disposing of Graves, Lorenzo continually dug into how Graves was ousted and by whom. He correctly assumed that Graves had gotten too cocky and divulged information to John Marconi's boys.

Lorenzo had planned the demise of Alex Mineo and Ben Moriani as surely as he would take over Marconi's territory, but there was more brain than muscle in these latest developments which sent him to his favorite group of "snitches" for answers and, more specifically, names.

Lorenzo had plants within the FBI's ranks as did every *reputable* mobster. From his informants he obtained the name of Matthew Winters, an investigative attorney from Gainesville, Florida.

By that evening, Lorenzo knew a lot about Mr. Winters as well as his law firm.

CHAPTER FIFTY-FOUR

BAXTER, BROWN, NEWMAN & WINTERS' BOARD ROOM GAINESVILLE, FLORIDA

"Gentlemen," said Brown, "we are meeting today on an urgent matter, and we need to be certain in our decision making."

"As you know the Federal Bureau of Investigation has elicited our help in several matters and Matthew Winters has stepped-up as not only lead counsel, but lead investigator for the client. While we recognize there is a certain amount of risk in involving ourselves with strictly confidential sources and informants, I feel that we are compelled at this juncture, to identify when and if our involvement continues or terminates. While I, as many of you, see representing the FBI as a great honor, we must now think in terms of the firm's security and the safety of our employees."

"With that preamble, the bureau has asked us to assist in the investigation of any and all persons, who may have had a part in the assassination of President Kennedy. The information we have had *confirmed*, reflects a connection between the Mafia, Cuba and its leader Fidel Castro, and James Hoffa, the controversial union organizer."

The silence in the room was palpable.

Brown continued. "The Mafia connection is believed to be that of one Carmine Lorenzo, Jr. of Tampa, which puts him all-too-close to our doorstep. I'll take any questions or comments you have at this time."

"What protection does the FBI offer Matthew or the firm for that matter?" asked one board member.

"None other than as much 'anonymity' as can be reasonably expected in a situation such as this. That to me says, 'none'." Brown replied.

Another board member turned to Matthew and asked, "How do you feel about continuing with this client?"

Standing to answer the question, Matthew simply said, "I have a sworn and vested interest in upholding the law, as does the FBI. While I recognize the risks, I have taken every precaution possible to insure my own safety and that of my family. This is a prestigious account for the firm, but I do not take the inherent danger lightly. We have produced some excellent results for the FBI and I would willingly proceed with them, if that is the consensus of this board."

"What can we do to further insure Matthew's safety?" asked yet another board member.

Brown stood and said, "We would take additional safety measures as suggested by the FBI. Those would necessitate some physical changes to the property, and 'bug-proofing' and anti-tampering devices would be added to our communication systems. As for Matthew in particular, we would provide a driver for him who is trained in combat and martial arts, Matthew would be certified in all applicable areas of self-defense training by the FBI, and we would increase the value of his life insurance."

Again the room went silent.

The only remaining board member who had not yet posed a question asked, "And how do you feel about all of that, Matthew?"

"I am not only capable, but I am willing to assume the risks involved, to maintain our relationship with this client."

"If there are no more questions, I propose we take a vote." Brown stated.

The vote was unanimous; the FBI would remain a client of the firm, and all FBI recommended security measures would be implemented at the firm's expense.

CHAPTER FIFTY-FIVE

ATLANTA, GEORGIA

1966–1970

Lily Marie Adams entered the world of Vera, David, Daniel, and Caleb Adams. Lily was beautiful and healthy and had been named for her paternal aunt who had died as a child. Vera was overcome with joy at the birth, even though her labor had been both long and arduous.

David was enveloped in love with Lily from the moment she entered the world. She was definitely going to have to learn to make her way in a family where the males outnumbered the females, but he silently swore he would see to it that no one harmed a hair on her head.

The Adams family was now complete. Vera and David had decided that three children was a blessing, and they would not try for more.

The great news about Lily's birth had traveled quickly through the Winters Clan. Telephone calls, flowers, and baby items were being delivered daily to the Buckhead home. It was a joyous homecoming when David was allowed to bring his wife and new baby girl home from Piedmont Hospital.

Amanda and Sandra were ten years of age now and were begging Marc and Lucy to take them to see their only girl cousin. Not to be denied, Marc and Lucy arranged a weekend getaway to Atlanta, where the twins offered to babysit, and Lucy helped with cooking and general household duties to allow Vera time to ease back into everyday life.

Joanie and Matthew flew up to Atlanta for the same weekend, along with Joanie's mother, Beatrice Bovier. The celebration was reminiscent of that Thanksgiving when they all first came together to pay homage to their collective blessings. For once, there was not a cloud of misery in their world.

After enjoying a family dinner on Friday night, the adults moved to the screened-in porch. The obvious first question was to Matt and Joanie.

"So when are you two going to have kids?" asked Lucy.

"Lucy," said Marc, "that's none of our business."

"Well of course it is. We're all family, and we all want the best for one another," she said, quickly turning her gaze back to Joanie. "So when?"

Joanie could feel her mother's stare fixated on her. She had been the first to ask of course and had been given an ambiguous attorney-like answer.

"Yes, darling, when?" said Beatrice.

She looked at Matthew for help, but he simply tipped his wine glass to her, saying nothing.

"Well...actually, we're trying," said Joanie very simply and sweetly.

Vera, Lucy, and Beatrice jumped to their feet and ran into one another getting to Joanie to hug her.

"Hey," said Matthew, "easy on the wife. She's not pregnant yet. We're just *trying* to get pregnant."

Marc walked over to his twin and shook his hand, with David following suit.

"I didn't realize it would be such big news," said Matthew. "Let's just hope we can get pregnant."

"Of course you can," said Beatrice, "and I've always told Joanie that I'd bet she will have twins. Wouldn't that be great?"

"Yeah, great," said a less-than-eager Joanie. "I'll have more wine now, please."

CHAPTER FIFTY-SIX

KONA, HAWAII

Riana and Jarrod Tavares were now thirty-eight and forty-three, respectively, and had been in Hawaii long enough for it to feel like home.

Jarrod kept up with the news from every source he could and knew that what was happening on the mainland was serious. He, of course, had heard nothing directly or indirectly about Alexander Mineo or Benjamin Moriani. Jarrod took that as good news. Since their names had not come up in conjunction with all of the information about organized crime, Jarrod assumed they had either been absorbed by another family or were dead.

The FBI agent who had met with Jarrod on a regular basis had backed off in the frequency of his visits but still pursued Jarrod by asking him direct questions about specific criminals. Jarrod had never been questioned directly about Alex or Ben, and he did not volunteer any information about his "boys."

The newspapers had been filled with stories about the presidential assassination, Jack Ruby (whom Jarrod knew), and E. G. Partin, the ousted union official who had cut a deal with the authorities in exchange for reduced jail time.

Jarrod candidly told the agent all he knew about the union situation and actually told them that Jimmy Hoffa was more than likely a marked man by the mob. According to Jarrod, Hoffa thought he could arm wrestle or buy his way out of anything, and the mob didn't operate on those terms.

Riana thought of the family she had left behind. She could not stop the dreams that appeared in the middle of the night and haunted her into the next day. Vera was always at the center of the dream, just as she had always been the center of the family. She silently prayed that Vera and David were indeed living their dream life together and that perhaps they were raising a family of their own.

Riana had started a small crafts business, learning how to make leis of flowers and shells. She spent many hours with the Hawaiian ladies who taught her their skills and shared their customs and traditions with her. The leis took considerable time to make, and creating them was a great way to occupy her time.

While Riana was obviously not of Hawaiian heritage, she was perpetually tanned from her long walks along the shoreline, and when dressed in Hawaiian clothing, looked quite at home.

CHAPTER FIFTY-SEVEN

NEW YORK CITY

Alexander Mineo and Benjamin Moriani were victims of a hostile takeover. Their entire organization was swallowed up by the Lorenzo family, formerly of Tampa and now of New York City. Carmine Lorenzo, Jr. and Francesco Patrone had used their influence with Chicago gangster Sam Giardeli, who organized and assisted in the bloody takeover. Once the skirmish ended, neither Alex nor Ben was left alive.

The takeover occurred in lower Manhattan before daybreak on a hot, humid July day in 1965 when Alex and Ben were lured to the borough for an alleged meeting with the local union workers. Rather than union workers, they were barraged with gunfire from a panel van that encircled their vehicle. Neither of them had a chance to defend himself, and they, as well as their bodyguards, were massacred. There was little news coverage of the incident other than the obligatory notice of machine-gun fire in the borough.

Carmine Lorenzo, Jr. brought in his brother Harrison to handle the family affairs in Florida while he and Patrone concentrated on New York. What Lorenzo did not anticipate was that a favor given meant a favor owed. Now he was indebted to Giardeli.

As with any crime lord, connections meant everything. Not only was Sam Giardeli now positioned to take over New York, his organization would have grown to the strength of the Legano family, a long-known and well-recognized rival family in Chicago.

The one thing that Sam Giardeli had over everyone else was patience. He would plan his strategy and then execute the plan. It did not have to mature overnight or even in a year; he would make sure everything was in place before he made his next move. And just as he had done with Alex and his organization, the takeover would be swift and totally unexpected. For the time being, he would let Lorenzo thump his chest and feel like the big man in town. He would also allow Lorenzo to do a lot of the dirty work for him. Yes, he had made a plan for that too.

CHAPTER FIFTY-EIGHT

TALLAHASSEE, FLORIDA

Detective Peter Sutherland had been made captain of the TPD as a result of his heroic work over the past several years. He had received numerous commendations and accolades as well as a sizeable jump in salary.

Pete no longer had to go out to investigate homicides or suicides or run of the mill disturbances. This was someone else's job now, and although Pete was grateful for the promotion, he missed his days of investigating. Pete often remarked that once investigating was in your blood, it was there for good.

Having worked so well with Matthew Winters, and having spent a good amount of time together as a result, the two had become quite good friends. Their budding friendship and mutual respect for one another led them to chat every couple of weeks.

Matt always remembered to ask about Detective Scott Wood, who was mentoring a younger detective now, having cut his teeth alongside Pete on several cases. Scott had learned from the best and had become quite a stellar officer. He asked the right questions of the right people at the right time and had matured beyond his years. Pete's tutelage was paying off.

Scott reported to Sutherland now and was the first to tell the newest members of the squad that he trained alongside the captain.

CHAPTER FIFTY-NINE

NEW ORLEANS, LOUISIANA

Jack Palace resigned as chief of police after a two-year stint and opted to retire with full benefits from the NOPD. Disliking the restrictive nature of the job, Jack opted to become a private detective after a three-month vacation, which had included a trip to Gainesville to see Matthew and Joanie and to do some fishing.

Jack named his new firm *Palace PI*, just because he liked the name. It was catchy, descriptive of what he was hiring himself out to do, and easy to remember if you were looking for a private investigator.

It wasn't beyond Jack to take on a protective case or two. He had a permit to carry a concealed weapon, a private investigator's license, and a dark sedan. He even hired a young woman named Carol to man the telephone at his office. While he paid Carol only minimum wage, it looked much more professional to have an office, and it was great to have someone to take care of the paperwork.

As a result of helping solve the murder of Jack Bovier, Palace, Sutherland, and Winters had all become friends. The three had maintained a relationship over the years, and when they could, they would assist one another on cases or simply supply information. It was a great network of trusted and dependable comrades.

Jack had at one point suggested to Pete Sutherland that he consider joining his PI firm, but without a significant number of new cases, the pay would be beneath that which the Tallahassee Police Department paid him. Plus, it would mean uprooting his family and moving to New Orleans, something Pete's wife Sylvia wanted no part of.

Jack Palace had maintained very close contact with Beatrice Bovier, even taking her out to dinner on occasion.

Beatrice was a lovely woman who Palace had admired greatly over the years. He was more than happy to spend time with her and do the occasional odd job around her house in the Ninth Ward. It seemed there was always something that needed to be done in that old house. Palace even suggested that she might want to sell it and move closer to Joanie and Matthew. Thinking he had her best interests at heart, it dawned on him one day that she might think he was trying to get her out of town. While that was the furthest thing from true, he managed to bring it up at their last dinner out together. He actually thought she seemed relieved.

NINTH WARD

Beatrice Bovier had just returned from her trip to Atlanta to visit Vera and meet the new baby. Arriving at the airport she opted to call Jack Palace for a ride rather than take a cab. He was happy to oblige and promptly left his office to meet her at the airport.

"So how was your trip?" asked Jack.

"Fantastic," said Beatrice. "Lily Marie is probably one of the most beautiful baby girls I have ever seen—well with the exception of my Joanie, of course."

"Of course," said Jack, "I remember when Joanie was born. She was a beauty, and I remember thinking then that she looked a lot like her mother."

"Why, Jack Palace, I think you just paid me a compliment."

"Guess I did; good for me. Are you hungry? Do you want to stop for something to eat on the way home?"

"No thank you. I'm ready to be home. As much as I enjoyed my trip, it's always good to be in your own surroundings." Beatrice was looking out the window of Jack's dark sedan as they sped along the highway. "So what have you been up to—any new cases?"

"A couple of new things, but nothing too demanding," answered Jack. "What are your plans?"

"For what, Jack?"

"Sorry, I just wondered if you would be around for a while so that maybe we could have dinner again or see a movie, whatever."

"I see. Well, I don't have any plans other than to unpack my things and settle into my normal routine, and, yes, I'd love to get together for dinner. But this time, I'd like to cook for you. Would you like that?"

"I would, of course; it's been forever since I had a real home-cooked meal, other than home-cooked by me, that is. But I don't want to put you to the trouble."

"No trouble, Jack. It's not so easy cooking for one, is it?"

"No, ma'am, it's not easy, and in my case, it's not very good!"

"Then it's settled. Why don't you plan to come to dinner on Friday night, say six thirty?"

"It's a date," said Jack as he pulled into her driveway. Realizing what he'd just said he leapt out of the car to get Beatrice's suitcase out of the trunk.

"Thank you, Jack," said Beatrice. "You can just put that inside the door," gesturing toward the suitcase. "I'll see you Friday night."

"Great, I'll be here; six thirty. Oh, and can I bring anything?"

"Just a good appetite," Beatrice said, simply waving goodbye and closing the door.

CHAPTER SIXTY

GAINESVILLE, FLORIDA

Matthew Winters had become a very busy man as well as a prominent attorney in his firm. William Brown was and would be as long as he lived, a friend and mentor to the younger partner. The two of them worked seamlessly together and occasionally enjoyed a social cocktail together with their wives.

Joanie Winters was still employed by the Florida States Attorney's Office and at this juncture, had a more appealing list of cases than her rookie years handed her. While it was nothing like Matt's private practice, she was up to speed on all the latest news out of Tallahassee and even made business trips there on occasion.

During one trip, Matthew accompanied her and introduced her to Peter Sutherland's wife, Sylvia, and their beautiful daughter, Gracie.

Joanie and Sylvia became fast friends, and Joanie loved doting over Gracie. She was a sweet, innocent child with expressive eyes that seemed to look into your very soul. Joanie told her at one point that she was going to be a real heartbreaker when she grew up. Gracie's charm and gregariousness made her the highlight of any visit.

Sylvia and Pete concentrated on teaching Gracie and were always ready with an answer to her eager questions. They had taught her manners and instilled respect in her since birth, making Gracie a six-year-old with a maturity bordering on age ten.

When asked what she wanted to do later in life, Gracie simply smiled and said, "I'll either be a veterinarian or a nurse." No one doubted she would grow to be whatever and whomever she wanted.

The Sutherlands and the Winters had become great friends and visited one another regularly. It was pleasantly unusual for two couples to have this close a bond, but all of them were grateful for their mutual friendship.

On their most recent trip to Gainesville, Peter had talked with Matthew about his unrest at the police department.

"I'm probably just getting old," said Pete, "but I feel like I've been promoted out of a job that I really loved and gotten dropped in one that will bore me until retirement."

"That's because you're the consummate investigator, and now you aren't the lead investigator on anything except maybe who left the coffee pot on the burner too long," Matt teasingly said.

"Yeah, or lining up a roster of who's to bring in the doughnuts," chuckled Pete.

"Ever thought about taking Jack Palace up on his offer of joining the PI firm? You'd be a huge asset to him."

"First of all, Sylvia doesn't want Gracie to grow up in New Orleans—thinks the schools here in Florida are better," said Pete, "but getting my investigative juices going again sounds good to me. I'm just not sure New Orleans is the best place for us."

"Then why not consider doing what Jack did in New Orleans here?" asked Matt. "Tallahassee isn't that far from Gainesville, but I think you'd do well here. As a matter of fact, the firm could use an outside investigator, and I'd be happy to put in a good word with William Brown."

"Certainly food for thought, I guess. I don't know how Sylvia would feel about moving anywhere. But we really don't have any family to speak of in the Tallahassee area; just an aging aunt on my side. "

"Where are Sylvia's parents?" asked Matt

"They're outside of Atlanta," answered Pete.

"Amazing—my sister lives in Buckhead!"

"Well, gee, Matt, I didn't know you came from a wealthy family."

"I don't. My sister married a man with a budding career as an architect. He bought her the house as a wedding present, no less."

"Sweet, but don't let Sylvia know that. She'll wish she'd married better!" Peter laughed.

At dinner that evening Matt asked Sylvia about living in Tallahassee. He was surprised to learn that she had moved there as a teenager, and when her parents decided to move to Atlanta, she had stayed. She had attended college there and had graduated with a BA in Education and a teaching certificate.

"So how did you and Peter meet?" Joanie asked.

"On a blind date," said Sylvia.

Pete jokingly said, "Yeah, they had to blindfold her to get her to go out with a lug like me."

"And I'll bet you supplied the blindfold," joked Matt.

The four adults laughed.

"So you don't really have any specific ties to Tallahassee?" Matt asked Sylvia.

"Sure I do, my husband works for the TPD," she answered.

"Well, your husband could get a job most anywhere, right?" Matt was pushing.

"What are you two up to?" asked Joanie.

"I was wondering the same thing," Sylvia said.

The two men looked at each other as if they'd been caught dead to rights doing something wrong.

"Oh, nothing, honey," said Pete. "Matt's always trying to get me to move down here where I can do all his investigative work, and he can sit back on Mahogany Row and get paid the big bucks."

All was silent for a couple of moments.

Joanie broke the lull by saying, "I think having you guys here in Gainesville would be a wonderful thing. I could see you all the time, Sylvia, and I could spend more time with Gracie. And when I get pregnant, you could help me understand what's going on…"

"Pregnant!" exclaimed Sylvia. "Are you pregnant?"

"No, just working on it," said Matthew sheepishly.

"Sorry. I forgot that I hadn't told you about that," Joanie said. "It isn't a secret. We just told Matthew's family a few weeks ago."

"Living in Gainesville is something I never thought about. Our schools are rivals you know," said Sylvia. "But if Pete wanted to consider moving, we could talk about it, I guess."

Matthew smiled across the table at Peter who wished he could give him a swift kick under the table.

Matt said, "I think you guys should consider it. It's not like moving out of state. You'd be near friends, near an airport with daily flights available to Atlanta, and a built-in babysitter for Gracie!"

Joanie rescued him by saying, "Who wants dessert?"

With the thought planted firmly in Pete Sutherland's head, he broached the subject of moving to Gainesville with Sylvia once Gracie was sound asleep.

"I think it's something we have to really think long and hard about, Pete," said Sylvia. "A move like this is a big step, and although it has its appeal to me, I would wonder about how easily we could replace your salary, not to mention uprooting Gracie from everything and everyone she has known since birth."

"I agree. I just think that with Gracie getting ready to start school, it would be the ideal time to make a move. That way she would start school here and meet new friends right away."

Pete began pacing the floor. "Honestly, Sylvia, I'm just not cut out to be the boss. I *can* do it, and I *am* doing it, but I hate it. The bureaucracy and the boredom are getting to me. I miss the intrigue of getting my hands dirty on a case—getting in there and looking for something I don't even know is there. If I could get some sort of guarantee of work, I'd opt to go for it."

"I guess I didn't realize how your job made you feel," said Sylvia. "Why don't you quietly pursue it with Matthew and see what, if anything, the firm could offer you?"

"I knew I married smart," said Pete as he wrapped his arms around her delicate waist. "I'll talk with him tomorrow, and then you and I can revisit it."

"Perhaps I could go back to teaching. As long as Gracie is in school and I can work out a teaching situation that would allow me to be able to pick her up after school, I'd be most happy to resume teaching," Sylvia said.

Although Matthew had not discussed anything further with Pete, he knew in his heart of hearts that the guy wanted out of being a captain in the police department. He arranged a brief meeting with William Brown and broached the subject of hiring an outside, independent investigator.

"We certainly seem to have enough investigative work to keep one busy," said Brown.

"I am quite honestly biased in favor of this guy, having worked with him on Detective Bovier's case," said Matthew, "but I would love for you to meet him, chat with him, and give me your honest opinion."

"That's fair enough," said Brown. "Why don't you ask him when he can come in and see me?"

"I will, sir. Thanks."

"Oh, and I'm assuming that you don't want to give up your sleuthing altogether?" asked Brown.

"No, I have a penchant for it too, but I could use the help with the FBI cases in particular."

"I hope it's safe to assume that the FBI won't have a negative dossier on Mr. Sutherland."

"I would stake my career on that one, sir."

"Fine, then let's invite Mr. Sutherland in—and thanks Matthew for thinking ahead and looking out for the firm's best interests and use of talent. That's good thinking on your part."

"Yes, sir—thank you."

By the time Matthew pulled out his desk chair, he saw the message on his desk from Pete Sutherland. Matt called the number, and Pete answered on the first ring.

After sharing his discussion with Brown, Matt invited Pete for a sit-down chat with William Brown.

"I didn't come to Gainesville prepared for a job interview, Matthew. I don't even have a coat and tie with me!"

"I can help you there," said Matthew. "You can borrow something of mine."

"OK, then how about tomorrow?" Pete asked.

"I'll get with Mr. Brown and set something up. I'll call you later. Maybe we can get together over a beer and chat about the opportunities as I see them?"

"Sounds great," said Pete. "Looking forward to it!"

Pete shared their conversation with Sylvia, who just smiled and shook her head. "I'm being railroaded here, aren't I, Pete?" she asked.

Pete simply smiled and hugged her tightly.

CHAPTER SIXTY-ONE

NEW YORK CITY

1966–1967

Having recently been released from prison, Chicago-born Sam Giardeli was going head to head with Vincent Barino of New York for control. Their feud longstanding, Barino had reportedly been kidnapped on his way to a scheduled appearance before a grand jury in 1964, and Giardeli had taken unofficial credit for that capture. He had given the order from his jail cell.

After Giardeli's release from prison, he temporarily fled the country to escape further prosecution. Anthony Aacardi came out of retirement to head the family and supervise Giardeli's territory in the interim.

Throughout the 1966–1967 time periods, Barino was in the Mafia headlines. After his abduction, he lay low, making a sudden reappearance and announcing that he was once again in command of his New York crime family. In a surprising move, Barino turned himself in at the US Courthouse at Foley Square in New York. Authorities had been looking for him for more than nineteen months, speculating that Barino was in Tunis, controlling the flow of narcotics in the Mediterranean. Nonetheless, by early 1967, Barino was reportedly running a narcotics trafficking route between Montreal and New York City.

In the months that followed, there was great upheaval in family hierarchy. Names like Joey Colombi, Joey Gallo, Johnny Dioguardi, and "The Genoveses" were on the lips of both law enforcement, FBI, CIA, and everyday Americans who were suddenly bombarded with news from and about the underworld.

CHAPTER SIXTY-TWO

MARTIN LUTHER KING, JR.

1968–1970

On April 4, 1968, Reverend Doctor Martin Luther King, Jr. was assassinated while standing on the balcony of his motel room in Memphis, Tennessee, where he was to lead a protest march in sympathy with striking garbage workers.

King's illustrious but short societal contributions to America began in 1955 when he became a member of the executive committee of the National Association for the Advancement of Colored People (NAACP), the leading organization of its kind in the nation. Subsequently he accepted the leadership of the first great Negro nonviolent demonstration of contemporary times. The *bus boycott*, lasting 382 days, moved the Supreme Court to declare unconstitutional the laws requiring segregation on buses. During these days of boycott, King was arrested and his home bombed, and he was subjected to personal abuse, but he emerged as a Negro leader of the first order.

At the age of merely thirty-five, King was awarded the Nobel Peace Prize—the youngest man to have ever received it. When he was notified of his selection as the Prize recipient, he announced that he would turn over the prize money of $54,123 to the furtherance of the civil rights movement.

CHAPTER SIXTY-THREE

PETER SUTHERLAND

Peter Sutherland was without a doubt a man's kind of man. Lacking little in the way of knowledge or experience, he was a team builder, an exceptional gentleman, and had mentored many a rookie cop trying to make detective.

Matthew Winters had found a best friend as a result of meeting him and working with him on his father-in-law's murder. And now Matthew had opened a door for Pete at his law firm.

Pete was trustworthy and had proven that to Matthew. What he said he would do, he did. Having grown up in a modest home among hard-working people, he learned family values by experiencing them firsthand, and was now instilling those same values in his daughter.

His father had been a cop, and had many accolades to show for his 35 years on the force. Pete looked up to his father and emulated him in many ways.

The one thing Pete had always wanted to do was work undercover. While he was trained in undercover techniques, he had always been more useful to his department as a lead detective. He was hoping the interview with Baxter, Brown, Newman & Winters would present an opportunity to fulfill his wishes.

CHAPTER SIXTY-FOUR

GAINESVILLE, FLORIDA
1968

Matthew and Joanie Winters welcomed twin boys Michael and James into the world. The Winters Clan now laid claim to three sets of twins: Matthew and Marc Winters, Amanda and Sandra Winters, and now Michael and James Winters.

Knowing that Joanie would need all the help she could get, Joanie's mother Beatrice Bovier had moved to Gainesville as soon as her daughter told her about the pregnancy. While Jack Palace wasn't too thrilled to know that Beatrice was now leaving New Orleans, he agreed it was best. He and Beatrice had become quite a duo in the last few years.

Vera was beside herself with joy over the twins' birth. She immediately got in touch with David, who suggested the family drive down to Gainesville after Joanie and the boys were home and settled. He agreed to find them suitable lodging so as to not be under foot, but be close enough to visit for a few days. That pleased Vera as much as David thought it would, and she eagerly agreed to get ready for the trip.

Joanie had suspected twins when during her pregnancy she became "baby round" very quickly. She and Matthew had purchased a modest but comfortable home in a Gainesville suburb and graciously said goodbye to apartment living. Their new home was completely unpacked and ready for the arrival of the boys, and for this, Joanie was grateful.

Along with their own changes, the Sutherlands had indeed moved from Tallahassee to Gainesville and Peter had been hired as an investigator at Matt's law firm. He had more than proven himself to William Brown and the other senior partners and was beginning to feel quite at home in his new position.

The FBI had run every check on Peter Sutherland known to them and found nothing but glowing reports. Based on the firm's past relationship with the bureau, and the personal recommendations of both Winters and Brown, the FBI put its stamp of approval on Sutherland, allowing him to handle some of the cases that were now regularly flowing through the firm.

Sylvia and Gracie Sutherland were happy in their new surroundings, and moving before the school year began allowed Gracie to start her elementary program in Gainesville.

Sylvia and Joanie had become best friends. Sylvia was the first to suspect Joanie's pregnancy and urged her to have a pregnancy test. When the results came back positive, they both cried with joy. And as soon as that moment of joy passed, Joanie cried with fear. The comforting friendship of Sylvia saw her through the morning sickness, the mood swings, and the swelling, but nothing had prepared her for twins.

1970

The kids of the Winters Clan were growing up quickly. Daniel Adams was now ten, Caleb was eight, and Lily Marie was four. Amanda and Sandra Winters were fourteen going on twenty-five, and the youngest twins, Michael and James, were just starting their most terrible twos.

Life as everyone knew it had changed. The war in Vietnam was on everyone's mind. Friends who had children only four years older than Amanda and Sandra were being drafted. Husbands of young wives were being sent to fight a war they didn't understand, and young men who weren't even old enough to vote were being drafted straight out of high school.

Amanda and Sandra were already thinking about college. Trying to hold onto them as long as she possibly could and wanting only the best for her girls, Lucy Winters told them they had to make good grades or else not make it into college. Sandra expressed an interest in teaching school, while Amanda said she wanted a job that would allow her to travel. Admittedly not knowing what kind of job that would be was the least of her worries at fourteen.

Daniel had expressed interest in one thing only: studying meteorology at Georgia Tech.

CHAPTER SIXTY-FIVE

CAMBODIA

1970

Halfway around the world a young ten-year-old girl was expressing her interest in one thing only: studying marine biology. Leaolani Barrett was the daughter of United States Marine Sergeant Olan Barrett and his wife Lelah, whom he had met and married in Vietnam in 1958. Marine Sergeant Barrett had been born in Hawaii and had been a career serviceman for the US Marines since he was eighteen years old.

Leaolani (pronounced Lee-ah-o-lah-nee) was simply known as Lee to all her friends. She had been given a Hawaiian name and pronunciation thanks to her paternal heritage. Its literal translation is "Heavenly Flower."

Lee was a precocious child, loved the ocean and everything that had taken its life form from water. She was an excellent swimmer and was more at home in the water than out of it.

Georgia Tech was in Atlanta—that's all she knew, except that the school offered a four-year degree in marine biology that was top-notch.

Lee dreamed of college as an escape from the terror that surrounded her and her family on a daily basis. Living as an American in Cambodia was difficult at best. Lee relied on her parents' gentle influence and uncompromising attitude that the three of them were there for a reason and a destined purpose to help, not hinder. There was never a doubt that they as a family would survive and move to the United States.

Lee had become fluent in three languages as a result of her family: English, Hawaiian (Mamaka), and Vietnamese.

THE VIETNAM WAR CONTINUES 1970–1975

After the attack on Cambodia subsided after sixty days and tens of thousands of casualties, herbicides containing Dioxin (which had been banned by the US Department of Agriculture in 1968) were being sprayed in Vietnam. The use of this product, later known as "Agent Orange," continued through 1971. Coined Operation Ranchhand, eleven million gallons of Agent Orange—containing 240 pounds of the lethal Dioxin—had been sprayed on South Vietnam, causing more than one seventh of the country's total area to be reduced to waste.

In 1972, North Vietnamese army artillery opened a shattering barrage, targeting the South Vietnamese positions across the Demilitarized Zone (DMZ). More than twenty thousand North Vietnamese troops crossed the DMZ, forcing the South Vietnamese units into retreat, thus throwing the Southern defense into complete chaos. With that success, the North Vietnamese soldiers pushed toward the city of Hue, defended by a South Vietnamese division as well as a division of US Marines. Within one week, the North Vietnamese were forced to halt attacks and resupply.

Spearheaded by North Vietnamese tanks, the attack eventually brought the northern part of the city under North Vietnamese control. But the South Vietnamese men defended the city, reinforced by elite airborne units. Launching furious counterattacks, American B-52 bombers joined in the fray, and within a month, Viet Cong forces withdrew.

Within weeks, North Vietnamese forces again battled, and defending South Vietnamese divisions retreated. By the end of April 1972, the North

Vietnamese overtook the cities of Dong Ha and Quang Tri City. In spite of US air support, the battles over the Binh Dinh province and its cities (now reduced to rubble) ended unsuccessfully on September 15, 1972.

The year 1972 ended with peace talks between the North Vietnamese and Americans breaking down. A successful new bombing campaign was initiated by order of the president, and after the United States dropped more than twenty thousand tons of bombs, North Vietnam suffered a mere 1,600 casualties.

It is widely believed that while US troops suffered great losses in both manpower and firepower, this *was* a turning point in the war.

By January 9, 1973, North Vietnam and the United States resumed their peace talks in Paris. By the twenty-seventh of January, all warring parties in the Vietnam War signed a ceasefire.

During March of 1973, the last American combat soldiers left South Vietnam, though military advisors and Marines who were protecting US installations remained in the country. For the United States, the war was officially over.

More than three million Americans served in the war; almost 58,000 were killed, and over 1,000 were missing in action. Additionally, more than 150,000 Americans were seriously wounded.

By 1974, President Richard M. Nixon resigned, leaving South Vietnam without its strongest advocate.

Meanwhile, the North Vietnamese rebuilt their divisions in the south and captured key areas. Taking over virtually every major city, although a blatant violation of the Paris peace agreement, the North Vietnamese successfully infiltrated and took over twelve provinces and more than eight million people.

In late April of 1975, US Marines and Air Force helicopters, flying from off-shore carriers began a massive airlift of more than one thousand American civilians and almost seven thousand South Vietnamese refugees.

On April 30, 1975, two US Marines were killed in a rocket attack at Saigon's Tan Son Nhut airport. They were the last Americans to die in the Vietnam War.

At dawn, the last Marines of the force guarding the US Embassy lifted off. Only hours later, looters ransacked the embassy, and North Vietnamese tanks rolled into Saigon, ending the war.

CHAPTER SIXTY-SIX

NEW YORK, BROOKLYN, CHICAGO

1970–1980

THE LAWLESS

RICO or no RICO, organized crime activity continued. Retainers for mob attorneys skyrocketed, and violence continued, internally as well as externally.

In June of 1971, Italian-American Unity Day organizer Joe Colombo was mortally wounded by an assassin's bullet in New York City. The hit was initially believed to have been ordered by Joey Gallo, but later was attributed to the Legano family.

In April of 1972, renegade Mafioso Joey Gallo of New York City was gunned down at Umberto's Clam House in Little Italy on his forty-third birthday. And in July, mobster Tommy Eboli was shot five times in the head and neck at his girlfriend's home in the Crown Heights section of Brooklyn.

July 1975, in a Detroit suburb of Bloomfield Hills, Michigan, Jimmy Hoffa met with his former underworld associates regarding his return to the Teamsters union as president.

Hoffa scheduled a meeting at the Machus Red Fox restaurant outside Detroit. It is generally believed that he was to meet Anthony "Tony Pro" Provenzano along with another Detroit mobster Anthony Giacalone. Some say Russell Bufalino was invited instead.

James Hoffa telephoned his wife at 2:15 p.m. to say he had been stood up. Hoffa was never seen or heard from again. Although investigators focused on Provenzano and Giacalone, each had alibis for the date.

Some theorize that Hoffa was killed to stop him from testifying in front of the House Select Committee on Assassinations. Ironically, or perhaps not, a fellow Mafia suspect in the John F. Kennedy assassination was murdered at the same time Hoffa disappeared.

March 21, 1978, at the age of only forty-eight, Manhattan gangster Salvatore Briguglio was found shot to death in Manhattan's Little Italy. Briguglio, Anthony Provenzano, and another kingpin were scheduled to go on trial May 1 in Kingston, New York, for a 1961 murder of a Legano family's protégé. Witnesses to Briguglio's murder said he was knocked down by two men in front of the Andrea Doria Social Club. The men allegedly drew weapons and shot Briguglio four times in the face and once in the chest. Briguglio, an official in Provenzano's New Jersey Teamster organization, had been questioned in connection with James Hoffa's disappearance.

Provenzano was convicted of *participating* in murder on June 15, 1978, along with his enforcer. He was later sentenced to twenty years in federal prison for labor racketeering. At the time of his sentencing, Provenzano was sixty-three years of age. During his incarceration in Lompoc, California, he died of a heart attack at the age of seventy-one.

CHAPTER SIXTY-SEVEN

ATLANTA, GEORGIA

1978

David and Vera Adams could scarcely believe their first-born son Daniel was now eighteen. Once the summer was complete, Daniel would begin college at his father's Alma Mater, Georgia Tech.

It had long been David's dream to see his son attend the school he had loved and served so tirelessly, and he knew that whatever field Daniel chose, he would be well prepared by the Tech professors. While David secretly hoped his son would pursue architecture, he knew that the boy's interest had always been in meteorology.

Throughout Daniel's teenage years, David took every opportunity to give him the Georgia Tech experience, attending sporting events or simply strolling through the campus. When Caleb came along, he was included on the outings with his big brother and Dad.

Daniel carried himself well and had a positive outlook on life.

Daniel knew that his father would love to see him follow in his footsteps, but architecture was not his first love. He loved following wind formation, ocean currents, and astronomical alignments; he couldn't seem to get enough information to satisfy his curiosity. There was always something new to learn. Everything that happed in nature made something else happen, and he wanted to know both the *what* and the *why*.

Daniel was interested in natural disasters and would have been an amateur storm chaser had he had the opportunity and had his parents allowed him to do so. Regardless, Daniel read everything he could get his hands on about tornadoes, typhoons, tsunamis, earthquakes, and volcanic eruptions. Daniel had garnered a great amount of knowledge through his private research and could literally carry on a meaningful conversation with someone more advanced in age and instruction.

He was driven by his ambition and singularly focused on his goal.

It had become customary for the Winters families to gather in Buckhead for a summer outing. David and Vera had enough room for everyone, including Beatrice Bovier.

This year, July Fourth had been chosen as the get-together date, and Marc, Lucy, and the girls would drive over, while the Florida contingent would fly into Atlanta. Everyone was eager to see one another, and Vera was thrilled that Amanda and Sandra would join them again this year.

The twin girls, now twenty-two, had graduated from Louisiana State University. Sandra was a teacher in the Birmingham Elementary School, and Amanda was interning as a design assistant with an interior designer in Birmingham. Still feeling the need to travel, Amanda felt that once she made it into the world of interior design, she could live and/or work virtually anywhere in the world.

Marc and Lucy Winters were finally adjusting to their "empty nest" and became closer than they had ever been. They were now in a position to downsize the house, move closer to Marc's job in Birmingham, and travel. They had toured Italy in the spring and were intrigued by the historic artifacts and buildings. Sipping wine in a gondola was a new experience for both of them, particularly during the middle of the day. They often laughed when they thought of what the good people of Birmingham would have to say about them if they knew.

James and Michael Winters were as different as twins could possibly be. While they were identical in appearance, their actions gave their identity away. They were ten years old, but extremely well-mannered, thanks to their strict yet fair upbringing. James was the more mischievous of the two, but both were good kids.

Joanie would comment privately to Matt that the boys were more than a handful, and they consistently gave her a run for her money. As amazing as it was, she had managed to pursue her own law career and care for the boys, working while they were in school and placing them in daycare or camp during the summer months.

Joanie and Matthew were good parents. Matt wanted his sons to have fond, lasting memories of their youth and a positive experience with him as a father. He himself had missed that growing up, relying on his sister Vera for both the attention and emotional support he needed

The family retreats were relaxed and comfortable, but there was always a mention of Ruth. No one had spoken about "Ruth and John" in the same sentence for a long time. Of course all of the nieces and nephews knew who Aunt Ruth was, as well as Uncle John, but all they really knew was that they had left one day and had not been heard from since.

CHAPTER SIXTY-EIGHT

KONA, HAWAII

1978

Riana Tavares had just turned fifty. She found it hard to believe that was possible. Jarrod teased her mercilessly on her birthday until she quickly reminded him that he himself was fifty-five and looked every day of it.

Riana had made quite a business out of her lei-making. She had ladies from Kona working for her now, and younger girls who wanted to learn the process would help gather flowers and shells for the jewelry. She had started to incorporate sea glass into her jewelry and found that cleaning and polishing the chards was therapeutic for her.

Devising her own cleaning solution made the process quick, but she was constantly cutting herself with the broken pieces or handing Jarrod an injured finger with a piece of glass embedded in it. He was meticulous in removing the chard of glass, trying not to hurt Riana. She told him it reminded her of the story of the lion who had a thorn in his paw. *He would lie around and roar at the top of his lungs, scaring away anyone or anything that might be of assistance to him, until one day the tiny field mouse walked up to the sleeping lion and, with one tug with its sharp front teeth, extracted the thorn*. While Jarrod didn't like being compared to a field mouse, he took the inference in stride and simply hugged his loving, talented wife.

Jarrod was meeting a newly assigned federal agent today, introduced to him simply as Jade. She was an African American beauty with long braided hair. After their private introduction and consultation, Jade was introduced to Riana.

Riana's initial reaction was surprise, though she successfully hid it from Jade as well as Jarrod. As soon as Jade left their home, Riana told Jarrod she had a feeling that she had met this woman before or knew her from somewhere. Though it sounded crazy, Jarrod took her seriously and vowed to look into it with the original agent.

Rarely, if ever, did Jarrod initiate contact with the FBI. He typically waited for agents to contact him, which they did with some regularity, but Riana's comment was troublesome. He and Riana had spent a great many years protecting their new identities, and he was not willing to take the risk that Jade might be someone from their past.

Jarrod placed the call, left the prescribed, agreed-upon message that would trigger FBI contact. Within the hour, Jarrod was meeting with his old agent—alone.

After conveying all that he knew, however slight, the agent simply thanked him, told him he had done the right thing, and promised to look into it. Now all Jarrod could do was wait.

For the first time in several years, Riana had a fitful night. She was dreaming of the ocean, but it was not Hawaiian waters. She tossed and turned so much that she awakened Jarrod.

When he woke her to get her out of her thrashing dreams, she could not remember what she had dreamed. "I think it was about her" was all Riana could say.

Reassuring his wife, Jarrod simply held her in his arms until she had once again dozed off to sleep.

The next day the answer came. Riana had indeed met someone who "looked like" Jade, but they were not the same person. Riana had no doubt about this and urged Jarrod to communicate that to his long-time agent.

The agent assured Jarrod and Riana that their identities had not been compromised and that the connection Riana had made with Jade was coincidental.

That did not satisfy Riana, but without remembering the details of the look-alike", she could not take this any further. She vowed to remember.

Again, Jarrod reassured his wife, urging her to take some quiet time and try to relax. Riana vowed to relax as soon as she solved this mystery. The woman was too distinct in her memory to be incidental. Riana left for a long walk along the shoreline.

Walking in the Kona sand was a real workout. Even experienced walkers found the sand difficult to pick up any speed against. The grains of sand were large and coarse; the edge of the water treacherous at high tide.

Riana had walked for a couple of miles when she saw a young boy playing in the sand. He had his plastic bucket and a shovel, and as she approached she noticed he was digging a large hole in the sand. As she stopped to speak to him, it hit her like a thunderbolt.

She had been walking along the shore near her home in Miami, when she suddenly went down, spraining her ankle. Before she could right herself, she was being helped up by a beautiful black woman with long, braided hair. She apologized and said that her son had dug the hole and she was coming back to fill it in when she saw her fall. Her name was...Crystal. Crystal—who turned out to be an undercover cop and whose body was found in Ruth and John's house after the fire!

Riana practically ran home to tell Jarrod. Her mind racing, she was trying to figure out how this woman who was dead had just been to her home in Kona.

"Jarrod, I remember," said a panting Riana. She related the entire story to him.

"This cannot be the same person," said Jarrod.

"The names are similar," said Riana. "Crystal and Jade? And other than looking a few years older, I'd say they were identical."

"OK, Riana, I'll contact the agent again; he can get to the bottom of this. Thank you for remembering, darling. Just try to relax now. Everything is fine."

When the agent returned to Jarrod's house, he had Jade with him. After reassuring both Jarrod and Riana again, they shared this information.

"Crystal was my twin sister," said Jade solemnly, her eyes downcast. "She was an undercover investigator for the Miami Police Department. It was she whom you met on the beach, and yes, it was she whose charred body turned up in the burned house on the beach."

"Jade volunteered for this assignment to seek retribution for the person or persons who we believe were responsible for incinerating the house in Miami. She in no way harbors any animosity toward the owners of that home," the agent stated.

"Well, I for one don't understand this at all," said Riana.

"Riana, my sister died as a result of a threat against you. She had received a tip that an innocent woman was about to be murdered in her own home and that the home would be torched to destroy all the evidence. She knew you to be Ruth Ward, period. She knew your husband had enemies and that you were in danger. The day you were walking along the beach, there was a semiautomatic rifle trained at your head. Innocently creating a hole for you to step in took you out of immediate danger and sent the assailant off to look for a better opportunity," said Jade. "I have sworn to protect and defend, and that includes protecting and defending you and your husband. Because of the two of you, we have successfully put a lot of crime lords out of business, and for that, I am grateful. I can only hope that the instigator of your attempted murder and the scum who murdered my sister is one of those."

"I'm at a loss for words, and Jarrod can tell you that's a rare occurrence," said Riana.

"I want you and Jarrod to know that if you want me reassigned," said Jade, "I understand, and I will take a reassignment and forget that I ever met you. I would, however, respectfully ask to remain as one of your agents to see this through." Jade quietly stood up and said, "I'll let the three of you talk, and I'll just wait on the lanai. Thanks for hearing me out."

"Riana, what do you think?" asked Jarrod.

"She seems sincere, but is this a risk in your mind?"

The agent simply said, "It's totally up to you. The Bureau believes Jade to be honest and straightforward; otherwise, they would have never assigned her to your case. "

"I've been a lot of things, including a fool, but I've always been a pretty good judge of character. I think she can continue to work with us with the caveat being that if we ever feel threatened in any manner, she's out." Jarrod looked at his wife and got a nod.

"Thanks to both of you," said the agent. Calling Jade inside, he relayed the news to her.

"Thank you, Jarrod. Thank you, Riana—you won't regret your decision."

After the agents left the Tavares home, Riana wrapped her arms around her husband's waist. "Now tell me what you really think."

"I've always said, keep your friends close and your enemies closer."

CHAPTER SIXTY-NINE

NEW ORLEANS, LOUISIANA

Jack Palace was busy with Palace PI, but not busy enough to stop thinking about Beatrice. He had been alone for so long, and while he thought he was happy enough with that, he had missed Beatrice since she moved to Gainesville.

Checking in with his secretary/receptionist Carol Rose, he was pleased to hear that Beatrice had called. He promptly returned her call and discovered she had called to tell him she was going to Atlanta for the Fourth of July.

"Wow, that's nice Bee. It seems that every time I chat with you, you're going somewhere farther and farther away." He tried to keep his voice light and airy, but she saw straight through that crusty facade.

"Why, Jack Palace, are you missing me?" asked Beatrice, all the while knowing the answer.

"I guess so, a little I mean."

"Why don't you meet me there?" asked Beatrice.

"I thought you were staying with Matt's family," he replied.

"Well, I could, or I could stay with you at a hotel," answered Beatrice.

"Oh—well. Yes, I guess we could do that. I mean, actually, that would be terrific. Do you think Matthew's sister would mind adding one to the dinner pot?"

“I’m sure she would be delighted. Besides, I’d like you to meet the family; they’re all so nice.”

“Count me in,” said Jack with a much lighter tone in his voice. “I’ll make all the arrangements and run them by you to make sure you agree.”

“Great. Vera and David live in Buckhead, so a hotel close to there would be perfect.”

“Yes—perfect. I’ll call you soon with details!”

Jack was ecstatic. This would be wonderful. He’d get to spend time alone with Bee, see Matthew and Joanie and the boys again, and he would actually be in the celebrating mood for the Fourth of July. Life was good.

Going into the office, Jack asked Carol to check out hotels in Atlanta near Buckhead and to call an agent about flying to Atlanta over the Fourth of July holiday. After a few more specifics, he told Carol that if she got him a good deal, she could take a four-day holiday with pay herself.

“Are you OK, Mr. Palace?” asked Carol.

“Never better,” he said as he headed out the door.

CHAPTER SEVENTY

ATLANTA, GEORGIA

By the time all the Winters Clan had assembled, it was afternoon. Lily was in her room; Caleb was listening to music, while Daniel and David worked feverishly on the veranda. Vera worked in the kitchen preparing for the onslaught of family. With the veranda set up to accommodate everyone a spot to sit, Vera's cooking duties were completed for the day. Tonight's meal would be simple yet ample, as Vera knew a thing or two about feeding hungry men and boys.

David set up long tables, and Vera covered them with white linen cloths. While it was picnic style, Vera wanted some sense of southern hospitality. Adding flowers from her backyard in large low vases, Vera thought the tables looked stunning. The final touches were votive candles that they would light during dinner.

Marc and Lucy were the first to arrive along with their twins Amanda and Sandra. Shortly afterward, Matthew, Joanie, Michael, and James arrived.

"Oh my," said Vera, "would you look at these boys? They are grown!"

"No one on the airplane thought so," said Joanie as she rolled her eyes. "When one went to sleep, the other one needled him. As soon as we could settle one, the other was fidgeting. It was not a very pleasant flight for any of us."

"I'm so sorry, but, Joanie, where is Beatrice?" Vera asked.

"Beatrice—Bee as *he* calls her—will be along later with Jack Palace," said Joanie with a wink. Then half whispering she said, "They're staying at a hotel on Peachtree Road and will be along shortly. Where's everyone else?"

"Hi, Joanie," said Lucy. "Let me see those boys."

"Hey, Matt," said Marc. "Where are the boys?"

Matthew put his hands on his hips and said, "Yeah, it's nice of you to be so excited to see Joanie and me, or have we been relegated to just token parents?"

"Get used to it bro," said Marc. "You're in the backseat. Right now the boys are changing more than you and Joanie are, so everyone's interested. Take it from one who's been there. Now when your hair starts to thin or gray or both, we'll be more eager to see you!"

Jack and Beatrice arrived just in time for a late afternoon cocktail. Vera was mixing mimosas while David poured bourbon.

The men congregated together as did the women until Vera heard the rustling sounds of children and went off to find her two youngest.

The holiday had begun in earnest, and even Jack Palace felt right at home, thanks to Vera and David and their hosting skills.

At dinner Vera served platters of southern fried chicken with sides of buttery corn on the cob and green beans freshly picked from a neighbor's garden. Then Vera passed around the baked hot biscuits with butter and honey for those who might want it. A simple wedge of lettuce with blue cheese dressing rounded out the meal.

Pitchers of sweetened iced tea, lemonade, and water were placed on an adjacent side board, and both white and red wine was available for the adults.

Midway through the meal Vera excused herself, returning from the kitchen with homemade peach cobbler—just out of the oven—and vanilla ice cream. Needless to say, no one left the table hungry.

"So, Daniel—have you decided what college you're going to and what you're going to study?" asked Marc.

"Yes, sir, I will be starting Tech this fall and will be working toward a degree in meteorology," Daniel replied.

The adults around the table were conspicuously silent, looking at one another with raised eyebrows.

Jack Palace was the first to speak up. "It sounds as though you have a really clear-cut idea of what you want, son. I wish you the best." He rose his glass to Daniel, and the others followed suit.

Beatrice squeezed his hand when he sat back down.

"I thought we'd all go to my office to watch the fireworks display," said David. "It's quite a view from the twenty-second floor.

"Awesome," said Caleb.

"Awesome, indeed," said Matthew. "OK, guys, let's clean off the table and help Vera in the kitchen. Vera—you tell us what to put where, and we'll take care of the dishes."

"Wow," said Lucy, looking at Joanie. "How did you train him to do that?"

"She taught him, not me," said Joanie with a nod toward Vera.

"And where was Marc during this training, Vera?"

"Absent, I'm afraid," Vera answered with a giggle.

The guys, now led by Marc, headed for the kitchen with plates and platters in tow.

Marc pulled Matthew aside as the other guys left the room.

"Hey bro," said Marc, "I had a very strange telephone call at the bank the other day."

"What do you mean *strange*?" Matthew asked.

“A woman asked me if Ruth Ward was my sister. Before I answered her I asked why she was calling? She said “I found her and I’m going to take care of her. What do you make of that?”

“Nothing good” Matt replied, “I hope you didn’t respond to that.”

“I didn’t and she immediately hung up. I haven’t heard from her since.”

“If you do, call and let me know.” Matt said, looking over his shoulder to make sure no one was within earshot. “Without giving you too much information, this isn’t good.”

“But Ruth’s been gone so long now, I can’t imagine why anyone would be trying to find her and even if they did, why they would call me?” Marc responded. “Do you think Ruth is in trouble?”

“No, but I’m sure if she wanted anyone – like us for instance – to know where she was, she would’ve been in touch. Let’s just keep this between the two of us, OK?”

“Sure, that’s no problem,” said Marc, “I didn’t even mention it to Lucy.”

“Good thinking,” Matt replied, “no use digging in old wounds.”

CHAPTER SEVENTY-ONE

SEPTEMBER

Moving day had come for Leaolani Barrett. Her father was still in Vietnam, but her mother Lelah had taken up residence just outside Atlanta awaiting his return and in support of her daughter beginning college.

Lee (Leaolani) was excited to be among the first handful of women who were now accepted at Tech. The entrance exams were tough and the culture different from any she had known, but she was eager to prove she was worthy of admission. She too, would be adjusting to dorm life.

Georgia Tech had set up a special orientation session for new and transferring students. There each student was assigned a faculty advisor in his or her area of interest. The advisor would work with new students on scheduling classes, being clear on exactly what courses were required, and then assist the student in getting into the class.

The opening session had begun, and Lee was feeling a bit apprehensive. Not only did she look different from the majority of other students, she was apparently the only freshman who was interested in pursuing marine biology.

Lee was beautiful by any account. Her long blue-black hair shimmered with a healthy shine, and her tanned and toned body was long and lean.

Daniel Adams sat in a separate auditorium across the hall from Lee,. He was surrounded by transfer students as well as incoming freshmen, all expressing an interest in meteorology. The transfer students had, for the most part, attended other schools to complete their basic courses and had come to Tech to hone their skills and pursue their Bachelor degrees.

The morning sessions came to a close, and the students had been introduced to the deans of all the colleges, given a packet of information about Tech, which included a detailed map of the campus and were given a break for lunch. The afternoon session was to convene in ninety minutes at which time all students were to return to the auditorium.

Strongly urged to be prompt in returning to the main auditorium, the entering class of 1978 was set free for lunch.

Daniel didn't need a campus map. He had virtually been raised on the grounds of Georgia Tech and knew every luncheon place that was within walking distance of campus. One of his favorite places and one of his father's as well, was the well-known Varsity, affectionately called the "V." They had burgers, hotdogs, and the best fries and onion rings in the world. His typical order included a "glorified," which was a dressed burger, as well as a "chili cheese dog" and rings. To appease his mother, he usually included a "PC" to drink, also known as Pure Chocolate.

Daniel gathered a few friends who he'd heard say didn't want to eat cafeteria food, and walked them to the Varsity. He was proud to introduce them to what was sure to become their new favorite hangout.

As usual the lines at the Varsity were long, but Daniel assured his new friends the lines would move quickly. He urged a few of them to get into other lines and they would meet up when everyone had their food.

Divided into areas of interest, these new friends parted ways with the exception of one young man named Joe who ended up being in the group where Daniel was assigned. Quickly recognizing one another they began to chat. Joe wanted to study meteorology as well, and had loved the Varsity, so a budding friendship was born. They were both dedicated to the same purpose, and finding a kindred spirit aspiring to the same goals was a good thing.

Getting their advisor assignment was yet another sign; they were both assigned to the same academic advisor, and happily trotted off to find him and make an appointment for their one-on-one meetings.

The afternoon session found Lee in a much smaller and more diverse group. She was one of the few females who had expressed an interest in marine biology and while the few other girls seemed a bit put off by the staggering ratio of men to women, Lee took it in stride.

Getting her academic advisor's name, Lee wasted no time in seeking him out and making her appointment for advice on what courses she should take. She was ready to get started and really didn't care if she was the only female in the program.

Shortly after getting her advisor assignment, Lee headed to her dorm room, hoping to get settled and establish a sense of order in her new collegiate life.

Reaching her room, the door was propped open, and a very tall, thin girl with hair that hung well below her waist was pushing a large box inside.

"Hi, I'm Lee," she said. "You must be my roommate."

"Yeah, I'm Celia Ann," responded the girl while continuing to push the box.

"Here, let me help you." Lee helped Celia Ann push the box inside the door. "My goodness, what on earth is in there?" Lee asked. "It's so heavy."

"Oh, it's just my books," said Celia Ann. "My major is music, and I have a lot of music books. What's your major?"

"I'll be studying to be a marine biologist," said Lee.

"Cool," said Celia Ann.

The two chatted aimlessly as they each unpacked their personal belongings. It seemed to both of them that this was a good pairing and secretly they were each relieved.

"So is Lee short for something?" asked Celia Ann.

"Yeah, it's short for Leaolani, a name from Hawaii."

"Wow, I've heard great things about Hawaii," said Celia Ann. "And by the way, most of my friends call me C. Ann. You can too if you'd like."

"Great! It's C. Ann from now on."

The girls finished unpacking their belongings and opted to go for a walk and find something to eat. C. Ann had heard about the Varsity and asked Lee if she wanted to go there. Not knowing much about her options, Lee agreed, and the two set out on their first excursion together.

Lee loved the Varsity as C. Ann thought she would. It was close to campus, food was inexpensive and totally unhealthy.

C. Ann told Lee that she had lived in the greater Atlanta area most of her life and knew the campus and the out-of-the-way eateries quite well. She committed to introducing Lee to all the good spots. Plus she told Lee that the cafeteria was closed every Sunday, and they were forced to find their meals elsewhere.

Lee asked C. Ann about her music and was surprised to hear that Georgia Tech was just a preparatory school for her, that she intended to get her basic collegiate courses completed here and then move on to Julliard or a similarly famed school of music and performing arts.

"Wow, you must be pretty talented," said Lee.

"I guess I am slightly above average, but I have to work hard and get a lot better at my craft to ever hope to audition for Julliard," commented C. Ann. "I've taken piano lessons as long as I can remember; I wouldn't know what it was like to *not* play. Actually, Lee, I think it would leave a big hole in my life if I couldn't sit at the piano and play."

"You must love it, and that's exactly how I feel about marine life. In Hawaii I was surrounded with all types of fish, sharks, whales, dolphins, and other sea creatures. I love everything about it. My mother says I must be part fish," said Lee with a giggle.

"You will have to tell me all about Hawaii, Lee. I've never been there."

"In a word, it's gorgeous. The temperature is consistent day after day, and unlike Georgia we have no humidity, even in the summer. We're islanders, and we always have the trade winds that keep us cool and keep the air clean," said Lee. "I could go on and on, but I don't want to bore you."

"Let's promise not to bore one another," said C. Ann with a grin. "I won't bore you with Mozart or Chopin, and you won't bore me with sea creatures."

"That's a deal."

On the walk back to Fulmer Hall—the first women's dorm on campus that had opened a mere nine years before—the girls chatted away. C. Ann pointed out buildings, explained some of the Tech traditions, and just as they got to the dorm asked Lee, "So do you have a boyfriend?"

"No, afraid there's no man in my life. I really haven't had the time or the inkling to find one either," answered Lee.

"Me either—there's this one guy I'm sort of interested in, but he doesn't know I'm alive," C. Ann said.

"Well, at least we can keep each other company on weekends, huh?"

CHAPTER SEVENTY-TWO

GAINESVILLE, FLORIDA

Baxter, Brown, Newman, & Winters was bustling with activity, and Peter Sutherland had become an intricate part of the inner sanctum, although he could never be a principal in the firm. Pete had earned the respect of clients and partners alike and was handsomely rewarded for his brilliant detective work on the firm's behalf.

Pete had used his skills in assisting the Federal Bureau of Investigation on the death of Sam Giardeli, who died at the same time Jimmy Hoffa disappeared. He was now investigating one John Gotti, not-so-affectionately known in police circles as "Teflon Don."

Pete's family was thriving in their Central Florida environment, and Gracie was flourishing in school.

Fleeting time had robbed Pete of his little girl. Gracie was now sixteen but acting twenty-five. She was as beautiful as she was talented, and Sylvia prayed for her to have wisdom and safety every single day.

Gracie was planning college and was considering all of the Florida universities. She still had aspirations of becoming a nurse with a fall-back career as a veterinarian. She had time to decide, and both Pete and Sylvia encouraged her to follow her dreams.

Sylvia and Joanie had maintained their close friendship over the past ten years, and often the two families would go out socially.

Gracie was tolerant of the twins, James and Michael, as she often caught the two ten-year-olds discussing something (and she did *not* want to know *what*) about her shape or hair or anatomy and dismissed it as nothing more than prepubescent boy thoughts. Gracie's stock answer to them was "Grow up, boys."

Michael and James were never rude; they knew rudeness would never be tolerated, but they too recognized changes going on inside as well as in the world around them. They were beginning to recognize through their relationships with both family and friends, that change was inevitable.

The hiring of Peter Sutherland had been well-timed. Shortly after he arrived at the firm, Matthew received his first threat.

An anonymous telephone call had come into the firm through the switchboard at the front desk. The caller, a woman, asked specifically to speak with Matthew Winters. When Matthew's assistant answered the call, a woman again asked for him. When she was told he was unavailable and the offer of taking a message was extended, the woman said, "Omerta is real." Immediately after uttering those three words, the line went dead and Matthew's assistant was left with a dial tone.

The assistant rushed into Matthew's office relaying both the story and the message to him. Matthew gave no reaction and said simply, "Thank you. Just leave the message with me please."

Doing as she was asked, the assistant left his office, closing the door behind her.

Matthew stared at the message, reviewed the time the call had come in and noted from the message it was a woman's voice. He then promptly notified both Brown and Sutherland.

Reacting immediately, Brown and Sutherland met in Matthew's office and after a brief discussion with him, asked his assistant in to relate the story exactly as she remembered it. Again, she was succinct in her response, giving them a verbatim account of the telephone call.

Sutherland's next stop was at the front desk, asking the receptionist about any calls that had come in and been transferred to Matthew's office. Again, the receptionist's response was the same as Matt's assistant had been; she had transferred a female caller who specifically asked for Matthew Winters.

The firm had upgraded their telephone network to include a tracking system for both incoming and outgoing calls. Calls were logged for billing purposes and with the new system, the accounting department could determine which calls made up billable time for the paralegals and attorneys. The duration of every call, made to or from the firm was there, as was the origin of the call.

If Pete got lucky, he would be able to tell where that particular telephone call originated. Recognizing the duration of the call was most likely too short to trace, Pete opted to check into the *combined* length of the call – from the moment it hit the switchboard including the hold time- through the time the call ultimately ended. Still, not enough time had elapsed to run a trace.

A new procedure was put into place instructing anyone who answered a call for Matthew Winters must now, without exception, route the call to his assistant.

Pete coached Matthew's assistant on how to handle any subsequent suspicious calls she might receive, noting that the longer the caller was kept on the line, the more likely it could be traced.

While tempted to think that Sutherland and Brown were overreacting, Matthew thanked each of them for their concern.

When Pete and Matt had a moment alone, Matthew related the fact that the now deceased Chief of Police in New Orleans had made the statement "omerta is real" in his suicide note.

Pete urged Matthew to follow the security procedures they had in place and to make mention of anything or anyone suspicious. That's when Matthew remembered his brother's telephone call and he shared that with Pete.

Pete shook his head. "Sounds as if someone intends to threaten, or at least create some chaos, for the whole family."

CHAPTER SEVENTY-THREE

ATLANTA, GEORGIA

Olan Barrett was finally home. One of the last to leave Vietnam, Olan was debriefed in Quantico, Virginia, for six weeks and subsequently had been admitted to Walter Reed Hospital in Washington, DC, for observation and a complete physical. In post-war times, this was standard operating procedure.

While active in the Marine Corps, Olan had earned the Vietnam Service Medal, the Armed Forces Expeditionary Medal, and the National Defense Service Medal, among other accolades.

Coming back from a structured military disciplined environment was almost torturous. Olan, like most of the soldiers who had returned from Vietnam, was having trouble adjusting to normal surroundings.

His debriefing had been arduous, and revisiting some of the indelible memories he had was difficult at best. He had seen men dying around him from both sides and had never had the opportunity to grieve. . He was now fearful that the scenes in his mind's eye would never come to an end.

Olan was happy to be a part of Lelah's life once again. Theirs had been a twenty-year marriage, with most of his tour of duty taking place separated from his wife and daughter. Visits were infrequent due to his rank of service, but they communicated with one another as often as possible.

Both Olan and Lelah longed for the peace and serenity of Hawaii and planned to move there once Leaolani had finished college. Both parents were extremely proud of their daughter, and each would have moved heaven and earth to support her endeavors.

While in the Atlanta area, Olan would complete his last tour of duty stateside and then look for gainful employment as a veteran. Lelah was currently working for a dry-cleaning chain in the area as their alterations specialist. While the pay was meager, it was sufficient. The Barretts had never led an extravagant lifestyle, always living within their means, but the cost of tuition and books for Lee had presented a challenge that could be met only by a dual income.

Lelah had insisted that Lee live on the Georgia Tech campus, even though she knew full well that meant additional money. She felt that Lee's life would be well-rounded by the experience, and that life lesson was priceless.

As soon as Lee heard that her father was home, she took public transit to see him. It was a joyous but tear-filled reunion. Lee was surprised at how much her father seemed to have aged since she had last seen him. Coincidentally, Olan was shocked at how mature his daughter had become.

Having a family meal together was a treat. Lee told her parents about her experiences thus far at Tech and told them all about her roommate, C. Ann. She asked if she could bring C. Ann over to meet them, and they both agreed that in time that would be a terrific thing to do.

Before Lee left to catch the bus back to campus, her mother pulled her to the side and said, "We need to give your father some time to settle in to this new life. Having C. Ann over would be a real pleasure, and your father and I look forward to it, but let's just give him a bit of time, OK?"

Lee agreed and gave each of her parents a kiss and a hug. Promising to call soon, she was out the door and on her way to the bus stop to return to campus.

Knowing only what her mother had said, Lee wondered what amount of time it would take for her father to feel settled here in Georgia. While Lee was an extremely bright young woman, she truly had no sense of what the war had done to her father and the soldiers with whom he had served. On the bus ride, she said a prayer for him, which was a ritual she and her mother observed every night they were away from Olan. She even said that while she had no idea exactly what she was praying for, God knew, and she asked for nothing but the best for both her parents during this transition.

CHAPTER SEVENTY-FOUR

NEW ORLEANS, LOUISIANA

Palace PI was doing a great business. As time went on, Jack took on a couple of employees—had them trained in the art of investigation—and paid for them to take the PI exam to become licensed investigators. He was now a full-fledged PI firm, and thankfully Carol Rose was still on board taking care of the appointment scheduling, keeping track of everyone, and running the office with ease.

The one request she had made of Jack was to hire a bookkeeper. She did not want to be responsible for the books. Realizing that an outside bookkeeper was a good idea, Jack hired a local CPA who was willing to take on the day-to-day accounting as well as the corporate, state, and federal taxes for the firm.

The only thing that Jack Palace was not happy with was being away from Beatrice Bovier. He made trips to Gainesville as often as he could, and she occasionally made a trip to New Orleans, but seeing each other infrequently was wearing on both of them.

While they truly cared for and loved one another, marriage was out of the question for them. Neither was willing to enter into marriage again, yet they did not like being apart.

Jack didn't have any family to speak of, and Bee had Joanie, Matthew, and the boys. Jack had grown particularly fond of Bee's "kids." He found himself missing them too. He decided to talk to Bee about it on their next visit together. That was a couple of weeks away, and he was traveling to see her in Florida. At least if she got upset with him, he had the option to leave.

Admittedly, Jack was a bit surprised to get the telephone call from Pete Sutherland. After the disconcerting phone call Matt had received, Pete opted to chat with Jack, asking about the suicide note left by the former COP in New Orleans.

Jack related all he knew about the incident, hoping that something could be gleaned from it.

Other than Graceffo, Jack had found no direct connection. He shared with Pete that in his opinion, discovering who Graceffo was working for was the best lead in understanding more about the suicide note and the veiled threat to Matthew.

Agreeing with that assessment, Sutherland asked Jack to review all of the former COP's records if he could gain access to them. Acknowledging that he was owed several favors, Jack felt confident he could make that happen.

CHAPTER SEVENTY-FIVE

GAINESVILLE, FLORIDA

Michael and James Winters were becoming more and more "unique"; not so much in appearance—they were identical which they used to their benefit—but their personalities and thought processes were eons apart.

Michael was undoubtedly the more studious of the two; James was more rebellious but within limits. James was more of a loner, spending time reading and pondering, while Michael was more outgoing and gregarious.

No one noticed the differences in the boys the way Bee did. She delighted in the fact that they were individual characters and had their own desires and needs, and whenever she could, she would nurture that.

The one thing that both boys loved and excelled at was swimming. Joanie accused them of being part amphibian, being as comfortable in the water as out of it. She noticed that neither of her sons had a fear of water, regardless of the depth, width, or condition. One of their favorite outings was a drive to Destin or Jacksonville to swim in either the Gulf of Mexico or the Atlantic Ocean. Daredevil James loved the Atlanta side of the state best; the current was stronger, the waves higher and more of a challenge. Michael liked either coast or even the neighborhood pool at the park in Gainesville.

It was likely that the boys would try out for the swim team in high school. James was already preparing for it.

Joanie and Matthew decided that their home would not be complete until they added a pool. After getting the specs and estimates from a couple of pool builders, they opted for an Olympic twenty-foot by forty-foot in-ground pool. The twins were ecstatic when they heard the news. This would allow the boys to swim laps and work on their stamina and speed.

The first question James asked was whether or not the pool would have a diving board. Reluctantly, Joanie had agreed to it. While the boys saw it as a necessity, she saw it as a liability.

The pool would be ready in time for the spring of 1979.

Beatrice heard from Jack and was looking forward to his visit. It was amazing that she had known this man for so many years, and while she had always been fond of him, she now realized that she truly did love the man.

Sharing the dates of Jack's visit with Joanie and Matthew, they opted to have everyone over for dinner. Joanie phoned Sylvia, who readily accepted. Thinking that Gracie might be more comfortable, Joanie also added that she was welcome to bring a friend along.

Jack arrived by car rather than flying in, which Bee thought unusual.

"Just needed a road trip," he said. "How's my girl?"

"I'm good, Jack," responded Beatrice, "and very happy to see you. It was a long drive, and you must be exhausted."

"No, I'm actually feeling really good, but I could use a walk. Want to walk with me?" Jack asked.

"Sure, just let me get a sweater," answered Bee.

The two had walked a few blocks along the street where Bee lived when Jack unexpectedly said, "You know I've been thinking that we're not getting any younger."

"That's a given," Bee said. "So?"

"So we like being together, don't we? I mean you know I like being with you."

"Yes, Jack, and I enjoy spending time with you," Bee replied.

"Well, what if we picked out a place to live together?"

"Wow. I didn't see that coming," said Bee.

"I know it's sudden—well not real sudden—but I just want to be with you, and I can't do that if I live in Louisiana and you live in Florida. The best we have are weekends or occasional visits, and that just isn't cutting it for me."

Bee and Jack stopped in their tracks and stared at one another.

Bee smiled and said, "But you have a business in New Orleans, and I have my family here."

"Right, I do. But my family is here too."

"Are you saying you would move here?" Bee asked.

"I would if you'd allow it," Jack responded.

"It's a lot to think about, Jack. Can we finish our walk and talk about this some more? I don't know anything about living with someone—well other than my late husband."

"Of course, Bee, whatever you need."

The two walked and chatted about their concerns and fears, the pluses and the minuses. They both agreed the pluses far outweighed anything negative. Returning to Bee's house, Jack made his way to the kitchen where he opened a bottle of wine and toasted their decision.

"To us—the new us," said Jack.

"To the old and new us," said Bee.

While the logistics were far from worked out, Jack and Beatrice decided to move in together. Jack wanted to buy them a home; Beatrice insisted on selling her house and putting that money toward the new home; Jack agreed and insisted that the home be put in both their names. He also proposed to keep his business in New Orleans for the time being. He could travel there once a month or so until he found the right person to either put in charge of running the firm or buying it.

Realizing there were many more details to work out, Jack and Bee opted to go out for a celebratory dinner and let the planning take a backseat until the morning.

Jack was an old-fashioned kind of guy, even though living together out of wedlock was the furthest thing from old-fashioned. He asked Bee if he could speak to Joanie about their decision, one on one. Beatrice phoned Joanie the next morning and asked her to come over. As soon as she arrived, Bee left the two of them together in the kitchen.

Fortunately, Joanie was a realist if nothing else, and she understood the couple's reasons for opting not to marry. She gave Jack her blessing and assured him that Matthew would concur. She did suggest that Michael and James hear the news from their grandmother, allowing them and her to voice any and all opinions they might have.

"She has a special relationship with my boys," said Joanie. "They love her and respect her. Why, the other day James even commented on what a neat grandmother she was. They will be much more understanding if she talks to them."

"Then let's ask her," said Jack. "Bee, it's safe to come in now," yelled Jack.

"Well?" said Bee looking intently at Joanie.

"Congratulations, Mom."

The two hugged.

Joanie pulled away saying, "There's just one thing you really have to do to make this work. Talk to your grandsons and tell them your decision. They may have a million questions; they may not even think a thing about it, but it's best coming from you," Joanie said.

Beatrice hugged her daughter and assured her that she would be happy to talk with the boys.

"So," said Joanie, "I guess our little dinner party this weekend has turned into something a bit more festive! Make sure you have told the boys beforehand so we can announce it at dinner! The Sutherlands will be so happy to hear the news."

"What can we bring dear?" asked Bee.

"Nothing but a nice bottle of champagne," Joanie suggested. "Now I should go. I have plans to make and shopping to do. Will you call the boys?"

"I will, and I'll make arrangements to spend some time with them later today."

"Great. Congratulations."

Calling Matthew at the very first opportunity was high on Joanie's list of things to do. He was somewhat surprised by the news, but not in the least unhappy about it. He knew Jack Palace to be a good and decent man. When Joanie told him she insisted that Bee tell the boys, he agreed that was a wise decision.

Matthew had shared the information about the anonymous telephone call with Joanie, but asked her not to say anything to the boys, or to her mother. She had agreed.

That day, the second call came in. This time, the message was: "I know what you did with John and Ruth, and after I take care of them, I'll come for you."

The first person Matt shared that with was Peter Sutherland. Without a moment's hesitation, Pete contacted the FBI.

For the first time since arranging their initial meeting with the Federal Bureau of Investigation, Matthew was talking openly to the bureau about his sister, her husband and their whereabouts. Matthew was assured that the lives of John and Ruth were protected, and that there had been no breach in security.

Without divulging specifics, Matthew was told that the information they had received from John was accurate and useful, resulting in several arrests.

The bureau vowed to "examine things" on their end to make sure none of their information had "been inappropriately" disseminated.

Jack and Pete managed a private meeting to review the now *copied* records kept by the late COP in New Orleans. Jack had reviewed them and found one recurring, but seemingly unrelated name: Jade, no last name given.

CHAPTER SEVENTY-SIX

ATLANTA, GEORGIA

Vera and David Adams were happy that Daniel was adjusting well to college life. They had suspected that would be the case, but hearing him on the telephone assuaged all their fears. He had phoned to tell them he would be staying on campus until the break for Thanksgiving, and while that seemed so far away to his mother, it was only a matter of a few weeks.

Thanksgiving in the Adams household usually involved out of town relatives. This year Vera's brothers, their wives, and kids would be coming to Atlanta. Marc's girls were off on their own adventures and, while they would be invited, were not expected to attend. Beatrice Bovier was coming, as was Jack Palace, and of course Matthew, Joanie, James, and Michael would be there.

Although it had been only a few months since everyone gathered in Atlanta, Vera saw this as a critical time. She saw her own kids growing up too quickly and realized that her household would never be the same again. She wanted as many "clan" gatherings as she could squeeze in before more of the kids were off to college.

Campus life was never boring for Lee or her roommate C. Ann. Due to her major, C. Ann was required to go before a music "jury" comprised of her teachers and the dean of the college of music once each semester. This was a stress-filled time for C. Ann, as she wanted her performance to be exemplary and flawless.

This semester she was to perform two pieces: Valse in C-Sharp Minor by Chopin and a Gavotte by Bach. She could be found on almost any evening in one of the school's practice rooms, and even while sitting in her dorm room, she would "finger" the notes in the air.

"C. Ann," said Lee, "let's get out of here for a while. I don't even care where we go as long as we get a change of scenery."

"Let's walk over to the Robbery," said C. Ann. The "Robbery" was also known as the book store and had not-so-affectionately been renamed by the students.

"Sure—fine with me. Let's go," Lee replied.

The bookstore was near the student center, which was always teeming with students, some sleeping, some playing games or reading, and some just hanging out to avoid their dorm rooms or studying.

As the girls browsed the bookstore, they separated, C. Ann heading for the music section and Lee wandering around the marine biology area.

Lee found several books of interest; one was a book of photographs of all species of whales and dolphin. Thumbing through the pages she enthusiastically looked to the day when she could actually work up close and personal with these marvelous mammals.

C. Ann found Lee about half an hour later sitting cross-legged in the floor at the corner of the marine life stacks. Lee was so engrossed in the subject matter she didn't even notice C. Ann had walked up.

"Lee," said C. Ann. "Lee."

"What? Oh sorry. I didn't notice you were standing there."

"I'm starving. Let's go to the student center and get something to eat."

"Okay," said Lee.

"What had you so enthralled?"

"Did you know that the humpback whale travels each winter from the Arctic North to the South Pacific to meet males, mate, and/or give birth to their young?"

"No, I can't say that I did know that."

"Yeah, and since they eat krill, which isn't available in the South Pacific, they don't eat anything during the whole migration down, back, or in between. Isn't that fantastic?" Lee was beaming.

"Okay, Jacqueline Cousteau, just come back to earth and don't order krill when we go through the cafeteria line," C. Ann laughed.

"What are you doing for Thanksgiving?" Lee asked C. Ann.

"I hadn't even thought about it," she responded. "I'll probably be expected to go home. What about you?"

"Home definitely. My father recently returned from Vietnam, and it will be the first time we have been together for Thanksgiving in several years."

"Wow, Vietnam. I heard lots of bad things about that war. My older brother was about to be drafted but was released on a hardship because his wife had a baby on the way," C. Ann said. "We were so afraid he would have to go to war—and more afraid that he would never come back."

"Yeah, my mom and I prayed every day for my father's safe return. And now he's home," Lee smiled.

"That's great," said C. Ann.

"I hope he's all right. He seems to be having some adjustment issues, but I suppose that's normal. He's been in Vietnam so long. As a matter of fact, that's where he met my mother."

"Really?"

"Yeah, that's how long he was there, minus a few weeks off here and there. I guess he's seen it all."

"From beginning to end," said C. Ann. "Wow, your dad is a real hero."

"He's certainly my hero," said Lee. "I'm just not sure he's feeling very heroic right now."

"Adjustments take time Lee, and now that he's back with your mom and you, I'm sure he'll be back to his old self in no time," C. Ann said.

"I hope you're right. Anyway, I'll definitely be home for Thanksgiving. I think they need me."

"I should go home too. It's just not something high on my list. My brother, sister-in-law, and their baby will be there and all of my mom's rag-tag 'I had nowhere else to go' friends. It's just always a bit too crowded for my tastes."

"I'd invite you over to my house, but I don't think that we're ready for company at this point," said Lee.

"Not to worry," responded C. Ann quickly. "I wasn't fishing for an invitation. And I completely agree. If your dad is trying to readjust to family life, he doesn't need to do it in front of a stranger."

"You've become a real friend, Celia Anne. Thanks."

Smiling and blushing, C. Ann said, "I think I'll go over to the music hall and see if there's a practice room available. I really haven't worked on my jury pieces at all today."

"I'll see you back at the dorm. I'm going to see what's going on in the student center."

Lee found that the student council was sponsoring a movie on the Vietnam War, and it was about to start. Not having any other plans, and hoping to learn a bit more about what her father had experienced, she opted to attend. All she needed to get free admission was her student ID card.

While the film was not terribly graphic, it produced a great amount of emotion in Lee. She learned much more than she had ever known about the political ramifications of the war, as well as the intensity in which it had been fought. More than a little distressed at the conclusion, Lee opted to sit in the student center for a bit before returning to her dorm.

"Hey, Lee, is that you?"

Lee looked up and saw her friend Joe walking toward her.

"Hi, Joe—how are you? I knew you were here at Tech, but I hadn't seen you around," said Lee, forcing a smile.

"Yeah, I love Tech. How about you?"

"I'm very happy here," said Lee. "Oh, hi," she said meekly to the young man standing next to her friend Joe. "I'm Lee. Joe and I are old friends."

"Sorry, Lee, this is Daniel. He and I are new friends. Daniel—Lee," Joe said.

"Nice to meet you, Daniel," said Lee.

Daniel returned the sentiment.

Joe said, "We just saw the docudrama on Vietnam."

"I saw it too; it was sort of disturbing to me," answered Lee.

"I know, me too," said Joe, "but now I sort of understand why so many students were actively protesting the war. Going there would be like going on a suicide mission."

The mere words sent chills up Lee's spine. "I know. I'm just glad that my father made it home safely."

"Oh, Lee—I completely forgot that your dad was there. Sorry about saying that. I'm glad he made it." Joe was red-faced.

"So, Lee—what branch of the service was your father in?" Daniel asked.

"He's a Marine—a decorated Marine, and he's only been back in the states for a short time. Thank you for asking, Daniel," Lee seemed a bit more comfortable now.

"So, Joe, what are you majoring in here at Tech?" Lee asked.

"Daniel and I both are majoring in meteorology," Joe responded.

"That's pretty impressive," answered Lee, smiling from one to the other.

"And what field are you studying?" asked Daniel.

"Marine biology," Lee answered proudly. "I eventually want to work in Hawaii as a marine biologist. My father was born there; my mother and I lived there for a while, and I thought it was the most interesting place on earth."

"The Hawaiian islands have extremely interesting weather patterns as well. The temperature extremes are amazing from atop the volcanic mountains to the oceans surrounding the islands. You can drive twenty miles and drop in temperature from a balmy eighty-six degrees Fahrenheit to chilling twenty-five degrees Fahrenheit. That is of course driving from the beach areas up the mountains." Daniel stopped himself. "I'm sorry; I just get caught up in that subject matter."

"I completely understand. I was telling my roommate about the humpback whales' migration to the South Pacific waters every year, and I realized

I was more excited about it than she would ever be," responded Lee, with a slight giggle.

"Right," said Daniel, "and I understand they fast for the duration of the trip back and forth and during their stay. No krill."

"That's exactly correct," said Lee with a huge smile on her face.

Joe interjected, "Lee, it was good to see you, and I'm glad you got to meet Daniel."

"As am I," said Lee. "Are you two staying on campus?"

"Yes, we're on the East Campus," said Daniel.

"So am I," said Lee, "but I guess all the freshmen are there. It was great to see you, Joe, and to meet you, Daniel. Hope to see you again sometime."

"Me too," said Daniel.

"See you soon," said Joe.

Mood elevated, Lee walked back to her dorm.

CHAPTER SEVENTY-SEVEN

KONA, HAWAII
NOVEMBER 1978

Riana was busily planning a Thanksgiving Pig Roast luau. She had made that her custom since moving to Kona. She always invited their neighbors, the ladies who worked with her in her jewelry and lei business and, of course, any of Jarrod's friends from the golf course who had no plans.

Jarrod had become quite the golfer in the last couple of years and, although he thought Riana was unaware of it, always placed a small wager with his buddies on every hole. That small bet and his alcohol consumption were the only two vices the man had left, and far be it from Riana to burst his bubble and tell him she knew about it.

Jarrod's golfing buddies were mostly native Hawaiians, and some were single either from divorce, being widowed, or being too set in their ways to involve themselves with a mate. Those were the ones who had ended up at the Thanksgiving luaus year after year, and Riana counted them in, regardless.

Jarrod and his friends had dug a pit in one corner of the Tavares' backyard where the pig would be roasted along with the locally grown vegetables.

Great care was taken in the selection of the pig—a task that Riana assigned to Jarrod. This year would be no different.

Traditional luau food was served, and Riana had worked very hard to master all the recipes. Her menu would include Haupia—a coconut pudding, Laulau—bundles of meat and fish wrapped in tea leaves; Lomi Lomi—a salad of tomatoes, onions, chili peppers, and salted fish (usually salmon); Poi—which is taro roots cooked and smashed into a paste; and Poke—a chopped raw fish such as yellowfin tuna, sprinkled with Hawaiian salt, ground kukui nuts and limu (seaweed). The star of the show, the Kahlua pig was covered with apple cider, sea salt, and ground ginger before a long, slow smoking process.

As her most favored side dish, Riana would prepare a Hawaiian rice pilaf, which included whole roasted macadamia nuts, garlic, red and yellow peppers, raisins, diced pineapple, and parsley. Jarrod's favorite desert had to be included—a macadamia nut pineapple banana bread slathered in coconut syrup.

Once again, Riana would outdo herself and have a truly one of a kind feast. Thanksgiving had become a very important holiday for Riana and Jarrod. They had never ceased to be thankful for their new and improved life, and celebrating the day with friends was the perfect way to express their joy.

Riana was still bothered by Jade and her presence in their lives, but to date, there had been no repercussions. Jade would come by at least once a month to talk with Jarrod, and while she was typically accompanied by another field agent, her presence made Riana a bit uncomfortable. She opted to take a walk or run an errand to avoid the issue.

Jarrod did not appear to be concerned and was continually providing the agency with the information he had knowledge about. The feds gave him just enough information to feed his curiosity and spur any background details that Jarrod might have otherwise forgotten to mention.

Jarrod knew the current Mafia kingpins: Vincent Barino and Sam Giardeli. He had shared as much information as he could about the two as well as their known associates. As an informant he was not allowed to ask specific questions, but he had pieced enough information together to determine that the Five Families were in trouble with one another and that the Feds were more than likely planning to make a move on them. Jarrod inwardly smiled at the thought of knowing their fate before they suspected a thing.

Since New York had been terrorized for more than twelve months with unsolved murders, one of the specific questions Jarrod had been repeatedly asked was whether he had any idea who might be behind those murders.

Jarrod admittedly did not and told the agents that based on what he had read in the newspapers and heard from television, this appeared to be a serial killer rather than a crime syndicate or Mafia hit. He explained his reasoning by saying, "The victims and the murders have too many similarities to one another that do not fit the mold. They're not intended to change anything or improve anyone's position. They're not mob justice—they're simply heinous murders."

And before the year was over, the serial killer David Berkowitz, code name "Son of Sam," was indeed tried and convicted of the mass murders in New York.

CHAPTER SEVENTY-EIGHT

ATLANTA, GEORGIA
THANKSGIVING

It was beautiful in Atlanta. The air was crisp and clear, and Vera had her family together. It was her favorite time of year, and she was relishing every moment.

As the family gathered around the oversized cherry table, they held hands with one another and returned thanks. Marc had been asked to lead the family in prayer. After expressing thanks for all the family had been given, he prayed for those in the family who were unable to be there. That, of course, included Sandra and Amanda as well as Ruth and John. When the prayer ended everyone stood silently for a moment longer.

Matthew silently gave thanks for his personal safety, the safety of his family and the firm's employees.

Across town another family gathering was taking place. Olan, Lelah, and Lee Barrett were spending their first Thanksgiving together in several years.

The three of them were blessed to have withstood the long bouts of separation and the ever-present fear of not being together again.

Olan was feeling a bit more at ease and was pursuing counseling through the Veteran's Administration. He attended both group and individual sessions and took comfort in group therapy since virtually all of the members of the group were Vietnam vets. They understood one another and had a bond that would inevitably last a lifetime.

At the dinner table, Olan expressed his thanks to both his wife and daughter for their love and patience. Lelah said she was most thankful for simply being together as a family again, and Lee said she was thankful for her life, her freedom, and that she had wonderful parents who allowed her to pursue her dreams.

While their meal was solemn by comparison to some holiday celebrations, it was out of reverence rather than angst.

CHAPTER SEVENTY-NINE

KONA, HAWAII

Riana and Jarrod hosted a fabulous luau and, prior to the carving of the pig, gave thanks to God for all their blessings. Riana silently prayed for her displaced family and asked God to bless each of them.

CHAPTER EIGHTY

GAINESVILLE, FLORIDA

"We should always return blessings," Pete had said each and every Thanksgiving morning for as long as Gracie could remember.

The Sutherlands celebrated Thanksgiving at the local homeless shelter, serving others who were less fortunate. It had become a tradition for the three of them, and Pete, Sylvia, and Gracie always left feeling blessed and more closely bonded to one another by the experience.

CHAPTER EIGHTY-ONE

1979

Some proclaimed that 1979 was the year of the beanbag chair, while others said it was the year the computer age began in earnest with the invention of the Atari 400 selling for a whopping $549. For Americans earning an average household income of $17,500 and a gallon of gasoline running 86 cents per gallon, this was an exorbitant price. *VisiCalc* became the first spreadsheet program, and business automation flourished. Later in the year, Sony released a diminutive but powerful technology to the private sector called the *Walkman,* which became a worldwide success even though it cost $200. And in the United Kingdom, Margaret Thatcher was the first woman to ever be elected as Prime Minister.

Mafia notables in the news included Johnny Dioguardi, Anthony Provenzano ("Tony Pro"), and Carmine Galante. Johnny "Dio" died of natural causes at a Pennsylvania hospital at the age of sixty-four. A longtime Mafia leader and labor racketeer, "Dio" was serving a sentence in federal prison for stock fraud. Provenzano was sentenced to twenty years in federal prison for labor racketeering, having been convicted of extracting payoffs from trucking companies in exchange for guaranteeing labor peace. And one day after Anthony Provenzano was sentenced to prison, former Barino underboss Carmine Galante was murdered at Joe and Mary's Italian Restaurant in Brooklyn. Of course, no one admitted to have witnessed the murder; in fact, no one admitted knowing *anything* about it.

For Matthew Winters, this was a pivotal year. Juggling work, home, twin boys and a gregarious wife was both a blessing and a curse. He was feeling the strain and it showed. He loved his life – all of it, but stress takes its toll. His once brown hair was now filled with grey, and the tiny lines around his eyes were becoming more pronounced.

The threats were ongoing, as was the investigation into who was behind them.

CHAPTER EIGHTY-TWO

ATLANTA, GEORGIA

Now in their second year of college, Daniel Adams and Lee Barrett had started dating. They had run into each other several times on campus, at the Varsity and at the Student Union, and Daniel had suggested that they see a new movie called *Every Which Way but Loose,* an action comedy starring Clint Eastwood, Sondra Locke, and Geoffrey Lewis.

That date was the beginning of a budding relationship between the two. Once they discovered their common areas of interest, with the exception of study hours and sleeping, the two became inseparable.

Daniel had invited Lee to meet his family, and the Winters Clan took to her right away. Daniel and Lee would often visit for dinner on Sundays since the campus cafeteria was closed.

Lee had introduced Daniel to her parents, and it appeared there was a seamless connection between them. Olan had a great deal of respect for Daniel, and Lee's mother Lelah thought Daniel was the perfect adjunct for her daughter.

C. Ann continued to room with Lee, and their friendship knew no bounds. She was now dating Joe and found him to be most intriguing. The four "roommates" would double date often, hitting Atlanta's discotheques, dancing to Donna Summer's *Hot Stuff* or *Bad Girls*.

The foursome pursued their studies with vigor, and all were producing exceptional grades, particularly by Tech's standards.

CHAPTER EIGHTY-THREE

GAINESVILLE, FLORIDA

Matthew had now received numerous threatening telephone messages and it appeared that Pete (and Jack) weren't any closer to unveiling the source of the threats.

As Matt was thinking about the whole situation, his assistant buzzed his intercom and told him his sister-in-law, Lucy, was on the line and that it was urgent. Dropping everything, Matthew answered the telephone to a very distraught Lucy.

"Matthew, I don't know how to say this" Lucy said through tears, "Marc has been shot and is in the Emergency Room as we speak. The doctors say they don't know if he's going to make it."

"Lucy, he will make it," Matthew said, "and I'll take the next plane out of here. You just take care of yourself and I'll be there as soon as possible. Tell me, do you have any idea how this happened?"

"No, not really" Lucy said sobbing, "I just know that someone walked into the bank and shot him. Why would anyone shoot Marc?"

"Don't offer any opinions to anyone Lucy. I'm on my way."

Matt immediately asked his assistant to book the next available flight into Birmingham for him.

He instructed her to book an open return ticket.

Matt then telephoned Joanie sharing what little information he had, and letting her know he was on his way home to pack a bag. He promised to telephone her as soon as he had any additional information.

As Matt sat aboard the airplane he believed without a doubt that the shooting of his twin was a direct result of the threats the two of them had received. He had telephoned Peter Sutherland and updated him before leaving for the airport, and he knew that Pete would make contact with the authorities in Alabama.

Hopefully, Marc would survive. Hopefully, the police had a lead on who had shot him, and even more so, this lunacy and the lunatic directing it toward the Winters family could be stopped.

Arriving at the hospital ER, Matthew quickly found Lucy. She was sitting in a waiting area with her head in her hands, crying. When he approached her she immediately threw her arms around him.

"I'm so glad you're here," she said. "Marc is in surgery and has been for the last hour. I've prayed so hard for him. I don't know what else to do."

"You're doing the right thing, Lucy. It's the best thing for Marc right now. Let's sit down." Matthew said.

"We can actually go to the surgical waiting room now that you're here. I didn't want you to have to look for me, so I stayed here. That's on the third floor – I'll show you the way." Lucy said walking toward a bank of elevators.

Once they reached the surgical waiting room, Lucy checked in with the nurse on duty, explaining who they were and who their patient was. The nurse confirmed that Mr. Winters was still in surgery and assured her she would update them as soon as she heard anything.

Over the next two hours, Lucy and Matthew talked about Marc. Lucy said that he was working too hard, spending way too much time at the bank.

Matthew sheepishly commiserated saying that both the Winters boys worked too hard. That comment, at least, made Lucy laugh.

The nurse called for the Winters family and Matt and Lucy quickly went to the desk. The nurse told them that Marc was out of surgery and was "holding his own". She also said the surgeon would meet with them as soon as he left the operating room, to discuss what had transpired. So again, they waited, but at least they knew Marc was alive.

When the surgeon came to the nurse's station, he called Matthew and Lucy. They met with him in a private area adjacent to the waiting room. There the surgeon told them all that he knew.

"Mrs. Winters, your husband suffered a gunshot wound to the chest which caused some internal bleeding that was difficult to arrest. The bullet penetrated one lung, causing it to collapse. The bullet barely, but fortunately, missed the heart. The thoracic cavity was damaged extensively by the bullet, but we are hopeful that the other lung will continue to function normally. In the meantime, we determined that Mr. Winters' breathing should be assisted, *if only temporarily*, by a respirator. His prognosis at this point is guarded, which basically means this could take a turn for the worse, or hopefully, for the better. The next twenty-four hours are critical. Do you have any questions or need me to explain anything further at this time?"

"When can we see him?" Lucy asked.

"He should be transferred to ICU soon. ICU patients can only be seen every three hours for about fifteen minutes. The attending physician will let you in to see your husband as soon as possible. Do you have any other questions?" asked the surgeon.

Lucy simply shook her head while tears flowed down her cheeks.

Matthew asked if Lucy would mind him having a private chat with the surgeon. She simply said "no" and turned and walked back into the waiting area.

Matt asked the surgeon if the police had spoken with him.

The surgeon simply replied, "Not yet."

He then asked what type of bullet had been recovered.

The surgeon met his gaze with a puzzled look on his face and said "a twenty-two". Turning on his heel, the surgeon said, "I have to go talk with the police now. Perhaps they will be able to answer you more specifically."

Matt said "Thank you for all you have done for my brother."

The surgeon simply nodded and walked away.

Lucy absolutely fell apart when she caught the first glimpse of her husband. Shaking violently and crying uncontrollably, Matthew simply wrapped his arms around her and quieted her as best he could. As soon as she was calmer she approached his bedside.

"Hi, my love. I'm here and so is Matthew. We know you're going to be fine, so get some rest and know that we'll be just outside the door until we can visit you again." Lucy said in as sturdy a voice as she was capable of.

Matt leaned over his brother, chest heaving, and simply said "Hang in there brother. We have a lot to talk about and a lot of living to do. I'll make sure Lucy gets some rest, so you do the same."

Three hours later, Matt and Lucy got another fifteen minute visit. According to the doctors, there had been no significant change in Marc's condition.

Lucy was in better control of her emotions now, and chatted away to Marc about family things, church, yoga class – anything she could think of. She just wanted him to know she was there.

Matt waited patiently by his brother's bedside and when Lucy looked to him for conversation he told Marc that he had contacted Vera – which he had done during the three hour lull between visits, and that she was sending up her most *potent prayers* for him. He again reminded Marc that he would be there if he needed anything.

The "whoosh and beep" sounds of the ventilator was deafening to Matthew. Seeing his twin brother lying unconscious in that hospital bed was maddening. Feeling his pulse quicken, Matthew left his brother's bedside, giving Lucy some one-on-one time with her husband.

As he paced in the waiting area, Matthew had one thought: *this is my fault*.

Deciding it was a good time to find out if the police had any leads, Matt opted to call Pete.

The news Pete had wasn't substantial; the police had not found anyone who admitted to being an eye witness to the shooting, and they basically had no leads other than the caliber of the bullet which narrowed down the type of weapon that was used. That wasn't much to go on.

Twenty-four hours later, Marc Winters awakened. The first thing he did was try to remove the breathing apparatus, which set off multiple alarms. Rushing to his side, the nurses calmed him and assured him they would remove the ventilator tube as soon as the doctor approved it.

Calmer now, but confused and disoriented, Marc Winters gestured for a pad and pencil. The nurses handed him a chalk board and he wrote "What happened to me?"

The nurse answered simply, "You've had surgery Mr. Winters, but it looks as though you are going to be fine."

"Where's my wife?" was the next question Marc scribed.

"I'll get her – she's just outside, with your brother. You relax and I'll go get them."

Joyful that he was awake and asking questions, Matthew and Lucy entered his room. Marc was awake, somewhat groggy, but he held out his hand first to his wife, and then to Matthew.

"Thank God" said Lucy. "I've never been so glad to see anyone in my entire life."

Marc reached again for the chalk board and wrote down "What happened?"

Matt immediately started responding. "You were wounded in a shooting at the bank. And no, before you ask, no one else was injured."

Erasing that question with his hand Marc wrote, "Was it a robbery?"

"We don't really know yet Marc," said Lucy, "and all that information will come to us in time. Right now, all we care about is getting you better."

Marc nodded his head and pointed to the breathing tube.

"How about I go see if the doctors are on their way to check you over?" Matt asked. "Maybe we can get some answers about removing that gizmo." As he turned to leave he whispered to Lucy, "Please, nothing about the shooting – not yet." She simply nodded.

When the doctor listened to Marc's chest, he nodded his head in an approving sort of way. "I believe we can detach you from this ventilator, Mr. Winters. Your breathing sounds very good from both lungs."

Asking Matthew and Lucy to step out of the room, the doctor and attending nurse removed the breathing tube.

The doctor said "That must be much more comfortable for you. I do have to ask that you refrain from talking a lot to give your throat time to heal from the trauma of the tube. And while you won't be able to drink fluids for a few hours, we will make sure you have some ice chips to quench your thirst."

Marc nodded in agreement; the nurse delivered the ice chips in a small cup with a spoon, and then left to tell Lucy and Matthew they were welcome to come back in. Explaining what the doctor had just told Marc – ice chips only – no liquids, she allowed them back into his room.

By evening, Marc was transferred to a private room, as requested by Matthew. At the door to the hallway, an armed guard was posted.

Lucy asked Matthew about the guard, but he explained it away as simply a precautionary measure suggested by the local police. Lucy accepted that explanation, taking her brother-in-law's word at face value.

In a scratchy voice Marc said "I feel like I've been run over by a truck."

"No," answered Matt, "just a bullet. While the doctors can give you more information, you were basically shot in the chest at point blank range, piercing one lung and barely missing your heart. I think that's enough information for now."

"Who –"was all Marc could utter before his voice gave way.

We don't know who yet," said Matthew, "but the police are investigating and will get to the bottom of it soon. For now, enough talking. How about you get some rest while you hold the hand of your lovely wife?"

Matthew made his way to a phone where he could talk at length with Peter Sutherland. Explaining his brother's condition, Matt made it clear that he was staying in Alabama until his brother's prognosis had improved.

Pete announced that he would be flying to Birmingham to work through the crime scene with the police. Pete was sure they had overlooked, or at least missed, something important, and he wanted to examine the crime scene and what little evidence there was.

Expressing his appreciation for the assist, Matthew suggested that Pete stay with him at the hotel near the hospital. Agreeing to do so, Pete said he would update Matt on his arrival time and see him then.

Calling Vera was the next order of business. She was undoubtedly frantic with worry, and reaching her with some good news would be a welcomed thing. Vera was thrilled to hear that Marc was awake and alert, out of ICU and off the respirator; all positive steps. Promising to keep her current on any developments, Matthew hung up and returned to Marc's room.

Marc was napping with Lucy at his bedside. She quietly arose from her chair and asked Matthew to step outside with her. She told him the attending physician had been in to see him and felt that he was improving.

Pleased to have good news, Matt told Lucy she should go home and get some rest. Avowing that she could rest there at the hospital, Matt convinced her that she should go home for a change of clothes. Having been at the hospital for more than a day and a half, she felt that might be a good thing to do. Reluctantly, Lucy left the hospital saying she would be back as soon as she could.

Sitting next to his brother's bedside, Matt said a prayer. He prayed that they would find out who committed this act and bring him or her to justice. As he said the prayer, a thought occurred to him that the shooter might have been a *woman*. Matthew headed out the door to the nearest telephone and called the police station. He asked for the detective in charge of his brother's case and when he reached him asked if the sex of the shooter was known. When the detective said "no", Matthew asked if anyone in the bank saw a suspicious *woman* in the bank on the morning of the shooting.

"Not specifically" said the detective, "why do you ask?"

"A hunch more than anything," answered Matt. "Do you have any idea of the height of the shooter?"

"No."

"Can that be ascertained from the bullet's entrance wound and trajectory?" Matt asked.

"Sure, we just have to get a copy of the x-rays from the hospital and send them to our crime lab. As a matter of fact, we should have already requested that information. I'll have the team assembled and see if we have all the pieces . I'll be happy to let you know of anything we may find. Oh, and Mr. Winters, I understand that we're expecting your firm's private investigator to join us on the case?"

"Yes, his name is Peter Sutherland. He should be arriving today." Matt said.

"We're looking forward to working with him, sir."

"Thank you detective. I appreciate all you are doing."

Returning to Marc's room Matthew noticed the guard appeared to be napping. When he touched him on the shoulder, the guard slumped over onto the floor revealing a stab wound just under his left arm.

Yelling for help, Matt quickly checked the guard for a pulse. There was none. He then rushed into Marc's room whereupon he found his brother, lifeless.

While Marc's body was still warm, he was not breathing. Matt frantically pushed the call button and help arrived within seconds. Forcing Matthew out of the room, the nurses called Code Blue. A crash cart, nurses, physician assistants and emergency physicians of every specialty came pouring into Marc Winters room.

The physician called the time of death at 3:30 pm.

Matthew leaned up against the hallway wall, sliding down it to a sitting position on the floor. He had to wait for Lucy. He would have to tell her that she was now a widow.

The funeral for Marc Winters was solemn and understated, as had been his wishes. Marc had created a living will and advance directives along with a prepaid burial plan. Lucy saw to it that Marc's wishes were carried out to the letter.

Matthew, Jack Palace, Peter Sutherland and three of Marc's best friends served as his pall bearers. A simple service was held at the church where Marc and Lucy had been long-time members, teachers and Marc a deacon. A simple graveside ceremony followed in the church cemetery.

The shooter, now a killer, had not been found.

Lucy Winters had not been alone since high school. She had fallen in love with Marc Winters the first time they danced together, at Ruth and John's wedding reception. She knew in her heart there would be no other man that she could love the way she loved Marc Winters.

An excellent provider, partner, lover and friend, she would grieve his passing *Day After Day*, but would carry his love within her very soul.

Lucy told Matthew how much her husband had loved him, and urged him to let go of the guilt she invariably saw him trying to cope with.

Reminding Matt that he and Marc were more than brothers, she asked him to turn those guilt feelings into positive actions, which is what Marc would have wanted.

Feeling comforted by his sister-in-law's unbelievable courage and benevolence, Matthew vowed to find the person who had left this gaping hole in their family, and see that justice was done.

CHAPTER EIGHTY-FOUR

ATLANTA, GEORGIA

Lee had long been a favorite person to Daniel's sister Lily Marie. Lily, as she now preferred to be called, had recently turned sixteen and to have a girlfriend in college was indeed a big deal to her. She secretly told Lee that she felt as though she was the big sister she never had but always wanted. Lee wisely told Lily that having two older brothers must be reserved for a very special young woman, and that she should be thankful to have brothers who would look out for her best interests.

Naturally, the family got around to twenty questions (each) about Daniel and Lee's relationship, but they both handled it with great diplomacy and pride.

Looking around, Daniel suddenly realized he had been abandoned. He gently kissed Lee on the cheek as he exited as well. The questions continued and—if anything—got louder. Finally Lee simply said that she and Daniel were in a committed relationship and that's all there would be until they graduated.

"Do you think you and my brother will get married someday?" asked Lily.

"That depends," said Lee, "on whether or not we both love each other enough to make that commitment." She smiled at Lily and said in a teenage voice, "And he has to ask me." The two girls laughed.

"If you did, we would be real sisters," said Lily.

"Yes, we would, but I love you like you were already my sister," said Lee, "and don't you forget that."

"Have you ever been in love?" asked Lily.

Smiling broadly, Lee said, "Only once."

CHAPTER EIGHTY-FIVE

GAINESVILLE, FLORIDA
1982

It was hard to imagine, but both Joanie and Matthew would each turn fifty this year. Looking blankly at Matthew one morning, Joanie said, "I don't think we should celebrate our birthdays this year."

"Why not?" Matthew asked. "I think we look pretty doggone good for five–oh."

"Don't say the numbers, you'll make them stick!" Joanie exclaimed.

"Baby, the numbers stick whether you want them to or not."

"I know. I just thought that if we just ignored it...well, it would go away," Joanie replied.

"Why are you suddenly so worried about this?" Matt asked.

"I don't know. I look at the twins and see the two of them turning fourteen, and it just hits me. How could we have been that old when they were born? Did I really *think* about having children when I was thirty-six? Didn't I realize I'd be in a wheelchair or on crutches for their high school graduation?"

"You won't be on crutches—maybe just a wheelchair," Matt scoffed. "And we didn't think about age then. It wouldn't have changed anything, would it?"

“Me in a wheelchair? I’ll probably be pushing you in one,” Joanie rebutted.

“That’s my girl,” said Matthew as he wrapped his arms around her, giving her a huge hug.

“I’m just having a moment, I guess,” said Joanie. “Oh, no—could I be entering—oh no, that isn’t supposed to happen yet.”

“Hello?”

“Menopause,” whispered Joanie.

“I don’t think so dear,” said the reassuring Matthew. “You don’t show any of the signs yet.”

“Mood swings—I have mood swings all the time.”

“And you have since I’ve known you, my love.”

“Oh, you wouldn’t understand. You’re a man. As a matter of fact, I’m the only female in this household. Maybe I’ll go visit my mother.”

“Good thinking,” said Matthew as he made a mental note to call and warn Jack.

James and Michael Winters had the opposite idea about age. Both wanted the years to go faster so that they could get on with their idea of living.

The twins were freshmen in high school and both had earned a spot on the junior varsity swim team.

James was the faster swimmer of the two, exhibiting more overall speed and endurance. Michael was a quick starter and performed very well in all of the relay races. He was always first off the block and seemed to propel himself further than any of his peers. Both young men enjoyed swimming and credited their talent to some not-so-hard work in their pool at home.

Bee and Jack attended every swim meet. These two made a handsome pair and were obviously happy about living together.

Bee had explained it all to her grandsons, and while they didn’t really say much or ask any questions, she felt there was total acceptance by Michael and a hesitancy to accept Jack by her grandson James. Nothing had been said; it was just a sense that she had.

James had become less sociable than Michael, to the point that he was at times withdrawn. Joanie had seen it happening and although she had tried to speak with James about it, he shrugged it off, saying she must be imagining it.

Michael was outgoing and popular at school. He was studious and seemed content with his world. Noticing that James was less so, he would try to include him only to be politely told "no thanks."

James preferred to swim, to read, and to do a lot of thinking. He just didn't want anyone to know what he was thinking about. The one thing that tied him particularly to his father was what he called the "planning" gene. He was a planner, if not a plotter, but only time would tell.

CHAPTER EIGHTY-SIX

GEORGIA TECH

MAY 1983

The graduating class of 1983 filled the auditorium at the Fox Theatre in Atlanta. Among the graduates were Daniel Adams and Lee Barrett.

Seated separately with their respective "colleges of study," the two could barely see one another through the crowd.

The spectators included everyone in the Winters family, plus Beatrice Bovier and Jack Palace, and next to them Olan and Lelah Barrett. It was a proud day for these two families and one for which they had all sacrificed to see to fruition.

David's Tech pride was obvious as he watched his oldest son cross the stage and receive his undergraduate degree. The "Old Gold" meant a lot to him, and he was honored that his son would follow in his footsteps. To no one's surprise Vera cried tears of joy as well as premature tears of the dread she would feel in saying goodbye to her eldest child.

Caleb, Lily, Michael, and James sat restlessly in their seats wondering how long the ceremony would take and making plans for what to do afterward.

Seated immediately behind them were Matthew, Joanie, and Lucy, all happy for the graduates but all-too-familiar with Vera and Lelah's separation anxiety.

Beatrice and Jack were sitting quietly in the same row feeling lucky to have one another and to have such a wonderful family to be a part of.

Lee's father stood as his daughter walked across the stage to receive her diploma. When she looked in his direction, he gave her a simple salute, expressing his love and admiration for what she had accomplished. Lelah stood beside her husband with her hand over her heart.

At the conclusion of the ceremony, people began gathering outside the auditorium, spilling out into the streets of Atlanta. Caps were flying, and families were struggling to connect and get photographs, and there was happy chaos everywhere you looked.

Finding one another before finding the families, Lee and Daniel took a long moment to kiss one another. They had both succeeded and in only four years, a rarity at a demanding Tech. Hugs and kisses came from their friends Joe and C. Ann, and soon they found their separate ways to their respective parents for their congratulations.

It was a bittersweet moment for the graduates. Recognizing the ending of one chapter in their lives was sad, but having the opportunity and the training to move forward to create the next chapter was exhilarating at the same time.

Lee and Daniel found themselves smothered in hugs and kisses from the families. Beautiful bouquets of flowers were given to Lee as well as a traditional Hawaiian lei that Olan had a local florist make for his daughter. Lelah's gift was one of placing her hand on the head of her child, then lifting her chin to look into her eyes, and bowing to her. This was the Vietnamese custom of honoring and recognizing the worth of your child. Lelah's bow meant that she now recognized her daughter as an adult.

Arrangements had been made to have a combined celebratory dinner at Pittypat's Porch. The legendary restaurant of *Gone With The Wind* fame was a traditional southern food fine dining restaurant. David and Vera Adams were hosting the dinner and had reserved the main dining room and the adjacent Rocking Chair Lounge for the evening.

Vera had contacted Lelah Barrett just after Christmas to invite the two of them to join in the celebratory meal. While Lelah was insistent that she and Olan contribute, Vera explained that this was their gift to Daniel and to Lee, and insisted that the two of them be there for the party. Having little recourse, Lelah offered to help in any way that she could and gratefully accepted Vera's invitation.

The décor at Pittypat's had been updated to include blue and gold helium-filled balloons and streamers hanging from the open-beamed ceiling. A large banner also suspended from the rafters read *Congratulations, Lee and Daniel!*

Drinks were served in the Rocking Chair Lounge, and the room was abuzz with laughter and congratulatory toasts.

Dinner was announced, and as the families made their way downstairs to the dining room, Lee and Daniel stole a private moment. Kissing one another tenderly, the two exchanged a long look into the eyes of one another. Daniel said, "We'd better go, but before we do, I just want you to know that I love you, Leaolani Barrett. I really love you, and I think I knew it the minute I laid eyes on you."

Not knowing if she was more shocked or exuberant, Lee said, "And I love you, Daniel. I was in love with you *from day one*."

"You know that's what my parents' wedding rings say inside?" asked Daniel.

"What?"

"I've loved you *from day one,*" replied Daniel. "Guess it runs in the family." He gently kissed her again and then took her hand in his and led her down the stairway to the dining room.

CHAPTER EIGHTY-SEVEN

NOVEMBER 1983
SIX MONTHS LATER

As usual everyone in the Winters family planned to gather at the Buckhead home of David and Vera Adams to celebrate Thanksgiving. Their extended family had now grown to include not only the Barretts; the Sutherlands of Gainesville were included, and were driving to Atlanta with their close friends Matthew, Joanie, and their sons.

Because of the sheer number of guests, Vera and David opted to hire professional caterers for the holiday feast. Not only would the caterer manage the cooking and serving, the group would also be there for the monumental task of cleaning up.

Predictably, Vera insisted that the catering staff share in the Thanksgiving meal, so that once the main course was served, they would take a place at the tables as well. While highly unusual, Mrs. Adams was the talk of the catering circles in Atlanta as a result of her thoughtfulness and generosity.

Dessert and coffee would come well after the feast, giving the staff time to remove all the plates and serving dishes. Tables of dessert selections would be placed on buffets, along with coffee, tea, sodas, and wine, and all of Vera's guests would have an opportunity to serve themselves.

The Sutherlands were at first reluctant to accept the invitation, knowing that they would have to forego their normal Thanksgiving shelter service, but with Joanie's pleading, they relented.

Joanie insisted that this could be an adventure if they rented and shared a van to drive the two families to Atlanta. By doing so, they could bring cases of wine and champagne for the feast.

Bee and Jack were flying to Atlanta so that they could make a side trip to New Orleans Lucy would drive from Alabama, and everyone else was in residence in or near Atlanta.

Vera and David Adams had a knack for entertaining large groups of people—perhaps because they had done it so many times before; perhaps because of their genuine willingness to enjoy their blessings with others. The Thanksgiving Day celebration in Buckhead was an annual event, but this year Vera sensed there was something special in the offing.

Among the first to arrive on Thanksgiving Day were Bee and Jack. They came into the house carrying large bouquets of flowers, candy, and champagne. Jack brought along his traditional bottle of Jack Daniels, which he ceremoniously handed to David.

Shortly behind Bee and Jack were Lee, Olan, and Lelah Barrett. They came carrying hostess gifts as well and some of Lelah's famous sweet and salty dessert bars.

Daniel bounded down the steps when he heard the Barrett family arrive. The sight of Lee absolutely took his breath away. She was wearing a simple but elegant azure blue dress with peep-toe pumps. Her hair was simply braided in one long braid down her back. She looked stunning.

Matthew served mimosas to everyone who was old enough to partake. After the adults were served and the teenagers had vanished into the den to watch the Thanksgiving Day Parade, he tapped his glass and got everyone's attention. He then introduced the Sutherlands to the other guests, teasing that there would be a test for Pete and Sylvia at the end of the first mimosa.

Everyone milled about talking and enjoying the day as well as the mimosas. Pete, being the investigator that he was exhibited his extraordinary ability to repeat back everyone's name as soon as his mimosa glass was emptied. Everyone cheered, and the next round was served.

The merriment continued into the middle of the afternoon when Vera announced that dinner was served. She had arranged the seating so that everyone was comfortable and while at different round tables, they were in close proximity to one another.

Dinner was served on the veranda overlooking the sprawling lawn. Outdoor heaters had been placed intermittently throughout the space in the event the weather was cold. Gauze drapes hung from the portico, and each table was meticulously set.

Once everyone found a seat, Vera asked that they stand together, holding hands with the person next to them, and she returned the blessing. As promised, once the main course and vegetables were put on the tables, the servers took their place at their table to enjoy the meal.

When everyone had eaten, David stood and raised a glass to toast the guests. He thanked the servers for their outstanding job and expressed his gratitude for his and Vera's many blessings. Asking if anyone wanted to share what they were most thankful for, he was a bit surprised to see Olan standing first.

"First of all, David, I know I speak for everyone in thanking you for this wonderful meal. Secondly, I am most thankful for my beautiful family—including now all of you as my extended family. I have been blessed to be a soldier who was allowed to come home and *express* my thanks. I have also been blessed to have such a smart, beautiful daughter who has chosen a brilliant, handsome man—your son Daniel." Applause was heard throughout the crowd before Olan could continue. "I'm also thankful to both David and Vera for teaching this young man to be honorable. God bless each of you."

Daniel was next to stand. "I am grateful for all the blessings God has given me, not the least of which is my family. But to be granted an opportunity to now have Olan's blessing is what I am most thankful for. I am thankful you are all here to share in one of my greatest moments." He turned to face Lee, lifted her to her feet, and asked her to marry him. When she said yes, he presented her with a lovely diamond ring.

Everyone stood—some crying, some laughing, some giddy from the moment and the sentiment that they had witnessed. The moment was breathtaking.

Crying tears of pure joy, Lee could not speak. She walked to her parents, hugged them both, and then held her left hand up in the air for everyone to get a glimpse of the engagement ring. Gliding back over to Daniel, she threw her arms around him and sobbed.

Daniel said, "I think she's happy, don't you?"

Everyone applauded.

Lucy stood next. "While that's a hard act to follow, I too must say that although all of us have been through more than our share of heartache and heartbreak, we are indeed a most fortunate group of people to live and love so openly and completely. Happy Thanksgiving."

Matthew followed. "There's not one new thing left for me to say other than I thank God for all of you and your place in my life. God bless us."

Joanie stood. "I want to say I am thankful to *be* thankful, and to be a part of this family. I'm also happy for my nephew Daniel and his new fiancée who can now carry on the tradition of hosting this gathering year after year." Everyone laughed loud and long.

Jack stood and said, "I am thankful for having Bee in my life and for the best friends a man could ever have. I love you all."

Lee stood and you could hear a pin drop around the veranda. "I'm thankful not to be crying anymore." Everyone chuckled. "I have so many things to be grateful for, I really wouldn't know where to start. I am thankful to be an American and to be happy and free. I am thankful to have found the great love I knew was out there somewhere for me, and happiest of all that I will be sharing my life with all of you."

Vera stood. "For everyone here, for our family members who are not here, I am thankful for your resolve to be a part of my life. Through the greatest joys and the most severe circumstances, you have been there. My life has been filled with great love and joy, thanks to you. And to my eldest son, congratulations; you have made an excellent choice."

Pete Sutherland stood. "Wow, had I known what I was getting into here," and he paused briefly, "Sylvia, Gracie, and I would have been here years ago." Interrupted by giggles he continued, "We're thankful people and grateful to be counted among your friends. God bless each and every one of you."

David Adams said, "A toast to the best doggone group of people in the world."

The catering staff wiped their eyes, sipped their wine, and then went about the task of clearing the tables and refilling the wine glasses.

"Daniel," said David, "you must have asked Olan for his daughter's hand in marriage, huh?"

"I did, and I was relieved when he said yes," replied Daniel.

"I'm proud of you, son," said David with a pat on the shoulder.

Vera made her way to Lee and Daniel, hugging them together and offering her congratulations.

"Mrs. Adams," said Lee, "I want you to know that I love Daniel very much, and I will be a very good wife to him."

"I'm sure you will be. You two are perfectly matched and well suited for one another," said Vera.

"We both knew that from day one," said Lee, waiting for a reaction from her future mother-in-law.

"*From day one,*" said Vera as she twirled her wedding ring on her finger, smiling all the while. "That's the perfect time to know, and I think you will find that it just gets better *day after day*." She simply smiled at both of them and walked away.

Just before leaving Gainesville, Matt Winters had received an anonymous telephone call, this time left by a male caller. The message was: "You took your eye off your brother and I got him. That was too easy. I have Ruth in my sights too. Who will be next – Ruth or you?"

The good news was that the call was longer in duration and the trace had worked. The call had come from Miami, Florida.

Peter Sutherland had contacted the Miami PD and the FBI with the information about the call. They were now within thirty square blocks of where the phone call originated, and zeroing in.

The Miami PD learned that a transient had been living in the area; no one knew much about him. The neighbors had heard him called "Jimbo" but had no last name. When the police knocked on Jimbo's door, he scurried out a back window.

Breaking in the door, the police discovered a digital voice distorter, tape recordings, a log of calls placed and a stack of ammunition. Having requested backup in pursuit of Jimbo, it was only a matter of time before he was caught.

Jimbo was arrested on several charges including possession of an unlicensed firearm, telephone harassment, and was promised the additional charge of attempted murder if ballistics confirmed this was the weapon used to shoot Marc Winters.

CHAPTER EIGHTY-EIGHT

KONA, HAWAII

It was probably imagined, but Riana Tavares felt a distant yet familiar tug at her heartstrings. Glancing over at the clock, the local time was 10:00 a.m., and she was putting the finishing touches on their traditional Thanksgiving luau. Without warning she realized it was 3:00 p.m. on the east coast—just about the time when her "former" family celebrated a Thanksgiving meal together. Shaking her head and silently shushing herself, Riana resumed her tasks.

It was a beautiful day, as were most on the island. With an ever-present trade wind breeze and a moderate eighty-two degrees, the afternoon promised to be gorgeous.

The roast pig had been in the pit for about eight hours already, and Jarrod and his golfing buddies were tending to the pork while imbibing with some local beer.

Riana made her way to the pit with local fruits and vegetables that would now be stuffed inside the cavity of the pig for its final hours of cooking. After supervising the placement of the veggies and fruit, Riana helped to cover the pig with palm fronds, attaching them carefully with skewers to insure they stayed in place. Satisfied that her work was complete, Riana headed back to her house for some quiet time before the other guests arrived.

She could not seem to stop the thoughts that were running in her head. She had secretly thought of Vera, Matthew, and Marc, but had been able to push the thoughts away by realizing and remembering the reason she had sacrificed her family ties. She said a prayer for each of them and for their families, spouses, and children—if they had any. Riana could only imagine what course their lives had taken. While she knew David and Vera had a child and that Marc and Lucy were married with twins, she wondered about Matthew.

He had been so studious and dedicated to his work; it appeared he had little or no motivation to find a mate. Perhaps that had changed. She would probably never know.

CHAPTER EIGHTY-NINE

ATLANTA, GEORGIA
1984

A June wedding had been planned and preparations were being made in earnest. Lee wanted an intimate wedding with just close family and friends, and Daniel agreed it would be large, even under that scenario.

Lelah Barrett had been instrumental in helping her daughter with the details, but asked Vera for a recommendation on a location for the wedding. Without hesitation, Vera invited Lelah and Lee to have lunch with her so they could scope out a possible location.

Driving through Buckhead and Five Points, Vera took the ladies to a private tea room for lunch and high tea and then to an area just north of the city known commonly as Chastain Park. When Vera stopped the car, both Lelah and Lee could barely believe their eyes. In front of them was a sprawling park whose absolute central figure was an amphitheater. It was indeed a breathtaking sight, steeped in tradition and charm, the lawn seating was vast and rustic.

Chastain Memorial Park, most commonly called Chastain Park, is the largest city park in Atlanta. Encompassing 268 acres, it includes jogging paths, playgrounds, tennis courts, a golf course, swimming pool, horse park, and amphitheater. It is also bisected in the middle of its wedge-shape by Nancy Creek which flows east to west. Surrounded by forested neighborhoods of the Buckhead region, it is located northwest of the original Buckhead Village.

"Now that you've seen it, what do you think about having your wedding here in the amphitheater?" asked Vera. "I was thinking we could set up tables of six in the pit and lower part of the orchestra section. We would do beautiful setups with great food, tablecloths, and candles and have not only the wedding, but the reception here as well."

"But how would we ever be able to get this place for our wedding?" Lee asked.

"Well, my soon-to-be daughter-in-law, my husband has a few connections with the coordinators that schedule the events here, and if we can let him know immediately, they will try to accommodate us."

Lelah thought the idea was grand. Lee agreed and all that was left now was booking the date.

By the following day, the venue was reserved, and the plans proceeded, thanks to a sizeable donation by David Adams. Thankfully, the Atlanta Symphony Orchestra did not have concerts the night before or the night of the wedding. As Vera had predicted, David made it happen.

CHAPTER NINETY

GAINESVILLE, FLORIDA

Michael and James were sixteen years of age and old enough, according to Florida law, to drive a car as long as a licensed driver accompanied them. This was Joanie's nightmare coming true. After six months—age sixteen and a half—the boys could take the driving test and would either have a legitimate license to drive or not. Naturally, both boys passed the exam, with Michael scoring a perfect one hundred and James squeaking by with a seventy-five percent.

Of course both of them wanted their own car, to which Matthew said "no," and to which Joanie said "hell no." Harmony was lost in the Winters household until Matthew made them a deal. He would purchase "a" car for the twins to share *if and only if* they both made the honor roll for a full semester. They would be seniors in the fall and could have a car to use if they made their last semester of their junior year a banner year in grades.

Michael thought that was a fair deal while James complained; no one was surprised.

James made the mistake of making a negative comment about it within earshot of his mother, Joanie, who promptly informed him he would have her help in making those good grades because he was grounded until further notice.

As time went by at a grueling rate for James, he asked if he could earn his way out of being grounded. His mother, taking this as a good sign, agreed to lengthen his chore list in exchange for his grounding period. Joanie quickly reminded James that if she heard another disparaging word, he would be starting his grounding period over from the beginning. All was quiet.

By the time the semester was over, and cousin Daniel's wedding approached, both Michael and James had received their licenses as well as the mutual use of a used but reliable vehicle. Naturally the two boys thought it would be cool if they drove it from Gainesville to Atlanta for the wedding. Not unexpectedly Matthew and Joanie gave an emphatic "no way" to that.

As a second choice, Michael and James offered to go to the ceremony in the company of Grandma and Jack. They were undoubtedly planning on taking some of the driving burden off of them. Joanie simply said, "Ask Grandma." They did, and they were accompanying Grandma and Jack to the wedding.

Joanie and Matthew opted to drive as well and asked the Sutherlands to go with them. Two cars, four adults (almost) seemed like a good idea.

After giving strict instructions to her mother about James and Michael and their lack of experience in driving, Bee agreed to let each of them drive "for a bit" on the interstate with Jack riding shotgun.

"No driving in or near Atlanta," said Joanie.

"No, absolutely not," replied Bee.

When Joanie shared the plan with Matthew he simply said, "I'll say prayers. I also want to get a two-hour head start on that group. They can call AAA if they run into trouble."

"Matt—what a terrible thought! We should give them the head start so that we can bring up the rear in the event they do have problems," said Joanie, attacking him with a quick love slap to the arm.

The Miami PD now had proof that the gun in Jimbo's possession was the gun used to shoot Marc Winters.

Jimbo turned out to be Jim Bonetti, a hired gun who had a lengthy rap sheet. He pled guilty to shooting Marc Winters, but refused to admit that he had killed him.

Marc's autopsy revealed that he was injected with a lethal dose of a barbiturate called "Allobarbital", which acts as a depressant to the central nervous system.

While the police were pleased to have Bonetti in custody, this meant not only was there a boss who hired him to kill Marc, there had to be an accomplice who had access to a barbiturate and knew how much to inject for the desired result.

Bonetti refused to identify his boss, but when threatened with life in prison asked if he could broker a deal to get less time.

Between the court-appointed attorney and the district attorney who was prosecuting the case, Bonetti was promised a reduced sentence if he identified his boss and agreed to testify against him/her in court.

Bonetti named Crystal Westley of Miami, Florida as his boss. When asked who his accomplice was he repeated the name, Crystal Westley.

CHAPTER NINETY-ONE

ATLANTA, GEORGIA

Daniel Adams had asked Joe to be his best man; Lee had asked C. Ann to be her maid of honor. It would just be the four of them, plus the parents of the betrothed who participated in the ceremony. The minister was the pastor from the church that Daniel had attended since birth.

Daniel had been working for the Gannett owned WXIA—Channel 11 in Atlanta as an apprentice in the "11 Alive Weather Center." There he was gaining hands-on experience in the latest interactive radar, regional satellite information, storm watches, and storm warnings. Part of his job entailed keeping an eye on the satellite images that came into the weather center. His boss had trained him in the use of the image monitors and told him what he should be looking for. It was Daniel's responsibility to alert his immediate supervisor if and when changes occurred.

While the position wasn't glamorous, Daniel was learning valuable skills and was ahead of the learning curve in understanding the fast-growing use of computers and simulators as they pertained to weather. In a market the size of Atlanta, and with the backing of Gannett, WXIA was a front-runner in the technology race. Watching radar images encompassed most of the hours in Daniel's work day, and he loved it.

With his degree in meteorology, Daniel was now gaining hands-on experience that would lead him closer to his career goal. He enjoyed what he was doing and had virtually everything a young man his age could hope for. He felt blessed.

CHAPTER NINETY-TWO

THE WEDDING OF DANIEL AND LEAOLANI
CHASTAIN PARK, ATLANTA, GEORGIA

The day could not have been more perfect. It was partly cloudy that morning, and the forecast—which Daniel had predicted himself—indicated clearing skies and an absolutely beautiful evening.

Lelah made sure the place cards were set along with the wedding favor at each seat. Lee's parents had flown leis in from Hawaii, and they were not only beautiful but deliciously fragrant as well. All of the men received a *Maile Lei* that featured deep green leaves, while the ladies received the traditional lei of *Plumeria* in yellow-throated pinks and whites.

The head table sported *Orchid with Rose leis* for the bridal party, along with *Maile leis* for the gentlemen, including the fathers of the bride and groom.

Just below the stadium seating for the reception, the amphitheater stage was adorned with a wedding trellis covered in white orchids and deep-green ivy. On either side of the stage were three tiki torches, which would be lit prior to the ceremony.

The two rows closest to the stage were reserved for the wedding guests and had been festooned with white and gold toile. All other seating had been removed for the event.

As family and guests arrived at Chastain Park, they were greeted with the Hawaiian music of Israel Kamakawio'ole—better known as "IZ." Though unknown to most of the contiguous United States, IZ was well known among his people as a champion of family values, saying no to drugs, and spreading the Aloha Spirit. The recording had been chosen by Lee and Daniel, and everyone found the musical styling of IZ to be fascinating and delightful.

Once family and friends were seated, the tiki torches were lit, and IZ's rendition of "Somewhere over the Rainbow" began to play. Daniel and Lee met under the trellis and were married. While Daniel kissed his new bride for the first time, the music of IZ was once again heard. He was singing "What a Wonderful World." There was not a dry eye in the amphitheater.

David made the first toast to his son and his daughter-in-law, followed by the best man, Joe. Olan Barrett made the next toast, teary eyed but firm in his resolve to get through the act of turning his daughter over to another man. Vera and Lelah stood together as mothers, and each spoke their own written prayer of thankfulness for this union. C. Ann was the last to toast, stating that she had made not only a friend for life, but now felt an integral part of a lovely family.

After dinner had been served and eaten, the happy couple rose from their seats, walked to the front of the amphitheater's stage, and thanked everyone for being such a meaningful part of this day. They each blew a kiss and left the stage to begin the rest of their lives as man and wife.

CHAPTER NINETY-THREE

ATLANTA, GEORGIA

1985

The year had flown by for Daniel and Lee Adams, and change was afoot. Lee's parents, Lelah and Olan had moved from suburban Atlanta to the Island of Maui in Hawaii.

Longing for the life they had shared as a young married couple, the Barretts had opted to return to the islands and spend the remainder of their lives in the manner in which they had begun their lives together.

Leaving their daughter in Atlanta had been a difficult decision, but Lee assured them that it was inevitable that she and Daniel would make their way to the South Pacific Island chain. Even if they successfully relocated to another of the inhabitable islands, it would be an easier commute than across country plus five hours of additional flying time.

Lee's life had been a virtual whirlwind since her arrival in Atlanta. Now she was married and again physically separated from her parents, but her career was taking on new life. She landed a job with NOAA—the National Oceanic and Atmospheric Administration in Atlanta. And while this assignment meant there was some travel involved—mostly on the spur of the moment when a calamity or marine mammal anomaly occurred, she was ready for the task.

Daniel had been promoted a couple of times at WXIA and had moved into the weekend meteorologist's position. Gaining great exposure plus on-air experience improved his resume, enhancing his chances for better positions in larger and better market areas.

By the end of 1985, Daniel was positioned for just that sort of move.

Lee was working in conjunction with rescue resources for marine life as well as those that were more specialized in atmospheric conditions. Daniel was able to coach her on that part of the business, and she found it fascinating as well.

CHAPTER NINETY-FOUR

THANKSGIVING, 1985

The tradition continued one more year with all the Winters Clan making the pilgrimage to Atlanta for the Thanksgiving Holiday Feast. While the numbers were dwindling, every adult without exception commented on the changes the collective group had been through.

Caleb Adams was now twenty-three years old and was attending Georgia Tech, just as his father and older brother had done. He proudly took a seat at the table next to his sister Lily Marie who was now a beautiful nineteen-year-old who had entered Emory College in the fall.

Daniel and Lee were in the midst of everyone, helping Vera with last minute chores and making sure everyone had something to drink. Both were thankful to have the day off, even though Daniel would be reporting the weather for the upcoming weekend. So far Lee had not been called by NOAA and was really hoping to have a couple of days' respite.

Joanie and Matthew Winters's twin boys, Michael and James, were in their senior year in high school and toiling with being seventeen. They knew everything there was to know *about* everything and invariably found their parents to be uninformed or just naïve about *their* real world. Michael was still the more studious and settled of the pair, while James was rebellious and fought "the system" at every turn.

They no longer looked like identical twins with James's hair grown long and unkempt, while the more conservative Michael kept his hair cut, styled, and—as their mother was quick to point out—*clean*.

Michael's grades were above average, while James fought for Cs, but both had clear-cut plans for the future. Michael wanted to be an attorney, and James wanted to be free of pressures and rules and live a wealthy life.

Lucy Winters was present along with Sandra and Amanda (née Winters) who were now each married with children of their own, and their husbands and kids rounded out the original Winters group.

Bee and Jack had just returned to Gainesville from a train trip across the United States, which they thoroughly enjoyed, and were excited to return to Atlanta to their extended family with pictures in tow.

The Sutherlands came as well, minus their beautiful daughter, Gracie, who was now serving as a missionary nurse in Guatemala, serving with Nurses without Borders.

Looking smaller than the previous year's group, an eerie silence had fallen on the mass. But once everyone had seated themselves, they once again carried out the tradition of expressing what they were most thankful for. Predictably, most repeated they were grateful for family, friends, and God's blessings.

After everyone finished, David stood and gave thanks to God. As he prayed, he asked that the Lord take care of those who were missing from this year's table, asking that He watch over each of them and put an armor of protection around them. Vera wiped a lone tear as David said Amen.

The after dinner conversation ranged from Daniel sharing information about the earthquake that measured an 8.1 on the Richter scale in Mexico City to Matthew and Pete discussing that a big-named Mafia boss—Paul Castellano—had been shot on the orders of John T. Gotti, better known as the "Teflon Don" because no one could seem to make felony charges stick to him.

Matthew said, "Ironically, Paul Castellano had been part of the old school of Mafia leaders who actually were against dealing in drugs. Gotti, a member of the same *family* had recognized something had to go—either the millions of dollars in drug profits being earned by his associates, or Godfather Castellano. The execution of a godfather was against the code of the Mafia, but obviously Teflon Don did not play by anyone's rules except his own."

"How do you know so much about the Mafia?" Michael asked his father.

"It's been an interest of mine for a long time son. Pete and I like to keep up on what the other side is doing, right Pete?" Matthew replied.

"Right," Pete responded. "Keep your friends close and your enemies closer—at least know without a doubt what they're up to."

Caleb commented on the emergence of a Corporation called Microsoft that had released the first version of a "user-friendly" operating system for the personal computer—*Windows 1.0* and that there was a registration of a *dot com* which he believed was the beginning of a technological revolution.

Lily's contribution to current affairs related to the now rampant Aids epidemic by stating the Food and Drug Administration had just approved a blood test for AIDS.

When Joanie asked James what he knew about current affairs, he stated that compact discs had finally been put in US cars. "Yeah that, and there's a new drug now that people are getting into—it's called crack."

"And how do you know that?" asked his father.

"Come on, man, everybody knows that crack is the new cocaine," replied James.

"Remind me to follow up on that with you, son."

"Yeah, whatever," James said.

Michael quickly changed the subject by saying that the space shuttle Atlantis had been launched and that the biggest and best musical artists of the day had recorded a song called "We Are the World" as USA for Africa to raise money for famine relief.

Bee recanted tales of the train trip across the country and shared their photographs with everyone who would sit long enough to see them.

As the crowd dispersed, Vera felt a sense of sadness. She knew in her heart of hearts that no other Thanksgiving celebration would be the same nor would the guests around her table.

Taking note of her mother's silence, Lily Marie put an arm around her waist and hugged her in the way only a daughter can do. Vera returned the hug with a silent kiss on the head as they watched their guests leave. "It will be OK, Mom, I promise," was all she said.

"Everyone who can be here is welcome for brunch tomorrow," said David as people filed out the door to go to their respective lodgings.

"Count us in," said Daniel and Lee.

"Sorry, Uncle David, we're all leaving for home tomorrow morning," said Sandra. "Amanda and I want to leave early while the kids are asleep! It was a great day—thanks so much."

Looking a bit forlorn, Vera looked at Joanie.

"We're not going anywhere. I'll get the wine and meet you on the veranda," said Joanie.

"What time, David?" asked Bee as she and Jack Palace made their way to the door.

"Anytime after eleven," said David waving goodbye.

"See you then," said Jack as he helped Bee put her coat on.

A silent Vera stood at the entryway of her Buckhead home looking forlorn.

"Are you OK?" asked David.

"Just feeling a bit overwhelmed," answered Vera. "I love seeing everyone come here and hate seeing everyone leave."

"But they'll be back," said David as he wrapped his arms around Vera and hugged her while he nuzzled her neck.

"I'm fine. Go on out to the veranda—I'll be along."

Vera stood for a moment in the entry foyer looking up at the spiral staircase that she and her children had climbed every day since their births. Day after day she had climbed those steps praying that life would always remain the same. But now, there were no more babies to put to bed, no more toddlers to fight with over naps, and only memories up those stairs. After uttering a silent prayer of thanks, she made her way to the veranda.

CHAPTER NINETY-FIVE

GAINESVILLE, FLORIDA

1986

Matthew was reading the transcript of the Bonetti trial, looking for answers that he still did not have. The trial of Jim Bonetti in Miami resulted in him being sentenced to life in prison, without the chance of parole. His plea bargain had been revoked when the Miami police department learned that Crystal Westley had been killed in a house fire several years prior.

Angry that his plea bargain was thrown out, an insistent Jim Bonetti swore that "Crystal" was alive and well, and that he had talked with her the day he was arrested. Swearing her existence, Jimbo could not produce an address or a telephone number where she could be reached. He had stated that she always called him because of her work, and because there was a time zone difference. When questioned about the time difference, Bonetti was unable to elaborate.

Pouring over all the details was maddening to Matthew. These people were literally holding his family hostage, and wherever this "Crystal" was, she was capable of hiring locals to do her dirty work.

Recognizing the danger he had agreed to put himself in, had jeopardized the safety of each and every member of his family, Matthew had no choice but to drop everything else he was doing, work hand in hand with Peter Sutherland and solve this before anyone else was hurt.

Matt shared his decision with the other partners in the firm, asking that his FBI cases be reassigned wherever possible, and on those cases that were close to resolution, he be assigned a back-up prosecutor to clear it out. The partners unanimously agreed.

When Matthew spoke with his primary FBI contact, he explained his reasoning for backing off some of their cases. To his surprise, the FBI contact said that they might be in a position to help him in his search, if they could speak with Jim Bonetti.

Matthew arranged the meeting and he, Peter Sutherland and his FBI contact visited the state prison together.

CHAPTER NINETY-SIX

ATLANTA, GEORGIA
1986

Friends and family of Daniel and Lee Adams began the year on a bittersweet note. Word that Daniel had been offered a position as chief meteorologist at KITV in Honolulu, Hawaii, spread quickly through the pipeline. KITV had long been a news and weather leader in the market with a longstanding reputation as a well-managed television association. KITV first aired as KULA on April 16, 1954, and had been going strong ever since.

Daniel was beyond excited, as was Lee. While Lee would be the trailing spouse, being in Honolulu would invariably intensify her chances for a position at a marine aquarium or marine biology research institute.

The two planned to move in June so that Daniel could begin at the station on July 1, 1986. They would enlist the help of Olan and Lelah Barrett to find a suitable home for the two of them. While the Barretts lived on the neighboring island of Maui, the commute was immensely easier and more economical than flying from Atlanta.

Daniel had made the trip to Honolulu alone for the interview and scarcely had time to have a quick tour of the island of Oahu. He had loved what he had seen, and his only request was that he be within a reasonable driving distance of the television station. What little he had seen of Oahu, which was scarcely more than a cab ride to and from the airport and to and from the station, indicated to him that driving in this growing area of Hawaii could be time-consuming. Unlike the other Hawaiian Islands, Oahu was the only one with any sort of interstate system, and even with that, traffic could be bottlenecked during peak hours. That, Daniel decided, would simply remind him of his Atlanta home.

Needless to say the Barretts were overjoyed at the news that their daughter and son-in-law would be in such close proximity to them.

Under strict instructions from Lee, the two of them would "house hunt" for the newlyweds and take photos of prospective properties to send back. Phone calls and photos would have to suffice since properties were not plentiful, and prices were steep. Giving them a strict budget as well as a description of the ideal setting would guide the Barretts in their search for the perfect home. And so the search began.

Within a matter of a week, the Barretts had made a trip to Oahu and with a real estate agent researched all of the homes available within Lee and Daniel's budget and other must-haves. The realtor sent photos via overnight mail to Atlanta, and within another couple of days, Daniel and Lee chose what they hoped would be their new home.

The real estate transaction took place via facsimile, and by the end of May, the couple was ready to close on their new home. David and Vera sent the couple to Honolulu in advance of the closing, just to be sure that Daniel and Lee were as satisfied in person as they had been looking at photographs. As predicted, they loved the home, closed on it, and celebrated with the Barretts.

While in Honolulu, Daniel and Lee purchased furniture for their home, planning to move only what they had to. Olan and Lelah surprised them with a new washer and dryer for the house as well as a gift certificate for incidentals.

Realizing that they would need at least one vehicle—and shipping one to Honolulu wasn't practical, the two opted to purchase a late model used car during the trip. Once they were officially living on the island, they would purchase a second vehicle.

All that was left now was the move.

CHAPTER NINETY-SEVEN

HONOLULU, HAWAII

JULY 1986

KITV was an ABC affiliate and was a full-power station licensed to Honolulu and aired on Channel 4. Its signal covered most of the Hawaiian Island chain including the inhabited areas of Molokai and Lanai located on facing areas of Oahu and Maui. Transmitters on the western end of Kauai allowed signal reception as well. With an excellent reputation for timely news and weather, the station was a perfect fit for Daniel Adams.

When given the option of selecting an on-air name, Daniel decided to use "Dan" Adams as opposed to Daniel. The station execs thought it had a more youthful connotation but was still a powerful enough name to exude professionalism and elicit confidence. The on-air promos and ancillary promotional material would announce the newest addition to its weather team: Dan Adams, Chief Meteorologist, KITV in Honolulu.

The move from Atlanta to Honolulu went as smoothly as it could have. It entailed shipping virtually everything that would not fit in a suitcase. This process helped Daniel and Lee purge excess items that they had hoarded, and the experience amounted to a good lesson in learning to be frugal. By the time the two reached their seats on the airplane, they were exhausted and ready for the multi-hour flight to Honolulu.

The Barretts were waiting—leis in hand at the Honolulu airport for the couple. While relieved that their long flight was over, the two were suddenly charged with energy to begin their new lives. The Barretts pointed out the billboard on the interstate as they traveled to the house. It was a life-sized picture of Daniel, and the caption said, "Aloha, Dan Adams, Chief Meteorologist—Channel 4." Daniel beamed upon seeing his face above the freeway.

For Daniel, saying goodbye to his mother had been the hardest thing he had ever done. She suddenly appeared frail, a characteristic he had never seen in her before. He hugged her tightly and assured her that they would visit at every opportunity.

Lee invited her in-laws to visit them in Honolulu as soon as they could and assured them they would always be welcome. Lee shed tears with Vera at their airport parting. She too had seen the frailty in Vera. It was almost as though someone had let the air out of a balloon or taken the wind out of her sails; her regret was obvious.

Now, with luggage in tow, the Barretts, their daughter, and new son-in-law made their way to the house where Dan and Lee would make a home together.

The Barretts were prepared to spend a couple of nights with Dan and Lee just to help them unpack and get settled. Their generosity was appreciated, and Lee took advantage of her mother's shrewd shopping skills to fill her pantry with staples.

Olan was relegated to handyman status as Lee kept finding little things that needed to be done. He was good with his hands and happy to help in any way he could. Most of his chores involved moving furniture; first here, then there, as directed by Lee and her mother. Dan was happy to go to work and praise all the progress when he returned home.

As an Aloha gift, Lelah and Olan had purchased a low-mileage used car that Olan had specifically checked out for his daughter. By the time the

Barretts had Lee drive them to the airport for their short flight back to Maui, the house was in order, the pantry stocked, and an Aloha mat adorned the front stoop.

Leaving the airport, Lee realized that for the first time since they had moved to Honolulu, she and Daniel would be having dinner alone. She would be sure to make it special.

Once everything was done in her house, Lee felt eager to look for work. She had spent time driving through the principal areas of the city and felt confident in her ability to get most anywhere on the island that she needed to go.

Glancing through tourists brochures, she had seen an ad for the Waikiki Aquarium in Honolulu. She decided to check it out. She could certainly play tourist, and if she found it interesting, she would inquire about any open positions.

Lee was fascinated with the history of the aquarium and wanted to be a part of its team. She made immediate plans to contact the personnel department to try to secure an interview. Within three days of her first visit to the aquarium, Lee Adams was hired as an associate marine biologist at the Waikiki Aquarium.

CHAPTER NINETY-EIGHT

SEPTEMBER – HONOLULU, HAWAII

Living anywhere in Hawaii came with some natural weather concerns that didn't affect most of the contiguous United States. Hurricanes were possible, as were tsunamis, although both were considered "occasional" rather than frequent. While hurricanes happen virtually everywhere, tsunamis result from earthquakes, and the tidal ripple effects often result in wave/water surges on islands that are in their path.

Daniel had studied the recent earthquakes that occurred around the globe, closely following those that resulted in tsunami activity hundreds and even thousands of miles across the oceans. There had been an abnormal amount of seismic activity in areas such as San Salvador where 1500 had lost their lives during the past year, and Mexico City in 1985 with 9000 fatalities. Additionally, there had been sizeable increases in typhoon and hurricane activity. Daniel was convinced that the tornados, typhoons, and hurricanes were directly related to the depletion of the earth's ozone layer, which resulted in abnormal temperatures, weather patterns, and uncommon conditions that the depletion created.

An earthquake on or near the coast of California created a strong possibility for a tsunami in the South Pacific islands. And unlike hurricanes or typhoons that produce storm surges, tsunamis literally pull the water off the shore, creating an effect called an *Alluvium Plain* or a flat spot that was once under water. A tsunami current begins at the point of the earthquake and fans out somewhat like a radar or sonar signal across the ocean floor. As the pressure mounts, so does the strength of the undercurrent "wave." When a tsunami approaches land, as in approaching an island chain, it encircles the land mass, pulling out the water from the shoreline, and sends it back in successive waves that can be powerful and all-encompassing, based on the land's position to the incoming waves or a direct hit.

Daniel knew that most people in Hawaii were familiar with a tsunami, but visitors had no idea how lethal they could be. By the same token, if you were on the opposite side of a land mass, the tsunami waves would be lessened in strength based on the amount of time it took the wave to reach the other side of the island. In that case, a tsunami would be little more than an interesting event to behold.

Part of Daniel's job involved educating people on how best to prepare and react in the event of a hurricane, typhoon, or tsunami. Islanders typically head for the highest ground on their island in the event of a tsunami, abandoning the coastal beaches. Hurricane force winds—typhoons—give greater lead time for preparation, which includes hurricane shutters to cover all exterior glass or, in most cases, economical plywood from the hardware store.

Islanders knew full well that preparedness was a must. Hardware stores often ran out of plywood and having more shipped in took days or sometimes weeks as all the deliveries came by boat. The same was true for batteries, gasoline, and basic necessities like drinking water and food. Barges do not deliver to the islands in the wake of a tropical storm.

Weather was constant only in that everyone had weather, period. The diagnostic tools were improving year after year, and technology was providing a bigger picture for meteorologists like Daniel to observe and forecast from as a result.

Lee's job at the aquarium was fascinating as well. The few full-time employees who were on staff were knowledgeable, friendly, and eager to make their aquarium the best in the world.

One of the first tasks Lee took on was volunteering to work with the educational programs for volunteers. She set up a six-week curriculum for those who wanted to be hands-on *docents* (trained guides) for the aquarium and who would commit to volunteer at least ten hours per week. The curriculum involved a half day once per week for the six weeks and included time with Dr. Taylor as well as the heads of the various departments within the aquarium.

The docents in training were briefed on every aspect of the aquarium, including the species of animals on exhibit, interesting but little-known facts about the animals, their patterns and behaviors and what the mission of the aquarium was. They would have information at their disposal about everything in the aquarium by the end of their training and be confident in their ability to answer questions that often came from the clientele. Upon completion of the course, each docent would receive a certificate as well as a monogrammed Docent of the Waikiki Aquarium golf shirt in azure blue. The shirt simply was a thank you but did recognize them as trained volunteers.

One of the biggest perks in being a docent was that, as a trained unpaid assistant, the docent could be called upon to assist in animal rescues, recoveries, and even in the virtually inevitable task of monitoring recovering animals after their rescue. It gave the volunteer a real opportunity to help sick and/or injured fish and mammals.

The docent program grew and flourished under Lee's tutelage. Dr. Taylor spoke highly of her assistance in regard to the volunteer efforts of the aquarium. Lee took great pride in his endorsement and recognized it as an indisputable career achievement.

CHAPTER NINETY-NINE

KONA, HAWAII

NOVEMBER, 1986

Riana and Jarrod each had a bout with what they thought was the flu. Jarrod had the worst of it with night sweats and chills, even in balmy Hawaii. Riana was trying her best to take care of him, while not feeling well herself.

Jarrod refused to see a physician—a trait he had long exhibited. Riana knew he would refuse any help other than hers. After several days had passed and he was not improving, she called a pharmacy to inquire about over-the-counter medicines that might be of help. After trying everything including homemade chicken soup, she was ready to take him to the emergency room. It was then that Jarrod made a startling comment to her.

"I think I'm being poisoned" he said.

"Poisoned? With what and by whom?" asked Riana.

"I think it's," Jarrod weakly tried to reply, "I think its arsenic."

"Arsenic? Why would you think that, Jarrod? Are you hallucinating?" Riana was confused by this sudden conclusion her obviously very ill husband had reached.

"Take a look at my hands—they're discolored. It's a tint I've seen before. And arsenic is odorless, dissolves quickly, and when ingested over a long period of time, can be deadly. Take me to the hospital. Please—don't ask me how I know. I just *know,*" he said with his weak hand clutching her arm.

Riana immediately started helping Jarrod get dressed.

CHAPTER ONE HUNDRED

HILO EMERGENCY ROOM

HILO, HAWAII

It took a good half an hour to dress and transport Jarrod to the hospital. As soon as Riana got him into admitting she told the physician on call that her husband suspected he had been poisoned. She described his progressive illness over the past few days and with Jarrod's feeble contributions was able to make the physician understand that he was confident that he may have ingested arsenic.

That of course put Riana under immediate suspicion. After all, she was the only other person living with Jarrod and with whom he had daily contact. Although knowing all this, Riana did not have time to worry about that at this point. She was more interested in saving Jarrod.

As predicted, a toxicology panel was run and with the results pending, the police were called. They arrived to meet Riana in the waiting room and proceeded to ask her very pointed questions. She answered them as best she could and since she had nothing to hide, felt her answers were straightforward and well received.

"How is your relationship with your husband, Mrs. Tavares?" asked the detective.

"Excellent. We have been married since 1951," she replied.

"Why does your husband believe he has been poisoned?" he asked.

"I am not at all sure why he believes that. When he mentioned it to me I thought perhaps he was delirious with fever."

"But you brought him to the hospital?"

"Yes, of course. I have wanted him to see a physician for days, but he was insistent that he would be OK."

"And you, Mrs. Tavares, are you well?"

"Actually, I have had some of the same symptoms as Jarrod. We both thought it was a case of the flu."

The detectives chatted privately and then returned to Riana.

"Would you be willing to have a toxicology screening as well, Mrs. Tavares?"

"Of course I would, if you think that is necessary."

"We do. If you have both been exposed to something toxic, we need to know that."

"Then by all means, let's do the testing."

Moments later, blood was being drawn from Riana's arm. After four vials were filled, she returned to the waiting room.

CHAPTER ONE HUNDRED ONE

GAINESVILLE, FLORIDA

Matthew had made a mental note to talk to his son James about his comment on "crack cocaine." While he wasn't naïve enough to think that the high school in Gainesville didn't have an active drug exchange, he had never thought his own son might be involved—until now.

Matt so wanted to confide in his friend Pete, but knew that Joanie would have a fit if she ever knew he talked to anyone other than her about this. Matthew also knew that was the right thing to do, and he would talk with her at his first opportunity.

Pete Sutherland was extremely busy dealing with the federal agents who had just "busted" the five families in New York. He had done a lot of undercover research and had done a fine job in providing the agents with exactly the information they had been hoping to find. Thanks to Pete, the arrest warrants held, and even though "Teflon Don" was out, he was in for more questioning and possible jail time.

Nothing ever happened at an appropriate time, but Matt's mentor and confidante, William (Bill) Brown had suffered a heart attack and was hospitalized. Matthew knew that the stress from the firm weighed heavy on Brown's shoulders, and he knew that all he could do at this point was say prayers for his recovery.

After dinner that evening, Michael and James disappeared, going their separate directions with friends, giving Matt the opportunity to chat with Joanie.

"How could you possibly think that one of our sons could be involved in drugs?" was her first question to Matthew.

After explaining that he had a concern more than a suspicion, Joanie became more rational and said that he was right to question the comment.

They chatted about how James and Michael were so vastly different in mood, temperament, interests, and ambitions, and after talking about all the "what ifs," they opted to ask James about it.

Michael was the first one home, of course. While both parents were tempted to talk with him about James, they realized that would be totally unfair to both boys.

James sauntered in the door—half an hour beyond his curfew—to find both of his parents up and waiting for him. He gave the reticent shrug of disapproval, which absolutely infuriated his mother when she saw his reaction to them.

"James—we need to talk about our concerns," said Matthew.

"And what concern would that be?" James asked.

Joanie said, "We want to know if you are involved with illegal drugs."

James threw his head back and laughed out loud. "Yeah—of course. You want to know if I do drugs."

"Actually, that isn't what your mother asked you," said Matthew. "She asked if you were *involved* with illegal drugs—not necessarily taking them, although we need to know if you are."

"So you think I'm a fence or what?"

"James, can you please stop beating around the bush and give us an honest answer?" Joanie asked.

After a longer than expected period of silence James said, "Yeah, I'm into everything bad that your precious Michael isn't. How's that for an answer?" James attempted to make a move to leave the room but was stopped by Matthew taking a stance to block his way.

"James, we are your parents whether you like it or not, and if you have any involvement whatsoever with drugs, we have to know about it," Matt said.

"OK, well I'm not. I'm not involved with drugs, although I could be and make a lot of cash really fast. Can I please go crash now?"

"OK, James. If you say you're not involved with drugs, we choose to believe you," said Joanie, "but if you ever *are* involved in something illegal, and we have to learn about it when you're arrested, we're not going to be so accommodating about it."

"Yeah, whatever," said James as he walked out of the room.

Joanie and Matthew were stunned into silence. They looked at one another hopelessly, both wondering if they had done the right thing and wondering if James had just lied to them.

"I can't believe he made that ugly reference to his brother," said Joanie.

"I hate to believe he really feels that way about his brother," said Matt. "There's no resolution to this tonight. I do believe we're going to have to be more vigilant when it comes to the boys," Matthew said.

Just then the telephone rang. Matthew answered it, knowing that any call coming at this time of night was not good news. He was correct: William Brown had died.

Tomorrow was to be the day that Pete, Matt and his contact with the FBI visited the state penitentiary to talk with Jim Bonetti. Matthew knew that if William Brown were alive, he would urge him to maintain his schedule. He could just hear Brown saying, "Son, you may not get another crack at this Bonetti guy, and I'll be dead forever!"

With a heavy heart, Matthew decided to keep to his schedule.

Having been informed of Brown's passing, Matt's contact called to express his condolences and to ascertain whether or not they would maintain the meeting with Bonetti. Pleasantly surprised that the meeting was still on, the agent volunteered to pick Matthew and Pete up at the firm.

During the ride to the penitentiary, Matt asked what Bonetti might be able to contribute. The agent simply said "I'm looking for a description of Crystal Westley. If this guy has ever met her face to face, he should be able to tell me exactly what I need to know. Listen Matt, this may not pan out, but I'm going on a hunch here, and if Bonetti can describe anything about her to me, I'll know if I'm on the right track or just barking up the wrong tree."

"I'm all about hunches myself," said Matthew, "I had a hunch that the shooter was female because of the height of the shooter. Without taking into account there are vertically challenged hit men out there, I was sort of right!"

"Hunches are often all we have to go on Matthew, so don't be too hard on yourself." Pete Sutherland said. "You hunches have paid off in the past."

All three men had to surrender their concealed weapons upon entering the prison facility. They were given "visitor" badges and asked to follow the guard. After being led through a series of locked doors and down several hallways, they were seated in a conference room that included a steel-topped desk with handcuffs attached to it for the prisoner, one chair adjacent to the cuffs, and three chairs on the opposite side of the table. Within minutes Jim Bonetti was brought into the room, seated and handcuffed to the table. The guard who had brought him in moved to the corner of the room.

The FBI agent gave Bonetti his name and told him he wanted to talk with him about Crystal Westley.

Bonetti stared at the ceiling and said, "Why would you ask me about Crystal. Everyone told me she doesn't exist. I know better, but none of you flat-footed cops believe me. "

"What if I tell you that I *do* believe you Jimbo? Because I think you'd be stupid to make up a name of a person who was dead when your freedom was at stake. So let's just say that I believe you may have worked with Crystal

Westley, OK?" The FBI agent stared at Jimbo until he shook his head in agreement. "Good" said the agent, "now we can begin."

"Who's this guy?" Bonetti asked, pointing to Matthew. "He looks familiar."

"I'm Matthew -"

The agent quickly interrupted Matt by saying, "Matthew Smith, my associate. And this is Peter Jones, another associate. Sorry I didn't introduce you. Matthew, Pete, this is Jim Bonetti."

The trio simply nodded to one another.

"How long have you worked for Crystal?"

"Off and on for a few years – nothing steady, just on an as-needed basis, you know." Bonetti replied.

"And so, you two must have met on several occasions, right?"

"Most of our communication was over the telephone." Bonetti said.

"But you've met Crystal, right?" The agent was nudging him.

"Sure, but it's been a long, long time ago. It's been a lot of years since I've seen her, and back then she wasn't the boss, she was just like me – a hired hand."

"I see" said the agent. "And can you describe Crystal to me?"

"Sure. Hot chick – if you're into the African American type. The last time I saw her she had braids – like that actress Bo Derrick had in that movie. Except Crystal's braids were long – halfway or more down her back. Yep, she's a looker."

"So, when you worked with her, was that in Miami?"

"Yep - Miami and Dade County. We were busy back then." Bonetti boasted.

"And who was your boss then?"

"Look, I don't know what you're angle is here, but I've been ripped off by your kind one time too many. We little peons in the organization don't always know our bosses by name, and even if I did, why would I snitch on them after all these years? Look around you, man."

"Sorry Jimbo. I'm just trying to help you by finding Crystal and proving that she does exist. Now if you don't trust me – I get that. But I *can* get your sentence reduced if I find her. Without the name of her old boss, I don't have much to go on, now do I? Let's see, a hot African-American woman with braids. That'll get me somewhere, won't it?" The agent was pressing Bonetti for more.

Bonetti rubbed his hands together, all the while shaking his head from side to side. "Why should I trust you?"

"Why not? What do you have to lose? If you trust me and give me what I need to find Crystal, your story stands up and you have a chance to reduce your time. What kind of chance do you have of that now?" Pausing for a minute, then looking at Matthew, the agent said "I think we're wasting our time here. Let's let Mr. Bonetti get back to whatever it was he was doing." The agent stood, pushing back his chair; Matthew and Pete followed suit. "Thanks anyway Jimbo."

"Wait, wait. Just give me a minute to think." Bonetti said.

None of the men sat down.

"OK, look," said Bonetti, "the guys all referred to him as Lorenzo Junior. That's all I know except that he was from Tampa, not Miami."

The three investigators took their seats.

This was a huge break and they wanted to keep their momentum. The FBI agent asked Bonetti a series of other questions that both Pete and Matthew knew were related to Carmine Lorenzo, Jr., a well-known mobster and head of a growing crime family. Listening intently, Matthew committed as much information to memory as possible. Once the agent had finished his questioning, he stood and told Bonetti that he would be back to see him when he had found Crystal. Once that happened he would make good on his promise to get the life sentence reduced.

Once their guns and personal items were retrieved, the threesome headed back to the law office. The FBI agent explained nothing of his interrogation to Matthew or Pete, except to say that he now knew who Crystal was and he was confident he knew where to find her.

For once, Matthew left the office that day feeling positive about their progress.

CHAPTER ONE HUNDRED TWO

HILO, HAWAII

The toxicology screen came back positive for both Jarrod and Riana: poisoning by arsenic. The detectives from the Hawaii police department were informed of the results by the physician in charge of Jarrod's case. Now they had to find out who was poisoning who, and where the arsenic was coming from.

When Riana heard the news, she wanted to see Jarrod immediately.

"Jarrod, now that we know this is arsenic poisoning, we have to know where it came from," said Riana in a hushed voice.

"No question in my mind," said a weakened Jarrod. "Jade."

"I thought of that," whispered Riana, "but how?"

"Easy enough to do if she has access to the arsenic," whispered Jarrod.

"What would you have me do?"

"Don't do anything, Riana," said Jarrod as strongly as he could.

"You can't expect me to do nothing, Jarrod. The police believe I have been trying to poison you!"

"I know. But you and I both know that if Jade gets wind of this, she'll be around. When she is, I need to be ready for her."

"Jarrod, you're scaring me now."

"Don't say anything to anyone other than to say that I was somehow poisoned with something. Make sure you tell everyone that I'll be here for a few days' treatment, and then I'll be fine. Now go home and take the medication that they will prescribe for you. Come back tomorrow, and we'll talk more. And Riana, do not eat or drink anything that is in the house; it could be contaminated."

"If you think that's best," said an anxious Riana. "I'll do as you ask. But then, haven't I always? I love you, J." Riana kissed him and left the room.

Meeting the physician in the hallway, Riana told him that unless she was needed for something else that evening she was going home. The doctor followed her to the lobby, gave her a prescription, and told her to start taking it as soon as it could be filled. Promising she would follow doctor's orders, she left the hospital.

CHAPTER ONE HUNDRED THREE

GAINESVILLE, FLORIDA

As one of the principals in the law firm, Matthew was called into an emergency meeting of the partners regarding the passing of William Brown.

Without a doubt, Brown was not only a founding father of the firm, he was admired, loved, and respected by his peers and colleagues. When the partners convened in the boardroom on what Brown had lovingly referred to as *Mahogany Row,* the sadness in the air was palpable. As second in command, Phil Baxter called the partners' meeting to order.

The discussion was mandatory since their chairman of the board has passed on. They were to nominate and elect a new chairman who would not only serve as head of the board but also be in charge of the day-to-day operations of the firm. Phil Baxter was nominated and elected by a unanimous vote.

His first official act as chairman was to ask the partners to nominate and vote for a vice chair, as well as a secretary/treasurer. Nominations were accepted and a vote taken. Once those key individuals were in place, Baxter moved to close the office on the day of Brown's funeral, allowing all the employees an opportunity to pay their respects. Once that was agreed upon, the meeting was adjourned.

The partners would, of course, send flowers in memoriam to William Brown as well as make a sizeable donation to his favorite charity, Big Brothers/Big Sisters of America, on behalf of the entire staff.

The funeral service for William Brown was a somber event. The partners were pall bearers. The service was simple and filled with William Brown's favorite music, performed by a lone guitarist.

After leaving the gravesite, Matthew walked slowly to his car accompanied by Joanie and the twins. When they got to the car, Matt handed James the keys and asked him and Michael to drive them home. Matt got into the backseat with Michael, Joanie in front. During the twenty-minute ride home Matthew wept.

Neither of the boys had ever seen their father so outwardly distraught, even during his own brother's funeral. They were afraid to speak about it and had the good sense to let him have his time to grieve. Michael simply put a hand on his dad's shoulder, while James drove his family home in silence.

Later that evening, James asked his father about the tears. "I've never seen you cry," he said.

"No, and I hope you never have to see me cry again," replied Matthew. "There's nothing wrong with crying, son. It's a natural thing to do, but it does take a lot out of you. Sometimes you're just so sad that there's no other way to let it out other than to just cry. Does that make sense to you?"

"Sure, I guess so. I just thought guys didn't cry," James replied.

"Some think that a guy crying is a sissy thing to do," said his father, "but crying is good for the soul. I loved that man that I watched being buried today, and I'm going to miss him every single day for the rest of my life."

"Why did you care so much about him?" James asked.

"Well—a lot of reasons, but the main reason is that he saw something in me that no one else recognized, and he gave me a chance at a great career and then helped me achieve it. He was my mentor and my friend, and more like a father to me than anyone else."

"Including your old man—uh—I mean your father?"

"Yes, including my own father. I know you don't hear me talk about my parents much, and it's because they just weren't too available to us kids. Your Aunt Vera always looked out for me and for Marc when we were growing up. She took up for us and was sort of a mother figure. It was a different world then, James, believe me. You and Michael have both of us—one hundred percent of the way. I didn't grow up like that."

About that time Michael knocked on the door and asked to come in. James started to leave the room.

"Don't leave on my account," said Michael. "I just came to make sure Dad was OK and to say goodnight." Turning to his father he said, "I'm sorry about Mr. Brown's death. I know it hurt you a lot."

Matthew just winked at Michael and said, "Thanks, son."

The two boys left the room. Michael went upstairs, and James bounded out the front door.

CHAPTER ONE HUNDRED FOUR

KONA, HAWAII

Riana worked diligently to clean out everything in her house that she believed could have been contaminated with arsenic. She opened every drawer, every cabinet and carefully inspected everything she touched.

She knew that arsenic was a wood preservative and after looking through the house, she went to the garage to see if there was anything there that could contain arsenic. She did find a substance called creosote, which was a wood preservative, and she immediately disposed of it according to the package directions. In removing it she noted that it was a thick yellowish-to-brown oily substance that had a foul odor and whose fumes were intense even at a distance. While she assumed it had arsenic in it, she did not find it listed on the label.

Deciding that could not have poisoned both of them, Riana kept looking through the garage shelves. After an exhaustive search, she found a small box of rat poison in the very back of a lower shelf that appeared to be relatively new. As she eyed the box, she knew that Jarrod would tell her not to touch it, which would put her fingerprints on the box. She found a stack of cleaning towels in the corner and carefully wrapped her hands in it to lift the box from the shelf. It felt as though most of the contents were intact.

Hiding the box in her car trunk—where she knew no one had access to it—she returned to the house. She would tell Jarrod what she had done and get his advice on what to do next.

Opening the refrigerator door, she saw the familiar pitcher of "sun" tea that she always kept on hand. When she started to pour it, she immediately stopped and placed the container on the counter. Inspecting it carefully, Riana noticed that the rim of the pitcher appeared "dusty," and she felt that she had found the dispenser for the poison.

Placing the pitcher back in the refrigerator, Riana headed to the hospital to talk to her husband.

CHAPTER ONE HUNDRED FIVE

HILO, HAWAII

Riana rushed to her husband's room only to find him sitting up in bed chatting with his contacts from the FBI. Stopping dead in her tracks, Riana put two and two together and came up with attempted murder.

As she composed herself, she entered Jarrod's room. Fortunately, she had picked a bouquet of flowers from their garden and placed them on the table next to Jarrod's bedside. When she did, she kissed him on the cheek and quietly whispered "I found it" to Jarrod.

Jarrod replied, "Thanks. I'm so glad you're here."

It took every ounce of restraint Riana had to be polite to these people. They were supposed to be assisting them in their efforts to live a peaceful life, and unless she was mistaken, one or both of these agents was trying to kill them. Riana had been in similar situations through the years with Jarrod, and she knew exactly how to present herself now.

Turning on her charm, she openly discussed how the local police had been so ridiculous as to assume that someone was trying to poison Jarrod, and even suspected her originally. She added that once they found that she too had been poisoned, they had backed off. "Can you believe that anyone would think that I could poison my own husband? How ridiculous," Riana said.

Jade spoke up, saying, "I'm so glad that you're getting better, Jarrod, and you too, Riana. It's a shame this happened. Will you be going home soon?"

"In a day or so," replied Jarrod.

"We'll come by to see you once you are home," said the male agent. "We don't need to talk to you about anything else at this point. We just wanted to check on you." He offered his hand to Jarrod, and after they shook hands, the two FBI agents moved toward the door.

"I'll walk you two out," said Riana, as she moved next to Jade.

Jade turned and said, "Feel better, Jarrod."

When they reached the hallway, Riana said, "How did you two even know Jarrod was here?"

The male agent said "Jade mentioned that one of her friends works here and that he had told her Jarrod was admitted last night on emergency."

"I see," said Riana, "how kind of him. Thank you both for the visit. 'Bye now."

When Riana reached Jarrod's room, he held his finger up to his lips as if to tell her not to speak. He then got out of bed and uncovered a listening device that had been put under the lip on the nightstand table. When he immersed it in water, he checked further but found nothing else. Taking the cue, Riana suggested that if Jarrod felt up to it, they should take a short walk down the hallway and back. He agreed, and the two left the room.

Riana told Jarrod exactly what she had found and what she had done. They both agreed that Jade was most likely the culprit. Jarrod told Riana to leave the pitcher in the refrigerator as it was. He also told her to pour the rat poison out of the box and replace it with baking soda, which was similar in appearance. He also applauded her for not contaminating it with her fingerprints and urged her to either use gloves when touching the box or to wrap it in paper or a towel.

Wondering what he was planning, Riana said, "So you want her to think we don't know about the poison and that we will still be ingesting it?"

"Absolutely," replied Jarrod. "I want her to think she has outsmarted us. Chances are good that once I get home she will try to poison me again. If she thinks we don't know about the rat poison, and she finds it just as she left it, she will use it again. It takes repeated doses of arsenic to kill a person, and she knows that. She won't stop until she's caught or we're dead—this I know."

"I'll do whatever you say," said Riana.

"Remember this Riana—until I get home and take a look around, do not eat or drink anything that you have not prepared from scratch. And before you cook anything, scrub every pot, dish, glass, and utensil. Who knows where she has put the poison. And, if something has a screw on lid, throw it out. That's the easiest place to plant arsenic that would go undetected. Touch the lid, then your mouth—you've just ingested poison."

"Do you think you will be getting out of here soon?" she asked.

"I would guess I'll be released as early as tomorrow."

"I'll be back in the morning. If you need anything between now and then, call me."

"I will, Riana. You had better be very careful tonight. I don't mean to scare you, but Jade could be up to more than poison." Jarrod kissed his wife and watched her walk to the door.

"Sweet dreams," she said.

"You too—safe, sweet dreams."

On the drive from Hilo to Kona, Riana kept watch out of her rearview mirror. She was more cautious than fearful; Jarrod's words rang in her ears.

Reaching home she pulled into the garage. Carefully wrapping the poison, she took it out of her trunk and placed it back where she had found it. Moving quickly into the house, she secured the baking soda and returned to the garage to switch the contents. She carefully removed the poison from the box by pouring it into a plastic bag, and then replaced its contents. Carefully, she positioned the "faux poison" on the shelf where she had found it, checking a couple of times to make sure it was exactly as she had first discovered it. Satisfied that she had done just as she was told, she left the garage.

Riana spent most of that evening washing dishes, utensils, pots, and pans and tossing out every jar that had been opened with the exception of the sun tea.

It was late by the time she completed her tasks. Exhausted emotionally and physically, Riana drifted off to sleep in her chair in the living room.

Awakened by the barking of a neighbor's dog, Riana looked at the clock to see that it was 4:30 a.m. Without turning on any lights, she armed herself with a butcher knife and walked to the rear door of their house. She didn't see anything at first. Then she saw a flicker of light in the garage. She thought she was seeing things, but when she saw the same light flicker again, she knew that someone was in there. Without making a move, Riana waited and watched. She caught only a slight glimpse of a person leaving her garage. She couldn't be sure, but she thought the size and shape of that person fit Jade's build and height. Waiting by the door for an interminable length of time, Riana finally moved away from the door after re-securing the locks. If she was right, Jade had checked to make sure the "poison" was where she had left it in the garage. And if Riana had done things correctly, Jade would believe it was in its place and had been undisturbed.

There was no more sleep for Riana Tavares. She sat in her chair, flipping through the television channels. It would be daylight soon, and she would dress and go to Hilo to get Jarrod.

While channel surfing, Riana saw a promotional ad for KITV's new weather man. She was struck by his name: Dan Adams. She recognized the name as being somewhat familiar, but just assumed she had seen the ad before.

Riana picked Jarrod up from the hospital, and as she arrived, his release papers had just been completed. The orderly wheeled him out to the car against his expressed wishes. Once the two of them were in the car, Jarrod told her he had replaced the "bug" where he had found it on the nightstand. Perhaps whoever was listening would just think it had malfunctioned.

Riana shared the story about the shadowy figure leaving their garage at four thirty in the morning and said she believed it was Jade. She also explained that she had followed his instructions to the letter so that if Jade were looking for the poison, she would have found it intact and "just as she'd left it."

Once home, Riana pointed out the box to Jarrod who looked at it intently, but did not touch it. She then showed him the rim on the jar of tea, and he agreed that it could very well be the transfer device. Now Riana wanted to know what Jarrod's plan was.

"It's simple—we're going to let her think she's winning. I'll get sicker and sicker—or so she will think—and I'll refuse to go back to the hospital. When she tries to slip me more, she'll think she has succeeded. Who knows, I might even keel over in front of her. "

"Jarrod—you would scare me to death," said Riana.

"You'll know that I'm faking. I actually think I'm pretty good at faking people out; well, at least I used to be good at it. Now that our lives depend on it, I'll be sure to be convincing."

"But how are we going to nab her?" asked Riana.

"That's the beauty of my plan—she will nab herself, and right in front of her partner."

"Why in front of him? He could be in on this," said Riana.

"I don't think so. He's been around for years and never once made any sort of move to hurt me. No, ma'am. This all began with Jade."

"OK—I'll go along with whatever you say. Just tell me step by step what you want me to do, or say."

"You've always been a good wife, Riana. We'll win this one just like we've won before."

Jarrod explained the plan in great detail to Riana. He told her to go over it again and again until all her movements, actions, and words were precise and comfortable. As soon as Riana was ready, Jarrod would be ready.

CHAPTER ONE HUNDRED SIX

ATLANTA, GEORGIA

At times the Adams household was bustling and harried with Caleb coming back and forth from Tech and Lily Marie darting in and out from nearby Emory College. At other times Vera thought she would lose her mind in the silence.

So much had happened in such a short amount of time. Her kids were virtually grown, her brothers were in other states, and now her oldest son was living in Hawaii. While proud of their achievements, Vera was feeling alone. These were the times she could not help but wonder about her sister. More than anything she wondered if Ruth was alive.

The typical family gathering for Thanksgiving did not happen this year. With Daniel and Lee in Hawaii—along with her parents, Matthew's friend and mentor William Brown's passing, and a myriad of other conflicts, Vera had only her husband, son Caleb, and daughter, Lily Marie, for Thanksgiving dinner.

Opting to act on her boredom, Vera decided to do something she had always dreamed of—learn to play the piano. She called a few friends who had used various piano teachers for their children and got a couple of names and phone numbers. That very day, Vera Adams scheduled her very first piano lesson. Just in time for her first lesson, an electric keyboard was delivered to the Adams residence and set up in the finished basement of their Buckhead home. Although intimidated, Vera vowed to learn and practice so that she could enjoy making her own music.

The lesson came and went, and Vera thought there had been too much explanation and not enough hands-on play. Being the kind of person she was, she accepted the lesson, re-read the material after the teacher left, and anxiously awaited her next lesson.

Deciding there was no harm in it; Vera turned the keyboard on and hit a couple of notes. At first it seemed loud and overpowering. She looked around the room hoping no one had heard her. She then settled in and started randomly plunking the keys. She quickly discovered she had an "ear" for the notes and had plunked out a rough version of "Mary Had a Little Lamb." Feeling quite pleased and eager to tell her instructor, she turned the machine off and went upstairs.

"I played 'Mary Had a Little Lamb' on the keyboard today!" Vera told David.

"Wow—at this rate, you'll be a pro in no time," David said, hugging his wife.

CHAPTER ONE HUNDRED SEVEN

GAINESVILLE, FLORIDA

Returning to the office was dismal for the friends and partners of William Brown. Each person seemed sad, tense, and mournful. Working without William Brown, returning to anything resembling "normal" would take time.

Matthew met with Peter Sutherland to get a pick up on his latest investigation.

Sutherland was still working with the US Attorney's office and the FBI to uncover enough palpable evidence to send John Gotti, aka "Teflon Don," to prison.

While Gotti was a conspicuous figure in New York, sporting his $2,000 suits, the mainstream media had suddenly turned Gotti into one of the most recognizable "celebrities" in Manhattan. His headquarters was a well-known entity and had been named the "Bergin Hunt and Fish Club" in Ozone Park. Every Fourth of July, Gotti would sponsor an event with rides for the children and hot, free meals for whoever chose to attend. He further made sure that there were enough members of the non-Italian ethnic groups on hand who would advertise that the "new" Mafia was an equal opportunity employer. Each year the event ended with a huge—and illegal—fireworks extravaganza.

"Ironically," Pete said, "there are always dozens of cops patrolling the area to make sure no one tries to interfere with the festivities. That's a slap in the face to law enforcement and to the mayor's office. The cops I've heard from are livid about having to protect a godfather's right to break the law."

"I'm confident the FBI sees it as a slap in the face as well," said Matthew.

"True, and it is serious enough that it's been pushed up to the president's office for help," Pete added.

"How so?" asked Matt.

"President Reagan has a guy on board named Rudolph Giuliani. He's an aggressive attorney from New York, and he's actually the number three person in the Reagan Justice Department. Giuliani is in charge of all the US Attorneys and has vowed to get involved. I guess Giuliani grew up in New York City and hated the Mafia for reasons that have not been explained to me."

"I see, so where are we in all of this?"

"The plan is that Giuliani is going to resign his high-ranking position in the Justice Department and take the subordinate position of US Attorney for the Southern District of New York. Giuliani feels he will then be in a better position to go after the Mafia," Sutherland explained.

"Sounds as though the plan is in action," Matt commented.

"Yes, sir, and who knows where it will go from here."

"And where are things with this Crystal Westley character?" asked Pete.

"I'm waiting to hear back from the bureau," said Matt, "and I can't hear soon enough. Unofficially Pete, I'm worried about what happens next."

CHAPTER ONE HUNDRED EIGHT

NEW YORK CITY

Rudolph Giuliani became the US Attorney for the Southern District of New York. From his office, Giuliani launched an unprecedented attack on the five Mafia families that had an iron grip on the labor unions, the garment industry, the waste management industry, the Fulton Fish Market, and many other viable moneymaking industries in the City.

Giuliani successfully prosecuted the "Commission Case" in which the leaders of all five families were indicted.

Gotti was placed on federal racketeering and murder charges by the US Attorney's office for the Eastern District of New York—where Gotti's headquarters was located.

When the jury was selected for the trial, a man named George Pape was included in the jury pool. Pape was a friend of a man with alleged ties to organized crime, namely "Sammy the Bull." That juror selection led to a hung jury in Gotti's trial.

"I'm free and will continue to be free," said a prideful Gotti. "I'm a businessman first and foremost, and there's nothing wrong with that. My public supports me."

The efforts by Giuliani, the FBI, and the office of the president had been thwarted.

CHAPTER ONE HUNDRED NINE

KONA, HAWAII

DECEMBER, 1986

Everything was quiet in the Tavares household. Jade and her partner in the FBI had been to visit Jarrod a couple of times without incident.

Jarrod feigned increasing sickness. Riana told the agents she had tried unsuccessfully to get him to go back to the hospital.

The agents chatted with Jarrod about John Gotti, but Jarrod had no new information to help them in their investigation. While aware of what was happening in New York, Jarrod was just too "ill" to be of any help.

"I understand that you weren't feeling well enough to have your traditional luau for Thanksgiving," said Jade, "or did my invitation get lost in the mail?"

Riana quickly spoke up to say, "Jarrod just wasn't doing well, and I didn't want him to stress out over a holiday."

"I was just kidding about the invitation. I am sorry to hear that you aren't feeling better. Maybe you should go back to the hospital or at least to your physician?"

"No more doctors. They're all nuts and just into the money they charge folks like us," a fragile Jarrod uttered.

"I know this isn't up to me," said the male agent, "but your skin is discolored more than it was before. Aren't you concerned that you're getting worse?"

"Well I am," said Riana, just as they had rehearsed. "He just won't listen to me anymore."

"Why should I listen to you—you could be trying to poison me!" said a weak but agitated Jarrod.

"I can't believe you would even think such a thing, least of all say it, Jarrod Tavares. How dare you!" said Riana as she stormed out of the room.

"Jarrod, look," said Jade, "if you really think someone is trying to poison you, why don't you let us check it out. We could look into for you—no problem."

Jarrod silently said, *Yes* while showing no emotion.

The male agent said, "Yeah, we could have a look around—see what's what and let you know. At least you'd rest easier knowing whether we find anything or not."

Jarrod motioned for the two agents to come closer. When they did he said, "Check the sun tea in the refrigerator."

Jade responded immediately. "I'll get it."

In a matter of minutes Jade returned without the pitcher. "It wasn't there, Jarrod."

"She's probably making more of her concoction. I won't drink anymore of it, regardless," said Jarrod. "I'd rather drink ice water anyway. Surely she won't poison that."

Jade looked at her fellow agent questioningly.

"We'll just do a little checking around if you don't mind Jarrod. We wouldn't want anything untoward to happen to you," the male agent said.

"Thank you. You don't have any idea how much I appreciate it."

Jarrod watched them both turn and leave the room.

He went to the window and signaled Riana who was waiting in the garage and watching for his signal.

"Riana," said the male agent, "do you mind if we look around the garage?"

"Why would I? Help yourself."

Both FBI agents sifted through the garage contents. Jade was careful to take the side that housed the rat poison.

"Nothing here," she said.

"Nothing here either except an empty can that once had creosote in it. That's more of a fire hazard than anything else," said the male agent.

"Riana, are you making more sun tea?" asked Jade.

"I am. How did you know?" asked Riana

"Oh, Jarrod just sent me to the refrigerator to get him a glass, and I noticed the pitcher wasn't in there."

"Yes, Jarrod does love my sun tea," Riana said.

Jade looked at the other agent raising her eyebrows.

"I tell you what, Jade, come with me, and I'll show you exactly how I make it. Come on." Looking at the other agent, Riana continued, "Then the two of us will catch up with you in Jarrod's room, if you don't mind hanging out with him for a few more minutes."

"No problem here. OK with you, Jade?" the agent asked.

Jade said, "No problem. I'll meet you in the house."

This was the moment Jarrod and Riana had planned and waited for. As Riana left the garage with Jade, she signaled to Jarrod who was waiting by the window.

GAINESVILLE, FLORIDA

Matthew and Joanie needed a break from their hectic schedules, but a vacation didn't look promising in their near future. Joanie had suggested visiting Hawaii—taking the twins there to see their cousin Daniel and making a family vacation out of it. Matthew said he would think about it.

Joanie knew exactly how to get to her husband. After dinner that evening, she poured him a glass of red wine and said as only she could, "You know, darling, it's the kids last year in high school, and then they'll be leaving for parts unknown."

"Yeah, and not a moment too soon if you ask me," replied Matt.

"I know—having kids has been a handful, but don't you think that we should do something as a family before they move out?"

Matt sipped his wine and said, "Like a family vacation to Oahu?"

"Wow," said Joanie, "that's a great idea. Maybe we could plan it during their spring break? I hear that April is a beautiful time in Honolulu. And besides that, we could make it an educational trip. We could visit the Arizona Memorial, and the boys could gain some firsthand knowledge about the attack on Pearl Harbor."

Coming as a complete surprise to her, Matthew said, "Sure, why not?"

"What? That's great. I'll make all the arrangements. Thanks, sweetie—you're the best ever," Joanie said, scampering off like a child herself to find the boys and tell them they were going to Hawaii.

Finding both boys in their rooms was an anomaly, but she did, and when she shared the news, they both jumped for joy. After all, Hawaii was the other side of the world, and the beaches were endless—not to mention teeming with young, beautiful women.

Telling them she would try to arrange the trip during spring break, she cautioned them that the trip could easily be canceled if their grades were not exemplary and up to par. She left the two of them in James's room strategizing what all they would do.

Joanie left the room feeling as though she had just pulled her twin boys back together and that she and Matt were giving them a trip of a lifetime in the process.

CHAPTER ONE HUNDRED TEN

KONA, HAWAII

The male FBI agent returned to Jarrod's room to find him sitting in a chair looking recovered and refreshed.

"Wow, Jarrod—you look so much better!" he said. "Did you find a miracle cure?"

"Listen to me," Jarrod said, "and don't interrupt me with stupid questions. You know that I know a lot about poison. While I didn't like using it as a weapon—thought it was time-consuming and messy in my business—I know what arsenic is, how it's transmitted, that it takes a while to detect, and so forth. What I also know for a fact is that Jade is behind my poisoning. I'll give you particulars, but we don't have much time."

The agent interrupted, "Jade? Why on earth would you suspect her?"

"Long story short, she's not *Jade* at all, she's Crystal—the twin sister. She tried to kill my wife in Miami but was unsuccessful. The guys behind that attempt thought that she had gone soft and asked to meet her at my Miami house. She sent her twin sister there to take her punishment for a botched job. She sent her twin sister—the *real* Jade—into that house to be torched and that's exactly what happened." Jarrod took a deep breath. "This was *before* we became the Tavares couple of Hilo, Hawaii. The real Jade was a law-abiding citizen who could've gotten a government job easily—no criminal record, not even a parking ticket. Posing as her dead twin allowed this one to infiltrate the FBI and to find me. It may not make sense to you yet, but I do have proof, thanks to Riana."

"Proof—what kind of proof?" asked the agent.

"First of all, *your Jade* attached a bug to my bedside table in the hospital and was in cahoots with one of the orderlies who spied on me, letting her know I had been admitted. Prior to that she had planted a box of arsenic in my garage, laced the jar lid of the sun tea, and added it to who knows what else. When Riana found the poison in the garage, I had her wrap it—to avoid transferring her own fingerprints to the box—empty it and refill it with baking soda to the exact level she had found in it. She then placed it back where *Jade* had stored it. Within the next twenty-four hours, while I was hospitalized *Jade* came out here in the wee hours of the morning, and when she found the box 'undisturbed,' she left. Riana saw her leaving the garage, but *Jade* wasn't aware she'd been seen."

"But, Jarrod, why did you keep getting sicker if you weren't being poisoned?"

"It's called acting, and it makes the predator think they're winning. It's worked, and now you can confiscate the box, run prints on it, and you'll find no one's other than *Jade's*. She has added what she thought was poison to the pitcher of water, the sun tea, and who knows what else. Riana and I don't consume anything she has had access to. So when she and Riana come back in here, you need to handle this situation—because I'm telling you now, I'm an old man, and I have nothing to lose. If you don't handle it, I will."

"I understand, Jarrod, but these are serious accusations. I think we should allow this charade to continue while I look into it. Would you and Riana be willing to do that?"

"We'll give you forty-eight hours to assemble the ammunition you need, but no more. This woman is out to kill me, and while that may not bother you, it bothers me and my wife, and we've done nothing but what you and the rest of the FBI has asked of us," Jarrod responded firmly.

"OK, but how will Riana know we're extending the time line?"

"I'll get back in bed, and give her a signal. She will know not to say anything out of the ordinary. We've rehearsed this scenario more than once."

Sounds from the women chatting warned them of their approach. Jarrod resumed his position in bed. When Riana walked into the room, she said simply, "How are you feeling, honey?"

"I'm sure you don't really care, but I think I'll be better in no time," Jarrod feigned.

"Jarrod, I got to watch Riana make the sun tea. It's quite a simple process—just really letting nature take its course," Jade replied.

"Nature has a way of taking its own course, and we just have to take advantage of it. Can I get any of you some sun tea?" asked Riana.

All three of them hurriedly said, "No thanks."

When the agents left the house, Riana watched them drive away. It was only then that she approached Jarrod. Jarrod got out of bed, holding his finger to his lips to silence Riana. He checked the room out completely looking for a listening device, but found none. They walked to the kitchen where he did the same thing and sure enough, found a bug on the top of the refrigerator door. He simply pointed to it so that Riana could see it was there. He then motioned for her to follow him outside.

When they were out of earshot of the bug, Jarrod told Riana what had transpired. She agreed to play along for a couple of more days but told him she was weary of the whole ordeal.

The next day the FBI agent came to visit Jarrod without *Jade*. Before Riana let him in the door, she stepped out onto the lanai and whispered to him that a bug had been planted by *Jade* in their kitchen. He nodded and whispered back to Riana that she should show him where it was. The agent looked it over but did not touch it, nor did he utter a word.

Riana broke the silence by saying, "So you're here to check on Jarrod again?"

The agent replied, "Yes, I was in the neighborhood and remembered something I needed to tell him about the Gotti case. Is he up for a visit?"

"I think so. Just let me turn this fan on—it's so hot in this kitchen today. There, that will help. Please, come with me." Riana winked at the FBI agent, who simply nodded.

Closing Jarrod's door as quietly as possible, the three carried on their conversation in whispered tones even though the droning sounds of the oscillating fan muddled the sound the bug received. The news was that the box of poison had been dusted for prints and those prints matched *Jade's*. The FBI was planning to make an arrest but did not want Jarrod or Riana involved in the incident any further.

"She tries to kill me, and I don't get to see her taken down for it?" Jarrod asked.

"This is the way the agency wants to handle it, Jarrod. My hands are tied."

"So how will I really know she's been arrested?" Jarrod asked. "I'm sure it won't be in the newspapers."

"I will personally let you know," said the agent. "She won't get away with this, and she doesn't have another twin sister to throw under the bus for this one."

"What?" asked Riana.

"The woman on the beach in Miami said her name was Crystal, and she was telling you the truth," said Jarrod. "Crystal was—up to that point, very good at carrying out orders from her superiors, but when she botched the job of killing you—she sent her twin sister, Jade, to our house, and it was Jade who was killed in the fire."

"I'm confused," said Riana.

"Crystal was a soldier for the mob. She was sent to kill you in order to get to me. When that didn't pan out, she had her twin sister—the *good* sister—take the fall for her screw up. She then waited for a time, applied for government credentials, assuming her twin's identity, and maneuvered her way into the FBI. Wanting to get back at *me*, she pulled this stunt."

"And what I wonder now is whether or not this was something she did on her own, or was she secretly working for someone on the other side," commented the agent in a whisper.

"I'd be dead by now if she was providing information about me to the Mafia," Jarrod said calmly. "They don't wait for arsenic poisoning to work. That's old school and neither efficient nor effective."

"I will worry about this from this day on," said Riana. "I thought we were in the clear."

"We'll interrogate Jade or Crystal or whatever her name is," said the agent, "and get to the bottom of it. In the meantime I'll order surveillance for the two of you, and the bureau will arrange to replace all of your food and supplies that could have come in contact with the poison."

"Just take care of *her*," said Jarrod. "If she sets foot on my property again, she'll be carried away in a body bag. I'm done."

The agent left shortly thereafter, but not before removing the bugging device with his handkerchief. He placed it in a cellophane bag used for gathering evidence and waved goodbye to the couple.

"Jarrod, I just had a horrible thought." Riana said. "If Jade knew who you were all this time and wasn't reporting about *you* to whomever she was working for, who was she trying to find out more about?"

"I hate to say this, but I think she may have been doing double duty to find out how you and I ended up under FBI protection. I believe she may have been trying to find out about your brother, Matthew."

"And all she had to do was read your case file or ask another agent; she'd have the whole story. That says to me that Matthew is in great danger."

"Reluctantly, I have to agree with you my love. What I need to figure out is who Jade's associates are or were, and then get word somehow to Matthew or at least his firm. He needs to be extremely careful."

"How can you make that happen? " Riana asked.

"Once I know more, I'll find a way to make it happen. I owe your brother my life, and I don't take that debt lightly."

A few days later, Jarrod and Riana heard from the agent again saying that "Jade" was being indicted and was under suicide watch in the Hawaii jail.

She would be transferred via military plane to Los Angeles and then to Washington, DC, for her formal interrogation.

"I'm going to have to talk with my FBI contact about Matthew." Jarrod told Riana. "I don't know who Jade was working with, although I suspect I might have figured that out. Regardless, before she was discovered, she could have caused some trouble for your family. I'm going to call him and have him come here. "

"I just pray you aren't too late," said Riana. "I don't have a good feeling about this."

Jarrod made contact with the FBI through the normal channels, and once he had, awaited the telephone call from his contact. Within minutes, Jarrod's agent called and headed to Kona to see him.

"I think it best that you take a walk, Riana," said Jarrod, "and let me talk with the agent alone. It makes no sense, to involve you at this point. After I explain things to him, I promise to share everything with you."

"I hate this," said Riana. "It's tearing me apart."

"Walk – say your prayers, and we'll deal with whatever we need to. Trust me, as you always have, to make the right decisions." Jarrod said, wrapping his arms tightly around his wife.

When Jarrod's agent arrived he was accompanied by a second male agent. When Jarrod answered the door, his expression of surprise was evident.

"Jarrod, this is one of my associates in the FBI. You can call him 'Tom'. He is here on special assignment from Florida, and has some questions for you."

"Come in," said Jarrod, opening the door wide. "Please, take a seat."

"Thanks."

"Jarrod, I want you to know that you can be totally open in front of Tom."

"Good, because I have an issue to discuss that affects Riana's family. We have lived up to our promise of *no contact* with anyone from our past. In light of what has just happened with Jade, I have to advise you that I am ninety-nine percent sure she was working for Carmine Lorenzo, Jr. of Miami."

"That's entirely possible," said Tom. "Go ahead."

"When I turned down the offer to work for the Lorenzo's, everything changed. My house in Miami was destroyed which is when Jade/Crystal came on the scene. After my wife and I met with her brother, Matthew Winters, we opted to start anew and met with your bureau for new lives, new backgrounds and a new start. Things were fine until Jade came on the scene, and while I don't have all the pieces of that puzzle, I know she was out to hurt everyone in our family. My specific concern is for Matthew, my wife's brother, as well as the rest of the family. She obviously did not see fit to tell Lorenzo who and where I was, for whatever reason, but I fear her knowledge of Riana and me has endangered Riana's family. "

"You're right, Jarrod" said Tom, "she has indeed made moves on your wife's family. I'm sorry to tell you this, but Matthew's twin brother Marc was killed on her orders."

"And Matthew?" Jarrod asked.

"He's fine. He has received a series of threats, but he is being carefully guarded." Tom replied.

"I'm sorry about Marc, and I don't mean to sound insensitive," said Jarrod, "but we owe Matthew our lives. That's a debt I take very seriously, and one I may never be able to repay."

"We know that Crystal Westley hired a hit man named Jim Bonetti. Have you ever heard of him?" asked Jarrod's agent.

"Yes, I knew him as Jimbo, and he was a soldier for Lorenzo."

"And what about Lorenzo, any thoughts on him?"

"He's sloppy and careless and all he wants is money and power. He'll step on anyone to get to the top of the heap." Jarrod replied. "And my senses tell me that he must have gotten involved with someone bigger, bolder and smarter to get to the position he has attained."

"Like?"

"Probably Gotti or Giardeli perhaps. He's trying to screw over someone to be the number one Mafioso in the country. But if he's dealing with either of those guys, he'll be squashed like a bug once his usefulness is used up."

"Why do you think Lorenzo would take revenge on your wife's family?" asked Tom.

"Only one reason Lorenzo does anything - to flex his muscle in an effort to impress a higher-up. From what I read at the library, Lorenzo has taken over some territory in New York and probably New Orleans, if I had to guess. He most likely learned that my brother-in-law was the key to my freedom, and out of pure spitefulness and hate, wanted to get back at the family. He's not smart enough to realize that getting me out of New York opened a world of opportunity for him. He should be thanking Matthew Winters, not trying to destroy him."

"Jarrod, you have been a huge help in giving us your insights."Tom said.

"Jarrod and Riana have been instrumental in helping us over the years." Jarrod's agent said.

"Thanks, but let's get one thing perfectly clear here. There is nothing, absolutely nothing I won't do to help Matthew Winters. If I can help in any way, even if it means losing my freedom, I will not hesitate to do it".

"Understood." The agents stood to leave.

"We would ask you to please maintain your status here with Riana. While we feel very sorry for her loss, it is impossible for her to reach out to her family. Do you understand?" Jarrod's agent asked.

"I do, and she will too. I'll find the right time and the right way to let her know." Jarrod said. "You have my word."

CHAPTER ONE HUNDRED ELEVEN

CHRISTMAS 1986

The time had crept up on everyone. Christmas was always celebrated and revered, but this year seemed to be a time of introspection. So many things in the world were changing at a rapid pace, and most were not to the betterment of anyone.

Looking back over the year, one had to recall the United States had bombed Libya in protest of its sponsorship of terrorist organizations that resulted in the explosion of the crowded La Belle disco in Berlin, Germany.

John McCarthy, a British TV journalist had been kidnapped in the capital of Lebanon, Beirut.

In Russia, the Soviet nuclear reactor at Chernobyl exploded, causing the release of radioactive material across much of Europe, while violence continued to escalate in Northern Ireland with more innocents killed.

When President Ronald Reagan's administration sold arms to Iran—an avowed enemy, the Iran-Contra Affair was named.

The Swedish prime minister had been murdered, but at the forefront of every American's mind, was the Space Shuttle *Challenger* that had disintegrated after its launch, killing everyone on board. It was a sad time for the world and the United States in particular, and celebrating the season was beyond the scope of many.

Nineteen eighty seven was eagerly awaited by many as a new start, yet feared by others who believed in the possibility that it may bolster more of the same.

CHAPTER ONE HUNDRED TWELVE

GAINESVILLE, FLORIDA

1987

Being somewhat typical nineteen-year-olds, James and Michael Winters were looking forward to the new year. They would be graduating from high school mid-year and were most excited about their upcoming spring break trip to Hawaii.

That meant warm sun, swimming, and surfing, *and* young women—mostly young women.

While both young men were on the school swim team, James had excelled in the sport and had managed to take some additional courses at the YMCA to get his scuba certification. He encouraged his twin to do the same, and while Michael enjoyed diving, he was not as keen on it as his brother, feeling somewhat claustrophobic in the pool where they were trained and were certified as divers.

James assured him that diving in Hawaii would far exceed his expectations, and that made sense to Michael. Being in an ocean surrounded by sea life would feel much less claustrophobic than the confines of a pool. To prove the point, James suggested that he and his brother drive down to Homosassa where they could dive in Crystal River and swim with the manatees.

Early in 1987 the twins did just that and had a wonderful day diving in the caves and watching the hundreds of manatees gather in the warm waters of Crystal River. Fed by underground springs, the river maintained its seventy-two degree water temperature, which the manatee loved.

The caves in Crystal River were interesting but could also be dangerous to the novice diver. James wanted to go deeper, explore further, but Michael gave him the "no" signal and indicated they should surface. Disgruntled by his twin's hesitancy, James reluctantly agreed. The two had accomplished what they had set out to do. Michael was more comfortable in an open-water situation, and both had accomplished their goals.

CHAPTER ONE HUNDRED THIRTEEN

KONA, HAWAII

Jarrod and Riana were once again settled into a routine. "Jade" who was actually "Crystal" had been indicted, convicted, and sent to a maximum security prison. Jarrod now had a new FBI contact whom he was beginning to accept and trust.

Riana, having become jaded by recent events, no longer trusted anyone other than Jarrod. What had transpired over the past year had frightened Riana and reminded her to hone her instincts and believe in them.

What still lingered in Riana's mind was that advertisement for the television station broadcasting from Oahu and that young man's face—Dan Adams—a meteorologist. She needed to follow the hunch she had, but feared doing so. She decided to find out quietly as much as she could about this young man.

Making a point to watch the weather forecasts, Riana saw more and more indicators that validated her suspicions: an expression, a lightly tripped over word that sounded almost *southern,* a certain way he held his head when talking—it all reminded her of Vera.

Visiting the local library had given her all the information she needed. The dossier on Daniel (Dan) Adams indicated that his home town was Atlanta, Georgia, and that his wife, Leaolani, had gone to school with him at Georgia Tech. As Riana read on, she learned that Daniel's parents were David and Vera Adams of Buckhead, in Atlanta. The only other information about the parents was that Daniel was the son of a famous architect and a stay-at-home mother with two other children, Caleb and Lily Marie.

Riana kept her information silent. She had learned how to withhold information quite well, but did not like the inevitable feeling of deceit. Keeping secrets from her husband had never been good, and it wasn't good now.

After a couple of weeks, Riana asked Jarrod to watch the evening's weather forecast with her, taking special note of the young, very handsome meteorologist, Dan Adams.

Jarrod watched the entire segment before making any comment. He turned to Riana and said simply, "I don't think you want to go there." Riana knew immediately that Jarrod had seen and sensed the same likeness that she had.

"He is indeed my nephew," Riana said. "I found that out at the library when I used their computer to get information about him."

"Then we consider ourselves blessed in knowing he's alive and well, and we steer clear of any contact with him," answered a stoic Jarrod.

"But he could tell me about–"Riana refused to utter the name.

"And we could be dead as a result," answered Jarrod. "Please promise me you won't contact this kid. If for no other reason, it could bring harm to him and to his family."

"I'm sorry, Jarrod. I hadn't thought it through. You're right; I cannot contact him. My heart leapt when I saw him the first time. I think I knew even then," said a distraught Riana. "I also know that his parents are Vera and David Adams and that he has two siblings, Caleb and Lily Marie," Riana said with her head bowed and eyes closed. They're my *family* and that's all I know."

"I realize more and more how much your love for me has cost you, Riana. The look on your face speaks volumes. Please forgive me for taking away such an important part of your life," Jarrod said solemnly.

Riana turned quickly to her husband of so many years and assured him of her love. She wrapped her arms around him and whispered in his ear. "I have never regretted the choice I made, and I do not regret it now," she said. "I love you and I always will. You are right; I will let *this information* be enough."

The couple had been through seemingly insurmountable trials in their thirty-six year marriage. They had not only escaped death to be together, they had made a life where none existed. They were bound to one another and embodied the true meaning of their marriage vows. And, on top of everything else, they were still very much in love with one another.

While he had never shared the information with his wife, Jarrod Tavares already knew that Dan Adams was the son of David and Vera Adams. He also knew that Marc had been murdered, leaving behind two twin daughters and a wife. There had never been a "good time" to tell Riana, and though guilt-ridden, Jarrod maintained his silence.

CHAPTER ONE HUNDRED FOURTEEN

HONOLULU, HAWAII

Daniel and Lee were doing exceedingly well in their careers. Lee's docent training programs at the aquarium were flourishing, and Daniel's career was taking high flight.

Lee had recruited enough volunteers to begin a second phase of training, and the new aquarium director had initiated an in-house training program for those docents who wanted more hands-on experience with the animals. While this program featured much more educational information, he had asked Lee if she would conduct the sessions, with him auditing it and performing backup responsibilities. This would cover any unforeseen liability on the part of the aquarium.

Lee accepted and furthered her career aspirations by doing so. There was a feature article written about the aquarium in the Honolulu *Star-Bulletin* and a good bit of the article was devoted to Lee, highlighting her achievements in her short but successful tenure with the facility.

Striving for mutual career success had not left the young couple time to start a family. But with the new year, came new and more involved dreams, and the happy couple opted to start trying to conceive. They committed not to tell anyone in their families about their decision, opting to announce the event when it became a reality.

By spring, Lee was indeed pregnant, and she and Daniel made the telephone calls to both sets of parents, giving them permission to share the news to the extended family members. Everyone was overjoyed at the prospect of a new baby on the way.

Both Lee and Daniel were ecstatic and started making plans for the baby right away. At every available opportunity, Lee worked to convert their third bedroom into a nursery. Lee was gifted at decorating and found that her mother was more than willing to aid her in any way. They painted murals on the walls and shopped for baby furniture and before Easter had arrived, were well on their way to having a completed nursery.

CHAPTER ONE HUNDRED FIFTEEN

GAINESVILLE, FLORIDA

Matthew and Joanie were nearing their long-awaited and eagerly anticipated trip to Hawaii with the twins when they learned of Lee's pregnancy. Opting to stay in a hotel so as not to crowd the expectant couple, Matt found them a charming hotel on the outskirts of Waikiki beach. James and Michael didn't care where they stayed, as long as it was on a Hawaiian island surrounded by water and young females.

When the time came to leave, it was difficult to know who was most excited.

Matt and Joanie had invited Bee and Jack to meet them in Hawaii to celebrate Easter there. Bee felt it was too expensive, but Jack eagerly agreed and purchased tickets for them to leave shortly after Matt and Joanie left. They rented a place in the same hotel and agreed to call as soon as they arrived.

The telephone threats had ended finally. Crystal Westley had been found, apprehended and sentenced to life in prison with no possibility of parole. She had been charged with murder, extortion, racketeering and tax evasion, as well as identity theft.

Matthew had learned through his FBI client that she had posed as her twin sister to gain access to a confidential informant. Without having it spelled out, Matt knew she had found his brother-in-law and sister and wreaked havoc on their lives. He also knew they were well. He hoped the pain and torment that began so many years ago was finally over.

CHAPTER ONE HUNDRED SIXTEEN

HONOLULU, HAWAII

Both Daniel and Lee met the family at the airport, sporting leis of their own and holding one for each of the six who were arriving virtually minutes apart.

Once everyone was properly greeted, they made the trek to the baggage claim area to collect the mountain of luggage that everyone had brought.

Astutely, Matthew had rented a van for his crew and their luggage, while Jack had rented a convertible for him and Bee.

After everyone had secured his or her belongings, the group made their way caravan style to Daniel and Lee's house for a traditional aloha breakfast. Lee's parents were there and had everything prepared for the family's arrival.

The twins were eager to eat and leave for the hotel, and a stern Joanie told them to mind their manners or she would send them home, half wishing she could. In her mind *that* would be a real vacation! The boys settled themselves and walked around in the warm sunshine outside their cousin Daniel's home, talking incessantly about their *plans*.

Matt asked Daniel what he would recommend that they do while in Hawaii. Listing the must sees, Daniel included Waikiki Beach, Diamond

Head, and the King's Palace in Honolulu. He also suggested the Arizona Memorial and a walking tour through the old city of Honolulu.

For the twins, Daniel urged Matt and Joanie to get them surfing lessons, which were readily available and safe on Waikiki Beach. He also said that parasailing was fun, but Joanie had already put her foot down on that one, stating the risks outweighed the rewards.

His last suggestion was that the group would enjoy traveling to other Hawaiian islands via the local Hawaiian airliners. On the Big Island of Hawaii, the volcano tour was tremendous; on Kauai, the scenery was legendary for soaring waterfalls; and Maui was the friendliest of all with all of the above.

Pledging to look into the cost of travel to and from, Matthew secretly thought that he and Joanie might take a trip to one or more of the other islands, leaving the twins in the capable hands of their grandmother and Jack. A night or two away would do wonders for them.

Arriving at the hotel on Waikiki, the twins could barely wait to unpack their bags and get to the beach. Expressing caution about the tropical sun went unheeded as the two bounded out of the room as soon as they unearthed swimming trunks in their ill-packed luggage. Joanie simply shook her head and went about unpacking her things.

Matthew wandered over to Joanie, still unpacking, and wrapped both arms around her waist. Kissing her softly and tenderly, he ran his hand up her back to her neck and bent her backward for a long, enduring kiss. When she righted herself, she looked pleasantly amazed at her husband's face.

"Well, Counselor, that's been a long time coming," she cooed.

"Just the appetizer, my darling. I'm headed to the concierge desk to inquire about the activities here. Would you mind unpacking while I do some investigating?" Matt asked.

"Don't mind at all as long as you come back soon and we can pick up where we left off," said Joanie.

"I'll be back before you can miss me."

Matthew returned shortly with stacks of papers and brochures in his hands.

"So did you just clean out the racks?" asked Joanie.

"No, just the pertinent stuff. Here's info on the aquarium where Lee works—looks like fun. And there's a brochure on the Arizona Memorial, the King's Palace Tour, a walking tour—"

Before Matt could finish his sentence, Joanie had wrapped herself around his waist.

"How long before the boys come back?" Matthew asked.

"Days, I hope," said Joanie, as she kissed him eagerly.

"Did they take a key?"

"I didn't give them one. Did you?"

"No."

"Then lock the door with the dead bolt and meet me over there," she said nodding toward the king-sized bed.

"Yes, ma'am—as you wish."

Once their love making ended, the two lay in each other's arms for a short, but precious few minutes.

"So?" asked Joanie.

"So what?"

"So what's next? I liked that tour!"

"Next I guess is to straighten up the bed and go find our offspring. By now they've most likely gotten into something we wouldn't approve of." Matthew was pulling the covers up.

"OK, I guess we have to act like responsible adults for a change. I'm surprised Mother and Jack haven't been by."

"Me too, but I don't think I would have heard them if they had knocked, would you?"

"No, nor do I care," Joanie said with a snicker.

Dressed for the beach, the couple headed down toward the water feeling the warm, thick brown sand beneath their toes.

It was so different from their Florida sand which was almost pure white and fine, like powder. This was coarse, thick sand that was difficult to walk in at best. There was also the fact that the constant sun had made the thick sand scorching hot—even underneath.

It was only moments before Joanie and Matt caught sight of Jack and Bee sitting under a rented tent, sipping a cocktail. Waving to them, she and Matt headed in their direction.

"Hi, guys. You look cozy. Seen the boys?" asked Joanie.

"Yes, we paid for them to take beginner surfing lessons over there," said Jack, pointing down the beach a short distance.

"They couldn't believe they had to start on the sand like everyone else," said Bee. "I guess they thought they'd start in the water."

"They'd be more upset if there weren't a couple of young women about their age who are trying to get the hang of surfing too," snickered Jack. "These boys have even become gentlemen on the trip over. They've helped the girls up every time they've fallen."

"Yeah—trying to cop a feel," said Joanie, louder than she had intended.

"Joanie," said her mother in a disapproving tone.

"Calm yourself, Bee. They're her kids and she knows how guys are at that age. Besides, I think she's right; they are just trying to cop a feel."

"Jack Palace, you're talking like a dirty old man."

"I am a dirty old man," he said, sipping his cocktail.

Bee slapped him on the knee and smiled.

"So what have you two been doing all this time?" Bee asked.

"Checking out everything there is to do here," cooed Joanie. "Matt came up with some wonderful suggestions."

Jack looked over at Bee and said, "Unless you want to call your precious son-in-law a dirty old man, drop the questions."

Bee slapped him again but stopped with the questions and sipped her cocktail.

A bit later the twins came by and introduced them to their new friends: the taller of the two blondes—Maggie; the shorter—Penny. They were there on spring break with their parents who were best friends and traveled together frequently. The boys added that Maggie and Penny were freshmen in college at Ole Miss.

"Didn't someone in our family graduate from Ole Miss?" asked Michael.

"Yes, your Aunt Ruth and your Uncle John," responded Matt.

Looking at the girls as if to explain, Michael said, "They just sort of disappeared a few years ago. I've never even met them."

Joanie leaped into the conversation asking the girls what they were majoring in, all the while noticing that Matthew had become quiet and was staring at the sand.

Maggie asked Joanie and Matthew if the guys could have dinner with them and their parents at a luau their hotel was having. Although Joanie thought that was too expensive an invitation, Matthew agreed as long as her parents were OK with two more mouths to feed.

Decision made, the foursome walked the beach, swam in the warm water, and said they'd check back in before too long.

"That hit you the wrong way, huh, Counselor?"

"What do you mean?"

"When Michael asked about Ruth and John. I could tell it upset you."

"Nah—just hadn't thought about those two for a while. It's no big deal. Want a cocktail, Mrs. Winters?"

"Yes, please. Why don't you and Jack go fetch us drinks, and Mom and I will decide what we'd liked to do for dinner."

Learning that Jack and Bee had plans for an intimate dinner for two, Joanie conjured up her own plans.

Arriving with drinks that sported brightly colored umbrellas, Matt and Jack sat next to their partners and made a toast to sun, surf, and some much needed rest and relaxation.

Shortly after the drinks were gone, Matthew drifted off to sleep. Joanie simply smiled and lathered him with additional sunscreen to protect his back from the elements. She then closed her eyes and napped as well, while Jack and Bee walked the beach.

The couple was awakened by the boys and their new friends; the girls heading for their hotel and the boys asking for a key so they could get ready for the luau.

"What do you wear to a luau?" asked Michael.

"A Hawaiian shirt and shorts, dummy," responded James.

"We don't have Hawaiian shirts, *dummy*," replied Michael.

"Well, we will as soon as we go buy a couple. There's a place right over there in that market. See, they're hanging everywhere. Come on."

Joanie interrupted the foray and told them they should be on their best behavior, not to stay out late, and asked where the luau was being held. Giving their mother the details of the hotel and its location, they stood in front of her, both with their hands out.

Matthew handed them each some cash and told them he wanted them at the room no later than 10:00 p.m. Explaining it had been a long day and they all needed to rest, he sent them on their way with a key to the room and money in their pockets. "Call if there's any sort of problem," said Matthew. Neither boy seemed to pay attention, but nodded as they scampered off toward the marketplace.

"Were we ever that obnoxious?" asked Joanie.

"Not me, Vera would've had my head on a platter, and that would've been the good news."

"Good thing Mom and Jack weren't around to put in their two cents."

"Right, I would've had to extend their curfew and I'm not sure I'll make it 'til ten."

"Speaking of making it—we're on our own for dinner, Counselor."

"Wow. Room service never sounded so good."

Dinner was early and romantic, and for once in their lives, the twins had made their curfew without excuse or incident. It had been a very good day in Hawaii.

Being touristy wasn't what Michael and James wanted. They had no interest in the Arizona Memorial, although they were required to go on the tour with their parents. The walking tour around Honolulu was dull and boring in their eyes, but Matthew and Joanie forced that cultural information into their heads anyway.

Rescued by their grandmother and Jack, the twins set out for a couple of days of nothing but sun and surf.

Giving Joanie and Matthew the opportunity, the two took a flight over to Maui where they spent a couple of days sightseeing, eating, and drinking.

Joanie loved the West Maui Mountains and how their starkness was juxtaposed with the lush sugar cane fields below. Renting a convertible, the couple drove the well-maintained, but curving roads that encompassed the island. Much of the beauty of Maui was its nature; driving along the ocean and feeling the spray from the surf was delightful, and catching the glimpse of a humpback whale breaching in the not-so-distant water was breathtaking.

There were places along the highway where you could park your car and wade out into the water for snorkeling. Joanie and Matthew did just that at mile marker thirteen—where all the locals snorkeled and enjoyed the close proximity of the reefs just off shore.

The coral was intricate and colorful; the water an azure blue like neither of them had seen before. This was indeed paradise.

Drying during the ride, Matt and Joanie headed into Lahaina Town for food and drinks. Slowly creeping along Front Street, they saw a two-story, open-air building whose sign read "Cheeseburger's In Paradise." As soon as they could find street parking—which was just sheer luck—the two parallel parked and walked back to the restaurant. The hostess took them upstairs to a bar where they could either wait for a table, or eat at the bar.

The trade winds wafted through the open air bar, causing the ceiling fans to turn. And from the bar one could look down on either the water lapping the shoreline or onto Front Street from the second story.

All around the bar, license plates adorned the walls. Many states were represented, and most were vanity plates that said something about sand or surf or simply Aloha.

Matthew asked the bartender for a recommendation on their order. He said quickly, "Split a cheeseburger with chili cheese fries and Maui onions." It was delightful.

Reality began to set in as the two left the restaurant to drive the short distance to their hotel. They were leaving Maui tomorrow, heading back to Honolulu, but they would be taking Maui's memories with them.

Spending their last evening alone in the privacy of their hotel room and its balcony overlooking the harbor, Matthew and Joanie made love under the stars of Maui. The gentle breezes, the scent of Plumeria blooms, and the rushing tide only enhanced their lovemaking. Vowing to return to the beautiful, friendly island of Maui, Matt and Joanie drifted off into a peaceful sleep.

CHAPTER ONE HUNDRED SEVENTEEN

OAHU, HAWAII – HONOLULU AND WAIKIKI BEACH

With their Hawaiian vacation coming to an end in two days, Joanie asked the twins what they wanted to do with their time left. The answer from both was the same: a cruise out to deep water where they could dive.

Feeling somewhat fearful, Matt and Joanie agreed they would go with the twins and stay on board while they went diving. Matt made the reservations and took the boys to the Frog Man Dive Shop to secure the necessary equipment.

Both boys had to show their certification papers from the mainland (which amazingly each had brought with them) and were told they would have to be recertified to dive in Hawaii. While tedious, it was the rule, so both boys went with the dive master to the local beach where they would demonstrate their skills and abilities. Both passed and were granted recertification. The trip would be in three hours, and the dive master would meet them at the launch with all of the necessary equipment.

The trip was "tense" for Matthew and Joanie, although they enjoyed the boat's speed and being on the open water. They realized this was as safe a way to dive as one could get, but breathing underwater for a long period of time was foreign to these parents.

The boys were accompanied with dive instructors acting as each boy's "buddy" to ensure the safety of the novice diver. Taught always to stay with their buddy, the twins did as they were told. They viewed an array of underwater sights they never expected to see; schools of dolphin swam around the boat; moray eels peeked out of their coral hiding places, and the thankfully disinterested piranha were abundant. They saw sharks, jellyfish, and a school of stingrays, all within a matter of minutes.

When the dive master gave the signal to surface, the twins could not believe how long they had been down. Wanting more, but obeying the dive master, the boys surfaced.

Joanie had never seen either of them so animated and excited. Describing all they had seen and experienced, James said it was the best thing he had ever done. Michael agreed, and said it was phenomenal—a word his mother had never heard him use before.

Everyone's expectations about Hawaii had been exceeded. But now it was time to go home.

CHAPTER ONE HUNDRED EIGHTEEN

GAINESVILLE, FLORIDA

Getting back into the routine of normal living was necessary but not embraced. School days were waning now for the twins, as spring was turning toward summer, and graduation loomed ahead.

Matt's practice was ramping up with new cases and extensions on old ones, and his duties on the Board of Directors weighed heavily on his shoulders.

Joanie's practice was not as hectic but had its moments, and in thinking about the impending graduation, she could not help but wonder where her family would be this time next year. Would the twins want to go to college? Michael definitely would, but with James, who knew? Would they both leave home? Would James want to hang out and mooch off his parents until he *found* himself? It was all too much to take in. She knew she wouldn't be able to stop working any time soon—that was a given.

Jack and Bee were as happy as any couple could possibly be.

The Winters maintained their close ties to the Sutherlands—one of the best things that had ever happened to either couple—and Gracie was exceeding all expectations that her parents ever dared have for her.

Sharing an evening out with Pete and Sylvia could not have come at a better time. Joanie and Matt shared their Hawaiian trip memories with them, along with the vow they took to return to Maui. While Pete and Sylvia had never been to Maui, they had traveled to Kauai and related similar stories with Joanie and Matt.

No evening was complete for the four of them without at least one emergency call from the firm. It came, almost on cue, and this one was for Pete. There had been a break in the investigation on "Teflon Don," and he was needed ASAP at the office to talk with the FBI. As Pete excused himself from the table, he kissed his wife and told Matt simply, "It's one of those meetings with the people we can't talk about who use initials for everything." Matt simply nodded and assured Pete that he and Joanie would see Sylvia home safely.

Graduation came and went with a tearful Beatrice Bovier, who proudly stood next to her twin grandsons for a photo. They had just come off the auditorium stage holding their diplomas and there was Grandma.

Mom and Dad followed—embarrassingly holding up the line of graduates who wanted to meet their parents as well.

A celebratory dinner was held at the boys' favorite restaurant and invariably the questions began.

"What do you want to do?"

"Get out of here right now."

"Do you plan to go immediately to college?"

"Not until September."

"Do you plan to work?"

"Not unless we have to."

Parents, grandparents, and friends of the family could be maddening.

Regardless, the twins were now officially out of high school and able to pursue their dreams, assuming they had dreams. Joanie and Matthew didn't know anything anymore. Just ask either of their sons.

As it turned out, both of the twins went to college in the fall; James to Florida State in Tallahassee; Michael to the University of Florida in Gainesville.

Rival schools, Joanie thought. *Who would have predicted that?*

CHAPTER ONE HUNDRED NINETEEN

OCTOBER, 1987

As October rolled around, Lee gave birth to a handsome baby boy whom they named David Olan Adams; honoring both of his grandfathers.

The decision about Thanksgiving was easy this year; the Adams family of Atlanta was trekking to Hawaii to meet the youngest member of the clan.

Wishing the entire family could be there as well, Joanie and Matthew chose to invite everyone not going to Hawaii to their house in Gainesville to celebrate Thanksgiving.

Lucy agreed; the Sutherlands were in, and even the twins agreed to make an appearance. Jack and Bee would, of course, be there, and Joanie enlisted her mother's help in the dinner preparation.

Recognizing how time was slipping by quickly, the Thanksgiving toasts included well wishes for the upcoming year. It was almost 1988, and though 1987 had not been a good year for family and friends, they still had much to be thankful for.

1988 THE WORLD

While the world waited to see what would happen in Iran, the Iraqi war ended after eight years and 1.5 million people were killed. Meanwhile in Iraq, a poison gas attack on the Kurds took thousands of lives. In Scotland a suspected Libyan terrorist bomb exploded on a Pan Am jet over Lockerbie, killing all 259 on board and an additional eleven on the ground.

Of special interest to Dan Adams, the Hubble Space Telescope went into operation, exploring deep space and making available data and photography never before seen. The antithesis of that good news was that an earthquake in Armenia killed sixty thousand people. Earthquakes and other weather-affecting anomalies were occurring on a more frequent basis, and meteorologists along with other scientists were trying to find out the cause(s). Hurricane Gilbert devastated Jamaica, and then turned its wrath toward the Yucatan Peninsula two days later.

The leader of Panama, General Manual Antonio Noriega, was charged with drug smuggling as well as money laundering. This accusation led to even more investigative work between Matt's law firm, his chief investigator, Peter Sutherland, and the FBI. A connection to organized crime in the United States was suspected.

The United States Shuttle program resumed after its two and one half year hiatus after the *Challenger* disaster. In the United States presidential election, Republican nominee George H.W. Bush defeated Democratic candidate Michael Dukakis.

CHAPTER ONE HUNDRED TWENTY

NEW YORK CITY

Organized crime had added a new drug to its arsenal with the appearance of "crack"—a derivative of cocaine. Thanks to the crime lords, the drug became popular in virtually every American city. Since it was "cut" from cocaine, and could be combined with various additives, it was more often than not lethal to its users.

Crack became the sweetheart drug because it was an inexpensive yet highly addictive substance. Users who were fortunate to have "clean-cut crack" became heavily addicted and sought out virtually anyone who would supply their habit. Many users became dealers in order to further their own addiction, while making money to perpetuate their habit.

With drug use escalating and street competition tightening, the underworld seduced users by adding gambling, pornography, and prostitution to the mix; a sort of one-stop deviant shopping experience. Multiple addictions meant more money for each crime syndicate, and turf wars became once again commonplace.

Lower Manhattan became an underworld capital. Nightclubs were not fairing as well as they had in the '70s, and alternative sources for corrupt revenue were explored.

"Pop Art" became the rage, and in a short amount of time, the underworld pulled its next victims into a subculture of the New York nightlife.

Pop Art relied on everyday, commonplace subjects, i.e., Andy Warhol's Campbell's Soup can. Clubs that referred to themselves as "Art Galleries" often dealt with drugs, sado-masochistic sex rituals, and even some involvement of the occult.

Artist Robert Mapplethorpe got his start in a New York Club called Max's Kansas City—a Warhol-revered establishment. Max's Kansas City was a place where stars and "wannabes" of the art, fashion, and music world gathered to interact off each other's creativity. Unknown musicians such as Billy Joel, Aerosmith, Bruce Springsteen, and Patty Smith first plied their craft inside the walls of the infamous club.

Within a short amount of time Smith was a star of the new "punk rock" genre, and Joel, Aerosmith, and Springsteen became rising pop stars on the Music Billboard charts.

CHAPTER ONE HUNDRED TWENTY-ONE

FLORIDA

The Winters twins were in their second year of college. Michael was excelling, and James was struggling to make the grade. Though Joanie and Matthew tried reasoning with James, no amount of talking, threatening, or cajoling seemed to make a difference with him. He disliked school, but loved living in Tallahassee and did not want to come home. He was living the good life without responsibility, and this had long been his dream.

Seeking counsel from their family and friends, Joanie and Matthew decided that tough love was the only alternative. They would tell James that he must make his grades or come home and go to work to earn money.

James ignored their edict, and at the end of the semester, his grade point average (GPA) was an astounding 1.5—failing. Driving to Tallahassee with a U-Haul in tow, Joanie and Matthew brought their almost twenty-year-old son home, literally kicking and screaming.

Proclaiming himself an *adult*, James in turn threatened his parents that he would leave home, and they would never see him again. Matthew simply said, "OK, son, then how will you live?"

Life with James in the house was best described as "miserable." Forced to secure a job, he got a part-time position with the YMCA as a lifeguard. Paid only minimum wage, James was still indigent, but at least was doing something he enjoyed.

Vowing to earn enough money to move out, James scrimped and saved every penny he could get his hands on.

His parents had told him they would feed and house him, but anything beyond that was up to him. It was a tough line to hold, but they managed to do so by relying on one another for support and crying together secretly at night.

After a few months, it seemed that James was more personable—not the James they raised, but a better James than they had seen in months. Both Joanie and Matt were encouraged to the point of being optimistic. James had been working at the YMCA for several months now and had actually had some additional hours added to his schedule. He had also gotten a merit increase in pay, although it was nominal.

Now the end of the school year, Michael appeared more and more often at the house. While he lived in the dorm during the school year, he and some friends had leased an apartment near campus, and he was staying there over the summer.

Michael's grades were excellent, and he was working part-time for an investment firm in Gainesville. While his desire was to be an attorney, he felt that getting into a corporate environment would be beneficial. It would have been inappropriate for him to work for a law firm that competed with his father's, and therefore this seemed to be his best option.

Michael's relationship with his twin had deteriorated, as had everyone else's. The exception to that was Bee, the twins' grandmother.

Bee had accepted James just as he was, even though he hated school. While she subtly tried to nudge him in a more productive direction, James never "heard her" as critical.

Joanie would regularly talk with her mom about James, seeking her advice. The recommendations she got were always the same. "Give the boy some emotional support—he's not Michael. He's James, and they are two different people. "

Talking with Matthew late that evening, Joanie shared her mother's advice. His reaction was similar to hers. They both felt they were emotionally supportive; both felt a sense of failure on their part as his parents. They didn't realize until much later that they would have to learn what being emotionally supportive really meant.

CHAPTER ONE HUNDRED TWENTY-TWO

HONOLULU, HAWAII

1989

Dan Adams was now chief meteorologist for the television station. While that meant more money for him, Lee, and now two-year-old David, it also meant more time away from them.

Depletion of the ozone layer had been discovered above the North Pole. Scientists like Dan were examining what would ultimately be coined the "greenhouse effect," and in addition to his other responsibilities at the station, Dan was researching all of the weather anomalies that were occurring around the world.

Earthquakes in Iran had killed 50,000, while one in the Philippines (measuring 7.7 on the Richter scale) had taken 1600 lives. The Loma Prieta earthquake was 7.1 on the Richter scale in the San Francisco area of California, killing 63 people. Daniel kept a close watch on the waves generated by the quake in the event a tsunami warning became necessary.

The technology for weather was swiftly being perfected, but a constant eye on current conditions was still Daniel's first line of defense.

HILO

While Jarrod maintained contact with the FBI, his usefulness to them was decreasing. He had been out of the loop too long, didn't know all of the current players, and knew less about the new strategies that were being employed by the crime syndicate.

Jarrod was playing less golf, was spending more time alone, and seemed out of sorts. Riana encouraged him to get out more, to go for walks with her, all to no avail. Jarrod just wasn't up to it anymore. Not only was he tired, he was feeling old and used up.

And in the spring of 1989 at age sixty-six, Jarrod Tavares passed away in his sleep.

Riana held a small, intimate memorial ceremony for him, inviting only their closest friends from the island.

The love of her life had ultimately been taken away from her, yet she harbored no regret. They had lived together in peace and serenity for nearly thirty years on the Big Island of Hawaii.

Jarrod never told Riana about Marc's death. During his last days he thought about it time and time again, but decided that love sometimes meant keeping things to oneself.

CHAPTER ONE HUNDRED TWENTY-THREE

ATLANTA, GEORGIA

A chill ran across Vera Adams as she sat playing her new Baby Grand piano. She stopped as if to savor that moment, though she had no idea what precipitated it. She occasionally experienced these moments and attributed them to an innate psychic ability that she never pursued.

Vera had always been an accomplished woman. She was highly regarded by her friends and family and could easily fit into any social situation she encountered. At age fifty-nine, Vera looked back on her life as meaningful and blessed. She had three beautiful adult children and now a grandchild, thanks to Daniel and Lee.

Caleb would soon turn twenty-seven and was seriously dating a lovely young woman. His younger sister, Lily Marie, was twenty-three and knee-deep into politics. She had graduated from Emory but had a penchant for the wrangling of "the" political structure. Too involved in her work to be bothered by dating, Lily Marie was single and happy to be unattached.

Because of her strong faith, Vera would pray for each of the family members daily. She was praying particularly for James, as his loyalties to the family were strained. She knew a bit of what he must be experiencing. Thinking back she recognized that her own loyalties had been tested, and maintaining a balance wasn't easy.

Feeling compelled to arrange at least one more family get-together, Vera contacted Matthew to set a plan in motion that would take some time and effort to bring together; a family retreat to Hawaii in the spring or summer of 1990. All that was left now were the details, and Vera committed to find a home or cluster of homes where everyone could stay together.

CHAPTER ONE HUNDRED TWENTY-FOUR

GAINESVILLE, FLORIDA

As the word about a family trip to Hawaii spread across the Winters Clan, there was a discernible change in James's behavior as well as his attitude. He became more respectful, more cooperative with his parents, and genuinely appeared to be trying very hard to work and save his money.

Needless to say, Joanie and Matthew were so pleased with these positive changes, they didn't look for any hidden meaning behind the improvement.

As James became more compliant, so did Joanie and Matt. Life in the Winters household was infinitely more pleasant.

While James and Michael's interactions had been at a minimum, they did converse about Hawaii. James expressed his excitement about scuba diving again, and while Michael agreed that it would be fun, he was more interested in getting the whole family together. Michael had obviously inherited the "togetherness gene" from his Aunt Vera.

Matt was extremely busy at the law firm. He and Peter Sutherland were working closely with the Bureau to garner any evidence available on John Gotti. Gotti had become *the* person of interest in the organized crime community.

For years now, Rudolph Giuliani had been trying to put Gotti away. Gotti had beaten two trials since his first encounter with Giuliani in 1986, and it seemed as if no charges would ever stick to him.

Matt and Pete were investigating one of Gotti's closest allies, Sammy (the Bull) Gravano. If they could find enough evidence to indict and convict Gravano, they hoped he would roll over on Gotti to save his own neck.

Through their investigations they discovered that Gotti had a career Mafia defender on his payroll named Benjamin Brafman. Brafman was a criminal attorney who had well served the organizations he represented. He was ruthless and beyond slimy, but wore expensive suits to court, looking every bit the part of a well-versed professional, all the while having *something* on every judge he came before.

CHAPTER ONE HUNDRED TWENTY-FIVE

ATLANTA, GEORGIA

Vera had been researching locations for the family "reunion," as it was now being called. She found what appeared to be the perfect setting on the island of Maui in the Kaanapali area, a golfer's paradise community on the northeastern side. Kaanapali was laced with hotels, condominiums, and private residences that could be rented weekly or seasonally.

Researching prices tended to be an arduous task, so Vera enlisted the services of a travel agent. Giving her all the information about the number of people, the cities from which they would fly and a rough guess of dates, she asked that the agent get back to her as soon as possible.

The agent responded within the week, and Vera passed the information along to her brothers. After no more than a matter of days and a few telephone calls, the "reunion" plans were set. The Winters Family would spend the last week of May and the first week of June of 1990 on Maui.

The travel agency sent brochures and confirmations to Vera for her to distribute to her family. When the package arrived, it was like opening a Christmas gift for Vera. She had never realized there was so much to see and do on Maui. It had indeed been a good choice.

The island offered tours of a pineapple plantation, several state and national parks, golfing, tennis, boating, whale tours, snorkeling trips, scuba diving, nature trails, arboretums, helicopter tours, an "S" curve drive to the unique Maui town of Hana—situated in the middle of the rain forest on the opposite side of the island, and much more. There appeared to be something for everyone on Maui.

The family had opted for a cluster of single family houses that were available during this particular time, and since it was considered the "shoulder" season for Maui, the prices were more reasonable.

Each family reserved a vehicle, allowing everyone to have ready access to do what they most wanted to do.

Vera sent maps and brochures to everyone, and she called Daniel to advise him of the time when the family would be coming to Maui. Dan and Lee would try to arrange vacation time during that two-week period when they could fly to Maui. There would be room for them to either stay with Vera or with Lee's parents. Olan and Lelah were splitting the cost of a house with the Sutherlands to be in the same compound as the rest of the family.

Jack and Bee would stay with Joanie and Matthew, and Lucy rented a house that would accommodate her twin girls and their husbands.

Everything was set: reservations were made, deposits were paid. Now came the hardest part—eagerly waiting for the late spring of 1990 to arrive.

CHAPTER ONE HUNDRED TWENTY-SIX

THE WORLD

1989

In the year that George H. W. Bush became president, thousands of students occupied Tiananmen Square in Beijing, China, protesting for democracy, while the Chinese government declared martial law, and hundreds of demonstrators were killed. Following this event, the United States and other countries around the world placed sanctions on China.

In technology, the first of twenty-four satellites of the Global Positioning System were placed into orbit. Nintendo began selling its popular *Game Boy* in Japan, while the 486 series of microprocessor was introduced by Intel to US consumers. A bundle of Microsoft's office applications including *Word* and *Excel* was released as *Microsoft Office.*

Scientists made the declaration that 1989 was the warmest on record, possibly a sign of the ever-emerging "greenhouse effect."

Hurricane Hugo struck Puerto Rico, St. Croix, Guadeloupe, South Carolina, and North Carolina as a Category Five storm and claimed over eighty lives, making it the costliest hurricane (in financial terms) to its date.

In Bangladesh, one of the deadliest tornadoes struck Saturia, killing as many as 1300. And in Alaska's Prince William Sound, the Exxon Valdez spilled 240,000 barrels—*eleven million gallons*—of oil after running aground.

In Florida, serial killer Ted Bundy was executed.

1990

The United States entered a major recession, while the Berlin Wall "falls," reuniting East and West Germany.

Industrialized countries around the world agree to stop dumping waste into the oceans of the world, and Tim Berners-Lee publishes a more formal proposal for the World Wide Web, and the first web page was written.

Saddam Hussein ordered Iraq's invasion of Kuwait. Following the Iraq invasion, *Desert Shield* begins as the United States and United Kingdom send troops into Kuwait.

CHAPTER ONE HUNDRED TWENTY-SEVEN

NEW YORK CITY

Thanks to the efforts of undercover detectives, the FBI arrested both John Gotti and Sammy "the Bull" Gravano on charges including gambling, tax evasion, and murder.

The indictments were the result of secretly taped recordings made in a building in lower Manhattan where Gotti and his associates gathered to conduct business.

Gotti and Gravano were each held without bail while awaiting trial. Gravano, as expected, hired criminal attorney Benjamin Brafman as his lawyer. Before going to trial, Sammy the Bull made the stunning decision to plead guilty and testify against Gotti in exchange for a reduction in his sentence. Gotti's fate was further sealed when the judge in the case barred Gotti from using attorneys Bruce Cutler and Gerald Shargel, citing both attorneys had been named by Gotti on the secret tapes.

During Gravano's testimony at trial, Gotti made a motion with his right hand as if he was injecting a drug into his left arm. The gesture was made to allude to Gravano's expensive anabolic steroids habit, and most likely as a threat to Gravano.

The *anonymous and sequestered* jury found John Gotti guilty on all charges, and he was sentenced to life in prison without parole.

The Godfather Gotti was sent to the federal penitentiary in Marion, Illinois, where he was kept in solitary confinement.

Sammy the Bull however would soon be a free man, receiving a prison sentence of only five years for the life of crime he confessed to, which included nineteen murders.

Conventional wisdom said that the Mafia would track Gravano down—wherever he was living in the world—and assassinate him.

CHAPTER ONE HUNDRED TWENTY-EIGHT

HAWAII

At last the Winters Clan had gathered in Hawaii—specifically in Maui, Hawaii. The cluster of houses that Vera had secured through her travel agent were so closely situated, it appeared a compound of sorts.

Naturally, Vera, David, Caleb, and Lily were the first to arrive, viewing all the properties and putting their stamp of approval on each. Carefully Vera chose which family would stay where and had everything planned by the time the next group arrived.

Family by family they gathered, and the noise from their chatter was at times deafening. Cousins were seeing each other for the first time in years; spouses were introduced and midmorning cocktails had begun to flow.

Sandra and Amanda and their spouses were staying in a house with their their mother,   Arriving shortly thereafter was Joanie, Matthew, their twins, and Bee and Jack. They had rented an SUV along with a convertible so that they could accommodate everyone's tastes and needs. They arrived after having stopped at the Safeway in Lahaina, stocking in provisions as well.

Among the last to arrive were the Adamses of Oahu and Lee's parents. Their in-state flight had several daily schedules, and they chose to take the later of the flights.

As each vehicle entered the "compound," the reunion began in earnest. And when everyone had arrived, Vera gathered them in a group on the front lawns of the homes. Saying a prayer of thanksgiving, she and David, standing arm in arm, wished them all an "aloha" and thanked everyone for spending their time and money on such a trip.

Naturally, Vera had T-shirts made for everyone that said "Winters Reunion, Maui, 1990," which she proudly handed out. Although even she thought it cheesy, it was something tangible that would commemorate the event.

Group by group they gathered, then dispersing, everyone seemed to be thrilled to begin this family adventure.

Vera and Matthew had determined that it would be best if everyone agreed on a time to collectively gather each day so that no one got lost in the shuffle. That would be the dinner hour, at which time everyone would come together for a meal. Naturally, it would be hosted at Vera's. Everyone agreed and then allowed to go off on their individual and/or collective adventures.

Things began splendidly though chaotically. Everyone appeared to be excited, happy, and eager to take on the sights and sounds of the island. Once all of the sleeping quarters were determined, the parents, less Daniel and Lee, who were allowing themselves some time away from little David, were gathering for cocktails.

Dinner hour came, and so did the clan. Once everyone was accounted for and fed, several chose to drive into Lahaina town and take a stroll along the streets. Warned as they knew they would be about drinking and driving, Lily chose to be the designated driver. She settled herself behind the wheel of the SUV that Matthew had rented, and they were off!

By the middle of the week, everyone was tanned and brown from the sun. Many of the clan had never snorkeled until this trip but were now the furthest thing from novices. James and Michael had been scuba diving a few times by boat, accompanied by Daniel and Lee who were certified divers.

Whale tours were sometimes disappointing this time of year since the mating and birthing season had ended in mid-April, but the twins Sandra and Amanda enjoyed the boating experience along with their husbands. They would frequently catch an up-close-and-personal experience with the spinner dolphin of Hawaii, who performed a graceful display, simultaneously breaching the water and spinning in a rolling side-over-side motion. As if choreographed, they would leap out of the water, spin exactly the same number of revolutions, and then dive back into the water. Smaller than bottlenose dolphins, they would range in pod sizes of sixteen to thirty-five.

Additionally, some of the cruises included supervised snorkeling in which one could swim with the giant green turtles of Hawaii as well as with the plethora of colorful fish that filled the blue water. Through boat to boat communication, captains took their passengers to areas where the turtles and/or spinner dolphins had been sighted, giving their passengers a rare opportunity to swim, snorkel, or simply observe these magnificent sea creatures.

On this particular day, James and Michael opted to snorkel along the shoreline of Kaanapali. The surf was calmer than usual, and the sand bar dropped off quickly along this particular patch of beach. By doing so, both boys saw huge green sea turtles and viewed firsthand the jagged coral that teemed with fish and sea grasses.

When they came back in they were literally exhausted from the swim and fighting even the mild current, but they were also energized by it.

At dinner, James shared the experience with everyone, urging them to pick up boogie boards (to assist them if they grew tired from swimming) and come along the next day. Amanda and Sandra wanted to go, so their somewhat reluctant husbands said they would join in as well.

The following day, they waited for the tide to go out before venturing into the water. Beginning along Black Rock in the Kaanapali area, they swam out and around its edge, catching great sights of coral and fishes. The girls had brought boogie boards along just as a precaution, and simply attached them with Velcro to their wrists. Naturally the men opted to forego the boards.

After a time, James led the group up the Kaanapali beach to the area he and Michael had snorkeled the previous day. While the water was shallower, the sights were nonetheless intriguing. There were nooks and crevices along the coral shelf large enough for eels and manta rays to hide in, and they actually saw several large green eels resting there. Careful not to disturb them, the group meandered up and down this section of the coastline for some time.

Amanda grew tired and signaled that she was going ashore. Sandra followed, as did their spouses. James gave Michael the thumbs in and up indicating they would all meet on shore.

Gathering on the sand, the sisters were talking nonstop about what they had seen and how exhilarating it had been. Their husbands agreed and were literally panting to catch their breath. This had been a hard swim.

Turning around they saw Michael coming slowly out of the water onto shore but none saw James. He was not leaving the water, nor could they see him.

Michael joined the group not recognizing that his twin brother was not behind him. When he reached them they all asked about James.

Turning around quickly, Michael sprinted toward the water and yelled to the group that they should call for help. Swiftly realizing there were no lifeguards on Kaanapali Beach, Amanda ran toward the nearest condominium complex to get help.

Michael swam to where he had last seen James but caught no sight of him. Swimming furiously, diving desperately, Michael felt as if James had simply disappeared.

When the coast guard boats arrived, they encircled the area along the shoreline where James Winters had last been seen snorkeling. Minutes later, coast guard helicopters swarmed overhead. Search and rescue for James began in earnest.

Hearing the noise from the helicopters, Vera instinctively knew something was wrong. About that time Lucy's telephone rang. It was Amanda, crying, in a panic, telling her mother that James was missing in the water.

The family gathered on shore as the rescue team diligently and methodically searched the water for James. Volunteers from the local fire stations arrived by the dozen, using inflatable rafts to get as close to the water's edge as possible. There was no sign of James. One half hour later divers were brought in; some in helicopters, some canvassing the water behind the inflatable rafts. Still, there was no sign of James.

Joanie and Matthew stood in the hot sand, willing James to survive, willing him to surface. A guilt-ridden Michael stood slumped over in the sand alongside his parents and his grandmother, praying, offering any deal God wanted of him, just to spare his brother.

Minutes lapsed into hours.

Vacationers offered Joanie and Matthew chairs and umbrellas to make them more comfortable. Condo owners brought them food and water.

As evening approached, James had not been found. A remorseful coast guard officer told Joanie and Matthew they would resume the search at first light; but it would then officially be a search and *recover*.

"I am very sorry, ma'am, sir," were the words they had been left with. No James, just words.

EPILOGUE

For over thirty years the Winters Clan has gathered together, sharing not only the happiest times of their lives but the saddest ones as well. The sorrow began with the sudden disappearance of Ruth Winters Ward and her (mobster) husband; then there was the murder of Detective Bovier at his daughter's wedding; next was the brutal and senseless murder of Marc Winters, and now the shocking disappearance of James Winters off the coast of Maui. The family's fortitude has been repeatedly challenged, and another family gathering has now ended in tragedy. Their resilience is again being tested to survive yet another horrible incident. Only their deep and enduring family love will help move them onward day after day.

www.ingramcontent.com/pod-product-compliance
Lightning Source LLC
LaVergne TN
LVHW050922080826
845145LV00001B/178

* 9 7 8 0 6 1 5 7 5 6 4 1 7 *